Praise for

NIGHT IN SHANGHAI

"Both of them young and awkward, but gifted and smart, [Thomas and Song] make for an odd but brilliant pair of lovers. They light up the pages of this novel . . . *Night in Shanghai,* an intelligent historical romance, shows off with forceful insight, terrific characters, and a telling sense of detail. And, folks, it swings."
— Alan Cheuse, *All Things Considered*

"You read *Night in Shanghai* impressed by its meticulous research and drawn in by its sweep — those crowded, humid Shanghai streets seem to live and breathe." — *Seattle Times*

"This thrilling, sexy novel reveals some little-known facts from that time. The strands of the story weave together as the themes and rhythms of the jazz her protagonist plays."
— *Christian Science Monitor*

"With a magician's sleight of hand, Nicole Mones conjures up the jazz-filled, complex, turbulent world of Shanghai just before World War II. Mones has re-created a feast for the senses, transporting us to the rich, decadent city in which the lives and loves of expatriate musicians intertwine with the growing tensions between the Communist Party and the Nationalist Party, while the ominous threats from the Japanese stir the winds of war. A rich and thoroughly captivating read." — Gail Tsukiyama, author of *The Samurai's Garden* and *A Hundred Flowers*

"Every page in Mones's compelling, sexy, and richly textured novel reveals some custom, some costume, some trick of language that exposes a fascinating moment in history — the Japanese invasion of Shanghai on the eve of World War II. Mones weaves the multiple strands of her story much the way themes and melodies are woven into the jazz her protagonist plays, with subtle and suggestive undertones of human greed, power, and passion."

— Marisa Silver, author of *Mary Coin*

"Mones's vivid account is animated by the real historical personalities it digs up and resurrects. More than ghosts, they're born again protagonists at the vanguard of a musical movement too brilliant to be made up." — *Time Out Beijing*

"Extraordinary . . . Comparisons to James Clavell's epic Asian sagas are appropriate. Never has history sounded so good."

— Robert Anglen, *The Arizona Republic*

"Mones works seamlessly with a large and disparate group of characters — gangsters and Communists, jazz men and diplomats — always with a sympathetic hand. Music jumps from every page; even if the reader doesn't know quite what it means to flat the 7th, the sound comes through just fine in Thomas Greene's voice. A touching story and highly recommended." — *Historical Novel Society*

"*Night in Shanghai* is a riveting, entertaining, and illuminating look at a moment that has largely been lost from history."

— *January Magazine*

"The novel excels in its flamboyant portrayal of Shanghai as a Noah's Ark of musicians, gamblers, drug addicts, poets, triad members, and prostitutes. Page after page, the multiple faces of Shanghai's nights are outlined; the worlds of the underground and entertainment tango provocatively." — *Asian Review of Books*

"Mones's engrossing historical novel illuminates the danger, depravity, and drama of this dark period with brave authenticity." — *Booklist*

"Breathless and enlightening . . . [An] ambitious book."

— *Kirkus Reviews*

NIGHT IN SHANGHAI

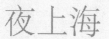

NIGHT IN
SHANGHAI

夜上海

Nicole Mones

Mariner Books
Houghton Mifflin Harcourt
BOSTON · NEW YORK

First Mariner Books edition 2015
Copyright © 2014 by Nicole Mones

www.hmhco.com

Library of Congress Cataloging-in-Publication Data
Mones, Nicole.
Night in Shanghai / Nicole Mones.
pages cm
ISBN 978-0-547-51617-2 (hardback)   ISBN 978-0-544-33445-8 (paperback)
1. Jazz musicians — Fiction.
2. Americans — China — Shanghai — Fiction.
3. Organized crime — Fiction. 4. Shanghai (China) — Fiction. I. Title.
PS3563.O519N55 2014
813'.54 — dc23
2013045640

Designed by Chrissy Kurpeski
Typeset in Fournier MT Std

Printed in the United States of America
DOC 10 9 8 7 6 5 4 3 2 1

For Ben and Luke

I reached the international city of Shanghai in July, with the sun beating down on the Bund, the harbor full of Chinese junks, foreign liners and warships from all over the world. It was hot as blazes. I didn't know a soul in the city. But hardly had I climbed into a rickshaw than I saw riding in another along the Bund a Negro who looked exactly like a Harlemite. I stood up in my rickshaw and yelled, "Hey, man!"

He stood up in his rickshaw and yelled, "What ya sayin'?" We passed each other in the crowded street, and I never saw him again.

—Langston Hughes, *I Wonder as I Wander*

一寸光阴一寸金
寸金难买寸光阴

An inch of time is worth an inch of gold
An inch of gold cannot buy an inch of time

—Chinese adage

Part I

内忧外患

DISORDER WITHIN,
DISASTER WITHOUT

. . .

*The years before the war forced everyone in Shanghai to choose:
Nationalists or Communists? Resist the Japanese invaders or
collaborate with them? Even passivity became a choice, a gamble, a hand consciously played. As for me, Song Yuhua, my
hand was forced—I belonged to Du Yuesheng, and though I
served him in public, through my education, rather than in private, as did other women, I was his indentured property, to do
with as he pleased until my thirty-third birthday. Only in my
secret mind was I free, so it was there, naturally, that I staked
everything of my life that mattered.*

*It was 1936; war was coming. Conflict with foreign pow-
ers had been eating at China for a century, since the Opium
Wars first partitioned port cities such as Shanghai into foreign-
controlled districts. We had already grown accustomed to being
colonized, but then Japan's southward expansion from its base
in Manchuria turned into an all-out invasion. The Japanese
ate up more and more of the northeast, and drew dangerously
close to Peking, yet still Chiang Kai-shek did not fight them.
His Nationalist armies fought only the Communists, who he
believed posed the greater threat. When the Imperial Army
pushed hard enough, he simply withdrew and conceded terri-*

tory to Japan. The wrath of heaven and the resentment of men could be felt everywhere. To so many of us, Chiang's policy, "first internal pacification, then external resistance," seemed like treason.

What choice did I have? I joined his enemies on the left, so secretly it was ren bu zhi, gui bu jue, neither known by man nor felt by ghosts. At last I was living for something, and by then I didn't care if it led to punishment or even death. I knew I was going to die anyway, maybe in the war that was about to engulf me and Lin Ming and Thomas Greene, or maybe, if my secret was betrayed, at the wrong end of a gun in some Shanghai alley. For all the glitter of its golden era, the city during those years dealt death and life in equal measure.

Ye Shanghai was what everyone called that time and place—Night in Shanghai, after the popular song by Zhou Xuan. It was a world of pleasure, permission, and nightlife, which was destined to evaporate the moment Shanghai fell to Japan. Jazz was the sun around which this paradise revolved, the rhythm that drove its nights, and agents like my brother Lin Ming made it possible by recruiting jazz men from across the sea and managing their lives in Shanghai. Those were the years of the great black orchestras from America who filled the ballrooms, bringing a marvelous sound that had never been heard in China before. For years after the Americans were gone, people remembered them, especially Thomas Greene. I used to hear people say they'd heard him play, or they'd danced to his orchestra, or they had it on good authority that he had been born in a cotton field. I knew all this was nonsense, and kept quiet, for almost no one really knew him. I did, knew him and loved him, more than this life would ever allow me to love any other. This was the one secret I never gave up.

.   .   .

1

T HOMAS GREENE AWAKENED on his first morning in Shanghai to the creaking wheels of a cart and a man's low-pitched singing call. For a long and dearly held moment he thought he was young again, back in Baltimore, with his mother still alive, hearing the cry of the strawberry man who brought his mule-clopping cart up Creel Street in the summer. But then he felt the snap of winter air against his face, and he remembered he was under silk quilts, in China.

The cry sounded again, this time answered by the crowing of neighborhood chickens. He slid out, shivered over to the French doors, and parted the curtains to look down. It was a night soil collector, his musical cry opening doors up and down the lane as housewives set out their night stools. Thomas's house had modern plumbing and pull-chain lavatories and many other extravagances since, as Lin Ming had put it the day before when they'd pulled up to the place in a motorcar, the Kings were one of the most popular orchestras in Shanghai, and he was their bandleader.

A forest of pops sounded from the south, over the rooftops. Later he would learn it was Japanese soldiers at firing drills on the proving ground below the Hangzhou-Shanghai railhead, but on that first morning, since Lin Ming had told him all about the Japanese invading China, he thought for a chaotic and dreamlike moment that the time had come.

But then it grew quiet again, and he saw the night soil man continuing up the lane unhurried, and the women still opening and closing their doors. No war today. Just his first rehearsal at nine o'clock, when within eight bars, the rest of the orchestra would know he was a fraud.

Not that he was unskilled; on the contrary. He started classical training young, with his mother, then other teachers, and finally in the classrooms at Peabody, where colored students who had shown exceptional promise on their instruments could sit in the back and learn harmony, notation, theory, and composition, so long as they kept quiet. The piano was what people aspired to in his family, a line of ambition that ran through his mother, his grandmother, and now him. When he was small, before his father died in the Great War, his mother used to take him to private salons over in Washington, D.C., to hear polished black musicians play chamber music for hushed audiences. By the time he was nineteen, he himself was performing in starched evening wear. But just a couple of years later, the stock market crashed, and it seemed like no one'd had a nickel to spare since. Teaching dried up, and accompanist work, and playing for church choirs. For a time he got by playing piano for the movies in the theater, but then the talkies came in, and that was that. No one was up in the money, except them that were already rich.

But finally, luck got him work sight-reading the classics at a rich man's party in Guilford, and word of mouth got him some more. He did not land many jobs, just enough to give his mother a respectable sum toward their rent and food. He should have been happy with that, times being so hard, yet he was always on eggshells because some of these engagements came his way on account of the fact that his looks were light enough to confuse people. He may have been caramel-toned, with eyes as dark as ink, but his features were fine-drawn enough to attract second looks on the street. If he shaved his hair close, he had people asking his nationality. It didn't hurt that he was a classical player, whom everyone expected to be vaguely foreign, possibly European, though surely from one of the southern countries. When asked his background, he always weighed his answer, since as colored, he got two dollars, but it was five when he performed as a Turk, or a Portuguese—which he did, whenever he thought he could get away with it.

He cracked the wooden wardrobe painted with Chinese scenes to find his meager stack of folded clothes, which seemed to have been arranged on the shelf yesterday before he even made it up the stairs. At home he had been proud of these suits, no, depended on them; they were his badge, the uniform that showed him to be a man of gentle education, fluent in the music of Europe. He had spent his whole life mastering the role, and now—he was here. He knotted his tie and buttoned his threadbare jacket like he was going to a funeral. In a way, he was.

Downstairs, he came upon the servants eating at a round table in the kitchen, but they waved him insistently into the dining room, where he found a table set for one, with china on white damask, all because he was the bandleader. Chen Ma bustled in to serve him some of the rice gruel they were eating in the kitchen along with buttered bread and enough eggs for six men. Hunger overwhelmed him, and when he had satisfied himself and started to slow down, Uncle Hua came in from the kitchen to stand over him.

"Master clothes b'long low class," Hua sniffed.

"No kidding." Thomas lifted a shoulder in response, and went on eating with real silver that felt heavy as liquid in his hand. He had seen silverware, of course he had, in rich houses where he had played at parties, but this was the first time he had eaten with it. His mother would be proud; she had made their little place an island of manners and gentility, with her fringed lampshades and her handmade antimacassars, and the exquisite sonatas that trilled out from her parlor every evening. She played the organ and taught piano at the church, and between the two of them, they made do, at least until she got sick.

It came on quickly, but word got out and her friends came to visit, all dressed in their best hats and gloves as she would have been. Even his cousins from his grandfather's side in Easton, across the Chesapeake, came to see her. Thomas had not seen them in years, not since he last traveled as a boy to their small patch of land, hand-cleared out of the dense, mosquito-whining woods, to stay in their brick house with two rooms downstairs and two up. It was jarring to see them full grown now, as he was, and he shook their hands and embraced them and let them all have a few minutes in the bedroom with her to reminisce about the summers when he and his mother rode the colored bus all the way up to Delaware and then back down the Eastern Shore to see them. He had built forts in the woods while she made pies in the morning, before the day grew hot, after which she passed the afternoons on the screened porch with her mother, who had been her own childhood teacher, just as she had been his. Now the years had passed under the bridge like slow water, the Great War come and gone, the 'twenties too, and he and his cousins were full grown, and his mother lay dying.

He never returned to church after the first Sunday of her illness, when the silence of the great pipe organ announced her absence as nothing else could, not even Reverend Martinson leading the congregation in a prayer for her recovery. *Who will play at her service if she passes?* was what he heard in his head during the prayer, a thought that shamed him like a wrong, discordant note.

When he got back that day, the apartment was already filled with food, as friends and neighbors swept in and out with their home-cooked stews and casseroles. She thanked them for coming, her hand light and bony in theirs. They emerged from the bedroom with their reports: "Had a rough night, I see." Or "Looks worse, maybe the doctor's right."

At the end, everyone grew strangely more positive. "Looking peaceful," said Mrs. Hazell from downstairs, and Reverend Martinson, his mother's friend and employer for decades, said, "Good Lord's smiling on her today."

Thomas was in the small kitchen heating up the meals the women had brought so he could put them out on the table by the stack of plates. The living room was full of church ladies, trading stories and gossip, passing in and out of the bedroom and telling each other, *She looks more at ease, yes, there's less pain today. I'm certain of it. Let's let her sleep.* Then they descended on him like a warm, powdered, half-sour old flock of birds, hugging him and blessing him and saying they would be back to see his mama on the morrow.

And then he was alone with her. He finished the dishes, let the sadness drain through him as he emptied the sink. Though he had been born in these rooms and lived here all his life and knew every floorboard and wallpaper seam, it was over. If she died, he would have to move. Where? A boardinghouse? Out west? People said there was work in Seattle.

He took a deep breath and pushed open her door, braced for the odd, sweet smell of sickness. It was there, and over it another note, perhaps a perfume carried in by one of the day's visitors. "Mama? How you feeling?"

He paused. Should he let her sleep?

His eyes adjusted to the low light and he saw she was so rested, she looked like she had sunk right down into the bed. "Mama?" he said once more.

He laid a hand on her arm and jumped back as if he had touched a hot stove. Cool. He touched her again, slowly this time, everything breaking inside him. *He'll come to your house, he won't stay long.*

"Master?" said Hua, standing impatiently over him.

You look in the bed, find your mother gone. Right, his clothes. After selling everything, even the piano, he'd had nothing left but these two suits, his shoes, and his leather briefcase which had belonged to his father, stuffed now with his favorite music, his personal canon, his life's work. "These are all the clothes I have."

Uncle Hua shook his head. "Tailor come tonight."

"I don't have money. I have not been paid yet."

Hua blinked, exasperated. "Master paycheck fifteen day, tailor chit thirty day due never mind."

"I see," said Thomas. His clothes were something he had never been able to worry about before. "All right, I guess so."

Just as he spoke, Little Kong, the household errand boy and most junior servant, burst into the room with a spatter of Shanghainese. Before anyone could reply, an older fellow sauntered in, at ease with his rolling gait in a way that Thomas, since leaving Seattle, had decided was peculiar to Americans. The man's hair was a gray grizzle, and his brown-eyed gaze kind and good-humored as he surveyed the dining room. "Well now, aren't we the grandee?"

"I was thinking the same thing." He stood and extended a hand. "Thomas Greene."

"Alonzo Robbins. Bass player. Seeing as today's your first rehearsal, I came to take you."

"Thank you."

"Didn't want you to have to walk in all cold by yourself."

"Very kind of you. Den of lions, eh?"

"Oh no." Alonzo grinned. "'Course not."

"Breakfast?" Thomas indicated platters, half-demolished.

"Thanks. I've eaten."

"Well." No more postponing it. He shrugged on his worn light-brown wool, inadequate for the cold and clearly a rag next to Alonzo's fine topcoat, and picked up the briefcase he took everywhere.

The lane was alive in the winter sunlight. Local women sold food from a cart, and one lifted the lid of a wide shallow pan to show them steam-fragrant rows of dumplings. "Tell me about the Kings," said Thomas, "where they came from."

Alonzo nodded. "Well—the first members were some guys who played with Bennie Moten's gang at the Reno Club in Kansas City. But then last year Bennie died having his tonsils out, and Bill Basie took over—you've heard of him, people call him the Count because he carries this card around that says 'Beware, the Count is here.' You know the Count?" They had come to the end of the lane and Alonzo raised his hand for a conveyance.

"He brought in new players from back east, like Hershel Evans, so he had to drop some guys too," said Alonzo, "and those guys joined us, along with a couple of fellows from Walter Page's old group, the Blue Devils. That's where the Kings came from. We had been playing together in Kansas City about six months when Mr. Lin showed up and hired us over here."

"I didn't know he went as far east as Kansas City, looking."

"Lucky for us he did, I'll tell you that. Hell of a place! Where'd he find you?"

"Seattle," said Thomas. That made it sound simple; it had been anything but. By the time he made it to that mist-shrouded city, he was broke and starving, and when the Blue Rose on Yesler Way offered him janitorial work, he did everything but fall to his knees in gratitude. The jazz club opened every night in the basement, and he cleaned it daily in exchange for meals and a small room at the back.

In the afternoons, his work done, he returned to the now pristine basement and its baby grand. In those last hours before sunset, when weak light slanted in through the dust motes in the air, his piano playing would make the owner, Big Lewis Richardson, along with anyone else who happened to be in the house, stop what they were doing and drift down the stairs to listen.

He understood that they were not used to hearing this kind of music in the house, read from the page, at this level of difficulty. "It's a *commitment*," his mother used to say, with a hush, as if art stood above all else. But what had this commitment brought him? Two dollars a night if he was a colored man, five if he was not.

She had not minded about him passing, but she was always afraid he would be distracted by the sounds of stride and Dixieland. "You're not playing that Saturday night music, are you?" she would say. "Put that sound right out your mind." She didn't even like it when he embellished his classical pieces with extra ornaments, or a little too much rubato. "Don't doctor it up," she would tell him. "You think you know better than Mendelssohn?"

But when it came to jazz, she need not have feared, since he could not play it. He had heard it sure enough, wailing underground in clubs and speakeasies, all through Prohibition, hot, polyphonic, toe-tapping, full of syncopated rhythms and bent, naughty notes—perfect for small and secret spaces. Now that alcohol was legal again, the music was changing, along with the very character of the night itself. Swanky clubs and ballrooms opened, featuring larger, dance-hall-type orchestras. With so many more instruments, especially on top in the reeds and the brass, songs had to be tightly arranged, by skilled bandleaders. This meant work, and it was considerably closer to Thomas's own playing than the exuberant Dixie-style polyphony of the 'twenties had been—but still out of reach.

This was clear to him after he heard the top bandleaders like Henderson and Ellington, who played whole orchestras like instruments. Thomas could play, but they were titans, and there was never a moment when he did not know the difference.

Big Lewis certainly knew. "You play nice," he said, that first week in Seattle. "But where you going to get work playing like that?"

"That's the problem," said Thomas.

"What you need is to learn the standards, with a little swing." Big Lewis launched into singing "About a Quarter to Nine," a popular song from the film *42nd Street*. "Go on!" He waved toward the keys.

Thomas shrank, humiliated. "I can't play that way. Reading is all I can do."

"You serious? That's it?"

"Yes. If it's written, I can play it. Let me get the music for that one and look at it." So Big Lewis advanced him five cents, and Thomas went down to Jackson Street for the sheet music, came back, and read it through. When he did, it was so simple he was embarrassed. In playing it for Big Lewis, he did his best to embellish it so it would sound more presentable.

But the older man was unimpressed. "Swing the rhythm! Let it go!"

Thomas started again.

"No! You turned the beat around again. Where are you, in

church?" Big Lewis gave a slam to the nearest tabletop and scuffed off.

Each night Thomas listened closely to the jazz in the basement, especially the piano work of Julian Henson, which was tightly controlled even when he improvised. There was restraint to it, a kind of glassy hardness. *If I could play jazz, I would play like this fellow.* But when he tried it at the piano the next day, it still eluded him.

Big Lewis heard. "You're trying too hard. It's variations on a song. Think of it like that, a song." He showed Thomas how to use the blues scale to force what he called the worried notes, especially the flatted third and seventh, over a major chord progression. When Thomas could not hear how to layer these up with counter-rhythms, or how to build chords from dissonant intervals, the older man sang him through it and showed him, using his voice, how to dance around his improvisations and get off them as quick as a grace note. By the end of that week Thomas could play at least a few of the popular ballroom numbers, like "Body and Soul" and "I Can't Get Started," and his renditions sounded respectable, if not exactly right.

"Will I get by?" he asked Big Lewis.

"No. Not around here—too many good musicians. Now, in a small town, I 'spect your sound could get over. You want that to happen, you got to work, and work hard."

So Thomas threw himself into practicing dance numbers every afternoon, and though he got better, he knew he was still well shy of the mark when Big Lewis pulled him aside one night at closing time and told him there was an agent in the house, a man from China, who needed a piano player.

"To play in *China?*"

"Shanghai. I've heard tell of it—fellows get recruited."

Thomas stared. Shanghai! It was alluring, dangerous; there were songs about it. "Is that him?" he said of the tall, rangy fellow who was the only Asian man left in the place now that it had emptied out. He had a narrow face, doorknob cheekbones jutting beneath his long, dark eyes. Thomas noticed his hair was combed straight back and pomaded down, while his suit still showed creases from the steamer trunk. He dressed like a gentleman, which struck Thomas as a promising chord of commonality.

"Go talk to him," Big Lewis said.

"What if he—"

"Say you're a pianist, then just play. Don't say anything else."

He looked down at his overalls. Maybe it was a good thing, a lucky thing, the way he was dressed. "Play what?" he said nervously.

"The *Rhapsody*."

Thomas closed his eyes for a second; yes, genius, Big Lewis was right. *Rhapsody in Blue* was the one piece he had memorized which was flat-out impressive and also danced at least a little bit close to the music he had to pretend to know. So he crossed the floor, still littered and sticky, and set his mop and bucket down with a neat slosh. "Name's Thomas Greene," he said. "My boss tells me you're looking."

And now he was in Shanghai, beside Alonzo, coming to the end of the lane, to Rue Lafayette, where they paused before turning. Thomas studied the older man's face. "You look like you like it here."

"Best thing ever happened to me. All my life I knew what I deserved, but Shanghai is the only place I ever got it. You'll see." With those words, Alonzo raised a casually crooked finger, and a panting coolie ran up with a rickshaw. Alonzo climbed up onto the rattan seat and slid over, making room for Thomas, who stood frozen. The older man had been here a year and knew all the holes and corners, sure, but should they really be pulled along by a poor, unfortunate man in a harness? Even the slaves had not done work like this. But the bare-armed coolie stamped impatiently, slick with sweat in the cold air, his sinews ropy, his legs strong. He wanted to resume running.

Alonzo was looking down with compassion, and Thomas understood that he too must have crossed this particular threshold on arrival. The city was cruel. Maybe all cities were cruel.

"You know what?" Alonzo said to him. "Man's got a right to choose his master." He patted the seat.

And Thomas climbed up beside him.

They swayed and jostled down the street, the gasping, heaving coolie pulling them at a steady rhythmic lope. Thomas felt almost sick, sweat popping out, though whether it was his discomfort with the coolie or the rocking motion roiling his overambitious breakfast, he was not sure. Alonzo seemed wholly undisturbed, placid almost, as he gazed down at the traffic, so Thomas forced his mind off the rickshaw puller, instead ranging back over what other musicians had told him about Shanghai before he left Seattle.

"Freest place on earth," Roger Felton had said. "Pleasure every damn place you look, and your money just as good as any white man's. Think on *that!* Fellows earn a lot, no two ways about it, but there isn't a one of them I've seen come back with a penny. They spend it all."

Not I, had been Thomas's silent reaction. *I can save money.* He had been much more sobered by what Roger had said when he asked about politics. "Say the Japanese fighting the Chinese, and the Chinese fighting each other. Say gangsters running the city. People disagree, they end up dead, so you best play your music and keep clear of it. Hear?"

The money Lin Ming had quoted him seemed to override such concerns, not to mention his own insufficient skills: fifty dollars a week for band members, and one hundred dollars a week for him, the leader. Granted, those were Shanghai dollars, worth only a third of American, but Lin had said Shanghai prices were as low as dirt— twelve dollars for a tailor-made suit, two for dinner in a restaurant, three dollars for a woman, all night. And in Shanghai he could have any woman, no race laws, a thought that would not stop tugging at him as they steamed across the Pacific.

At home, in Maryland, he'd had his share of white women. Sometimes, when he played a party, he got lucky with a good-time girl afterward, and once in a while, when he was performing as an Egyptian or an Argentine, that girl would be white. None of them were the kind of girls he could know, or call on; they were janes, party girls, girls with bobbed hair and short flapper skirts who liked to be drunk every night, and were still young and pretty enough to do it. Actually there were very few girls back in Baltimore that he could call on, because he had never earned enough money to court the kind of respectable girl he wanted. He hoped Shanghai was going to be different.

On the ship, in his tiny metal-riveted cabin, in the small mirror screwed to the wall, he assessed his face as he tried to put his hopes in order. He took after his father's family, everyone always said so, light-skinned people. His father's mother had been a teacher, and her father a chemist and an officer in the Twenty-fifth Infantry regiment in the Indian Wars. He had inherited his father's looks and his mother's ear for music, which came in turn from her own mother. But that grandmother fell in love with a landowning man during the Reconstruction years and became a farm wife outside Easton on the Chesapeake's far shore. She never wavered, his grandmother; a cream and tan beauty in her youth, she played the rest of her life on a parlor upright, performing works that asked hard, crashing questions with no easy answers, pouring through open windows to dissipate in the tangled woods. He had loved that place.

But it was gone, separated from him first by a continent on the rails, and now by the blue Pacific. He had never been at sea before, or on any vessel larger than the flat-bottomed scow he and his cousins had used to explore the tributaries of the Chesapeake up and down Talbot County. He stayed in his cabin that whole first day aboard ship, so afraid was he. It was not until the sun was dropping into the December horizon that he heard the thump of music from Lin Ming's cabin, and stood with his ear to the metal wall. He knew the song, he had heard it on the radio, back on Creel Street—"Memphis Blues," by Fletcher Henderson. In a rush of longing, home came back to him, the velvet air, damp and biting in winter, sweet in summer. He almost heard the far-off roar of the crowd at a baseball game, the slipping, satisfying ring of leather shoes on white marble steps. He had left that world, but not its music, for that had crossed the ocean and was here with him, making him bold. He stepped out and knocked on Lin Ming's door.

His knuckle had barely touched the metal when the door swung back. Lin looked at him like a thirsty man seeing water; farther along, Thomas would understand how much the other man hated to be alone. "Come in! I thought you would never be emerging. What?" He followed Thomas's gaze to his ankle-length Chinese gown, slit up each side for easy movement, worn over trousers. "You never saw one? It is freedom. Try sometime. You like Fletcher Henderson?"

"Very much," said Thomas, always appreciative of the musician's formality and control.

Lin looked pleased. "He is high level. And to me, he sounds like someone who works from the sheet music. Like you. What's wrong? You look like you want to show a clean pair of heels! Don't be embarrassed. I could see that you work by the reading and writing. Now here." He piled a stack of seventy-eights into Thomas's arms. "Take these to your room. Take my gramophone. These are songs the Kansas City Kings play, and we have twenty-two days to Shanghai, enough time for you to write them out. At least you can arrive with something."

Raised on obstacles, Thomas felt the surprise of gratitude almost like a blow. In his experience, one got help from friends, from family, not outsiders. "Thank you."

Lin waved him away. "Don't thank me yet. I am taking you to China, where things are as precarious as a pile of eggs. Japan is invading us, they need land and food and the labor of our millions. They already occupy part of the north and are pushing south. China should be united to fight them, but we are divided into the two sides who want to kill each other — the Nationalists and Communists."

"Whose side are you on?"

"Neither. And I tell you why. The Nationalists and Communists may be poles apart, heaven in the north and the earth in the south, but they do agree on one thing — they think jazz is a dangerous element, and must be banned. So! How can I support either side?"

"Ban jazz?"

"I know." Lin shook his head. "The arrogance. One hundred mouths could not explain it away. And how could the government ever ban any type of music anyway? This is the age of radio! But Little Greene, listen." He had started using the nickname on account of Thomas being twenty-five to his twenty-eight. "When you get to Shanghai, Japanese people will try to tell you we Chinese are incapable of governing ourselves. That is their superstition, that we are lazy and disorganized, stupid, we are children who need them to take care of us. They will tell you that we want them there."

"I don't think they'll tell *me* anything. I'm a musician."

"Just remember, no matter what they say, do not believe it. They want us as their slaves." He stretched, settled his gown, and said, "I am dying of the hunger. Let us go to dinner."

It was the twentieth of December when they finally steamed up the Huangpu, watching from the rail in the cold as lines of coolies carried goods to and from the docks at the water's edge. They sailed around a turn in the river and the Bund came into view, an imposing colonnaded line of eclectic façades topped with cupolas and clock towers. Behind it crouched a city of low brown buildings.

The ship dropped anchor, and passengers lined up to board the lighter that would take them to shore. He could see the Bund was thick with traffic, its sidewalks crowded. The energy seemed to come right through his feet the moment they bumped the dock and he stepped on the ground again, dear solid ground; he dodged through the crowd behind Lin Ming. All around them passengers swirled away to meet friends, relatives, and servants, then dispersed across a narrow strip of grass directly onto the boulevard.

"No customs?" said Thomas, for they had simply walked ashore, without even showing their identification.

"A free port," Lin said proudly. "All are welcome."

On the sidewalk, the air rang with a dozen languages. They were surrounded by men in Chinese gowns and padded jackets, and wand-like women in high-necked dresses and sumptuous fur wraps. Other men passed wearing tunics from India and robes from Arabia, some with faces darker than his own. Suddenly he was not different any-more, everybody was different. No one looked twice at him, for the first time in his life. And no one cared that he stood right there on the sidewalk, neither deferring nor giving way nor lifting his hand to tip his hat, which was in itself a marvel. Even a few pale foreign women in their tick-tock heels and woolen coats walked right past him, un-concerned. He could feel a grin growing on his face.

"Over here," Lin Ming called, and Thomas saw him holding open the door to a black car. Rarely had Thomas ridden in a private car, but he slid in now, the smooth, fragrant leather and the murmur of the engine enveloping him. Shanghai was a fairy world, he decided as they drove along the river with its endless docks and braying vessels of all shapes and sizes.

The city was mighty, yet Thomas could see hints of the war Lin had described, too: clots of soldiers in brown uniforms standing along the wharves, puttees tight to their knees and rifles hooked casually on their shoulders.

"Japanese," Lin confirmed.

"I thought you said they had only taken over the northeast."

"Yes. Shanghai still belongs to China. But there was trouble four years ago, in 'thirty-two—fighting—and the foreign powers forced a cease-fire by promising that only Japan could have troops in Shang-hai. China could not."

"No Chinese troops here? But it is a Chinese city."

"Correct." Lin dripped dark irony.

"How could foreign powers force China to accept a thing like that?"

Lin almost wanted to laugh. "You are forgetting what I told you on the voyage. Shanghai is the city of foreign Concessions. Little colonies, each owned by another country. The city seems very free to you foreigners, but we Chinese must serve someone else. Do not forget that. You are a *jueshi jia,* a jazz man, you of all people should understand that we are not free. Up ahead, you see that row of docks? The Quai de France? That is the Frenchtown. This part now, we pass through? This is the International Settlement, belongs to Britain and America."

"Like foreign colonies," said Thomas.

"Concessions," Lin corrected him, and said something musical in light, tapping tones to the driver, who made a right turn. "And here is the Avenue Édouard VII, the border of Frenchtown."

Thomas saw that the street signs on the right were in Chinese, while suddenly on the left, he read Rue Petit, Rue Tourane, Rue Saigon. The buildings here had red stone façades with tall French doors and wrought-iron balconies, and between the cross-streets, small lanes led away. Peering into these, he saw women carrying vegetables for the evening meal, young girls in groups with their arms linked, grannies shepherding little children. It was as foreign as it could be, yet faintly familiar.

The false sense of welcome evaporated when Lin cut into his thoughts. "There is one thing you must know about the International Settlement, the district we just left behind — there are race laws."

"What did you say?"

"It is shared by England and America, but they have the American race laws. Like your South."

"Like the *South?*" Thomas felt his head squeezed. Here? On the other side of the world?

"Now, now," said Lin, "do not react so. You are seeing a serpent's image in a wine cup. It is only in that one district, and they will love you everyplace else, especially here, in Frenchtown, where they are crazy for musicians like you. Everyone will think you are exotic."

Thomas sank back into the seat. Only one district? There was no way he was going to avoid the International Settlement, for it included the center of the city, the downtown, the docks, the Bund. He mulled this new worry as they rolled through Frenchtown.

"Look," said Lin, "here we are." They had stopped before a wrought-iron gate leading to a small front courtyard and a large house. Its European-style stone façade and tall windows were topped by upturned Chinese eaves; four or five bedrooms at least, Thomas thought, nothing like the small apartment in which he had been brought up. *We are gentlefolk,* his mother had always said, but that had been more a philosophy than a reality. The longing stabbed through him to have his own room; that would be a fine thing, after all the cramped and crowded places he had rested his head since his mother had passed. "How many of the fellows live here?"

Lin was already up the front steps. "Just you," he said over his shoulder.

Impossible, he thought, stepping up just as the door opened to a middle-aged Chinese man in a white tunic. Two other men and an older woman formed a hasty line behind him.

"Who are these people?" said Thomas. Through the door he glimpsed rosewood wainscoting and an expensive-looking porcelain bowl on the hall table.

"Your servants," said Lin Ming. "This is Uncle Hua, your steward."

"Servants?" The first word Thomas attempted to speak in his new household was so thick with disbelief it stuck in his mouth.

Uncle Hua joined his fists before his chest, and lowered his eyes deferentially. "Yes, Master," he said.

Jesus, was it only yesterday? was his amazed thought as he and Alonzo dismounted from the rickshaw in front of the Royal. The older man unlocked the lobby door, and dropped the brass key in Thomas's hand. "This was Augustus's key."

It felt heavy and cold to Thomas. The bandleader he was replacing had died of a heart attack, in a brothel, and as he slipped the key into his pocket, he understood with a lurch that the house, the servants, the piano in the parlor, even the bed with its silk quilts must have belonged to Augustus too. Now their footsteps were shushing across the empty marble floors of the lobby, through the arch. Across the ballroom, on the stage, ten other men waited in a pearly circle of light, their legs crossed, loose-trousered, instruments on their laps.

Thomas got up beside the piano, one hand on the lid to cover his tremble. He knew he was a liar, and soon they would know too. "First, before anything else, my sympathy to every one of you for the loss of Augustus Jones. It was a shock, and I'm sorry. But now we have ten days before the theater reopens on New Year's Eve. I know fourteen of your songs. That's not enough, and I aim to learn the rest just as fast as I can. Hope you'll bear with me."

A resentful mumble circled the room.

A squat, short-legged man with a French horn cradled in his lap said, "How come you don't know the songs? Where'd you play before?"

Sweat trickled as Thomas tried to deliver the answer he had worked out earlier. "Various places. Pittsburgh, Richmond, Wilmington." In fact, with the exception of Wilmington, Thomas had never even visited those places. He was hoping none of the band members had either. "Let's start with your signature tune—'Exactly Like You.'" The 1930 song, perennially popular on the radio, was sweet and simple, easy to play. He had practiced it. But as soon as he started it, instead of falling in with him, the others stayed in for only a phrase or two, and dropped off. He stopped. "What?"

"You gotta be kidding," said the other horn player, whose jowls seemed to hang straight from the point of his chin to his collar.

"All right, sir," said Thomas. "You are?"

"Errol Mutter."

"Pleasure to meet you. Why don't I count you off, and you play just a few bars of your version so I can hear it?" And before anyone could protest, he ticked backwards until they started. Within two bars he heard how his accent had been on the wrong beat, and he came back in on piano, this time more or less correctly, if without the proper swing. He saw Errol exchange a look with the other horn player, and felt the drops track down his spine as he bent his face closer to the keys. It was not until the end of the song that he realized Lin Ming had come in, and gone up to the balcony to watch.

Lin was not alone in his box above the stage; he had come to observe with his sister-by-affection, Song Yuhua. She sat very straight beside him in her closely fitted *qipao* of stiff blue brocade, her hair bound at the neck with flowers, the way Du Yuesheng liked it. He wanted the women in his entourage to look sweet and old-fashioned.

Song was not one of Du's wives, only an indentured servant, if an educated one. She was versed in the classics, at home with literature, fluent in English, and passable in French. She could play a simple Bach invention. For Du Yuesheng, who was illiterate, she was not only a translator but an accessory of incalculable value; for her he had paid a considerable price.

Lin Ming was the boss's illegitimate son, so to him Song was family, and also the only person in Du Yuesheng's inner circle he could really trust. "What news of Chiang Kai-shek?" he asked, for as soon as the ship docked, he had heard how the Nationalist leader had been kidnapped by his own allies in the north.

"He refuses to even talk to the Communists," said Song. "He keeps insisting he will fight them until they submit to him, and only then will he resist the Japanese. His kidnappers are threatening to execute Chiang if he won't stop fighting the Communists!"

"And what does Chiang say?"

"He says no! He just repeats that the Communists have to submit to him. Then he goes in his room and sits on his bed and reads his Bible."

"Speak reasonably!"

"I do! Every word is true. They are at an impasse. Maybe they will kill him," she said, her voice faintly hopeful.

He shot her a look.

"Someone has to do something," she protested. "Look how close Japan's army is to Peking and Tianjin. If those cities fall, we have no hope. We are fish swimming in a cooking pot."

"If," Lin repeated. "For now, they are still far away, and as long as that lasts, as long as the city crowds into our ballrooms to dance to *mi mi zhi yin*," decadent and sentimental music, "we will be here. And so will my American *jueshi jia*." He nodded toward the stage below, where Thomas Greene had just come to the end of a song and risen from the piano bench to address the others.

"Now, with Augustus," they heard Thomas say, "which did you-all follow? Scores or charts?"

"Scores?" said Cecil Pratt, the trumpet player. "Charts? We just followed Augustus."

Snorts of laughter rose. "Hell to pay if you weren't there by the second measure, too!"

"Do you like it that way?" Thomas said, sensing an opening. "Because I'll tell you, I cannot play without either a score or a chart, for the life of me. So if there's anyone who would like written music . . ."

A wondering quiet spread. "Man," came the voice of the violin player. "You'd do that?"

Watching from above, Lin and Song exchanged worried looks.

"You'd write out all that stuff?" said the drummer.

"I would," Thomas said.

Up in the box, Song said to Lin, "You have to get him a copyist."

"Immediately," Lin agreed. Thomas needed someone who could shadow the band at rehearsals, and write scores and charts all night. As was generally the case with servants in Shanghai, the cost would be insignificant, chicken feathers and garlic skins.

"How many want scores?" Thomas was saying, on the stage below, and hands went up. These were the ones who could read music. "Charts?" The rest of the hands rose. He made a note and then sat down to play the opening chords of the next tune, and the musicians, mollified for a moment, moved with him. Reeds were moistened, brass lifted to the ready, and they set the pace for him to follow.

By the time rehearsal ended at six, the box where Lin Ming and Song Yuhua had sat was empty, a fact Thomas could not help but notice as he went out to the lobby to say good-bye to each man, repeat his thanks, and stress again his sympathy for the loss of Augustus. He was deliberately warm to the horn players. And he was surprised by how, up close, the two brothers who played reeds looked even younger than he had thought. He wondered how they had gotten themselves over here with the Kings in the first place.

"Don't you worry," said Alonzo, beside him. "Those boys cause more trouble than six men, you'll see."

"I will, eh? By the way — did you see Lin Ming in the box up above stage left?"

"'Course I did," said Alonzo. "That's the big boss's box. Once in a while he'll show up late at night. You'll know who he is when you see him."

"Boss of what?" Thomas said, confused. "The company?"

"Company?" Alonzo gave him a long look, speculation drifting to amusement. "Is that what Mr. Lin told you?"

"He said his father was head of the Tung Vong Company, and that they owned a controlling stake in the Royal." Thomas was pretty sure that was what his new friend had said.

Alonzo was laughing, in his gentle way. "Well, that's probably true. And about the Green Gang holding some big old part of the Tung Vong Company, you can forget I ever told you, if you like —"

"No, of course not." Thomas was embarrassed. He had to adjust, take in everything, or he would fail. Probably he would fail anyway. "Tell me."

"The Green Gang is who Mr. Lin works for, make no mistake. It's the biggest Triad in China, and his father runs it."

"His *father?*"

"He didn't tell you that?"

"No." Thomas tried to stay composed. "And a Triad is —"

"A gang, but bigger, and more like a secret society. These fellows swear their lives, forever."

Thomas felt his eyes blind over as these new facets of his world turned before him. *You don't know anything yet.* Still he had to play the boss right now, the bandleader, and so he turned a calm expression to

Alonzo, who was twenty years his senior, and clearly knew all about Shanghai, and said, "Thank you for telling me." He reached up to switch off the lobby lights. "But to my mind, that's Lin Ming's affair. Like you said about the rickshaw coolie, man's got a right to choose his master. Right? See you in the morning, then. And thanks for today. I mean it." And they buttoned their coats up high and walked briskly in opposite directions, fedoras pulled down low against the cold.

Thomas was freezing, and all he wanted was to get home to that big, lonely house so he could practice for the next day. This time he would not hesitate, not even look twice at the coolie; he would leap right up on the seat, and tell the boy *chop-chop.*

2

BEFORE THE REHEARSAL ended, Lin Ming left with Song, and after putting her in a rickshaw, he crossed Frenchtown to see his father, who was at the Canidrome. Lin loved this part of the evening in Shanghai, the first hour of true dark, for night was when the city's enchantments beckoned, from the genteel to the most depraved, anything, so long as you could pay. Shanghai at night was not a place, exactly, but a dream-state of fantasy and permission, and to Lin Ming, no place embodied it quite like the Canidrome.

The entertainment complex was by far the biggest place of its kind in which the Green Gang had a stake, though its profits were dwarfed by income from the Gang's much larger criminal empire. Still, with its ballrooms, restaurants, gambling parlors, mah-jongg dens, and a full-sized covered dog track, it was Shanghai's grandest and greatest palace of nightlife.

Lin Ming approached the grounds by the Rue Lafayette gate. "Who goes?" came the gruff voice of Iron Arms, one of the guards.

"Your mother's crack," Lin shot back genially. "I just came from her place."

"*My* mother's? Someone as puny as you would get lost in there. *Ma gan,*" Iron sniffed, sesame stalk, a nod to the long skinny frame Lin had in common with his father, Du Yuesheng.

Lin took the remark placidly. He knew he looked startlingly like Du; no one who saw the two of them together ever doubted their relationship.

"Pass," Iron Arms said, gruff but indulgent, and Lin vanished into the dark path that led under bare-branched trees to the rear of the dog track. The air was cold, and he was well inside the walls, but still he could smell Shanghai — rotting waste, temple incense, diesel oil, perfume, flowers. He may have had no real home, owing to the fact that he had no clan behind him, but the smell of Shanghai was his anchor, festering, sweetly fecund, always drawing him back. He crossed the dog-track arena, an oblong bowl above which banks of louvered windows rose to a high, steel-trussed ceiling. Rimming the track were the tiered observation stands, finished with iron rails and matching light posts in old gas lamp style, every row jammed with gamblers talking and jostling.

The shot popped, the fake rabbit screeched off, and the dogs bounded after it. The noise of the crowd rose to a long roar, deafening, a wall of prayer and hope that fell away as fast as it started when the finish was crossed and the dogs fell back, slavering. The winners' numbers were called off in a string of languages.

In the next building a long hallway led to the back of the ballroom stages. He had two bands at the Canidrome, the Teddy Weatherford Orchestra, which played from seven thirty to two in the large ballroom, and what remained of Buck Clayton's Harlem Gentlemen after Clayton himself had been let go as a result of a brawl. In the matter of his dismissal, Lin's hands had been tied, though fortunately the man had been able to find other work in the city to start earning his fare home. When it came to the rest of the Harlem Gentlemen, Lin simply waited a decent amount of time and hired them back, and they played the tea dances in the afternoon and early evening. Tonight, since he was here to see his father, he skirted the ballrooms and went directly upstairs.

He found Du behind a polished desk, chatting with H. H. Kung, who lounged in an armchair opposite him. Kung was the Minister of

Finance, the Governor of the Central Bank of China, and an indecently rich man. For the moment, while Chiang Kai-shek was being held prisoner in the north, he was also the acting head of the Chinese government.

"Young Lin," he said warmly, and grasped Lin's hands, temporarily parking his cigar in his mouth to do so.

"Pleasure to see you," Lin said. They understood each other well. Dr. Kung had studied at Oberlin and Yale, Lin Ming at boarding school; both were at home with the English language and the West-ocean mind.

Next he turned to his father, sitting straight and gaunt in his Chinese gown, skull clean-shaven as always. "Teacher," he said politely. Du had founded a conservative school for Chinese boys, and he liked to be addressed this way.

Du accepted his obeisance without remark, and turned directly to the news Kung had brought. "The Generalissimo's wife, and her brother T. V. Soong, will fly to Xi'an tomorrow with a large amount of money to purchase Chiang Kai-shek's release. They will get him out."

"Your in-laws," Lin said to Kung respectfully, since he knew the man was married to the eldest Soong sister, Ai-ling. "I hope they are safe."

"Oh, they're safe enough," said Kung. "The problem is getting old Chiang to listen to the demands of his kidnappers. He has to give up on beating the Communists now, and fight Japan."

Du did not conceal his shock. "Give up fighting the Communists?"

"For now," said Kung, puffing on his cigar.

"But I shall continue to execute them."

Kung smiled, because Du Yuesheng would execute whomever he chose, and there was nothing anyone could do about it. "As you will," he said amiably. "But your attentions are needed against our Japanese invaders, old friend. This is another reason I came to see you tonight — to tell you that a new, high-ranking officer has arrived from Japan. An Admiral."

Lin strained forward with interest—an Admiral would automatically, at this moment, be the top-ranking Japanese officer in Shanghai.

"Morioka is his name," said Kung.

"Our new Viceroy," Du said sarcastically. "Yes, I know."

"You do?" said Kung, drawing and relighting. "Regrettably, I have heard nothing personal about him yet."

"Wait a moment." Du knocked three times on the side of the desk, and one of his many secretaries came in, a senior Cantonese named Pok. "Sir," he said to Du respectfully, and then again to Kung, "Sir." Lin Ming he ignored. His fluent Shanghainese was stretched by the drawling tones of his home dialect as he spoke. "One of my men has an informant who works in the officers' section of the new Japanese Naval Headquarters."

Kung drew his brows together in thought. "The old Gong Da Textile Mill they took over and reinforced, that one?"

"Yes. The new Admiral has his apartments there. Here is what your servant has learned: Morioka goes out at night and drinks, but is never drunk. He is married, but his wife and children did not accompany him, nor does he have their pictures."

"There will be something he cares for," Du insisted.

Kung nodded. "His weak spot."

"Yes, Teacher," said Pok. "You are correct. There is indeed a thing he loves—music. His quarters are filled with gramophone records."

"Really." Du's cold, serpentine gaze lit with interest, flicked to Lin, and then back to Pok. "What kind of music?"

"Jazz," said Pok.

"You don't say," Kung said in English, sending a twinkle toward Lin Ming, not yet seeing how the news was strangling him with terror. "And for you, Teacher," Kung went on, back in Chinese, "What a bolt of luck! You don't have to do a thing. He'll come to you."

Lin stood in the center, feeling everything around him crashing. He did not ask for much, just to bring music from over the sea, to shepherd his musicians, to be with his favorite girl, Zhuli. He did not expect to be free; he understood that his father, and the Green Gang, controlled his life, and might even end up choosing the time and manner of his death. He also accepted the fact that he personally was powerless to stop Japan. But his musicians, his flock that he'd brought from America and nurtured here in Shanghai's endless night—they should be left alone.

Pok backed out, with Du's thanks. Du always treated his secretaries well.

"Lucky. As for you, do not worry so much," Kung said to Lin. "There is no reason why they should sacrifice the plum tree for the peach tree."

Kung's kindly joke in turning the phrase around—in the old saying, the plum tree *did* get sacrificed—failed to allay Lin's fear. Meanwhile, Du Yuesheng nodded approvingly, for ancient military strategy was the kind of traditional tidbit he loved.

Lin stood motionless. "Please," he heard himself say, small and squeaky.

"What?" Du looked over sharply.

"There are so many jazz men in Shanghai, others could serve as bait—"

But his father held up a silencing hand. "It is not up to us. It is he who will decide. No one can resist Shanghai for long, including Morioka. He will be like a bird hovering over a field of flowers. Sooner or later he will light, and then we will have him." He looked hard at Lin. "Wherever he comes to rest."

Lin ducked his head, burning with hatred—for his father, for Japan, and for himself most of all—because he knew that no matter what order he received, even if—when—it put one of his own in danger, he would have to obey it.

Thursday was Christmas Eve, 1936, and after rehearsal, Thomas decided for the first time not to go home and practice, but to go out. He was not homesick, far from it; he remained glad to be far from

America. Things here put his homeland to shame. Every day he woke up expecting to feel some nostalgia, yet it never came. He missed his mother, but that was different, for nothing was going to bring her back.

On Christmas Eve, he could not take the big house with its hovering servants. He had no privacy there, and no real company either. So he buttoned his overcoat and walked from the theater to Avenue Joffre, lit up with shops and restaurants. "Little Russia" was what the other musicians called this stretch, and beneath the signs in Cyrillic letters, the shop and restaurant windows were bright with holiday lights and crèches. The joy of it was touching; from the door of one restaurant, as it opened and closed around a laughing couple swathed in fur, he could hear clinking glass and the strains of a piano. Everywhere there were parties tonight.

Back on Creel Street, there would be lights in all the windows, and carolers up and down the sidewalks, and warm turkey smells in the hallways. A sharp sting went through him at the thought, and he pretended it was the cold, and clutched his coat collar a little closer.

He would go to hear another orchestra. Over in the International Settlement, which he had not yet visited on account of its race laws, white jazz groups from America were playing at clubs like the Vienna Garden and the Majestic Café. Those clubs, according to his band members, employed dance hostesses, mostly White Russians, which put them a rung below French Concession clubs like the Royal, the Saint Anna's Ballroom, the Palais Café, and the Ambassador. Tonight he would pick a place in Frenchtown, with a black orchestra.

With the help of a city map he had bought, he saw it was a reasonably short walk to the Canidrome, where Teddy Weatherford was about to end his long engagement and move his orchestra to Calcutta for the winter season.

When he arrived, the gate to the complex was wide open, and most of what had probably been intended as lawn was filled with rows of boxy parked cars. He was able to stroll right in through the front door, which still exhilarated him. The Chinese hostess welcomed him with a smile, and, when he mentioned Teddy Weatherford, directed him toward one of the ballrooms.

By now, Thomas knew what to do. As soon as he entered the ballroom and spoke to the headwaiter, he had a tab, just as he did in every reputable establishment: Shanghai's chit system. You signed for whatever you wanted—purchases, food, drink, women, anything that money bought. At the end of the month, messengers would come around with the totals, and he would dispatch Little Kong, the most junior of his servants, with payments. In this way, still awaiting his first paycheck, he was ushered to a table like any man of means, and a cold bottle of Clover Beer and a chilled glass were set in front of him.

The men in his own band had praised Teddy Weatherford, and he understood why as soon as the man strode out to cheers from the crowd. Weatherford answered them with calls for a Merry Christmas, then hopped on the bench and launched the set with a body-shaking burst of brio. Out walked his sidemen in a color-coordinated line, and Thomas recognized Darnell Howard on violin; he had seen him once with James P. Johnson's Plantation Days Orchestra. They raised their instruments in perfect sync, while Weatherford drove his own piano storm system, thundering, crashing, clouds breaking, sun shining.

Thomas watched, mesmerized. He would never play with that kind of power. They were electrifying, and as soon as they took a break, he hastened over with congratulations.

Weatherford turned, whiskey in hand, face split in his trademark smile. "'Bout time you came up and said hello! Boys! This here's the new bandleader over to the Royal."

"Hello," he said, "Thomas Greene." He shook hands with each of the men who crowded around. "You were all terrific. I'd give anything to know how you do it. And you," he said to Darnell Howard, trying to fluff up the appearance of connection, "I saw you on tour with James P. Johnson. Fine playing. Pleasure to see you on stage here. But I'm curious." He turned back to the bandleader. "How did you know who I was?"

"Come on!" Weatherford laughed. "You think there are so many of us here? I knew you for fair soon as I saw you. Not Harlem, though — not from the look of you, or the way you talk. Am I right?"

"You are," said Thomas, wondering what else about him showed. "I'm from Maryland, the Eastern Shore." He was afraid to say Baltimore, in case Weatherford knew any musicians in the scene there. "A little place in the countryside near Easton." At least that was true, for his grandfather's farm was such a place, and a sort of home to him.

"Maryland! What'd I say?" Teddy exulted. "All-American, though." Beneath his suit, congenially unbuttoned, Weatherford's shirt showed spots of piano-sweat. "Let's sit down," he said, and they moved to an empty table. "Mr. Lin taking care of you?"

"Sure." Everyone seemed to know Lin Ming.

"And you have somewhere to go tonight, for Christmas Eve? 'Cause you can go on out with us after midnight, if you want to stay around."

"You're very kind." Thomas did not want to admit that he had nothing to do, that the only people he knew here were the fellows in the Kansas City Kings, none of whom had invited him over tonight. "I'm sorry — other plans. So tell me, where else do you play?"

"The whole circuit," said Weatherford. "Here in the summer months, to the winter holidays. Then to the Grand Hotel in Calcutta, and the Taj Mahal Hotel in Bombay. Midwinter's the big season there. In between we go up the Malay jungle."

"You mean to Singapore?"

"We sail to Singapore. But then we get in cars and drive up the jungle."

"To where?"

"Big rubber plantations. British planters. Man, they give balls you wouldn't believe! White folks coming from hundreds of miles around, gowns, tuxedos, diamonds, glamorous as you please, ballrooms with marble floors and great big chandeliers bigger and finer than what they got here — out in the jungle! They love the way I pound it!"

NIGHT IN SHANGHAI · 33

"So do the people here," Thomas said, rounding up the ballroom in a glance. "What about the International Settlement, with the race laws?"

Weatherford shook his head. "Mr. Lin tells everybody to be careful, and I've heard of a few fights, but sure, you can go there. You might want to steer clear of the big hotels or restaurants, they won't let you in the front door, but private parties are no problem a-tall. The Brits have villas out there with lawns and gardens out of a fairy tale."

"What about Japan?" Thomas nodded toward a small group of uniformed soldiers, lounging on the edge of the dance floor.

The bandleader gave them a long look. "They like jazz, don't get me wrong, but I've seen what they do when they take over. They seize Shanghai, we're taking it right off our circuit, man. Just like that."

"What have you seen? What do they do?"

"They take a city, they take over the nightlife and ruin it. They have this new drug they are pushing, heroin they call it, it comes from opium and they inject it with needles—that's why they want nightclubs. Don't do it. They take over, you get out of here. What?" He looked up at a signal from Darnell Howard, and drained his glass. "Sorry, man. I got to go beat out some blues."

"Thank you," said Thomas.

"To your sound," Weatherford said with a salute, and Thomas smiled as he tried to quell his anxiety. He had no sound, and he probably wouldn't be finding it in the next six days, either. The Kings had a sound, a big one; their songs rode on riffing, bluesy backgrounds, punctuated by spontaneous solos from the reeds and brass. Arrangements were already tighter now, under him, but as yet he had no idea what his piano could bring to it.

After the third stunning set he left, and stood shivering on the street, hand up for a rickshaw, thinking that he had work to do. This time he did not even blink at paying a man to haul him through the cold like a beast of burden; all the best people did it. He already knew better than to tip, too. If you tipped, they lost respect for you. As for being alone on Christmas Eve, jazz men were wandering men, men of the blues, and it was correct for him to be on the road. It fit.

On his front steps, he had barely touched the key to the lock when Uncle Hua swung the door back from inside. "Master have guest," he said.

"Thank you." Thomas stepped into the parlor, where the sight of Lin Ming, on the settee, sparked a grin. "Pleasure to see you!"

"You too," said Lin. "Did you hear the news about Chiang Kai-shek?"

"No." Thomas had heard people at the Canidrome talking about the kidnapping, but had not tuned in to it.

"They released him, because he promised to fight side by side with the Communists! And because H. H. Kung and T. V. Soong paid a huge amount of money. It is the big news."

"That's good, right? Maybe you can beat Japan now." Thomas was thinking of the ruination Weatherford had predicted if they took Shanghai.

"Yes! Drive those bandits out!" Lin was reaching around inside his padded jacket. "Ah! Here." He found the bottle he had been digging for, and uncorked it. "Tomorrow is Christmas, and that is another reason I came—I have nowhere else to go. Sit, Little Greene. Drink this with me."

On opening night Lin Ming arrived early. The great curved ceiling was hung with cascades of light, and the clamshell behind the stage shone in radiating bars of ivory and gold. White-coated kitchen staff adjusted camellias in bud vases and straightened starched linens, and Lin saw that every one of them had his face scrubbed and hair slicked back. All his workers were refugees who had streamed in from the Japanese-ravaged areas up north, starving, desperate; every day there were more. War was written all over the faces of the jostling, sharp-boned workers who came begging for employment. He could have hired and fired every day if he wanted. *Kuai ma!* he cried with a handclap, spur the horse!

Zhou, his floor manager, had overseen so many cabarets that he rarely indulged in even a flicker of excitement anymore, but the size of the well-dressed crowd waiting outside made him catch Lin's eye and mouth the words *Zhen ta ma jue,* damned incredible. When the hour came, they opened the doors to men in suits, tuxes, and long Chinese gowns, to *qipao*-clad Chinese women, and white ladies in full-length evening dresses. The wealthiest Chinese entered with pods of Russian bodyguards, rogue kidnappings and ransoms being a constant threat to anyone of importance. At exclusive venues like the Royal, thugs with guns on display were the norm.

The patrons were a mix of Chinese, foreigners, and Japanese, twenty thousand of whom lived in Shanghai. Among their ranks were not only jazz lovers but also the best jazz players in Shanghai, next to the Americans — not that Lin would ever hire Japanese jazz musicians. They had their own clubs up in Zhabei, now a heavily Japanese area. But he welcomed them as patrons the way he welcomed all people, for this was one of the unwritten rules of *Ye Shanghai:* politics and affiliations were left at the door. All were welcome, all were equal.

A parallel and less attractive truth was that no one wanted to face the facts of war, especially after dark, the time for enjoyment. To make this easier, people referred to every incursion, every skirmish-and-annexation as an incident: the Mukden Incident, the Great Wall Incident, even what people called the January Twenty-eighth Incident here in Shanghai, which was what led to the Japanese being the only ones allowed to bear arms in a Chinese city. But as long as each thing was an "incident," people could go on working and playing and spending their money the way they were going to do tonight. "Hello," Lin said to each guest who passed him. "Welcome to the new Royal."

He recognized the head of the Hong Kong Shanghai Bank, and behind him the *Tai-pan* of the big trading house Jardine's, with his longtime French mistress, whom he squired about openly these days now that his wife had passed over. The man had grieved long and decently, and now even the flintiest matrons tolerated the ripe, heavy-lidded Héloïse on his arm. Lin never ceased to find amusement in the habits of white people.

His smile lit even brighter when he saw the composer Aaron Avshalomov. Born in Siberia, the Russian had spent most of his life in China and wrote concert pieces blending Western and Chinese music; he was admired as a composer, and his presence here raised the tone. He was dressed as he often was in a black silk Chinese gown, which paired oddly with his large, forward-set blue eyes and his angled, leonine face. "Hello, Ah Fu! So nice to see you," said Lin.

They closed the doors when every seat was taken and the dance floor was crowded with people talking, standing, waiting for the lights to dim. When they did, a single spot bathed the center of the stage, and Lin stepped up with raised arms. "New Year's Eve!" he shouted, and a roaring cheer enveloped him. "Your waiters are ready to bring the finest food and the best liquors, as we bring in nineteen thirty-seven! The dance floor is yours!"

The crowd screamed again. Behind him, the first musicians strode out in their blue suits. He prayed that Thomas was going to be ready, and spread his arms wide. "Please welcome back the Kansas City Kings!"

The room exploded, and the words were lost as Thomas stepped out behind him into the light, somehow tall and imposing even though he was a man of slight and ordinary build.

He slid into place at the keyboard, under the spotlight, raised his right hand, and ran off a complex, instantly impressive Lisztian phrase that sent a gasp through the hall. As abruptly as the line had started, it stopped, a warm-up. The same hand lifted again, and tapping time with his feet, he counted down the opening bar of "Stompin' at the Savoy," which needed only a few notes to send the crowd prancing onto the floor in delight.

Good. Lin heard how the arrangement drew attention away from Thomas's piano, which, after the showy intro, became all but invisible, keeping time, no more. He was young, green, just out of his thatched cottage, but he was already doing something fresh by quoting the classics. Lin hoped it would reassure those who still thought of jazz as a savage and dangerous current in the *yang bang he*, the river of foreign culture. No one listening to this could see jazz as something wild that came from the jungle. Yet despite Thomas's style, the Kings were hot, especially the toe-tapping, knob-kneed young brothers, Charles and Ernest Higgins, who broke the song's theme over and over on their saxophones in tight harmony, while the brass called out melody lines and the guitar slapped a rhythm underneath.

And the money was flowing: two songs in, the ballroom was over capacity and they were turning people away. Every time Lin passed the business office, he heard the safe opening and closing. Du was going to be pleased.

The boss arrived shortly after midnight, when 'thirty-seven took off with an ear-rattling fusillade of popping champagne corks, and a chorus of "Auld Lang Syne." The band had just started back in with dance music when Du appeared. He had Fiery Old Crow and Flowery Flag on either side, and Song bringing up the rear in a tea-length *qipao* like some calendar girl from the 'twenties. "Little Sister," Lin said, and she gave him the warm smile they always shared as she vanished up the lobby stairs behind her master.

On the stairs, once Lin Ming was out of view, Song Yuhua matched her steps to the men climbing ahead of her, Teacher and his bodyguards. She always walked in last place in public, unshielded by his men. Not like the actress she remembered from a few years ago, whose dressing room door was always attended by a couple of Du's dog's legs. Each of his two most recent wives had her own security guard assigned to her apartments in the mansion, too.

Not Song. She lived up on the low-ceilinged top floor. Hot in summer, cold in winter. She had a bedroom, a small sitting room, and a tiny chamber just big enough to hold a cot for her maid, Ah Pan. Du had no intention of wasting either space or staff on her. All this because her father gambled away the family estate to the Green Gang, and Du Yuesheng, arriving to take possession, offered to take her into service instead.

As translator and arm-piece, she had tasks and obligations, but at least she was not one of his women. He had taken her twice that way, shortly after she entered his service at eighteen, and after, never touched her again. This was a blessing to her, and also a constant reminder of a failure she barely understood. Sometimes she watched the wives, and wondered what they knew about the house thing that she did not. Fourth Wife talked with her on occasion, and more than once Song had helped her look after the children, but though Fourth Wife was the youngest of the wives and closest to Song in age, they never spoke of private things.

Still, she was worlds away from the submissive girl she had been when she arrived in Shanghai. She had her own loyalties now. And this was where being out with Du had its advantages, for he was master of Shanghai, the fulcrum for all agreements legal or illegal, so she was positioned to overhear things. As she ascended the stairs at the Royal, last in line as always, she scanned the bubbles of conversation that floated out between the tied-back curtains of each box. Understanding English was her great advantage; foreigners babbled like fools in front of her.

Ahead of her Du paused at a box, and stepped inside to trade greetings. Flowery and Fiery assumed their positions. As she entered, she recognized the rotund form of H. H. Kung, and next to him a dissipated older Englishman she had seen in the papers—Sir Frederick Leith-Ross, sent by England to help China control its economy. *Bloodsucking ghost capitalist.* She looked with disdain at his few remaining white hairs combed over his bald head, at his face pouched and ruddy from drink.

Leith-Ross, meanwhile, was making little effort to conceal his distaste at the sight of Du's trademark large ears, bald head, and long gown. "Shocking that they let him in here! And in a box! It's a disgrace."

"Of course he is a blackmailer or murderer or worse," Duke Kung replied in his smooth English, "but my dear sir, one hundred thousand men in Shanghai obey his orders." That was an exaggeration, Song knew—the number was closer to ten thousand—but Kung was rolling, and his eyes gleamed behind his round tortoiseshell glasses. "The only reason the Nationalists can even hold Shanghai is because of Du and his men. Why, what choice do we have? He could create a disturbance at any moment!" Switching to Shanghainese, he turned to address Du. Called "Duke" because of his direct descent from Confucius, he lowered his eyes respectfully. "Teacher. I am always and ever will be your servant."

"Where? Where?" said Du, chiding him affectionately for his flattery, as was proper.

Kung switched back to English. "May I introduce Sir Frederick Leith-Ross?"

They both turned to the Englishman, who had now trained his rheumy eyes on Song. "Good God, his tart is young enough to be his daughter!"

Turtle egg. Stinking son of a slave girl. She stretched out a hand and spoke in English. "Forgive me, but I do not believe we have been introduced. I am Song Yuhua. You are . . . ?"

He choked on his spittle. "Sir Frederick Leith-Ross."

"Enchanted." She turned to Kung, who kept the play going by raising the back of her hand to his mouth for a pretend European-style kiss. "Duke Kung," she continued in English, "it is always a pleasure to see you." And then she smiled sweetly and stepped back as Teacher made his magisterial Chinese farewells and swept out, surrounded by his men.

What she'd said had been flawlessly polite, yet the man's choleric face showed that her arrow had found its mark, and Duke Kung was fighting down his laughter. Good; the foreigner was a toad, a parasite.

She settled into her chair in their box, and scanned the crowd as she always did, to settle the fear that she might see someone from her native place, where no one knew she had been sold to Du in payment for her father's debts. That night she saw no one from Anhui, but she did notice quite a few Shanghai luminaries, bankers and shipping magnates and real estate barons—even Ah Fu, the Russian Jewish composer. Everyone on the dance floor below had their eyes on this new ghost pianist, who did not, despite the Chinese-language advertisements that had been trumpeting the club's reopening for the past week, look like a man who had come straight from the cotton fields.

His playing had an upright feel that sounded familiar to her, carrying her back to when she was a child, and her Western tutor gave her piano lessons. Yet it was a dance orchestra too. She decided this was a fresh hybrid from America, and she liked it.

Sometime after two in the morning Lin Ming appeared in the box, his sleeves rolled up, exhausted, dazed. *"Mou qu bao li,"* he said, treasure and exuberant profit.

Du made a curt nod of acknowledgment, which was a lot for him, and Lin discreetly patted the sheen off his brow as he heard the first tinkly piano notes of the band's signature song, "Exactly Like You." They played it as an instrumental, with Charles and Ernest trading off voices, a two-saxophone duet of the melody Benny Goodman had made famous on the clarinet.

> *I know why I've waited, know why I've been blue,*
> *Prayed each night for someone*
> *Exactly like you.*

The song's end brought a cascade of applause and cheers, during which Lin Ming touched Song's elbow in good-bye and slipped out. Then the house quieted, and even the air hung still, suspended, as everyone held their breath for the encore.

The piano player lifted his hands. A spotlight circled him, as all else went black.

A rising cry from the clarinet sailed out of the darkness behind him and resolved itself into the famous first notes of *Rhapsody in Blue*.

Song recognized it from the radio, though she had never expected to hear it in a ballroom.

The clarinet walked atop the melody and the piano's first chords rained down. For a while she listened, her eyes half-closed, and when she opened them and looked down, she beheld something she had not seen before, ever: a dance floor full of people in expensive evening clothes, perfectly still, all quiet as shafts of light, listening, all under the spell. She too sat motionless, suspended. To think of the hardship he had come from . . . and now he raised a tapered, aristocratic-looking hand to bring in the horns.

She noticed that the musicians were staring at him too, surprised, almost awestruck. A few stumbled slightly, before finding their way into the rhythm, which the pianist, in this piece at least, had in his keeping. A few seconds later, they were in his time, following him. She could feel the shift.

Too soon it was over, and applause exploded through the ballroom for the last time that night. Song turned to Du and said, feigning modesty, "Not bad. Wouldn't you agree?"

He gave her a cold look. She should have expected it; jazz, like all Western music, was only noise to him. He wanted everything Chinese, and nothing foreign; everything old, nothing new. He was a gangster, a criminal, but in his mind he belonged to some lost aristocracy. He and his fellows hoped to silence composers, declare jazz dangerous, ban new plays, and remove dissenting editors from their posts. She hated him.

Most of the young people like her in Shanghai who joined the Communist underground felt as she did; they were struggling writers, actors, journalists, and musicians, living for the future. Whether they were of humble origins, or were the children of well-fed families who were leaning down to the workers' cause, they were idealistic, typical of young "urban path" Communists, as opposed to those who found their way to the movement along the "rural path," in the provinces. They were smart and passionate and sophisticated; they believed. That Song was one of them, secretly, made every day of her life worth living.

Du stood to go, and she rose with him, her lies contained and her surfaces flawless.

Two floors below, Thomas Greene stood by the brass-trimmed door. His head was spinning with relief as he thanked people and wished them well. The whole theater seemed to be surging toward him with compliments and congratulations.

"Happy New Year! Yes, thank you," he said. "So kind of you. Don't forget the rest of the Kansas City Kings, fine musicians, every one. Yes, thank you. The best for nineteen thirty-seven. Come again." Lin stood next to him saying the same things in Chinese, and everyone in the theater had to squeeze past them.

Atop the sea of heads Thomas saw one man taller than the others, tall as Lin Ming, but older, and he knew at once it was the father, the crime lord, Du Yuesheng. Should he greet him? But people said he spoke no English.

Du did not give him the chance. Refusing to look at him, he stared straight ahead as he passed.

But behind him, trailing in the wake of his bodyguards, floated a woman with the most brilliantly intelligent eyes, and gardenias fixed at the back of her neck.

Thomas watched as she was carried toward him on the tide, forced ahead, laughing. When she came abreast, he held her eyes, just for a second, and then the crowd bore her away. After one last moment of clinging to her with his gaze, he turned back to the line of people.

Lin saw him staring. "Don't look at her."

"Why not?"

"You deaf in your dog's ears? She belongs to him." And he slid back into Chinese with the next man in line.

"Is she his wife?"

"Nothing like that," said Lin.

Then like what? Thomas wanted to know, but he said no more, because playing his part properly meant giving in sometimes, as he had been taught from the beginning of his life. But that had always been irrelevant to what he thought, felt, and planned inside — and now he had noticed her, and he would be watching for her in the future. In his own time.

When at last the crowd thinned, he stepped outside, where musicians and well-wishers were still gathered. Among them he noticed a man Alonzo had pointed out across the ballroom, a slight, blue-eyed Russian Jew in a Chinese gown. Greene crossed to him and extended a hand. "Happy New Year. Thomas Greene."

They grasped warmly. "Delighted, and the same to you." The older man's accent was a mash of European tones. "Aaron Avshalomov. The evening was most wonderful. I always say one should go to the classics first. Your *Rhapsody* was resplendent! The essence of America, with all its brashness. I conducted it in Tianjin a few years ago with a Russian cabaret pianist, but to you he did not compare! You were marvelous. We should meet again. We must, I insist. May we please? Let us agree to it for the new year."

"I'd like that," Thomas said, riding the sudden swell of acceptance, wanting the same thing he had always wanted, the respect of serious musicians like Avshalomov, who, after a quick good night, was borne away in a rickshaw, his light, unruly cloud of hair bouncing above the folded-back awning.

Thomas turned to see the two reed players beside him, Charles and Ernest. "Come on, Tails," said Ernest — the nickname having arisen earlier that night on account of the cutaway coat he wore as bandleader — "You promised us on the night we opened, you'd go celebrate."

"You're right, I did." He ruffled the young head, grinning at the fact that all the doors seemed wide open to him, for the first time ever; he could drink, dance, and sample women, for he had money, and here, where all men were at last created equal, that was the only thing that mattered. "Let's go."

3

B Y EARLY SPRING, Thomas was keeping up on piano, though hardly delivering the irresistibly danceable keyboard lines the Kings required. This was overlooked partly because he was skilled at arranging and leading, and partly because the classical flights of fancy he delivered onstage brought such responses from the audience that even the brass section dared not raise a voice.

But he could feel things simmering, and one day in March, at the weekly rehearsal, brass player Lester Cole let it out. "When are you going to take a solo, Tails?"

"Well —"

"'Cause we're getting tired of the Uncle Tom business."

Thomas heard nothing for an instant save the buzzing in his head and his own sharp intake of breath, but then Charles filled the emptiness by speaking up. "That's not fair," he said.

"I agree," his brother Ernest put in. "I like the new sound."

Cole bristled. "What do you two know?"

"They know what we all know," Alonzo said, his sonorous voice drawing everyone's attention. "You got no call to say that. Whatever you think of the sound, I think we all know we have never had so many people on the dance floor. Not even close. Am I right?"

This brought a mumble of assent, and the logjam loosened enough for Thomas to push ahead, but the vibrato of anxiety stayed in his gut through the whole rehearsal. He called out the changes in the new arrangements, and played a minimally credible piano line beneath the Kings' bluesy surge, but everything was teetering. He was bringing too much of himself to the role. Back in America, he could never be light enough, never fully pass for European. He had always had to work extra hard on his precision and the subtlety of his touch to compensate, just as he had chosen his clothes and cultivated his manners in the same fashion. He had formed himself prophylactically, creating almost an exact shadow of his obstacles in the persona he presented. But to pass as a jazz musician, he was going to have to drop that, and be someone different.

To start, he had to offer something that sounded like solos, so using scores his new copyist Mr. Hsu had written out, he devised a series of elegant and unexpected elaborations. These impressed the crowd readily enough, but not his musicians.

He envied the way the other Kings could just take off and play, as if inspired to sing a line or two. It was the Kansas City sound, to have solos riffing above a driving, danceable bedrock in flat-four time. All of them could solo, except him. Even after he understood that it was part of the Kansas City sound itself, the way it allowed each man to stand up and stretch out and tell a story, horizontally, melodically, with the steady beat behind him, he remained jealous of what they could do.

And most of his bandmates had something else he was lacking — a girlfriend. Not that he was chaste; girls of every nationality were available, and some of those he sampled had pleased him. He took delight at first in being offered lovely bodies of every shade, in kissing mouths that spoke Russian and French and Hindi and Tonkinese and three or four different Chinese dialects, but in the end, he found it a lonely business, paying for a woman. On the other hand, he was always treated like a gentleman, which he loved, for respect was headier to him than sex, even the sex they had here—more affirming, more restorative, the root note that had been missing from his chord all his life. He made sense in Shanghai.

He had grown to envy the other Kings their women. Some of them were Chinese, two were Russian, one was Malaysian, and Alonzo even lived with Keiko, a Japanese woman he'd met through one of the guys in Buck Clayton's Harlem Gentlemen. He wanted a special someone too.

Yet it was hard to go out on the town when he got off work at two A.M., so most nights he went home and spent an hour shedding his life completely, no posing, no passing, just paging through the sheets of concertos and sonatas he used to play, and wearing his soft old union suits instead of the silk dressing gowns the tailor had provided. It was ninety days now, and he still did not miss America. He did miss the feel of Creel Street though, and one thing that took him back there was to sit in the concentrated, benevolent light of an oil lamp late at night. In their leanest years, after the War, his widowed mother had used a single hurricane lamp every evening when the power was off, carrying it with them from room to room. Thomas had used it in the last days in the apartment as well, after the electricity went off, and left it behind in the cupboard when he departed. Here in Shanghai, to his joy, he found one like it in a used-goods shop over by Suzhou Creek. Uncle Hua disapproved of the thing, calling it a fire hazard, but Thomas used it in the dead of night anyway, and was comforted by its glow.

He took stock of himself, those nights, and realized he could court a respectable girl, if he could find one. He had money to spend on a woman. Even with all he had dropped on ladies of the night in his first months, he still made more than he could spend, and he kept the excess neatly folded in his wardrobe, underneath his shirts, which were laundered, pressed, and folded to knife creases by Chen Ma. One March day when he was taking some cash out, Uncle Hua materialized in the doorway.

Hua watched for a moment, and said, "Pay my look see, Master."

"I think you already had a look see," Thomas answered. It had not taken long for him to understand that he had no privacy at all, a fact to which he was already resigned as he put the little money package back in its not-so-secret spot.

"Master. You give one hundred, bye-bye make pay one oh seven."

Seven percent? This caught Thomas's attention. "How?"

Hua's creased face went stubborn. "That b'long my pidgin."

"It belong my pidgin if my money's in it," Thomas retorted. "How?"

Hua's eyes narrowed. "Gamble place, my house."

"Is that so! You must do well, to offer seven."

"Can do."

"I see." Thomas thought, and pulled another hundred from the pouch. "We'll start small," he said, holding it out. "One ten, in a month."

"One month no can do. Three months. One seven five."

"Two months. One eight five."

"One eight."

Thomas considered.

"One eight five?" Hua repeated, and Thomas nodded. "Can put-tee book?" he said, barely able to contain his glee.

"Puttee book," said Greene. "It's a deal." He handed him the money and closed the cupboard. "And you stay out of my things, Uncle Hua." He faked sternness and his majordomo pretended to quail in response, but Thomas understood by now that this was theater, that people were playing their roles, just as he played his. He was getting the hang of it.

Or so he thought.

Every Saturday, Song Yuhua went downtown to collect Du Taitai's medicine. Seeing to the health needs of the supreme wife and matriarch was a task of importance, even if the old lady was an opium addict who had not left her room in years. The task fell to Song partly because no one else wanted to do it, but she always looked forward to her weekly afternoon abroad in the city, stretching an errand that could be done fairly quickly into several hours of doing what she wanted. She was in no way imprisoned in Du's mansion on Rue Wagner, for though always on call, she was able to come and go more or less as she wanted. But on Saturdays, Teacher knew she took care of his first wife's medicines, and so on that day, he never requested her services before evening fell.

On the sidewalks she heard two fur-clad Russian women quarreling, several groups of men speaking English, and bubbles of French and German. Polyglot vitality was one of the things she loved about Shanghai, even though it was the foreign capitalists who had turned Shanghai into a warren of occupied Concessions, enriched themselves, and then looked the other way, refusing to help, when Japan started to press its invasion. It had been one of her only real disagreements with the Communists, the fact that they, like the Nationalists, were so anti-foreign, but this divergence she kept to herself. To think of it was unwise, and to speak of it would be dangerous; one did not disagree with the movement. So she never spoke of liking Western music, or even of any fondness for the language in which she was proficient. Privately, she credited English with having given her a separate and entirely different engine of thought. And there was no getting around the fact that her English was exactly what made her valuable to Du, and therefore to the left, as a spy. It was her weak point, her vulnerability, and at the same time her greatest strength. Thinking about it was like sorting silk threads in a way that only entangled them further.

She pushed open the door to the dark apothecary shop, a room with floor-to-ceiling drawers and a wood counter trimmed in brass. The herb master, stout and fusty with a sparse white beard, bobbed his head when she came in. "Has Young Mistress eaten?"

"Yes, thank you. And you?"

"Yes." He smiled happily, and she knew he had. Though a loyal Party member—he took no small risk, hosting meetings in his shop between her and others—the old man did not believe in denying himself. He had not read Marx. He told her once that he was going to go see Marx when he died, and the great man could tell him all about it then. Right now, what mattered was resisting Japan.

He took her prescription and studied the flowing characters in the old doctor's elegant hand. "This is a complex formula. I suggest you take a moment's rest, Mistress, in the parlor. I will call for tea."

She nodded. "Thank you." They were always careful to say only the right things, even when they were alone.

He reached beneath the counter and pulled a lever so that a section of the wall sprang loose. He swung it back to show a windowless inner room of black wood chairs and side tables, lit by yellow pools of electric light.

When he said he would call for tea, it meant someone wanted to see her, so after he had closed the wall-door behind her, she sat in a warm haze of anticipation, watching the little coals glowing in the brazier. It was always exciting, being told she was wanted for a meeting, and then waiting to see if someone new would walk through the door. At a minimum, that would mean a fresh face to put into the puzzle, for the Party operated in secret. Most enlistees knew only the other members of their cell. Song's position in Du's household being too sensitive for a cell, though, she knew only her guide, and the others who came to her in these meetings. Someone new was always of interest.

And if heaven smiled, one day she might meet her comparable other, a man who lived his life as she lived hers, with a mind and will equal to her own. She had always believed in such a man's existence, even as a small child. Perhaps it was her training in Western languages and stories, this being a Western fantasy—but why should she not find him here, in just this way? The movement was the center of her life. There was never a time when she was called to a meeting that she did not flutter a little, inside.

She remembered the thrill of those early months in 'thirty-two and 'thirty-three when she first joined, going to many secret meetings at the so-called Foreign Language School at number 6 New Yuyang

Lu, off Avenue Joffre. The school advertised its French and Russian courses constantly in *Minguo Ribao*, the *Republic Daily*, but there were no such courses, even though the place was always full of young people; it was a center for training Communists. She still went there occasionally for high-level meetings.

The strange thing was that it was Du who led her to the Party in the first place. He had been having an affair with an actress, and to keep that fact from his newest wife, he began taking Song out with him in the evening for cover. In the fashion of the season, he invited the actress for coffee before dinner, and she chose the Vienna Garden, which in its late-night hours happened to be one of Du's favorite clubs.

Yet in the early evening, the Vienna was a meeting place for leftists, something Song discovered as soon as Du and his lady friend disappeared to their private room upstairs, bodyguards surrounding them. Alone with the actress's friends, she found the conversation instantly exciting, a plunge through white-water rapids. Never before had she been face-to-face with admitted Communists, people who in their aboveground lives were playwrights and musicians. Their sympathies were no secret, for the left-leaning playwrights created stage works that demonized foreign imperialists, just as the musicians wrote songs and motion picture scores with choral singing and stirring martial melodies. They eschewed the "you and me" lyrics of love songs for "we and us" lyrics of nationhood and progress. She had met such people before, but as to who was actually a secret Party member, usually no one was willing to say. Yet that evening, at the Vienna Garden, every one of those around the table said straight out that they were members. Her thrill was made even sharper by her awareness that Du, if he found out, would want to kill several of them — except that he could not, since they were people of reputation.

Ideas flew, not only from men but from women, which excited Song even more. They were all part of a theater world undergoing complete revolution, in which stage forms such as opera, stylized with male-only performers for centuries, were giving way at last to contemporary plays in which women could participate, and through which all the issues of the day could be aired. Theater could spread ideas not only quickly, but in metaphors the Japanese invaders did not grasp, which was why playwrights and producers took risks, and occasionally were assassinated. All theater people lived with danger, just by staging their work, and Song saw how for them, the leap to Communism was almost natural.

The real point was money, said a smart young woman from Nan-yang University. Was it not true that the foreign powers used Shanghai for profit, with no concern for whether Shanghai people were free or were slaves? Had they not rammed through the 1932 treaty that prevented China from having her own troops in Shanghai, just so they could make more profit? Money, always money.

At that moment, Song noticed an exceptionally beautiful dance hostess seated against the wall, her *qipao* slit to the lower thigh, showing off silk stockings and high heels. "That is Miss Zhang," said the man next to her. They had been introduced when she first sat down; his name was Chen Xing, and he was head of the League of Left-Wing Theater People. "She has become pregnant by Ziliang Soong," Chen said. "Do you know the name? He is the younger brother of Mei-ling Soong, Chiang Kai-shek's wife."

Song drew a sharp breath. She had heard about this in the halls of Rue Wagner, through which rumors always expanded like fog. Normally such a pregnancy would not be a problem, as the girl would be paid to get rid of the baby, but gossip had it that Miss Zhang had refused. *Look at her, she has nothing but a Soong baby inside her, and she fights.* "What is she asking for?"

"Why, Miss Zhang wants ten thousand," Chen Xing told her in mild surprise. "She says if she doesn't get it, she'll put the story in the papers."

"Unwise!" Song cried. It was reckless to demand so much money. The Soong family was much too powerful.

"You want to tell her?" Chen Xing said, his mouth a rueful pucker. "Really, you should not become involved."

His words were barely out when Du Yuesheng's bodyguards reappeared in the corridor.

Song dropped her eyes before her master came into view and caught her speaking to the man next to her. *These are Communists, and I know, and you do not.* She could barely contain the thrill that swelled inside her, for she had found a source of power, a way to live. And years later, it had led her here, to wait alone in a secret room behind the herb master's place.

A half-bald man in a rumpled gown whom she knew well stepped in — her guide. She hid her disappointment as he addressed her, using one of her false names. "Mrs. Ma, how are you? All is well?"

"Yes, Mr. Guo, thank you." She did not know his real name either.

"Do you have any news?" he said.

"I know Du gave two hundred thousand Chinese dollars to the Nationalists for the war effort. Even if Chiang did just agree to fight side by side with our army!"

They traded smiles. A deal had been struck and Chiang Kai-shek released; now the Nationalists and Communists would form a united front against Japan. "How are your relatives up north?" she said, code for the Communist stronghold and the frontline struggle to push back Japan.

He shook his head. "They can eat bitterness and endure fatigue to the end, but they are overwhelmed. They are starving. They have no —" He abandoned all pretense of talking about his relatives. "They have no ammunition. We need money."

She blanched. She had never been asked for money before, only information. It was impossible of course, she had no access to money. "I cannot imagine how I could help, Mr. Guo, but the cause is everything. I will go to the temple and pray to the gods to send a solution to your dilemma." A light knock sounded on the door, and she rose, her moves well studied. "My prescription is ready. Good day."

Out on the street, she tucked the packet of herbs away in a silk pouch she carried. How could she get money? Du's money was out of reach, for he knew the whereabouts of his every copper cash. He also had his hands in all the city's banks, holding a seat on their boards or simply controlling their directors as if by so many puppet strings. *Curse all lords and bosses like him, all the masters who steal and extort and drown the city in opium*. She may have willingly offered her life in trade for her father's debt to be canceled, so her clan could avoid poverty and her little sisters could be educated, but she was still a piece of property—on the outside. Inside, she had this, her life, her pledge to her country. *If they catch me, let them kill me.*

This was real power, and it lifted her lips in a smile as she crossed the street.

"You gave the house steward your salary?" said Lin Ming. He and Thomas stood outside the Cathay Cinema, on Avenue Joffre, waiting to see *Pennies from Heaven* with Bing Crosby and Louis Armstrong.

"He's done well, so far. Eight and a half percent."

Lin grinned at this proof that his bandleader was doing more than playing his role, he was thinking. He had deduced from the beginning there was something more to this one than met the eye. "That's higher than the bank."

"It was for that reason we reached a deal."

With a blink, Lin Ming realized Thomas was staring at the *shuoming shu* Lin had been perusing, the bastardized and unfailingly entertaining English-Chinese plot summary that was passed out at most Shanghai movie houses. No, he was mistaken, the American had to be looking at something else. The *shuoming shu*, with its sophisticated cult following, was strictly the province of Shanghai's cognoscenti.

"When you're finished with that, can I keep it?" Thomas said, dispelling all doubts.

"You *read* them?"

"I collect them." And they laughed together as the line started to move. Good. Lin needed something light to take his mind off the new danger posed by this Japanese Admiral.

Was this the time to warn Little Greene? The question teased itself into knots as they took their seats and spoke of small things, waiting for the lights to dim. Unquestionably, Lin would have to tell him, despite the danger to himself in subverting any plan of Du's. But he had to choose the right moment, and so far, there was no immediate threat. Lin's paid informants had assured him that Morioka listened to jazz only in his apartments, on his gramophone; he had not gone out. Not a single club had seen him cross the doorstep. Lin pondered until the lights fell and the velvet curtains cranked apart, and then it was too late. To bring it up now would only create fear, just as speaking of a tiger makes one pale.

"Are you coming to the theater?" Thomas asked him after the picture, when they poured out with the rest of the audience onto the rounded corner sidewalk, under the tall, narrow modern-style stacked letters CATHAY. The street down which they watched for a conveyance was lined with Gallic-style four-story conjoined buildings, three ornate brick floors above for apartments, and the first floor a twinkling line of shops, restaurants, and teahouses fronted by plate glass windows all lit up for the evening.

"Not tonight," Lin answered him, raising his hand to a rickshaw. "I have others to see to." It was his habit to excuse himself in this way, and on this night he had reason to be vague, since he was meeting H. H. Kung for dinner. Despite all his wealth and power, Kung remained at Du Yuesheng's mercy in many ways, and periodic ultra-private conversations with Lin Ming helped him keep up with the master's leanings.

"Has he talked about moving his assets yet?" Kung said from across the table at the Sun Ya. They were dining on bird's nest soup with pigeon eggs, whelk with chicken liver slices, frogs' legs braised with thin broccoli stalks for bones, and shad steamed in caul fat with a crystal sauce.

The question startled Lin Ming. Moving assets would mean he accepted that the Japanese would take Shanghai. It was true that it was now impossible to turn on the radio without hearing how close their army was to Peking and Tianjin in the north. And here in Shanghai, there were suddenly Japanese everywhere in the streets, not just sol-

diers but families, civilians, including many who came into his cabarets and ballrooms at night. But a Japanese invasion? "On that, he has
said nothing."

"His money and bullion can be moved quickly," Kung said, "but
our situation is different. We are disassembling whole factories and
moving them to the interior, trying to keep China on her feet through
industry. We cannot wait until they are at our gates." Kung shrugged
as he reached for choice morsels, his hands precise and balletic as he
loaded Lin Ming's plate before his own, like any good friend.

Lin felt his stomach turn. Duke Kung was twice his age and ten
thousand times more powerful, so if he sensed the invasion was near,
it probably was. "Is there nothing that can turn them back?"

"Possibly," Kung said. "Moscow has floated the idea, tentatively,
very *entre nous,* of organizing a group of countries to oppose Japanese aggression. Maybe even the Americans, though no one has approached them yet." He signaled for more wine. "I leave next week
for Moscow, from there to Germany, to discuss it."

"Germany?"

"I went to graduate school in Berlin, did you know that? After
Yale. I know people there, I can get things done, arrange meetings
at the highest levels. I will meet with Hitler. But I am also going to
check on my friends, Schwartz and Shengold, two men I went to
school with. Jews. Very powerful bankers. They have not answered
my letters. Have you heard anything of the situation of the Jews in
Germany?"

"Nothing clear," said Lin.

"My friend Dr. Ho Feng-Shan, the First Secretary of the legation
in Vienna, has been updating me. They have passed anti-Jewish laws
and seized Jewish property. I plan to find my friends, and if this is
true, I will bring it up with Hitler. But above all, I will persuade him
to join us in opposing Japan. That's my commitment."

They raised their glasses to it, and drank. "And you?" said Kung.
"What is yours? You have no clan, no place to sweep the grave-
yard — you're just the sort who could commit to something."

"Never," Lin said.

"Isn't that 'forgetting the war, forgetting the motherland'?"

Lin shook his head. "Of course I oppose Japan without question. I am Chinese. But I serve Du, remember."

"You're not a member of the Gang, are you?"

"No." The *Qing Bang* initiates were sworn for life. "I am his son. That's enough."

"And I suppose you'll never inherit."

"No." Lin was not a real son, born neither of a *nei ren*, an inside person, a wife, nor of a concubine, nor even of a mistress — but in the lowest possible way, of a whore. And his salary was stingy, just enough to keep his small flat in Frenchtown.

Regarding Dr. Kung across the stacked, fragrant platters, Lin remembered why Kung was under Du Yuesheng's power too: the Green Gang and the top Nationalist leaders were bound by a blood debt. It was Du Yuesheng who had carried out the 1927 Shanghai massacre that wiped out many high-level Communist leaders, lured to Shanghai by the Nationalists through the promise of peaceful talks. The bloodbath had cemented the power of the Nationalist clique and ended the Communists' long-term status as a legitimate wing of the Nationalist Party. Everything changed for the Communists then as they were driven underground, at least in the cities. In the countryside, they pulled back to Jiangxi, where Chiang's armies encircled them and drove them out. From there they set out on a long march to Shaanxi Province in north China, where they consolidated their new headquarters and continued to fight the Japanese.

It was thanks to Du Yuesheng that the Communists had been driven out of the true government, and the highest Nationalist officials would always be in his pocket because of it. Moreover, they were all a family, the Nationalist leaders, related by marriage to the Soong sisters. Soong Mei-ling was the wife of Chiang Kai-shek, Soong Ai-ling was Kung's wife, and Soong Qing-ling the widow of Sun Yat-sen. Their brother T. V. Soong was a former top Finance official. They brought the sense of a dynasty to the leadership of the Nationalist Party, and it seemed to cement their absolute power despite the fact that the Imperial system had fallen back in 1911. Whatever the case, they held China's reins, and as a family had grown fabulously rich — yet still they had to appease Du.

They also did not seem to be able to stop Japan. The fact that they had relocated their Nationalist government south to Nanjing and also prudently moved 640,000 priceless art treasures out of the Forbidden City seemed to signal that they expected Peking and Tianjin to fall to Japan. Would the enemy be allowed to occupy these cities, unopposed? If so, Shanghai would be next.

"If they take us," Lin said, "the night-world will wither and die faster than you can turn a head. The clubs, the money, the jazz — it will all be finished."

"Along with everything else," said Kung. "On that day there will be gloom in heaven and darkness below. That is why I must go to Moscow and Berlin and London, and you, my friend" — Kung's eyes ticked up, and Lin could see, behind his round glasses, the flicker of Christian compassion — "you must not interfere if they have a clear shot at Morioka. Do you understand? Even if he happens to be standing next to one of your men."

Lin's face hardened into a mask to cover the roiling sea of his awareness. This was the end of his fragile equilibrium.

"Agreed?"

Lin lowered his eyes. "Agreed," he lied.

That Friday was Du Taitai's regular visit from Dr. Feng. Song sat beside the physician at the bedside as he took the pulses of Du's revered first wife, and examined the whites of her eyes and her tongue. He wrote out a new list of herbs, and counseled rest in a darkened room — as if the Supreme One could do anything else in her opium-addicted state. Song thanked him respectfully and shook the last few silver dollars from Taitai's private purse to pay him.

When he was gone she showed Taitai the empty purse. It had never been empty before, and there was still the medicine to buy.

A white, clawlike hand came out to brush at Song's wrist. "There." The old lady pointed to the wall.

What? The painting in its frame? The striped wallpaper? Song leaned closer.

"Behind the painting."

Song was amazed; the old lady had never before said anything so coherent. In the frame was a cheap copy of a minor fan painting by the Ming artist Chen Hongshou, the sort of piece favored by middle-class Chinese aspiring to display good art.

"Behind," Taitai repeated, and Song pulled the edge of the frame away from the wall. Behind it she saw only the yellow rose wallpaper.

But the Supreme Wife continued to gesture with her curled fingers, and Song peered at the back of the frame itself, where she saw a small velvet pouch webbed to the frame with an ancient, dust-covered crisscross of thread.

"This?" She tipped the frame up so the old lady could see the pouch, glad the maid was out washing the sheets and no one was in the room at this moment but Taitai and herself.

"It's mine," Taitai whispered. "From my mother. No one knows, not even him."

Song separated the fraying threads and removed the pouch. "Here." She held it out to Taitai.

The translucent little fingers could only flutter weakly. "You open it."

It was closed with no more than a drawstring. Song leaned over the dark blue quilt cover, opened the bag, and gently turned it over. A small river of white diamonds poured out, capped by the sharp sound of her own breath.

"Take one," the lady said. "Trade it for the medicine. Will it be enough? No. Take two or three." She might sound more lucid than Song had ever heard her, yet she still seemed to think it would take two or three diamonds to buy a week's herbs.

Song was certain Taitai had forgotten about these diamonds long ago, for the story around Rue Wagner was that when she was younger, and first starting to use the Big Smoke, she and Du had many arguments about money. He limited her cash to try to slow her addiction. As sure as it was that she had forgotten the gems, it was just as sure that Du did not know they existed, for if he did, they would be gone.

Song stared at the stones, a pool of glinting light against the dark silk. It gave her a new jolt of power to think that Du was in this room at least once a week, visiting Taitai, sitting here on this bed, and he knew nothing of the diamonds.

When Du came, she knew he told his wife news of the family, as if she could still listen. To him, she was ill, for was it not true that millions used opium with no problems? As her husband, he took care of her, sitting by her for an hour a week, for which he was as faithful as the changing moon. Song could find no fault in how he ministered to his wife; it was something she had to admire about him.

The wave of sadness drowned her again, disappointment that she had been sold to an old man, one who perceived her not as a woman but as a tool. She was grateful for that, she did not want him anywhere near her, yet at the same time, it hurt that her womanhood had never been allowed to develop. Du would release her one day, but she would be past thirty then, and would have nothing.

Except for the Party.

She looked at the jewels, and remembered what she had said: *I will pray to the gods to send a solution to your dilemma.* Was this the moment to which her vows had led her? She rolled the diamonds in her hand, unable to take her eyes from them, thinking back once more to her reasons and her commitment.

Du's affair with the actress had continued for much of 1932, and she'd sat through many evenings at the Vienna Garden listening to Huang Weimin, a well-known editor and playwright who, she realized as they spoke around the cigarette-clouded table, was also a secret leader of the Communist underground. She remembered the whiff of danger, but above all the fun of interacting with a like mind as they spoke of literature, and matched each other with lines of poetry. She had been there for almost an hour when she realized the beautiful, bold, and pregnant Miss Zhang was not present. "What happened to that Miss Zhang?" she asked. "Did she give in and stop the baby?"

"No," said Huang, "she held her ground. In fact she was here, earlier this evening. I saw her."

So Song watched, curious, thinking the girl might return at any moment to join the others being paid dance by dance, ticket by ticket. The left-wing debate continued and the pregnant girl did not appear; instead, sometime later, Song saw Teacher, coming down the hall behind Flowery Flag.

"Zou ba," he said abruptly when he reached her, let's go. She jumped up and followed him, noticing that his other bodyguard, Fiery Old Crow, was not with him.

At the car, she saw Fiery was already inside, waiting in the front passenger seat. He leaped out to hold the door for the boss, who climbed in the back, next to Song, and they headed out Bubbling Well Road. The driver, as always, was Flowery Flag, who had earned his nickname by once having worked as chauffeur for the American Embassy.

But he did not take any of the expected streets back into the French Concession that night. Instead he turned north into the side streets, until he reached the banks of Suzhou Creek. He turned at the top of the bank, and followed the waterway out to the suburbs, where wooded stretches and farming plots alternated with huddles of darkened houses. No one spoke in the car, and she kept her face set, while fear clawed at her inside.

Flowery left the road and followed a short gravel driveway to the riverbank, where they ground to a stop beneath the bare trees. "Get out," Du ordered.

Around back, he unlatched the trunk and then stepped aside. "Go ahead. Raise it."

She did, and looked down into the agonized, pleading eyes of Miss

Zhang, the pregnant dance hostess, who shook, rags tied around her mouth, her ankles, her hands behind her back—

"Please," Song said, her voice cracking. "Don't do it."

"Step back," he ordered, each word a separate blow. "I want you to watch."

Fiery and Flowery bent over the trunk and attached cement blocks to her feet with lengths of chain while she squirmed and squealed through the rag. Song stood with tears running, hating herself for her powerlessness, while they hauled the girl out, still struggling, and then counted to three in a good-natured, almost boyish way over her muffled shrieks, swinging her back and forth in order to land her out in deep water, where she hit with a massive, heaving splash. The water boiled, and frothed with bubbles for a minute, before it settled and returned to its dark placidity.

Flowery and Fiery had already turned back to the car. She followed, trembling, agonized, certain she would never get the girl's eyes out of her mind.

"We call that 'growing water lilies,'" Du said.

In the car, riding back that night, staring straight ahead through the windshield, she had decided that this was the last time she would feel so impotent against evil. She would join. She would work the rest of her life against people like Du, and against Japan, as long as its army fought on Chinese soil. She remembered how a deep and unexpected sense of calm, of resolution, settled over her. It was the beginning of her new life.

Now, as she sat in Du Taitai's room, she made a silent vow to Miss Zhang, the poor dance hostess who had opened her heart to the son of a powerful family, conceived his child, and met her death while Song looked on. She had been a helpless girl then, no better than a slave, not the canny woman she was now. She would take these diamonds, and she would keep them for Miss Zhang. For herself, too.

She shook four diamonds into her hand like fractured light. She deserved them, she pleased the old lady. The maids said Taitai responded to her as to no one else, not even her husband. When Song was not present, she lay in bed, an empty seedpod, rattling on life's last puffs of wind. Song fixed the pouch back in its place and resettled the picture on the wall.

She turned to see Taitai watching her, puzzled. "Was the picture crooked?"

Song searched the old face, her heart pounding. *Already she has forgotten.* "A little," she lied.

Taitai gave the fan painting a blank look. "Pretty." The lucidity had been like a flash of light in a forest.

The maid came back in, and observed that First Wife was tired. They settled her more comfortably on the pillow.

When the Supreme One slept, Song tilted open the wooden shutter slats and cranked out the windows for a few minutes to release the heavy smell of the opium and bring in the scent of the city. She straightened the chairs and dusted the bureau, which held all that was left of Taitai's life: the wedding picture, a bronze pocket-plaque inscribed with sutras for some long-ago journey, a pair of jade earrings, and several books which had not been opened in many years. The old lady had lost interest in these things, in the room, in everything but the drug.

After the first couple of years, Song stopped asking herself what had made Taitai this way, whether it was the marriage to Du or something that came before; she saw only a sweet old lady worn thin as a ghost. She smoothed the paper-dry brow and turned the light down, sitting quietly for a while before she latched the window, darkened the shutters, and eased out.

In April of that year, the Kings lost their first member to the war when their violinist, Solomon Kirk, told them he was going home. This revelation came midway through an uncomfortable rehearsal, in which the brass players started talking disrespectfully about Mr. Hsu, who had not yet arrived.

Thomas got right up from his piano bench. "What was that?"

He knew it was Errol Mutter who had spoken. "You want to tell everyone?"

"I said, your boy's not here yet. Maybe you can't work without your boy."

"Mr. Mutter. Mr. Hsu is the reason I can give you written music." Thomas had slipped into his angry voice, crisp and a little controlling. He did not like to deploy it, it was not part of his jazz man persona, but Mr. Hsu worked tirelessly for his eight dollars a month. That was exactly the wage he had asked for, too; Thomas never once tried to bargain with him. He wondered how Mr. Hsu could survive on that amount, but Lin Ming had told him that the copyist lived in a *tingzijian*, a pavilion room or scholar's room, which was a small, closed-off loft above another room. "Of his skills none of you can possibly have the slightest doubt," Thomas said.

"But can you play without him?" Errol pressed.

"It's not him. It's written music I cannot play without. I told you that at our first rehearsal."

"He did tell you that." The voice came ringing down over the empty seats from Lin Ming, who had climbed the stairs quietly and taken a seat in Du's box without anyone noticing. "Mr. Hsu is here, standing in the lobby, you know. He just arrived. He heard what you said."

Appearing in the archway, Mr. Hsu let loose a stream of light, consonant-tapping Shanghainese.

Lin translated to the group. "He wants to know what is the meaning, calling him 'boy'?"

The men shifted in their seats. In Shanghai, male servants, hotel attendants, rickshaw pullers, and the like were called "boys" regardless of age, but Mr. Hsu was an educated musician, and they all knew it. Thomas waited for Errol to answer.

"It's an insult," Errol mumbled at last, and Mr. Hsu immediately turned toward the lobby door to leave.

"Wait!" Thomas said. "Please." He saw Mr. Hsu hesitate.

Lin Ming jumped in, cajoling Hsu with wave after wave of appeasement, until finally the man unrolled his paper, uncapped his pen, and sat down to work.

"You must be more polite to Mr. Hsu, or he will not stay," Lin said from the balcony.

"We will do better," Thomas said humbly, pretending to take the blame, because here, everything was vertical authority, and as bandleader, he stood for the behavior of his men. It was Lin's obligation to upbraid him, and Thomas's to absorb the blame.

The rehearsal had barely teetered back on track when Solomon got up and made his announcement, saying he was sorry to leave, but the Japanese were everywhere, and to him it did not look good. He had saved his fare — that was what they had all agreed to when they came over on the one-way ticket. He wished them well. They were braver than he. He played his heart out for the rest of the rehearsal, even though he would be gone by Saturday night.

The first night they played without Solomon was the night a pretty, dark-haired white woman came into the ballroom, wearing a simple but close-fitting satin gown. She sat alone, unusual for one so attractive, and Thomas noticed she refused several offers to dance, instead sitting regally at her table, posture perfect, eyes bright. He felt a pull to her growing stronger through the evening, until finally, after the last set, he took a deep breath and introduced himself.

She smiled and extended a slim, white hand. "Anya Petrova, of Saint Petersburg. Your playing is very beautiful."

"Thank you." *Saint Petersburg*. Those who used the old name were White Russians, he remembered, as he took in her shiny dark bobbed hair and disconcertingly pale gray eyes. "Not as beautiful as you." Normally, he was too worldly to say such a thing, but in her case, it was the truth.

"Pfft." Unimpressed, she flicked at the air with two manicured fingers. "Do you know, when I was a girl, I was the plain one in the family? My parents, the servants, even the coachmen, all they talked about was how beautiful was my sister Elena. Never me."

Servants. Coachmen. "Then they were wrong."

"Flatterer." She flashed a smile. "You are sweet. I must go now. Good night."

"Please come again." He watched her walk away across the ballroom, deliberately bewitching, moving her hips for him, making sure he would remember. It was a good bet she would be back.

She was, in less than a week, and he asked her to dinner after the show. Back in the dressing room, Alonzo said, "Who is that girl? I've seen her somewhere before."

"Her name is Anya."

"I know, I saw her on stage somewhere. She sings. Say—Mr. Lin was looking for you. Said he had something to talk to you about. He catch up with you?"

"No." Thomas bounced on the balls of his feet, encased these days in top-grade Italian leather; he was eager to get back to Anya. "You choose," he told her when he did, and she selected an all-night Chinese restaurant called Golden Tripod Kitchen, which surprised him. His expectations were further upended when, on their arrival, she greeted the staff in peremptory Shanghainese, to which they responded in the same tongue. Fascination bloomed. "How many languages do you speak?"

"Six," she said.

Back home, Thomas had never met anyone who spoke another language, other than high school teachers. It was not like music, which was everyone's second language back on Creel Street. Many people could play a simple song. The I-IV-V song form was easy, abbreviated; a child did not have to go on in music in order to know it. A song could be bent any which way and filtered through any kind of lens, but it was still a song, and still the spirit of America, as Thomas was increasingly coming to see. Strange he had to leave America to grasp it. So he had only this one language, music, the song, whereas she had mastered all these others. And she was beautiful. "Tell me," he said, his admiration pulling him forward on his elbows, across the table, closer to her. "Your languages."

"Shanghainese and English, you know—also Russian, French, Latin, and Greek."

"You went to good schools."

"Yes. It seems so far away now. And you? I hear a good musical education."

"Actually, I would not have been allowed to attend most music schools in America. In addition, I grew up in a very poor part of the city. My mother was a domestic."

Anya drew her brows together.

"A maid." Thomas hauled up his own reins and reminded himself to pay attention, since this was not the story he had told the other men in the orchestra. As far as they knew, he was a farm boy from Easton, on the Chesapeake's remote far shore. That had suited him well enough, since it put a believable framework around the naïveté of his playing relative to theirs. With Anya, he wanted to be a different kind of man, and he felt his way slowly with his story. "Though she cleaned rich people's houses for a living, she knew the piano, and she was my first teacher. She taught me to read the staff at the same time I learned the alphabet. And she showed me if you play well, people will appear along the way to help you." As he spoke, he realized he had learned this from America, not just his mother, and it was the first genuinely nostalgic thought he'd had about his country since coming to China.

"Were your family slaves?"

"All that ended seventy years ago," he answered, deliberately vague, because actually his ancestors had been free people of color, as far as he knew. But that was not a good story for Shanghai, where he was a jazz man; he should be from the crossroads, someplace cruel, preferably in the Deep South. The longer he was away from the U.S., the more detached he became from the actual facts of his life there, gaining the freedom to unfold himself anew in this city. Everyone in Shanghai had a story. It was that kind of place.

But Anya was eyeing him shrewdly. "I see why they love your music, the Chinese. To them you are marvelous, and also pitiable.

They themselves are slaves—to the foreign powers in the Concessions, and now to the Japanese. When they see you, they feel better,
because you were the same."

"Not exactly."

"In their eyes, yes. The Communists might feel something similar."

"Anya, really—"

But she held her hand up. "I predict it! Has one approached you
yet, a Communist?"

"No." On this Thomas was emphatic, because he had not met even
one. "People say one third of Shanghai is Communist—but I don't
know where they are, any of them."

She snorted with laughter. "Don't be silly, you have met them, they
are right in front of you. They lie, they pass as law-abiding people,
they are everywhere."

"Really." He sat back, unwilling to believe that he, the master of
appearances, could be so completely fooled. "What are they like?"

"They are bandits," she shot back, "crude and evil. They killed my
parents and my little sister."

"Where was that?" he said gently. He reached for her hands, but
she pulled them away.

"Russia."

"And then where did you go?"

"Mukden, in north China." She let a tremor go through her, and
then pushed the whole thing away, refashioning her face until it was
bright and gay again.

She changed the subject to music, and would say no more of her
family. She told him it was true, she sang in clubs sometimes, and she
loved jazz, though when he asked her whom she enjoyed, she could
not name a single group. He saw what she was doing, but it didn't
matter to him, he loved it, loved her, or at least loved spending time
with her. It was a joy to be with a beautiful, educated woman who was
here because she liked him, not because he was paying her.

The two of them talked and laughed until they seemed to be the
only ones left in the restaurant, which had grown quiet around them

as the night deepened. By the time they rose to leave, she had drunk so much she could barely stand, and was in need of a steadying arm. He bundled her into a rickshaw and climbed up beside her and together they swayed down Route Gustave de Boissezon beneath rows of trees, in a night-world washed of color. When they came to her front door, he bowed over her hand to say good night. She responded by rising on her toes to kiss his cheek, then took an uneven step and vanished inside, clicking the door behind her.

The light of infatuation was lit, but what Alonzo had said back at the theater about Lin needing to see him was still tugging at him as well. He decided to go by Lin's place on the way home, this being the time when Thomas knew his friend usually came home from his nightly circuit.

He threw a few small pebbles at Lin Ming's window, and sure enough, it opened up, the room's occupant still fully dressed and wearing a scowl which fell away as soon as he recognized Thomas down below.

"I'm glad you're here," he said when he got to the front door.

"Is something wrong?" Thomas followed him inside and up the stairs.

"Come inside," Lin said, latching the door of his tiny two-room apartment behind them. "Sit."

Thomas sank down on the couch and let his face sag into his hands. "I've been worried too. Solomon's leaving. I've got ten men still, and all of them are anxious for me to tell them if it's okay to stay here."

Lin nodded his understanding, and for the first time Thomas could remember, he shrugged and gave no answer.

"So what's going to happen?"

"As to that, no one knows, but—"

"Come on," said Thomas.

"—but powerful people expect Japan to invade Shanghai."

"What! When?"

"Who knows. Not immediately, but they are taking factories apart and moving them to the interior."

Thomas felt the blood drain from his head. "And what does that mean for us? The Americans?"

Lin shrugged. "I would think, if they tried to avoid hurting anyone, it would be the Americans. The last thing they want is a war with you."

"Would we be able to keep playing?"

Lin took a long, hesitant breath. "It is not a question of whether you and the Kansas City Kings can play. It is a question of whether *Ye Shanghai* will continue to exist at all. But Little Greene, right now we have a more immediate danger, concerning the new Japanese Admiral, Morioka. That's why I was looking for you. To warn you."

Thomas felt his eyes grow wide.

"First — swear to secrecy." Lin swallowed nervously. "If anyone knows I warned you, my life will be forfeit. Do you understand? They will kill me. Swear to tell no one."

"I swear," he said softly.

Lin tightened his mouth. A perceptible shiver ran the length of his body. "Listen carefully."

Through the next few days, Lin Ming could not shake the apprehension that he had crossed the line, and that retribution might come swiftly, at any time, and out of nowhere. He had disobeyed orders.

Lin was not so naïve as to think his physical parentage would be enough to protect him if he were caught; he was a son, but not a real one. Not that Du had ever denied having fathered him. Indeed he had acknowledged the boy as soon as he laid eyes on him, since he was childless then, his first wife, Du Taitai, having proved barren. Acknowledging Lin Ming was insurance, but the policy was never cashed, for Du was later to add wives who had more sons, sons of his line, born within his house and thus his legal heirs. But Lin Ming was conceived before all that, when Du himself was only fifteen and practically living in Lin's mother's room.

In her day it was the fashion for girls such as herself in the houses behind Avenue Édouard VII to claim to be from Suzhou, since that charming town of canals and gardens was known for its lovely and sweet-voiced girls — yet Lin's mother truly had been born and raised there. In Shanghai she was called a "one-two" because a man could drink with her for one dollar and pierce her for two. One-twos were not the lowest — those were the Cantonese saltwater sisters, who worked the docks, and the alley girls who let themselves be had against a wall for thirty cents — but they were far from the highest. A step up from them were the two-threes, and many tiers above *them* were the city's premier courtesans, perfectly formed, gorgeously dressed, able to sing, play, and hold their own in games of poetry and calligraphy with the very rich.

Lin Ming's mother was nothing like them. But Du was hardly more than a boy himself when he met her, and little better than she. He never paid for her; they were friends. That was another reason why, years later, when he heard about the tall, thin boy who looked so much like him, being raised in the Suzhou brothel to which Lin's mother returned after giving birth, Du decided to have himself driven to that peaceful garden town so he could see the child up close.

Lin Ming's whole world then was the brothel, with its successive courtyards, its butterfly flock of aunties, its vermilion Gate of Coming and Going. Beyond the gate, cobbled streets unwound beneath overhanging willows, soft in summer with green-dappled light. Canals were crossed by stone bridges whose half-moon arches made circles in the water. From the ponds and fields and wooded hills came peddlers with live flapping fish, caged ducks, bundles of freshwater greens, and tender shoots of baby green bamboo. All around were the lilting strands of Suzhou dialect. If it was Third Month, he would use the coins in his pocket to buy green dumplings stuffed with lotus root. In the autumn, at the festival of the weaver and the cowherd, he would eat the special coiled, sugary cakes. The world was his, and it passed in front of him in the stream of faces, the scudding clouds above the roofs, the crisp flapping banners of merchants. Back then he never thought about the future.

That changed the day his father came.

He remembered the way his mother entered his tiny room at dawn to awaken him. Normally she herself never arose before noon. "Get up, Sprout," she said; he remembered because she used his milk name. He yanked away from her.

"Bathe," she told him. "Put on your new blue gown."

"It's scratchy. I bathed last night."

"Put it on."

"Why?"

"Your father is coming."

He went still. She might as well have said the sun and the moon had changed places, for he had no father.

"Get on the horse," she said, smoothing the bedclothes as if she could take away all the bumps in the road ahead. "Time to be a man."

A clamor rose in the lane, the squawks of chickens, cries of children, rumble of a motorcar. He pulled on his clothes and ran to stand in the courtyard between Jiang Ma, the proprietress, and his mother.

The big square automobile puttered in and crunched to a long and extravagant stop. A knot of bodyguards climbed out, followed by a tall man with a shiny shaved head and a long loose gown that swung with his steps. He had crossbow cheekbones and big ears. *Ears like mine*. A hot knife of panic slid into Lin's middle.

The man looked at him for a long time without expression and then turned to talk to his mother. They had not seen each other since she left Shanghai during her pregnancy, but a wisp of affection was still evident between them as they turned away from Lin without a glance and walked toward the reception hall, already negotiating. A few days later he was sent to Hankou.

Much later Lin Ming understood that it was an investment. Du had enrolled him in Hankou's Lamb of God Missionary School so that someone in his sphere might understand the language and thoughts of the foreigners. That Lin had repaid the Gang's investment through profit was undeniable, for the jazz he arranged brought people into the clubs to dance and drink and dine, and many of them went on to spend even more money in the brothels and opium dens just outside, from which profits also flowed straight to the *Qing Bang*'s coffers.

Yet this success was due less to his parentage than to the fact that he had grown up in a foreign boarding school, with Western music. Every day there had started in chapel with the other pupils, singing hymns and learning their tempered twelve-note scale with its chords and intervals. Their music became another of his languages, and later his ticket to the night-world. Some rival agents around Frenchtown sniped that his success was due only to his proximity to the throne. *A waterfront pavilion gets moonlight first*, they liked to whisper. They were wrong. It was all because he and his *jueshi jia* listened to the same songs as children, hymns, the bedrock of the church. His ear was like theirs. They were brothers beneath the skin.

In his world, there had never been room for a wife. That was why Zhuli was the perfect girl for him, Beautiful Pearl, all his in the moment and yet after, not his responsibility. They understood each other. And walking through the brass-studded gate of the Osmanthus Pavilion in Stone Lion Lane, he felt the familiar flutter of anticipation.

Inside, high ceilings and flickering gas lamps might have signaled any fussy, old-fashioned city mansion, except for the fact that it was full of girls lounging in loose robes with free, unbound breasts moving for anyone to see. *"Lin Xiansheng lai le!"* they trilled when he came in, at ease, childish, for they knew he would never choose one of them. He came here for Zhuli, and her alone. When she was busy, he waited.

Tonight she signaled her presence at the top of the steps with a delicate cough, her hair freshened, her lips moist, her gray silk skirts rustling beneath a close-fitting vest of red brocade.

In her room they fell together, struggling from their clothes. He knew how many men she had here, and he did not mind. She was like him, a fellow traveler, able to give her heart freely to no one. He knew she would never ask any more of him than what they had together, never ask for his money or his protection; knowing this freed him. War was in the air, and it was all he could do to keep himself and his men safe.

They joined happiness and afterward lay back in the sheets. He always paid for the night, which meant he could sleep until noon.

She turned him over and began a soft kneading of the muscles in his back with a touch that was expert, professional, but also intimate. She understood where he hid his anger and his fear, surrounded it with gentle fingers and drew it out until all under heaven was peaceful. Was this love? he wondered, deep in the profound state of rest he always felt under her hands. Was this the feeling? She finished and lay beside him.

He had been conceived just like this, in a room not far from here, in a brothel. Lin always made a prideful point of insisting that he was nothing like his father, but here he was the same, and he knew it. He felt for Pearl just as his father had felt for his mother, though unlike his father, he knew he would feel that way always. With her, all his cares, even the fact that he had just broken ranks to warn Little Greene, melted away.

"What is it?" she said, turning.

"Nothing." He put her head back down, loving her. "Sleep a while."

That night, while Lin Ming lay twined with Zhuli, Admiral Morioka crisscrossed Frenchtown in the back seat of his curtained chauffeured car, looking for music. In his previous China postings, Peking and Tianjin, he had always been able to find some club where a jazz group, Japanese, Chinese, sometimes even American, was playing. And neither of those cities could compare to Shanghai.

Yet in his short time here, it already seemed to Morioka that the Chinese government tolerated Shanghai like a man tolerates a boil on his skin. Night in Shanghai made money, and so was allowed to exist, but what the Chinese government really wanted was to ban foreign music, not just jazz but all of it. Hopeless. A more useless goal for China's future Morioka could hardly imagine. It proved once again that the Chinese were not mature, strategic thinkers. Ban music? What next, forbid moving pictures? Yet this notion, of the toxicity of foreign culture, was promoted by both Nationalists and Communists alike. Amazing.

Morioka never ceased to marvel at China's two parties and the way they squabbled and fought each other, especially as Japan carved their country away from them bit by bit. *Clearly, they need us.*

He had his driver roll slowly past the Ambassador, the Canidrome, the Casanova, and the Palais, all the nearby places where jazz could be heard. His secretary had made a list for him, but so far, he had not ventured into any Shanghai ballroom. Tonight was the night that would change.

He consulted his list one last time. "Driver," he said, deciding. "Take me to the Saint Anna."

Song Yuhua walked down Nanjing Road, the most famous shopping street in Asia and a patchwork of Shanghai's international influences: Parisian bakeries, Balkan dairy shops, and Austrian-style cafés competing with shops dispensing nuts and dried fruits from central Asia. Her eyes always lingered on the international places, not the Chinese establishments like the Wing On and Sincere department stores. The foreign names were music in her mind as she read them off against the clicking of her spool heels on the sidewalk.

As a lonely child in a rural household, learning English from her tutor, she had sustained herself with fantasies fed by foreign books. She imagined herself a woman, grown, beautiful, traveling the world, speaking foreign languages. She had believed in love, in the kind of connection she had never observed in her clan compound in Anhui, and the language of this hope was always English. Now that she believed in the cause, she spoke English only when commanded, and otherwise kept it to herself. She did not really know what to do with her feelings about things foreign.

She stopped at the edge of the Bund, next to the Cathay Hotel with its green copper pyramid roof, and in front of her, along China's most celebrated boulevard, rolled a convoy of trucks filled with weapons and supplies, marked with the red sun of Japan. Her fists bunched and her eyes stung, not at this blatant show of fattening up the Japanese Army warehouses, but at the expressions on the soldiers' faces, placid, impervious, already sure of their victory.

Turtle eggs. Of course we ought to distrust all foreigners. She left the Bund and hurried up Sichuan Road to Avenue Édouard VII, the boundary street between Frenchtown and the International Settlement, with a number-three redhead Sikh on the pedestal in the center of the intersection, directing traffic. She watched him send motorcars, pedicabs, and buses through the intersection with his hand signals, and when a lull in the traffic cleared the avenue, she was startled to see the new American piano player from the Royal. He stood on the corner looking east, toward the river, which gave her time to study him. Though his renown in the city had already put ten thousand pairs of eyes on him, as people liked to say, he did not seem to stand out. His face was reserved, and did not announce him.

When the Sikh gave a burst on his whistle and signaled with stiff-stretched arms, she started across with the knot of pedestrians who had accumulated around her. She was within a few feet of him and was opening her mouth to speak when he turned and saw her.

"I almost walked into you," she said.

"What?" His mouth went slack. "You speak English!"

"Song Yuhua." She touched the tip of her nose with her forefinger in the Chinese style rather than extending her hand.

"Thomas Greene," he answered, looking at her through a daze. "Would you call me Thomas?"

She stared at him on the sidewalk, while people streamed around them, gamblers, office workers, painted-up prostitutes with their stout old amahs hurrying behind them, bald Buddhist nuns in ash-colored robes. "All right. And I am Song."

"May I ask where you learned such good English?"

"Tutors, at home." She could not unlock from his eyes, which were round and fringed and very dark in his milk-tea-colored face.

"All families in China do that?"

"Only wealthy people," she said, and in this unexpected moment, face-to-face with the American, she felt the protective shell of forgetting she usually kept around herself dissolve, and she saw her old life, the existence she had taken apart in her mind and stored away. There it was again, her home, the cistern quickening with its fantailed goldfish, the wall of fragrant wisteria, the plum tree court with rattan recliners. In the warm weather her mother used to lie back in her silk pajamas beneath the branches, and recite Tang dynasty poems. That was the last time she had felt truly understood by another, during those soft nights, answering those great classic lines with quick smiles of understanding; after that, her mother had died. And her father had started to gamble.

Thomas Greene held her gaze in his, as if he wanted to see all the way through, straight into her. "You're far away," he said. "Back home?"

"Yes." Her eyes lifted in surprise.

"I lost my home too. My mother passed away, and I had to strike out on my own."

"I'm sorry."

"Don't be," he said. "I wish you'd tell me how you came to be here, in Shanghai."

She noticed he was rocking from foot to foot, unsettled, forgetting himself. Maybe he felt something too.

But she was not free to feel anything. Du had thousands of men in Shanghai who would kill anyone who crossed him, including her, at his slightest signal. *We call this growing water lilies.* She was not even free to stand here with this American, two rocks in the human stream, face-to-face, visible to all. Even that was dangerous. "It is bad for us to be speaking like this, on the street."

"Somewhere else, then," he said. "I'll meet you."

"No," she answered. "Impossible. I am sorry." And she turned away quickly, so he would not see how much it hurt her to do it.

. . .

Thomas found himself endlessly checking the archway into the lobby that night, hoping she might appear behind Du Yuesheng. But the box remained dark. He had no idea when he might see her again, if ever. He told himself when he kept his eyes on the door that he was watching for the Japanese Admiral Lin had warned him about, but that was untrue.

On the third night he finally caught a movement of skirts in the lobby, and his heart almost jumped up his throat. He lost his way in the music, recovered. Errol and Lester sent him looks, always the first to notice his mistakes. He looked up again: Anya. It was Anya.

It had been more than a week since their dinner. She had not returned to the club, and though he had gone by her rooming house once and left his visiting card beneath her door, he had heard nothing. After his brief meeting with Song, Anya had frankly drifted from his mind, but Song was someone he might never see again, and Anya was here, beautiful in a floor-length white silk dress, smiling. Quickly he motioned to one of the waiters, a skinny fellow named Wing Bean, and in the toe-tapping space between two songs, he slipped him some money to go out for a gardenia.

When the band took a break, she came right over. "A joy to see you," he said, tenderly fastening the flower in her hair. "Our evening together was unforgettable."

Her face clouded. "Oh, dear. I don't remember anything—did I disgrace myself?"

"That would not be possible," he said.

"Why?" Her cashmere brows drew together.

"Because anything you did would be all right."

She smiled at this and said, "I received your card. I was out of town."

"Then welcome back." He caught her arm. "Stay," he said tenderly. "Stay until we finish."

She did, and as soon as the last set ended, they left the theater and rode a rickshaw directly to her lodging.

The place was smaller than he had imagined, only one room,

cramped by a bed, dresser, and chair, with one tiny gabled window. It also lay at the top of four long flights, but that he barely noticed; he would have climbed mountains to get to her, to have love in his arms for a night.

Anya filled a small cup with water from the old-fashioned basin and pitcher atop the dresser, detached the flower from her hair, and with thrifty care settled it in the cup. He had a strange sense of being back in Baltimore, in a narrow row house where vents were closed off to save all the heat for one room, and a child's clothing, when torn, was always taken apart to be stitched into something else. He had seen his mother linger for long minutes at the strawberry man's mule-drawn cart, finding what was bruised and crushed and talking the man into letting her have it for a few cents less.

He watched as Anya placed the flower by the bed and then peeled her dress from her milky shoulders. She turned her back with a natural ease for him to unhook her. He put his hands on her skin, different, satin to his velvet, and the pale feel of it was exciting to him. As he picked her up and laid her on the bed and undressed her, the greatest difficulty was holding himself back, and their first time was over all too soon.

But he awoke before dawn the next morning and they did it again, slowly now, and at leisure, until both were still and content.

He thought she might protest when he said he had to go, but she was sweet, acquiescent. "There's a clean washcloth on the dresser, and a towel. Beside the basin."

He washed and stepped into his clothes before he kissed her. "Thank you."

"No, no, all thanks is for you." She wound her arms around him and kissed him back, stopping just before she drew him down again.

It was getting light when he came to the house. He let himself in quietly, slipped up to his room, and stretched out between his sheets. Now he had what he wanted, a real woman. He folded a pillow behind his head and closed his eyes to enjoy the first early voices from the lane, the tinkle of cart bells, the crank-up cough of an automobile.

He was replete with love, so every sound was music to him, every noise an echo of beauty, doors opening and closing, wheels creaking, the burbled cooing of the spotted dove outside his window. But just before he surrendered to sleep, when the real world started to clank apart and disassociate itself into the other, it was Song's face he saw, not Anya's.

4

ANYA WAS HIS girl through that spring of 1937, and she came to the club most weekends. He loved having her sit up tall and lovely at his table, his for all to see. Song and Du still had not come in, and while at first he had watched in hopes of seeing her, now he was glad they had not returned. Anya was a lovely bird whose plumage was always on display.

She lifted his spirits, which he needed, because the war was chipping away at his Kings. Now Eddie Riordan, the drummer, had stopped going out and was eating at noodle stalls in order to finish saving his passage home. The trumpet player, Cecil Pratt, was starting to talk about the same thing. Cecil had a Japanese girlfriend, and he went up to Zhabei most nights to stay with her, in a sector that had become almost entirely filled with soldiers and civilians from Japan. Much as he hated to leave her, Cecil said the sight of so many men in uniform unnerved him.

On the nights Anya came to the club, Thomas went back to her room with her, always leaving before dawn so he could sleep at home. He liked it that way, separate. When Alonzo and Keiko invited them all over for lunch, he never mentioned it to Anya. Keiko was different, part of their lives, almost Alonzo's wife, though they all knew he had a real wife back home and children in college, to whom he sent most of his money. But here in Shanghai, Keiko was his woman and everyone's older sister, cooking Japanese food, homey in her scuff slippers and apron, shiny black hair tufting from her neck-knot. While Alonzo sat back in his chair like a potentate, she plied Thomas and Charles and Ernest with grilled fish, vegetables cooked in soy and wine and vinegar, and steaming mounds of rice. Those were happy afternoons, which he enjoyed without Anya.

But on his nights off, the two of them went out together, and he let her take him into other worlds, to be with dancers and drug addicts and gamblers, philosophers and utopians, and assorted secret plotters who hoped to take over China. In her company he met actors, artists, and poets, drinkers and pleasure seekers.

"And yet none of them are Communists," he said to her one night.

"Of course some of them are," she retorted. "We've discussed this. One third of Shanghai is—"

"I know," he said, "but who? I never seem to meet any."

"No one wants to *admit* it," she said. "They *kill* Communists."

"It's a conundrum. I cannot be sure they really exist."

"Listen." She leaned in and dropped her voice. "I know all kinds of people—people who know Shanghai's secrets. And you know what they told me? Very hush-hush? That the Foreign Language School at number six New Yuyang Lu is a Communist front."

"Truly?"

"Yes. It was whispered to me that they don't teach languages at all. Go there one day, and you will see, they look like everybody else."

He drank more than usual that night, and barely remembered going to Anya's room and finally arriving home at dawn. When he awoke at midday, it was to a thudding headache and a mouth that was swollen and parched. And something else, voices. He washed and hurried into his clothes.

Downstairs he found Charles and Ernest in his dining room, tucking into a lavish breakfast prepared by Chen Ma, grits and thick slices of ham and big creamy curds of scrambled egg.

"Oliver and Frank are leaving!" Ernest blurted through a mouthful of egg.

"What?" He sat heavily. "Those two? I thought they never saved anything." A bottom-class ticket cost 150 U.S., but that was 450 Shanghai, a lot to save when you made 50 a week, and Shanghai lay before you, arms wide, every night. Few had done it. "Where'd they get the money?"

"Dog track," said Charles. "Soon as they won, they got them two tickets. Say there is going to be a war here, we *all* got to get out."

"Well," said Thomas, leaning back for Chen Ma to serve his own breakfast, "there could very well be a war here, they are right. But I'm not sure we've all got to get out."

"You're not scared?" said Charles.

"Sure I'm scared. But I was scared back where I grew up, too, and I like it here better."

They exchanged a look. "Us too," Ernest said.

"If they invade Shanghai, we're going to have to lay low. It could be bad. But we're not in this war. And another thing — both sides love jazz. Whoever wins, however it comes out, we should still be able to play."

The boys exchanged looks. "We'll stay," said Ernest.

"Never going back," Charles agreed.

"Tails," Ernest put in, "where were you last night?"

"How do you know I was anywhere?"

"Because Uncle Hua told me you came in at seven."

"He did, did he? You're a rascal, Ernest." Thomas admired the boy; in a year and a half he had become agile enough at pidgin to rattle along endlessly with the locals, while Thomas had not learned more than a phrase or two of pidgin, and even less of Shanghainese or Mandarin, which were much harder. In fact, Thomas had not run into any American players in Shanghai who had more than a few words of Shanghainese or any of the other Chinese dialects.

Bright and enterprising though they were, the Higgins boys were too young to be alone. "Fellows, you can't live in that house by yourselves. I think you should move in here with me." As soon as he saw the relief on their faces, Thomas knew he was right. And he needed company, too. The house had too many empty bedrooms, and was oppressive now that the hot summer had set in. Zhu, the quiet man who in winter was the house's master of heat, now opened windows and positioned fans to make the house comfortable.

"I'll square it with Lin Ming," he told the two brothers. "Get your things. Sleep here tonight."

It was two nights after that, the third Wednesday in June 1937, when Morioka walked into the Royal for the first time.

Du Yuesheng was in the balcony box, along with Song, Lin Ming, and his bodyguards, but none of them noticed when he entered in plain, nondescript clothes, slid into a corner table, and ordered a whiskey. Their first inkling of his presence was a racket of footsteps, followed by Floor Manager Zhou yanking their curtain aside. "He's here," he said, panting, "the Admiral."

"Is it so! Where?" said Du, and followed Zhou's finger. "Ah! I see. Puffed-up plug!"

They all strained to see the dim figure under the balcony overhang opposite. "Motherless fornicator," said Fiery.

"Is it true he is going around the city opening field offices?" Flowery asked.

"Yes," Lin Ming answered. "Like Shanghai is already his."

They all stared together, hating him, united for once in ill will.

"Damn that scar of his mother's she calls a cunt," Du said, to murmured assent. "Damn her crack to all the hells."

"Let me take him," Flowery Flag said impulsively. "Tonight."

"Patience," Du said abruptly, and Flowery fell silent.

The boss sat for a long time, staring at the Japanese officer below with the reptilian flicker of possibility that passed for engagement in his expression. Then before he spoke, he glanced with favor at the bodyguard, indulging him as one would a favorite pet. "First we find his weakness, his opening. Then we look for the moment when his assassination will most throw them off. Then we kill him — not before. Teacher will see to it."

Lin's knees shook as he listened. Morioka's rapt focus on Thomas Greene was obvious; they could all see it.

His intestines chilled at the scene on the stage below, where Thomas, unaware of what was happening, was signaling a solo. Charles and Ernest took off on their reeds a major third apart, a bit of showmanship that, though well rehearsed, never failed to please the crowd with its sense of spontaneous intimacy and the simple optimism the major third interval always seemed to ignite. He was a good arranger, Little Greene, able to keep the band sounding polished even though he was down to nine, piano included. He was also popular, a moneymaker, and the first real friend Lin had found among his musicians in a long time. So why couldn't this whore of a Japanese Admiral turn his attention someplace else? The question sounded plaintively in his mind as he watched.

Song, seated in front of Lin Ming, was equally horrified, and she also saw what Lin could not — the look of icy calculation hardening in Du's eye as his gaze traveled from Morioka to Thomas and back again.

Down in the lobby, after the show, she followed her master's gliding form through the crush of people toward the door. Ahead, Fiery and Flowery formed a wedge to clear a way through the crowd.

None of them noticed Morioka bearing down from the other side of the lobby. Song did not catch sight of him until she had almost reached the door, where Thomas stood, thanking well-wishers.

Morioka stepped into the crush just a meter or so in front of her, and she jolted back, her entire being on fire. She saw the way the hair grew down in two points on the back of his neck, where his skin was brown from the Japanese sun. She caught his aroma. It was unbearably tense to be so close to him.

And then he started talking to Thomas in English.

"How do you find China?" she heard him say. "Really? But so

dirty, so primitive. No? That is why they need us, the Chinese, to keep order. Here—take my card. If you need help. Here." And he pressed his calling card into Thomas's hand before bowing and being carried by the crowd out the door.

Song glared after him. Keep order? How dare he? She let the crowd bear her to Thomas, averting her eyes from him while she checked the crowd in all directions, and then, in one quick, low, economical slice through the air that no one could see, she plucked the card from his hand and threw it on the floor. It disappeared beneath the crush of feet.

She kept her eyes straight ahead, but could feel the heat of his awareness as she passed.

Du felt it too, for at that instant, he turned to look back. *"Yuhua,"* he commanded.

"Wo lai," she answered, coming, and lowered her gaze once more, fully concealed, the good girl, *bu gou yan xiao,* no careless word or smile.

"What did he say to you?" Lin Ming asked Thomas the next day.

"That he thinks China is primitive."

"Fornicator. Piece of turtle dung. And you threw the card on the floor?"

"The second he moved on." Thomas said nothing about Song being there. He was thrilled to have had her cross his path, even just for that moment. No one had noticed her rip the card from his hand in the packed lobby, but he had been inches from her, and he caught his breath at the burn in her eyes, the glow that came from inside her. He seemed to be able to see straight into her in that loud, pushing crowd of people.

"You did well," Lin said. "But back to Morioka. If he approaches you again, say as little as possible. Do not ever agree to meet him anywhere."

"You've made that clear already," Thomas said gently, though he failed to see what a Japanese officer would want with him anyway. He thought it unlikely that he and Morioka would ever have another conversation.

But that little scrim of security evaporated less than a week later, when Morioka returned to the Royal. This time he did not stay long, only one set, but before he left, he ventured up to the stage. Thomas was frozen, only half-risen from the piano bench, watching Floor Manager Zhou and Wing Bean scuttle into position to eavesdrop.

"Very beautiful playing," Morioka said, somewhat formally, and Thomas answered, "Yassir, thank you, sir," vamping up the plantation accent for the benefit of Zhou and Wing Bean. Morioka said no more, bowed to him, and left. Zhou and Wing Bean seemed satisfied.

Thomas was shaky, though, and he went directly to Anya's rooming house and rang her bell. He rang over and over, and she never came down. The window light was on in her room, which usually meant she was out. Where? He checked his new gold watch. It was almost three A.M.

Yet much of Shanghai was still awake. In fact, though only two hours had elapsed since his conversation with Morioka, Du Yuesheng would by now have already parsed every word they said.

The next afternoon, Du summoned Lin Ming to Rue Wagner, and they met in one of the quietly carpeted second-floor studies, with wooden shutters tightly closed against the early summer heat. As usual, Du showed no discomfort, not even a shimmer of perspiration, and his voice was as cool as stone. "Twice in one week he has approached the American," he told Lin. "We are moving ahead."

"Moving ahead how?" Lin's voice strained its fragile film of normalcy. "If I may—"

But Du interrupted him. "Your man will be watched all the time for the right opportunity."

"Perhaps you don't need Thomas Greene. Isn't it excessive? Isn't it using Mount Tai to crush an egg?" He knew his father was ever vulnerable to a classical idiom.

"You are here because I am showing you the respect of warning you," Du said sharply. "Do not presume to question."

Lin said nothing.

"We have to kill the blood-sucking ghost. It will throw them into confusion and put us on top, like overturning the river and pouring out the sea. Naturally we will try to keep your American safe. In the end, though, that is irrelevant."

The words sliced through Lin. "And who is going to be watching him?"

"I'm bringing in an outside man for this job," said Du. "His name is Zhao Funian."

Lin Ming nodded, silent, thinking there was nothing left for him now except *bao tou shu cuan*, to cover his head and slink away like a rat.

That week, Avshalomov's boy came to the door of the house with a note inviting Thomas to a rehearsal of the composer's tone poem *Hutungs of Peking*. Thomas had the boy tipped and fed, as was proper, and a few days later sent back his own most junior servant with a reply that he would be honored. He greatly enjoyed his nights out with Anya, trawling the underside of Shanghai, but this was an outing of another sort; Avshalomov was a composer of stature.

They had seen each other six months earlier, when Avshalomov's piano concerto had premiered at the Lyceum, the concert hall where Shanghai gathered on Sunday afternoons to hear music before going out to dinner. The concerto was performed by Gregory Singer, Avshalomov's customary pianist, as the second half of a program that began with Beethoven's Fifth. Greene attended the concert and afterward sent Little Kong over with a warm note of congratulations. Now Avshalomov had responded with this invitation.

Thomas had seen that there was music all over Shanghai, from pit orchestras for the film and recording studios to the Shanghai Symphony. The city teemed with classically trained players. Some musicians were Chinese, some were older Russian Jews who had come years before, and now younger, immensely talented European Jews were arriving too, players who had fled persecution and found their way to the city's orchestras.

Avshalomov was different; he had been in China most of his life. "I am trying to capture everything you hear in the lanes of Peking," he explained. "The chants of the vendors, the buzz of the barber's fork, the temple bells, everything."

"I loved your piano concerto, by the way."

"Ah, thank you, I received your kind note. Did you notice the boy on the celesta? My son, Jack!"

Just then a loud buzzing tone filled the stage. "That is the *huan tou*, the barber's tuning fork," Avshalomov said. "That was how the barber announced his arrival in the neighborhood, and everyone who needed a trim or a shave would come outside. You could hear it from quite far away. Ah, we will begin now." And with a small Old World bow, he excused himself.

Thomas watched him in front of the orchestra, pressing the trombones and tuba for bigger sound, directing the temple blocks and bells and Chinese drums, asking the violins to come in softly and crest in waves like insects on a summer night. He led the musicians through, explaining, correcting, singing. "Here," he called out. "This is the operatic tune. I want that feel. Violins, play with one finger on the E string; accentuate your trills. Again."

At the end of the run-through Thomas complimented him, and they talked for a bit. "It is clear what your training is," Avshalomov said. "When you play, *ça se voit*. But this group you are in now — these Kansas City Kings — I feel this is the future. I hear jazz arrangements everywhere — do you not as well? Brass, more than anything else — in movies, on the radio, even in advertisements. I hear it but I do not always find beauty in it. In your playing, there is always beauty."

"Thank you," said Thomas. "But if I may ask, do you think it's safe for us to continue playing here if the Japanese invade?"

Avshalomov looked sadly at him, only in his forties but older from the weight of all he had seen, his expression grave beneath the light hair that floated in an untamed aureole around his head. "No," he said. "But if they take over, you will not want to play here anyway. I know. I am from the north."

That night, Song returned to the Royal.

At once his anxiety ignited, for Anya was here, languid and lovely at her usual table. Song came in with her eyes downcast, walking a few paces behind Du and his bodyguards, as she always did. Thomas willed his eyes away from her and kept them on the keys, barely breathing. He looked up at her two or three times while they were playing, but fleetingly, and in a way no one could possibly have noticed.

But Anya saw. That night, on their way back to her place from the theater, she brought it up. "Who is she?"

"I don't know who you mean."

"The woman up in the box."

"The box belongs to the gang boss," he said.

"I know. I'm asking about her."

"She comes in with him. That is all I know."

Anya still studied him, speculating as the rickshaw bumped and swayed along, but he went quiet, and so did she. Then when they reached her place, they flew at each other, joining on the bed in a frenzy.

Later, when they had quieted, she turned to him to speak. He thought she might return to the subject of Song Yuhua, but instead she surprised him by saying he could no longer come to her room at night; a "no visitors" rule had been imposed by her landlord. "He meant you," she apologized. "You have come so often. There is nothing I can do—"

"It's not your fault," he said, wondering where they would meet now.

"Perhaps where you live?" she said.

"I don't think that would do. I've taken in two young brothers from the band. They're just teenagers."

She gave him a look, because anyone could see they were far from innocent. "Well, then. Perhaps you should rent a room for us. We can meet there. Something small would not be more than seven or eight dollars a month. You can afford it."

True, he could, and why not? So starting that week, he secured a small ground-floor studio on the Huangpu, at the end of Peking Road, across from the docks, with cooling wood shutters to filter the river air. They went there together after hours, and slept in the pre-dawn coolness, and when the sounds of the day started to rise outside, he got up and went home. It was his last period of routine quietude before the world fell apart.

Song debated long and hard about giving one of the diamonds to the Party. If Du caught her, of course, she was dead, but if Du were to discover her secret affiliations in any one of a hundred ways, she was equally dead, so one more risk hardly mattered. What frightened her was something different, that the gift was so ostentatious for a leftist. A *diamond*. It would have been safer to convert it to cash first, except that then she would be exposed to even greater danger, for gossip from a gem dealer could easily get back to Du.

Still, to hand over the diamond would cement her commitment. This was wealth she found by chance, and it belonged not to her but to China.

One diamond, anyway. The other three would stay well hidden.

The midday rain had cleared, and she saw shopkeepers on both sides of the street reopening their lattices to the wet sidewalks, while sellers of books and magazines and curios moved their racks back out to the street. Men in light, sun-shielding fedoras and cotton gowns stopped to peruse string-bound volumes and old prints. The letter writers came back, small-town scholars who had failed the examinations and now waited for customers behind flimsy folding tables.

She felt for these men, since she too had received an education she could not use, except when she translated for Du. Before his gambling losses, her father had been set on making her a modern woman. He had engaged the best tutors for her older brother, and always insisted she sit in on his lessons. When her brother died of consumption, all the father's ambition transferred to little Yuhua, Jade Flower, an old-fashioned and ornamental name she had never liked. Nevertheless she wore the name he gave her, and studied hard to please him. Though only eight or nine, she could feel the family's future resting on her, and excelled, especially at English. Her younger sisters were but babies then, and she spent all her time with tutors.

But then, after her mother died, her father started going out at night, and reeling back, white-faced, in the mornings. Artworks were sold off: a pair of Yongzheng *mille-fleurs* bowls, a Qianlong white jade censer, a blue and white dragon dish from the reign of Chenghua, her late mother's green jade bracelets. Then other mornings he would come home with money in his pockets, and meaningless gifts. She saw what was happening, but she was only a girl with no more power than a grain of millet afloat in a vast sea. All she could do was watch. At last there came a day when he drew an unlucky hand, and forfeited the ancestral compound and all the land surrounding it.

That was when he begged her, crumbling inelegantly to his knees.

"*Ba*, don't," she said, shocked. "Get up." She disliked this memory. She preferred to think of the shady gardens, the round gates through which respectful servants passed with trays or basins or folded linens, leaving behind the slip-slop of their cotton shoes against the flagstones. That was the memory she allowed.

She had no desire to go back to her family. They had sold her and never made contact again — out of shame, no doubt, for the Songs were a locally illustrious family and their daughters had to marry respectably. Indeed, that was the story they put about, when she disappeared, that she had gone away to be married, and people believed it.

She was born and bred to be used, as surely as any peasant or worker. Communism had saved her, to her way of thinking, opposing as it did the feudal ways that had landed her in this servitude to begin with. Her beliefs elevated her; they connected her to the city.

She had heard it said that every block in Shanghai held a thousand souls, when you added up mothers, fathers, children, shop workers, and servants, and when she was out, moving through the lanes like this, she could feel the rhythm of their breathing like a single organism, hear the hum of their thoughts. This was *ren min* to her, the people, this pulsing urban honeycomb, and they were her real cause.

As she entered the apothecary shop, she brushed her fingers past the hidden pocket inside her dress to confirm for the hundredth time that the pouch was still there.

"Young mistress."

"Special prescription today," she said, and handed the old herbalist a blank sheet of paper, a prearranged signal that meant she needed a meeting. "Also the usual one."

"Mistress is tired," said the herbalist. "Take your ease in the parlor and I will send for tea. I regret that at this moment there is none here, I will have to send out, but it will only be a moment. Please." He gave one more careful look around the shop to make sure no one was watching, and pulled the lever to release the hidden door in the wall.

"Thank you." She entered and sat down with the impatient distraction of the young matron abroad in the city, until the wall of drawers shut again and she could relax from her role and dab the nervousness from her forehead. It was dim but for the small lamp, and cool, no brazier needed now to provide its halo of warmth. She knew it would take time for someone to fetch her current guide, the primary contact through which she reported any information she gleaned as a result of the evenings she spent by Du's side. For a long time it had been Mr. Guo, aboveground identity and occupation unknown.

Presently the inner door opened and he came in, out of breath. *He works nearby*, she realized. *He ran here in the heat from his place of work.* "Mrs. Ma," he said, with complete neutrality despite the urgency of his gasping. "How are you? Have you eaten?"

"Yes, thank you. You?"

"Yes." He mopped his face as he sat.

"Do you remember our conversation when we last met?"

He was lost. "No."

"You told me of your cousins in the north, their need. I said I would pray for a solution."

"Ah," he said. "The need." As they both knew, the situation in the north was even worse now. Japan's armies had been massed near Peking for weeks.

"The gods listened to me," she said, extending the tiny package she had removed from within her dress.

He took it, confused.

"Careful," she said, when he fumbled with the wrapper. The edge in her voice made him open the last square of silk attentively, after which his eyes all but fell from his head. A silence cloaked the little pool of lamplight between them.

"Your spittle is three feet long," she said gently, when he could not stop staring.

He looked up. "Sorry." The jewel vanished inside the silk, which he knotted over and over inside his handkerchief. "They will be most pleased in the north."

"It was luck," she said, hiding her elation. The north was the nerve center of the Party, their base. "Only one thing — enough must be set aside from this for the herbalist to provide for my mistress's medicines, permanently. No matter what happens. That should only be a small part."

"Agreed," he said, giddy at the stone's obvious value.

A tap sounded on the wall, and the hidden door released, with a wooden sigh. She rose. "My prescription is ready. So nice to see you. Please give my regards to your family."

On her way out, the herb master handed her a packet of the usual tonics and restoratives. She nodded toward the inner room, now sealed off again, and said, "Talk to him about payment." She walked out with a firm stride, pleased with what she had done. The *mo shou*, the "evil hand" of the aggressor, was bearing down on Shanghai, but she had done her part, today, to push it back.

· · ·

Thomas awakened a half hour before dawn, curled up to Anya and her warm smell. Soon he would get up and go home, where, a little after midday, he would have breakfast with Charles and Ernest. Right now, though, he liked it here by the river, the fresh air and splashing waves and the hollow bass bumping of the hulls. Dawn would bring the soft slap of river water, then slowly the city would awaken to its human music, the thousands of conversations bubbling up as people rose from their beds throughout the streets and alleys and even on the water, on the bobbing brown sampans. The first minutes of every day were always a genial simmer of voices, before the din of commerce, traffic, and engines took over.

He lay listening against lace pillows, hands behind his head. He could see her scarves spilled over the mirror, her clothing in the small closet, her shoes. In a wash of clarity, he understood that she was living here.

Suddenly, things clicked together: the way she had him take her out to dinner every night, the half-starved manner in which she ate. The way she never wanted to meet anymore in the neighborhood where her room used to be, because she no longer had it, and no money either.

When she woke he said, "You let go of your room."

"I cannot pay all that. Why go between two rooms? I have nothing." Her voice became sweet, appealing. "Can you not give me some cash every month? Not much. Just so I have something in my pocket. I haven't a *sou*, not a *centavo*, not a Chinese dollar. Look what you spent on dinner last night, just for one night . . . can you not help me?"

"Of course," he said, gathering her close. He felt ungentlemanly for not having noticed things sooner, and resolved to give her money regularly, starting with the clump of bills he left on the dresser that morning.

Yet as the days slid by, he started to wonder about it. Being a gentleman was important, but he did not love Anya, and had never thought of making it permanent. She brought him great pleasure and incalculable comfort, and obviously he should support her in return, but for how long?

"For as long as it pleases you to share her bed," Lin said to him at lunch a week later, as he paged through the menu at De Xing Guan, a second-floor restaurant overlooking the river. They sat next to metal-crank windows, which were open to the summer humidity and the bobbing thatch-fabric of sampans, lorchas, and junks. Large vessels passing in the channel traded groans from their horns — the bottom note to Shanghai's chord, a sound special to downtown Shanghai that Thomas had come to love.

Lin ordered the dish the restaurant was famous for, a rich, milky-white seafood chowder brimming with fish, shrimp, scallops, tofu, thin-sliced sea cucumber, and tangy mustard greens, touched by white pepper. To accompany this they had cold plates of pungent steeped cucumbers, gluten puffs with winter mushrooms and bamboo shoots, and *ma lan tou*, a minced salad of a local freshwater weed and savory dry tofu. Sensing his friend's inner disturbance, Lin ordered rice spirits for both of them, *bai jiu*, powerfully alcoholic, served warm in a small crock. "You look like you have a fishbone stuck in your throat. Out with it," he said, pouring.

"First of all, my men. We are down to a skeleton."

"I already told you, we can't replace any of them."

"But the ballroom is full every night! The money's got to be as good as ever."

"Money is unrelated. Would you have me bring new musicians over here now, in conditions like this?"

"Now we are getting to it. Should the rest of us leave?"

"How can I know? Each has his own decision. But you and I," Lin said, "and the others you have left, we are here. All of us know the risks. A new man, in America? No."

Thomas was silenced by this.

"Was there something else?" said Lin. "Anya?"

"How did you know?"

Lin smiled. "It shows. You foreigners are so sensitive when it comes to the house thing."

"Well . . . first she told me we could not be together any longer in her room, and that I would have to rent a room for us to meet. I did that."

Lin nodded; the strategy was well known to him, and he saw little wrong with it. "Why should two rooms be paid for?"

"That's what she said. Except that now I am responsible for her rent. And she wants me to give her money, too, every week."

"And how else do you expect her to get money?"

Thomas stared.

"You want her to go with another man?" Lin asked, serving his friend more soup. "Let me ask you: What work did Anya do when you met her?"

"I don't know. She had that room—she sang a little in clubs, she performed."

"That is not enough."

"So you're saying she got money from men?"

"As all women do, even wives. In my view, this is unimportant. What matters is, what kind of woman is she?"

"A good woman."

"I agree, and lovely too," said Lin. "By the way, what man did she see before you?"

He bristled faintly. "I wouldn't have any idea."

"But I would," Lin said. "It was an Italian, an embassy man."

"How do you know that?"

Lin raised his palms. "I have eyes. I live in Shanghai. You should not be so hard on her, you know—how else do you expect her to live?"

"I am starting to see your point," said Thomas, thinking that now it made sense—her wildly divergent social circles, the instant recognition she commanded from people, club patrons, doormen, waiters. She was just trying to get by.

The *bai jiu* had made Lin Ming professorial. "Actually, Little Greene, this type of woman is as precious as jade. She is not like a wife. Anya is there when you want her, not there when you do not. Who would not desire her, in Shanghai, especially in times like these?"

"What about your woman?" said Thomas. "You told me about her once—but not much."

Lin thought of trying to describe Pearl, but decided Thomas could never understand a Chinese woman. "Well water and river water do not mix," he said.

Thomas left their lunch and walked up Dong Men to Ming Guo Road, which circled the Chinese City and led him to the beginning of Avenue Joffre. The long avenue lined with shops and impressive buildings would eventually take him back to his part of Frenchtown. As he walked, every beautiful woman he passed made him think of Anya, and wonder what he ought to do. He had spent quite a few nights in the greatest intimacy with her, doing everything men and women could do, yet they were not really close. He was to blame, clearly, for he had kept her in a small, circumscribed part of his life. He had always gone home to sleep in his own bed. But that was because he did not love her.

So he would not go on like this.

The awareness was like a weight floating off of him, as he understood that their time together would end. He would make sure she was secure, and he would leave her happy.

He would miss her forthright hungers and her bliss in their joinings. He would miss the way she took him into Shanghai's back rooms and secret salons, even though through her, he still had not met a Communist. Maybe they did not exist.

He approached the corner of New Yuyang Street, and Anya's words came back to him: *Communists? The Foreign Languages School on New Yuyang.* He turned down the narrow road, lined with Shanghai's usual three- and four-story brick apartment buildings, dotted with groups of somnolent old men and gossipy grandmas, the only people out on this hot June afternoon, except for the rickshaw coolies who had no place to go, and were stopped here and there along the cobbled sidewalk, napping beneath their awnings.

Ahead, he saw a sizable building with a white sign out front, English words that made his midsection flutter in excitement: *Foreign Languages School*. He withdrew to the shade beneath some plane trees across the street and willed himself to blend in, straining to disappear against the green backdrop as he studied the doors.

The strange thing was that almost no one passed through the doors, at least no one he could see clearly; they all seemed to hunch over and get away as quickly as possible. He picked out a middle-aged, scholarly-looking Chinese gentleman, two threadbare office clerk types, and a young woman who looked like a student, and held a scarf over her face.

And then another woman stepped out, and he sank backwards. Her form and her elegantly controlled walk were familiar to him; even though her face was half-shielded by the hand she held up, he knew it was her, Song Yuhua.

He pressed against the ivy-thick wall behind him as she checked up and down the street, her shoulders pulled forward around her.

She's one of them. In a blazing instant, he understood the oddities, like the manic light in her eyes when she ripped Morioka's card from his hands, so at odds with who she was in the company of Du. She had another life, he saw it — in the trenches where the Communists fought Japan, and the Nationalists fought the Communists. *And she does it right under Du's nose.* He pressed back into the waxy leaves, breathless at her bravery, as he watched her hurry away down the street.

5

FRIDAY AFTERNOON, STILL reeling from his discovery, Thomas attended a lawn party at a Tudor-style estate in the western suburbs of the International Settlement, a wealthy area favored by Shanghailanders, as the white foreigners who had settled in Shanghai generations before liked to call themselves. Their guests were a Caucasian mix of business people, teachers, missionaries, and the interlopers of every stripe who were everywhere, seeking to explain East to West and vice versa. There were also a few dozen Chinese in gowns or business suits, and one or two oddities like himself. Everyone appeared prosperous, from the women in silk stockings and heels to the men in handmade suits with spectacles and timepieces of solid gold. Too successful-looking to be Communists, in his opinion, but then of course he remembered Song, encased in brocade with huge jewels clipped to her ears; she had fooled him.

He loaded his plate at the buffet, choosing from plump pink prawns and roast beef and rack of lamb, cucumber salads, and strawberries with clotted cream. He loved the food at these parties, which was why he often took advantage of the invitations pressed into his hand at the informal receiving line with which he ended every show. He also enjoyed being a guest in rich people's homes, just as he liked getting the same wage a white player earned.

But here in Shanghai, he did miss Western food. Chen Ma cooked only two things, Chinese food and Southern food. The first had wearied him, and the second he had never liked to begin with. With Anya, he had visited restaurants often, of every nationality and type, usually late at night, when he got off work. They had been faithful about eating at restaurants, because it was the only time when she ate.

It had not been easy to end things. Thomas took her to dinner after the show, as he always did, and by the time they were in a rickshaw, being pulled by a straining coolie back to his studio on Peking Road, it was 3:30 A.M. She rode pressed against him as she always did, unsuspecting; he had planned to say nothing until they were alone together, in bed.

He might as well have poured ice water on her. She was out from the sheets in a second, pulling down her scarves and dumping her fake jewels into a bag.

"Anya," he said, trying to pull her back.

"Stop it."

"Don't do that."

"If that is all I am," she swore, "even one wink I will not sleep here!" It took him more than an hour just to convince her she did not have to move right then, before dawn. He made it clear he would rent another place and pay for eight months, but this, of course, she quickly refused.

After that came apologies and accusations, tears, humiliations, and declarations of good intentions, until at last she accepted his offer of eight months' rent. An agreement reached, they fell into an exhausted sleep. The next day he helped her make arrangements, gave her the money, and she was gone. What surprised him was that he did not miss her, beyond the pleasures of sleeping with her, and the trips to restaurants.

He finished his food, and handed off his empty plate to a Chinese servant with an easy, absent smile.

Strolling the lawn as a *digestif*, he found himself talking with a trio of foreigners, British, German, and American. When he walked up, the American, a businessman from Pennsylvania, was holding forth about China and Japan. "You see how sloppy everything is here? How much everything has to be greased?" the man said. "It'll be cleaned up spit-spot if the Japanese win. Now *they* know what they're doing. Ed Rollins, Cleveland. Pleasure." He extended his hand jovially to the white fellow standing on Thomas's left, who turned out to be British, then to the other fellow, the German, and finally, almost as an afterthought, to Thomas himself.

Once acknowledged, Thomas responded to what he had said. "Do you really think it's all right for Japan to invade China just because they seem more organized?"

"Works better for us," Rollins quipped.

"I've heard Germany's pretty organized," Thomas shot back, keeping it serious. "Think they should take over the U.S.?"

"Now, wait a minute—"

"We would do very well," the German cut in, a grin stretching his blustery Hanoverian whiskers. "But all of you are missing the point. The danger to the world is not Japan. It is the Jews. And you here in Shanghai, you are letting them in! No other country in the world is so stupid to do that."

"My good man," said the Brit, pouring on the plumminess, "Shanghai is an open port. Everyone is welcome here. And so it will remain."

"Jews are good for work and labor," said the German. "No more."

Thomas stared, amazed he was hearing this.

"They breed," the German added.

Thomas closed his eyes, and back to him came one of those powerful, long-ago memories, dreadfully important but glossed over by scarring until now. He was nine but runty for his age, on account of his father having fallen in France and them running chronically short of food, so he probably appeared too young to be out on the stoop by himself, although he was not. What he was doing that day was sulking; his mother wanted him to play the first ten Bach inventions in sequence, and he wanted to be out with his friends. As he hunched on the steps, two white ladies walked by, which already made him cringe back in fear, because they had steel-colored eyes and wore dead foxes around their necks. They looked at him as if he were a strange animal, revolting but interesting, and one said to the other, "They breed," utterly careless of whether he could hear her or not. He remembered his sharp intake of breath, and his almost instantaneous decision not to tell his mother, who already suffered with so much.

Now, though, he spoke to the German. "Such claims have no place in Christian company, sir."

"But I am right," said the German.

"See here," the Brit interrupted forcefully, "I must insist you stop. I agree with my friend here, Mr. Greene"—the man nodded his distinguished white head at Thomas, and in a rushing instant, Thomas realized he was the host of this party, it was he who had slipped the invitation card into Thomas's hand a week before—"your comments are insupportable. This is my house, and my party. I insist you cease such talk."

"And I insist that you know nothing of Jews," said the German.

"There you are wrong," said the Briton, as he pointed across the crowd to a man with a cane. "That is my friend of twenty years, Sir Victor Sassoon. He is a welcome guest here, as he is everywhere in Shanghai." Now the silver-haired gentleman turned to Thomas. "Just like my friend here, Mr. Greene."

"Actually," Thomas replied, "I am not welcome everywhere in the International Settlement. I can't walk in the front door of a hotel or restaurant."

The Brit looked sad. "Ah, that is your American policy, not ours."

"The Jews are your problem too," the German said. "They are filth, not like us." With a generous gesture he included Thomas in the circle. "We are gentlemen."

"You are wrong about me," said Thomas firmly. "They are filth?" He steadied his gaze right in the German's eyes. "Then I am exactly like them."

· · ·

That night Kung's ship docked at the Bund, bringing him back from Europe, and Lin Ming went downtown to meet him. He wanted to hear about his trip over brandy and a few cigars.

The shock was Kung's deflated appearance, unexpected because sea journeys by their nature were restful. "Duke Kung, what's happened? Are you ill?"

"My pride and my hope are wounded," the older man said, "not my body, this time. Shall we go have a drink?"

"Precisely why I came," said Lin, and they scrambled into a rickshaw and swayed comfortably down Avenue Édouard VII, on their way to a coffee shop Kung favored on a small street off Boulevard de Montigny. There they took a private back room, and ordered an expensive bottle of Armagnac, and also a steaming pot of Iron Goddess of Mercy with two tiny teacups.

Kung clipped a cigar and lit it. "Unfortunately, though it was the Soviets who asked me to set out in the first place, their plan had been abandoned by the time I reached Moscow. Nevertheless, I continued on to Berlin—you know I hoped I could get the Nazis to help us."

"And?" said Lin.

"They will not."

"I see," said Lin heavily. "That is very bad."

"It is," said Kung, exhaling a tufting cloud of smoke. "But that is not the only reason for my fear. It's because of what is happening to the Jews! They are seizing their property, their fortunes. My friends lost their banks. They are passing laws against them."

"Are they all right, your friends?"

"Schwartz and Shengold? I still could not locate them. Their houses were locked up; I pray to God and Jesus they are safe. Young Lin, we must do something. This is a grave international crime. China has to take a stand against it."

"Other countries have not."

"All the more reason."

"Why do you say 'we'? What has this to do with me?"

"Your father is what it has to do with you. We have to help him see the importance of pressuring Chiang on this."

"I don't help Papa Du see anything," Lin said, using his father's popular local nickname. "He does what he wants."

"He wants to beat Japan, doesn't he?"

"No question." Du had donated millions to Chiang for the war effort.

"If we take a stand against Germany on the Jews, the West might come to our aid against Japan."

"Maybe," Lin said, and also thought, *but maybe not.*

"There is no reason for the Jews to be persecuted," said Kung.

Lin nodded; he himself had always had high regard for Jews, starting with Hiram Grant, one of his first recruits, a saxophone player long gone back to America. Hiram wore a gold Star of David around his neck which he never took off, and insisted that he was Jewish, though he was not. Hiram's grandmother had been taken in during Reconstruction by a Jewish family in Ohio, who sent her to college and financed her education. She educated her son in turn, and he educated Hiram, who was conservatory-trained. All of them considered themselves members of the tribe of Israelites, and wore its golden symbol around their necks. Hiram revered Jews. They had given the priceless gift of an education to his grandmother, the same gift Du had given to Lin Ming; the difference was that his father used it to control him, while the Jews in Ohio set the Grants free.

He knew it was right to stand with Kung on this. It was a kind of filial piety — going beyond his father, whom he could never venerate, to do something for his country, and for all the world's people. "Here is what you do. Invite the boss to a late-night dinner, you and him and Sun Fo." He saw Kung nod as the implications clicked into place; Sun Fo, a big supporter of Jewish rights in British Palestine, was also the son of Sun Yat-sen, the founder of the Chinese Republic, and therefore royalty. He was someone Du would take time to meet. "Then once you are there —"

"—persuade him to insist Chiang Kai-shek pressure the Nazis

about the Jews," Kung finished. "He ought to do it, you know—he is Master of Shanghai. He has ten thousand Jewish refugees in the city already, maybe twelve. More all the time. They are under his protection."

"The trouble is, he does what he wants."

"You're right." Kung puffed on his cigar. "But I have to try. Because if anyone can make Chiang go to the Nazis about this, it is Du."

"And if anyone can make Du go to Chiang, it is you," Lin answered. They squinted, barely able to see each other through the cloud of smoke, but they understood each other perfectly.

Eddie Riordan made his ticket money, and by the twenty-sixth of July, the Kings were without a drummer. Thomas scrambled things once again, moving Alonzo's slapping bass into the forefront for its percussive feel. There were eight of them left, and the lineup was top-heavy, with two reeds and three men on brass. Cecil Pratt, the trumpet player, would probably be the next to go, since he had been saving, but even then, they would still be out of balance. Thomas was bailing a sinking ship, and he knew it.

After midnight the theater became more relaxed, as it always did, the security at the front door a little less stringent, and this was the hour when Morioka walked in. They were in the middle of a Duke Ellington piece called "Blue Ramble" when Thomas recognized his blocky shape in the archway to the lobby. So did everyone else, for no sooner was he seated than Thomas saw Floor Manager Zhou and Wing Bean move into position.

Thomas played through the sweat, bending over the keyboard and the slow prance-rhythm of "Blue Ramble," propelled by the paddling, naughty-sounding circles blown by Charles and Ernest on their layered saxophones. Luckily the song was simple melodically—until that one moment in the twelve-bar B section when they came to the sudden sustained chord, six voices with a growling ninth on the bottom from the valve trombone, played by Errol Mutter. It was the key to the song, the unexpected ninth, the twist of fate, the turn, the dissonance. It was the misstep, the instant that changes the course of a life, and it came just at the moment Morioka walked in. They played to the end, and he called a break. Quickly the ballroom floor and stage emptied as dancers returned to their tables and musicians went off to refresh themselves.

The lights flickered up and Morioka rose and walked through the tables, Zhou and Wing Bean hovering as close as possible behind him. But once Morioka reached the empty dance floor, they could not stay so close behind, so they hurried around to the side of the stage where they could idle near a table and, from ten meters away, hear fairly well.

Morioka obliged them by talking loudly. "Mr. Greene, I give compliments."

"Thank you."

"I very like the jazz."

"Thank you for listening." Thomas felt himself shaking, as his voice pitched up a notch to match the Admiral's.

"Jazz records, I get from diplomatic pouch." Suddenly Morioka lowered his voice and spoke in a whisper, imperceptible from the distance at which Zhou and Wing Bean stood, his lips barely moving: "According my spies, some Chinese are watching you. They want to use you to kill me."

"Diplomatic pouch? Lucky man," Thomas said, in the same loud voice they had been using. Then, in the same thread of a whisper, he answered, "I know."

"Yes. So I bring you this." Admiral Morioka said at high volume, and held out a heavy, shellacked seventy-eight in a paper sleeve. "I present you." In a whisper he said, "I will invite you somewhere. Say you will go. Do not go. Understand? Do not go."

"You're too kind. A new record?" Thomas peered at the label, and whispered, "I understand." When he raised his face, he said, "Count Basie Orchestra! Several of my men came from his band."

"Is it so?" Zhou and Wing Bean had edged closer, putting an end to the whispering. Morioka went on, "Now they have a new saxophone player, the name is Lester Young. I never hear any sound like this before! Please. Take this. Listen this musician."

"All right," said Thomas. He turned the disc over: *"One O' Clock Jump." Count Basie Orchestra.* "Lester Young. I will listen to him. Thank you."

Morioka made a slight, crisp bow, and turned away.

Zhou and Wing Bean bore down on Thomas instantly. His insides were shrieking, but he managed to speak calmly. "You heard him. He complimented my playing, and gave me a new record." He held it up. "Told me to listen to this saxophone player, Lester Young."

They appeared to accept this, and he finished out the night in a state of controlled panic. What really shocked him was that this plot, this ultra-secret plan Lin Ming had warned him about, had already been penetrated by Japan. He knew that until he had it sorted out, he should tell no one of the words he and Morioka had just exchanged, not even Lin.

But he did hurry straight home after closing, so he could crank up the parlor gramophone.

The first half minute of the twelve-bar blues was a long, frisky piano intro, building atop a light, sibilant drum line. But then the whole orchestra came in, and on top of it the most fully expressive saxophone solo he had ever heard, touched with pleasure and regret. He rocked back on his heels in awe, and cried out for more when it ended far too soon.

This Admiral was a music lover, the real thing. As soon as the song was over, Thomas set the needle back to the beginning, exhilarated, certain this moment would always stand as a before-and-after mark in his understanding of music.

A wry trumpet line came in, and by the second or third listening, Thomas felt sure he recognized Buck Clayton's sound. It could be Clayton; he had finally left Shanghai after many months of saving while playing Yellow Music in an all-Chinese club. *They are fixing to have a war here,* he had said to Thomas over tea and blintzes at Rosie's on Rue de L'Observatoire, two days before he left, *and I want no part of it.* He had sat across the table as urbane and perfectly dressed as ever, but gray from worry. "I put it to the rest of the Harlem Gentlemen, those who are still here playing the tea dances at the Canidrome, and they all agreed with me, all except one," said Clayton. "They're all leaving."

"Who's staying?" Greene had asked, curious.

"Stoffer, my pianist. He's got himself hired on with Earl Whaley's Syncopators at the Saint Anna. Earl says he's staying in Shanghai, no matter what. Well, I wish him the best. You too." And they drank to their futures, about to diverge. Buck left, and now here was his trumpet on "One O' Clock Jump," like a clarion call. *Fixing to have a war here.*

It was almost four o'clock when the teenaged brothers rattled their keys at the front door. They came in rubber-limbed and slurry from drink, but stood at attention the instant they heard the new saxophone solo. "Who's that?" said Charles, and that was it, sweet land of liberty. They refused to go to bed that night until they had played the record at least fifteen times, hovering next to the sound box, its volume doors swung all the way open. Watching them, he could see a glimmer of the furious journey they were going to take with their reeds as they aged, and the music grew and changed with them. Their form was a young one, his was old. He envied them that.

And it was his job to see that they were safe.

In the third week of July, Du Yuesheng met H. H. Kung and Sun Fo for dinner at Lu Bo Lang, a venerable restaurant next to the Yu Garden in the Chinese City, to talk about the Jewish question. Du brought Lin Ming with him, for the same reason he often brought Song to these events, because men who had been educated abroad sometimes made references to that world, and used foreign phrases, and Du wished to miss nothing.

Over shark's fin and water shield soup, sautéed abalone, and tofu-skin pastries of minced quail and wild mountain mushrooms brought from Yunnan, only pleasantries about health and family were exchanged, as custom demanded, while the gentle net of *guanxi,* relationship, was sewn into place. Finally, when the dishes had been cleared, a crock of warm Shaoxing wine brought out, and Kung's first cigar lit, Sun Fo delivered a passionate denunciation of the Germans' mistreatment of their Jewish citizens, now streaming into Shanghai by the thousands. Du listened and said nothing.

"These people are under your protection," said Kung.

But still Du had no response.

"If I may, Teacher," said Lin Ming, and all eyes went to him. Du nodded permission. "Were you to succeed at this, you would be remembered as a great benefactor. Not just now. Throughout history."

As he had guessed it might, this kindled the glow of interest. Kung and Sun sensed it, and notched forward.

"What did Hitler say, when you raised this matter with him?" asked Du, since they all knew Kung had just returned from an audience with the *Führer.*

"He said, 'You don't know Jews.' It's strange, because he was an impressive man otherwise, quite smart." Kung's habitually calm expression was punctuated, as always, by the steady brilliance of his small eyes, which took in everything from behind his tortoiseshells. "But Chiang Kai-shek is his equal, his peer, he is the leader of China, so perhaps if he approached him . . ."

"What did Hitler say about helping us against Japan?" Du asked then, which was what they all burned to know.

Kung removed his round glasses, and rubbed his eyes. He was rich and powerful, but no longer young, and now he sagged with disappointment. "He refused," he said, and pushed his frames resolutely back into place. "His advice was, give up and join Japan's East Asian Co-Prosperity Sphere immediately."

"Hand ourselves over to Japan?" said Sun Fo incredulously.

"As if we would do that," said Kung.

"Never," Du agreed. To Sun Fo he said, "We'll do our part. Tokyo has placed a new chief officer here, an Admiral, and we are about to kill him. I have brought an assassin in from outside, a man with no ties or temptations." He turned to Lin, and indulged his shallow crescent of a smile. "And he is watching your piano player day and night."

As a result of handing over the diamond, Song was bumped up a notch, and assigned a new guide. Most Party members in the city belonged to cells, kept small, so that if one person was caught, the others could scatter and start over. Song had no cell, since she lived as a spy. Thanks to her, they had periodic reports on the money flow from the Green Gang to the Nationalist armies, and twice had learned of a Green Gang plot against them in time to avert disaster. When she was a new recruit in 1933 and Du maneuvered a hostile takeover of the Da Da Steam Navigation Company to gain a fleet of merchant and passenger ships, the Party knew about it even before the public did. She had always seen her contact one-on-one.

All she had been told about the man she was meeting today, her new guide, was that he was a person of some import in Shanghai's theater circles. She already knew she would be deferential, for the relationship was always vertical, never a meeting of equals. In this way the Party was like Confucianism, which unsettled her, because Confucianism was so traditional.

When she stepped off the trolley, she saw by the clock tower atop the Wing On Department Store that she was early; her destination, Cyrano's on Peking Road, was nearby. So she wandered into the store, past gleaming counters of merchandise and smiling attendants, and rode the elevator to the fourth floor. There, a dim, slow-churning dance floor of tightly pressed couples swayed to a Filipino band. These were not prostitutes; those were on the highest floor. These were dance hostesses, and couples who came looking for a dark place to embrace. She stood on the side, her arms crossed in front of her waist, watching them clutch each other, seeing love the only way she could, as a spectator.

Thomas Greene had broken it off with his Russian girlfriend; she had read about it in the *xiao bao,* the mosquito press, which, in addition to its cheap scandals and gossip, also ran some of the city's bravest anti-Japanese editorials.

So he and the gray-eyed Russian had parted company; she had set up a separate kitchen, as the Chinese would put it, and he had kept the studio by the river. And here, watching the anonymous couples press together in the false daytime darkness, she thought of him, and of dancing, something she had never done. She did not know how, just like she did not know how to do the house thing. Obviously she had done it wrong, because even Du did not come back for more, after he had bought her. She watched the dancers rock on their feet, embracing in public.

She thought of the meeting coming up, and moved her hand to her thigh. Her new guide was someone of known sophistication — there would be a conversation, reflections, thoughts. She missed those early years of talking with theater people in cafés while Du pursued his amours. She missed the companionship of people who thought and debated and visualized the future.

She remembered the day she was sworn in. Her directions took her up Henan Road, past the Mei Feng Bank of Sichuan, past Peking Road, and almost to Suzhou Creek before a young man she had never seen before fell into step beside her. She smiled as if she knew him, and they continued along the creek past the Shanghai Waterworks. Her sponsor, Huang Weimin, the editor and writer, had told her they were to look like any couple.

The man took her hand and led her into a narrow alley that ran between the Capitol Theater and Taylor Garage, where he knocked twice on a door that was quickly opened to a dim hallway. Down a corridor, up a narrow staircase, they came to an office where a man who looked like an ordinary clerk, the sleeves of his gown protected by cotton over-cuffs, looked up at them. "Yes?" he said, and put down his fountain pen. "Who is this? Eh, Huang Weimin's candidate." His eyes stayed on her as he picked up a memo with a few lines of flowing characters on thin, translucent paper. "He told us about you. Stand right there." And in just a few minutes, with no fanfare, no ceremony, and certainly no acknowledgment of the danger to her life, she was sworn in and registered to the Shanghai branch of the Communist Party of China. She had joined.

Magic pulsed from the orchestra in looping, sinuous waves as dancers pressed together in the dark, and she wondered why she kept coming back to places like this. To torture herself? She would be Du's for another ten years. She turned her back on the music and hurried out into the street.

At the café, she gave her name as Mrs. Gao, *Gao Taitai*, according to her instructions. She was always *Taitai* something or other, since women of her age were almost never unmarried. They seated her in a private room, where she ordered a pot of tea and two cups. When the tea had gone cool, she poured herself a cup and drank it, and after that, another. It was a full half hour past the allotted time when she finally heard footsteps in the corridor and the door rattled for a fraction of a second in its frame before opening.

The irritation she had been nursing died inside her as she looked into the face of Chen Xing. She had met him at the Vienna Garden during her early exposure to Communism; he was the one who had told her about Miss Zhang, the lovely and pregnant dance hostess who had been planted like a water lily, keening and begging Song with her eyes to save her life. Did he know what had happened to the girl?

Since that time she had seen Chen Xing's name in the press, and knew that he held various civic posts and served as director of some of Shanghai's biggest banks. He was also a producer of plays, a leader of the League of Left-Wing Theater People, and the host of a radical salon. He was famous for his scandalous affairs with women. But though he was left-leaning, no one knew he was a Party member.

She could see by the flutter in his eyes that he was just as surprised to see her. No doubt he had been told only that he was meeting a member who had come up with not just information but also a diamond. He certainly had not expected it to be someone he knew, and above all not her, someone connected to Du. She caught the note of admiration in his appraisal, and saw him assume she had stolen the diamond from her master. *Fool. No one steals from Du.*

"*Gao Taitai.*" His smile was effortlessly smooth and vacant. "So nice to see you."

She answered politely, "How is the family?"

Steps sounded outside the door. "Ah," he said, "here is Miss Wu now." And a girl came in, a child less than eighteen, cheeks firm and round like a honey peach. Who was she? His daughter? But a third person had never attended one of these meetings before.

In the next instant Song saw she was not his daughter, for she sat on his lap and curved her body against him, despite the fact that he was twenty-five years her senior. "Pleased to meet you," Song said.

"*Gao Taitai,*" the girl replied, and went right back to simpering in Chen Xing's ear.

He whispered back to her and fondled her through her clothes as if Song were not even there. She found it shocking. He was not even trying to attend to the business they had come to conduct.

Then abruptly, he pushed the girl off his lap. "Be a good child and go get an extra teacup and a basket of soup dumplings. No, two baskets. Wait for them and bring them back. You have raised my appetite." And he squeezed the firm round of her behind as she turned away.

Song endured bolts of humiliation as she forced herself to review how much time and care she had expended in dressing before she left the house today. Nervous as a bed of pins, she had tried on a dozen dresses, eventually settling on a plain *qipao* of gray cotton which made her look left-wing and serious, but still pretty. She wore her hair as usual, sweetly knotted with flowers at the nape, because to have left Rue Wagner any other way would have been to invite notice. In the end the look suited her, and when she walked out the gravel driveway and through the iron gates, she knew she was beautiful, ready for anything. And now she had to stare painfully at Chen Xing nuzzling this child-bauble. *Serene. Face of glass.* She watched Miss Wu walk to the door with the excessive, untrained switching of a young girl.

By the time the door clicked shut, Song was in control again. "Lovely," she said neutrally, hoping that now they could talk.

But what happened went beyond her expectations: he changed completely. The sophisticated ennui drained from his face. His spine lifted, his eyes clicked to a different and infinitely more focused shade of black. In one turn of the head she saw the theatrical producer, the salon host, the man of ideas. "She is spoiled and simple," he said dismissively. His voice had changed too, become level and grainy; gone was the oil-slick politeness she had heard before. "Easy to deceive. I always bring someone who is pretty and wooden-headed, so they can see the places I go and the things I do as I want them to. Forgive the intrusion. It is actually safer this way, and now we have a few minutes alone."

She stared. Which was the real Chen Xing, the rich, bored man of the theater, or this concentrated, severe figure who now sat across from her? "Any news from the north?" she said. By this she meant the advance of the Japanese, but also Party headquarters, where all major decisions were made. For the past two years, the top leaders had been operating out of caves in Yan'an. The brain trust was there, the future. One day, when she was free, she too would go there.

He leaned closer. "I do have news. Peking is silent as a tomb, everyone just waiting. Japanese troops are massed outside the city. They have taken Tianjin, and Tanggu, the port that serves both those cities."

"And will our troops protect Peking?"

"No. Chiang has ordered a withdrawal." It was like a blow to her chest. So Peking would be handed over to Japan without a fight.

"We must comply," Chen said sadly. "We are a united front with the Nationalists now — and also, Chiang is right. We could never hold them off."

The injustice of it flamed up, burning her, parching her. "Will they give Shanghai to Japan the same way?"

"No! Here we will kill them one by one, starting with that foul swine Morioka. I heard he showed up at the Royal again, to see that piano player."

"Yes, I have details." Though the story terrified her, she kept her voice even as she repeated what she had heard from Lin Ming. "He gave the American a new record, with a saxophone player called Lester Young. He gets them by diplomatic pouch. The American loves the song; I am told he listens to it over and over, and his own saxophone players, two skinny brothers, a couple of drainpipes, they listen to it even more."

Chen Xing sat back in his chair, momentarily silenced. "A song," he said, and paused again. "You know, *Gao Taitai,* you have learned more than the West-ocean language; you understand how they think."

She was taken aback. "I do my best to serve the cause."

"I know. You do a good job. Your skills are high. You have been noticed." She felt her insides chill, for he meant the diamond, as well as her English.

"I will serve in any way. Never speak English again if they want."

He raised a hand. "Just be careful. Now, the next thing we want you to do is support Du's plan to kill Morioka. Do anything you can to help it work."

"But they are our enemies. If they want to use an American as bait, we should work against them and—"

"Miss Song," he said, so surprised at her that he used her real name, "your opinion was not requested."

She blinked back.

"You will help this plan."

"Yes," she said, resistance hammering inside her.

"And also," Chen continued, "we still need money. So if there is any way that you can—"

The door opened, and Miss Wu sauntered through. "Food is coming," she said, proud of her competence in arranging this.

Chen Xing slid smoothly into his other self. "What do you mean, you think Hu Die is pretty? She's a great actress—did you see her in *Twin Sisters?*—but she's too noble to be pretty, almost like a carving, a face made of stone." He drew Miss Wu to him. "I prefer a real girl!"

Song sipped her tea, watching them laugh and trade banter, understanding that the meeting was over. Chen Xing wore his public face now, puffy-eyed, weary, brined in a thousand shallow nights—a complete change.

He looked up. "As I was saying, Mrs. Gao, if there is any way that you can again attend the weekly salon, we would all be so grateful. What you contributed was valued by all, last time. We hope you will return again."

She smiled neutrally. "I will try. Mr. Gao keeps me busy." She rose, aware that her dress was frumpy and out of date and that she herself was old. "Please give my best to your family. Good day. Good day, Miss Wu."

The girl looked up as if surprised she was still there.

She swept out, her final turn as the regal matron, and did not let her mask drop until she was outside, her heels tapping on the sidewalk, her profile echoing her in the shop windows she strode past. What was she going to do? She could not support a plot with Thomas as its bait. And what would she do with the diamonds, three in the wall behind her night table and at least twenty-five more in the pouch on the back of Du Taitai's picture frame? Du Taitai had forgotten them once again, and no one else knew of their existence.

Maybe, she thought, boarding the clanging trolley, she should take them and emigrate. And this strange, exotic thought stayed with her all the way home, to Rue Wagner.

The assassin Du hired, Zhao Funian, came highly recommended by the Nationalists' paramilitary force as a cold killer, though his background was ordinary in every way.

Zhao had been raised south of the Yangtze, in the painted beauty of

Zhejiang, where his father owned five *mu* of land—and also had five sons, prompting Zhao Funian to leave home at an early age. This was the modern world, and men no longer had to spend their lives serving their clans, especially fifth sons with no land and no wives of their own. So he went to Hangzhou, where he managed a numbers game and collected monthly bribe envelopes from merchants, eventually becoming bodyguard to the city's Beggar Boss. From there it was only a matter of time until the Nationalist Secret Police tapped him to eliminate collaborators. Competitive, clever, secretive, charming when he needed to be, he was perfect for the work.

"And the jazz man, is he to die too?" he had asked Du Yuesheng.

"Spare him, but only if you can." Du's eyes narrowed; they were dead eyes, Zhao noted, unencumbered by emotion. "The Admiral's life is worth any price, Chinese or foreign never mind."

Zhao knew this was the most important thing he would ever do. He spent excited hours in the little room he had rented in a house behind the Royal, smoking, stubbing out cigarettes on the windowsill, watching the back door and the musicians and the comings and goings of cooks and maids and waiters. He picked out the pianist easily, for he walked like a man in charge, and passed in and out without an instrument.

Still, Zhao Funian needed someone inside the theater to tell him what went on, especially any words that might be exchanged between Thomas Greene and that whore Admiral Morioka, and soon his crosshairs settled on a waiter named Cheng Guiyang. A few nights before, he had overheard him at a noodle stall near the theater after closing, speaking in the soft, sibilant accent of Wu, as familiar to Zhao Funian as his own voice. The man was from Zhao's part of northern Zhejiang, maybe even from Pingyao County itself. Zhao had paused nearby, pretending to study the turnip-shred-stuffed cakes in the opposite stall, listening until he was sure and even, in a stroke of the gods' favor, hearing the man's name when another waiter walked past and addressed him: Cheng Guiyang. Thus blessed by fate, he had been able to learn enough things about the fellow to create a spider-web of *guanxi* between them from the first hello. Cheng was a perfect target: he slept in a room of stacked bunks with seven other men, who called him Wing Bean; ate but twice a day; and sent every other copper cash back to his family.

Zhao made the opening move at two thirty A.M., after following the waiter to a food stall. Cheng was tearing into a plate of *xiao long bao*, soup dumplings filled with hot broth and ginger-scented pork. As he was passing, Zhao contrived to drop a handful of copper cash so that some would roll under Cheng's stool, forcing him to stop eating as Zhao picked them up. "You should be more careful," Cheng admonished him.

Zhao said, "Your accent—I know the speech of Wu. You are from Zhejiang?"

"Yes," said Cheng, annoyance evaporating into curiosity.

"The northern part, near the Yangtze?"

"Yes—"

"Wait! My friend, this is not possible!" Now Zhao had assumed the opposite stool, moving as lightly as a shadow. "I believe I recognize you. Could you be from Cheng Family Village on the Li River?"

"I am!" Cheng stared.

"Your father brewed vinegar, isn't it? The Tai Yang Company, that one? He was brew master there?"

Wing Bean's eyes widened. "You knew my father?"

"Yes. Such a good man."

"I don't remember you."

"I was from Guo Family Village."

He saw Cheng studying him, raking his mind for a memory. Time to play his high card. "About your father," he said, tilting his head in sympathy. "It's too pitiable about him passing over."

The younger man froze, stricken, and looked down at his half-eaten dumpling, the pork fragrance steaming up. He blinked, and closed his eyes for a second.

"There, my friend," said Zhao, and settled a warm hand briefly on the younger fellow's shoulder. "All will be well. The gods have watched out for you if they have brought you to Shanghai."

"No. They have not." Cheng lowered his head, and for a moment he looked no older than a child. "I work hard but I earn nothing. At home they need my help, but I can barely feed myself."

"*Ei,*" said Zhao. "It's like that, is it? Put yourself at ease." He too was speaking in their home accent, pouring it on nice and thick. "Persons from the same native place should stick together, isn't it so?" He held up some coins and called to the vendor for more dumplings. "Now, my friend — what is your name again? Your given name?"

"Guiyang. Cheng Guiyang. Everyone calls me Wing Bean."

"Guo Liwei," Zhao lied, indicating himself. "Now listen, Wing Bean." He moved closer. "I'd like to lay a proposition before you."

The next night, when Du's retinue walked out of the Royal at two A.M., Song slipped a scrap of paper into Thomas's hand at the door. Neither acknowledged the other or made eye contact; to all who observed, each gave the appearance of not even noticing the other. She walked right past him in her gossamer-silk *qipao* of ivory white, embroidered all over with pale pink butterflies, while he continued his conversation with a British man in black tie. Yet their hands touched, and when he took the paper, he touched her fingers quickly, reassuringly, in return. She vanished, and he moved the slip discreetly to his pocket as he went right on greeting people, burning inside. She had something to say to him.

And he knew her secret.

It was not until he was going home in the back of a rickshaw, his privacy assured by the open night air, that he unfolded the note, and felt himself soar:

Hua Lian Teahouse
Avenue Hing and Route Alfred Magy
29 July, Thursday, 3:00

When the day came, he found that the address was a considerable trolley ride away, almost to the western edge of the French Concession. As he watched the city stretch out and grow leafier from the clanking, rocking car, he ran through all the possible reasons she might have for summoning him. He disembarked early and covered the last stretch to Avenue Hing on foot, just to calm his pizzicato nerves.

The half darkness of the teahouse was cool after the blazing street, and no one was in sight, no staff, no patrons. He walked through a series of empty lattice-screened dining rooms until he came to a circular tower room, in which an old-fashioned octagonal window looked down through meshed trolley lines to the street below. He barely saw the rose-patterned wallpaper, the white damask set with a steaming teapot and two cups, because there she was, rising from her chair to greet him, face opening in a smile. "You came," she said, and reached across the table to clasp his hand in greeting. She wore a plain cotton *qipao,* the two-inch spool heels favored by Shanghai women, and no jewels except tiny pearls in her pierced ears.

The door clicked behind him and he was jolted to see they were alone together, for the first time. "Miss Song," he said.

"Call me Song."

"Isn't your name Yuhua?"

"That's a feudal name, Jade Flower. I have never liked it. My friends call me Song."

"All right, I will too." His big dark eyes clouded with concern. "Say, is everything all right?"

"Not really." She poured tea and pushed a cup across to him. "I asked you to come because there is danger to you, very grave. It concerns that Admiral Morioka who has several times come into your ballroom."

"That!" he cried. "Believe me, I know."

"You know?"

"Yes. It's not hard to figure out. They want to kill him, and here he is coming into my orchestra and sitting through set after set like a man in a trance! I get it."

She relaxed a little. "I know Du is planning something — I suspect Lin knows too. I didn't know if he had dared to warn you."

"It would be very dangerous for him to do that," Thomas said pointedly, as a way of explaining why he would not say any more. Neither would he reveal that Morioka also knew.

"I need not have come."

"Not at all." His eyes, fringed with curly lashes, were warm. "I'm glad you called me here. I want everything straight between us, everything honest. So — I know, okay? I know about you. But I won't tell a soul."

All her alarms screamed and she fought to keep her voice calm. "What do you mean?"

"I mean, I know. You are a Communist."

"What?"

"It's all right." He covered her hand with his. "No one will ever hear it from me."

She felt her mouth opening and closing, and no sound came out. He knew. Her life was ruined if someone knew. She had to change everything. "I must leave Shanghai immediately," she blurted.

"No! Don't do anything. I told you, it's all right. You are safe. I will protect this as carefully as you do."

She looked at him for a long time, desperately calculating. If he kept her secret, what would she have to give him in return? The instant the question bloomed in her mind, she saw herself, in an involuntary dreamlike instant, in his arms, an image she pushed away. Would that be his price? If it was, she would pay it. She looked at the gentle slope of his shoulders beneath his suit. "Can I trust you?" she said quietly.

"One hundred percent."

"Who else knows?"

"No one."

"Lin?"

"No one."

She was trapped, and she knew it. Tears stung behind her eyes and wobbled her vision.

He said, "Believe me. Even if we never see each other again after today, no one will know. I swear it."

She rose, deciding, and he rose with her, and they exchanged the brief embrace of a promise.

"Please be careful," she said into his ear. "My life depends on it."

"I will." They sat down again, Thomas electrified from that moment of holding her. "May I ask about this contract with Du? Lin Ming told me you have a contract related to your debt."

"My family's debt."

"Under that, you cannot—"

"No," she said miserably. "I cannot. Even though that is not what I am to him. He has other women."

His look was patient. "And how much longer does this contract last?"

She felt sadness spring up to prick behind her eyes, and she hated the answer she had to give, since it would extinguish all his desire. And she badly wanted his desire to stay alive. "Ten more years," she said.

She saw how he paled. Ah, there, she had him: deflated. He would have no further interest in her after this. Why should he? He would have better things to do for the next decade than wait around for a broken shoe such as she was. She corrected herself; the phrase was harsh, she was no prostitute, but there was no denying that she had sold herself, long ago, and now he knew. She half expected him to make excuses and leave.

Instead he said, "Ten years is a long time." His words sounded sticky, as if his mouth was dry. "Would there be any exceptions?"

"No," she said, smiling a little, in spite of herself, at his sweet persistence. This was a foreign thing she liked, the way he showed himself, and strangely, she felt safe with him, safer than she felt in the Party. She wished she could stay with him forever. The Japanese were coming, everyone said they were surrounding Peking at that very moment, waiting to enter, uncontested—the Chinese army had withdrawn. Tianjin had fought for only three days, and now Peking was not going to fight at all. Next was Shanghai. She wished she could be with him when it happened, instead of in her little room on the top floor of Rue Wagner, with her maid, Ah Pan. The words of an essay by Wang Tongzhao came back to her—*In both action and spirit, will you continue to resist or surrender to the enemy?* She would resist, she wanted to be part of it. If only Thomas were part of it too.

But it was not even his war. "If we see each other at the theater, you must look right through me," she told him. "We cannot talk, or meet . . . whatever you want to tell me, tell me now."

He smiled. There were no words really for his world, the marble steps of West Baltimore, the ringing sound of a piano in a conservatory practice room, his mother, his grandmother. It could be told in music; one day, if he played for her, he could make her understand. He could spin out the bent-note melody of poverty, the feeling of always being an outsider, an actor, of the turning road that had brought him across the United States and here to China. It was a kind of walking blues; he felt that if they were alone, and there was a piano, he would play it, and she would know everything about him. "We may not be able to even acknowledge each other. But I'm staying."

"You are staying in Shanghai?"

"Until they throw me out. And if you ever hear me play, it's for you. Remember that. And if anything changes, or you need help, come to me. I'm going to be here."

Her face seemed to crumple. "Why are you so kind to me?"

He picked up the pot and refreshed her tea. Because she had wrested freedom from servitude. Because she had brains to match her beauty, and no man had ever yet had the chance to make her happy. "I just want to be part of your life," he said.

· · ·

Lin Ming surprised Pearl by arriving at the Osmanthus Pavilion in the late afternoon of August eighth, when the mansion was just stirring and the girls in their bright flimsy silks were sitting together in the public rooms to play cards, and listen to Yellow Music on the wireless. As he opened the front door, Zhou Xuan's song *"Ye Shanghai"* was playing, and he felt a stab of fear for the fragility of his city's fabled nightlife.

"Lin Ming," he heard softly, behind him, and he turned to see his *qin'ai de Zhuli*, his dearest Pearl, waiting. He felt all the trouble and worry ease out on his breath as he moved toward her and took her in his arms, not even caring that they stood in the foyer, in full view. "Shall we go upstairs?" she said.

He nodded. "Yes. Order some wine, and an early dinner." She clapped for the maid, and he hastened up the stairs, anxious to escape to her room.

In the upstairs hallway, the madam intervened. "You will be buying out Pearl for the night?"

"Yes," he said, needing Zhuli beside him tonight, along with a warm crock of wine. The world was changing, the seas transforming to mulberry orchards and the mulberry orchards to seas, and he had no way to stop it, and certainly no power to protect Zhuli. But the Osmanthus Pavilion was the one place where that sort of promise was not required.

As soon as they were alone, she took off her robe and heavy earrings, leaving nothing but a clinging shift of apricot silk, and her glow of surprise. He rarely told her ahead of time when he would visit.

Food arrived, dark-marinated razor clams, fresh crab paste with leeks and chewy rice cakes, short ribs, and an herb-scented purée of broad beans. They served each other and ate as loved ones, sharing a cup of wine.

"I reached the age of twenty-eight last week," Pearl said casually.

He immediately understood. At twenty-eight her lifetime buyout price came down to five thousand. Undeniably there was a current of happiness between them, and an ease, something like what the foreign people would call love. In their most intimate joinings she sometimes whispered that everything of her belonged to him, which always lifted him to the heights.

And she was becoming more affordable now.

She lowered her eyes and went on eating, as if what she'd said was an observation of time passing, no more, when he knew her entire life depended on this turning point. She had asked him to free her, without asking.

He froze, stuck between tenderness and reality. First, where would he get five thousand? And if he got it, how would he protect her and see to her well-being all her life? Because if he bought her out, she would be his, as surely as any bondmaid. War was coming, and even in good times, women like her had no way to survive. Almost all of them ended up back in the flower world no matter how much money the man spent, and grew old there, the way his mother had done. It was an old story in Shanghai.

He took her in the same way they had done it for years and fell asleep beside her as always. When he woke it was six thirty. Normally he slept with her until noon, but today he rose quickly to dress for the early meeting Du had called. Maybe it was the click of his watch that woke her, or the slipping sound of his shoes on the floor, but just before he walked out, he glimpsed her watching him.

They both knew he was answering her, for it was the first time he had ever left without embracing her. He could not buy her out, and there was no use discussing it. She was awake, he knew it, but when he looked at her one last time just before he stepped out the door to leave, she had her eyes closed, pretending to be asleep.

He rode the trolley to the Cathay. Du was never awake at this hour; normally he began his days at noon in the steam baths, drinking hot tea while his back was scrubbed by Flowery and Fiery — it being unthinkable for a stranger to have personal access to the boss in a public place. But everything was different now, for Peking had been taken by Japan, surrendering in near-complete silence. Yes, lives had been spared, architecture saved, and most of the art treasures moved out, but it was still devastating. Lin, like everyone in the clubs the night before, was shell-shocked by it.

Meanwhile, the previous night had set a cash record. Even the most ascetic young students and partisans sought to lose their minds, float their senses, stay out all night—to *wan wu sang zhi*, play at trifles until one has exhausted one's will. Why should they do anything else? The dwarf bandits were sure to storm Shanghai next, and nothing could stop them.

There were also more foreign men in his clubs now than ever before, men who had been living in Shanghai with their families, but had now sent the wives and children home for safety while they soldiered on. Gloriously unencumbered, they arrived nightly with fresh young girls, pretty things streaming into the city, running for their lives. Riding the elevator up to the restaurant, Lin Ming decided the girls were a reliable barometer of the war's advance in rural China, just as the daily influx of Jewish refugees told of the conditions in Europe. Things were coming to a head, and that was surely why Du had called him at this hour.

The older man waited in a small private alcove that was really just a glassed-in balcony, tucked behind a waiters' station so that even from the main dining room, its existence was not apparent. Inside, it was a large-windowed box cantilevered to look over the river, with its great vessels at anchor, flags flying. Du was eating *xi fan*, rice porridge, and he immediately filled a bowl and set it next to Lin's spoon and chopsticks. It was jarring, the hint of family, and Lin had to remind himself that it was an illusion. Aside from sending him to an American boarding school, which had beyond doubt been the forging of him, Du had been no father at all. In control again, reality in place, Lin picked up his chopsticks and reciprocated by serving the boss with meticulous care, choosing from the onions, peanuts, pork bits, and pickled vegetables on the small condiment plates around the table.

When they had finished, Du spoke. "It is only a matter of time, now. But we *will* be defended—Shanghai is where Chiang will launch the War of Resistance. I have his word. We won't lie down like the north!"

"Can we possibly beat them?"

"Maybe not, but we can fight to buy time. Factories have to be dismantled and rebuilt, gold and silver bullion moved to safer places."

Lin felt his face twisting. He had been assuring all of his Americans that even if Shanghai fell, there would likely be no actual battle.

At the Royal, he had gathered the seven remaining Kings into the back room. "It's coming," he told them, "no way to deny it. You will have all heard that Peking and Tianjin have given up. Very little fighting. But next they will be coming to Shanghai. So each of you, one man, then another, you must tell me you understand. Because these are new conditions. If you have your fare and you wish to go, you have our blessings, never mind your contract, and please do not waste any time. So." He turned to Alonzo, the eldest. "Mr. Robbins?"

"Staying here," Alonzo said with ease. "We'll hunker down much as we have to." They all knew he meant him and Keiko.

"Mr. Cole?" Lin Ming said to the French horn player, and Lester answered, "Staying."

"Mr. Mutter?"

"Staying," said Errol. "I understand the risk."

Lin sensed the tightening in Thomas. Fate that his friend's grumbling brass section should hang on until the end. "Charles and Ernest?" he said to the brothers.

They looked at each other in confirmation. "We stay long as Tails stays," said Ernest. "We don't have the money anyway."

"Mr. Ames?" Lin said to the guitar player.

"Leaving Thursday," Will said. "Saved the tourist-class fare." His eyes flicked from Thomas to Lin. "I hope you'll give me my last paycheck a couple days early."

"We will. Mr. Pratt?" he said to the trumpet player.

"I'm going," said Cecil. "Same boat as Will."

"Fair enough then," said Lin. "That leaves you, Mr. Greene." He had not addressed Thomas that way since they left Seattle, but this was a formal roll call.

"Far and away the best place I've been," said Thomas. "Staying."

"All right. But you should understand that this nightlife, this whole world of *Ye Shanghai*, could vanish the minute they take over." Up in Tianjin, where Japan had held a concession for many years prior to conquering the city as a whole the week before, they had run heroin dens in which customers, once injected with this powerful new version of opium, were stripped of their clothes and their cash and dumped, unconscious, into the sea. Recently a reverse tide had washed 107 naked male corpses back up the river, exposing the scheme to a horrified public. The "mystery of the 107 corpses" was sensational at first, and then sickening. "They could shut us down in the turn of a head. And if that happens, any of you who live in Tung Vong housing"—he sent a glance to Thomas, Charles, and Ernest—"will have to get out right away. So please think carefully."

They assured him that they already had. And now, the next morning, here was Du telling him the city would not be giving up without a battle—a long, dangerous battle. "Perhaps if there was diplomatic intervention, we would not have to fight," he said.

Du turned his stony gaze on him.

"If Chiang can get Hitler to stop discriminating against the Jews, it will gain us the sympathy of America and Britain," Lin said. He was pushing it, but he could see the distant gleam of interest in Du's eyes.

Please, Lin Ming begged silently. It would make his father a hero, for there were great musicians among the refugees in Shanghai, also writers and doctors and scientists. Yet every Jew he had spoken to said the same thing. *We are only a few. There are so many more back in Germany.* He watched hopefully.

But Du Yuesheng shook his head. "Chiang Kai-shek has no interest in this. He still hopes Hitler will be his ally, despite what Duke Kung was told in *his* audience. Chiang will not push him on the Jews."

"And Hitler won't help us."

"No." Du spat out the word.

Lin pressed on, hoping to use Du's anger at least to gain protection for the Jews in their city. "Shanghai, then—that is yours. And you have many thousands of Hitler's Jews here, under your protection, already. I'm sure you have heard the complaints from the Germans in the International Settlement—they are demanding that you restrict your Jews, put them in a ghetto as they would do back in Germany."

"No!" Du thundered, his sphinx-like façade shattered in a second by cold fury. "This is our city, not theirs. Shanghai is a free port, no restrictions. So it will remain."

"Teacher," Lin said with a grateful nod of his head, acknowledging Du's commitment. It was something, at least.

"In fact," said Du, "you give me an idea. I have already moved the corporate seat of my shipping interests to Hong Kong, along with a few vessels."

Lin blinked back astonishment. This was the first clear indication he had heard that Du was actually preparing to flee Shanghai. *If he did that, all the cards would be in the air* . . .

"Just a few vessels to Hong Kong," Du was saying. "The bulk of Da Da's fleet will remain here, and continue to serve the Subei ports. Perhaps we should have Jews on the board, and as proxy owners, to prevent the Japanese taking Da Da over."

Lin made a note. In 1933 Du had engineered a takeover of the Da Da steamer line, whose merchant and passenger vessels dominated the "little Yangtze" routes between Shanghai and Haimen, Nantong, and Yangzhou, called the Subei ports. The Green Gang had already controlled the Stevedores' Union and the China Seamen's Union, holding sway over the docks and the sailors. Once they acquired Da Da, they were able to dominate the profitable regional shipping in and out of Shanghai. It was a business worth holding on to, even if one had to leave the country. His heart pounded at the thought; if Du left the country, he would be free. So would Song. "Are you planning to go?"

Du's look hardened again. "Even though we remove Morioka at

exactly the right moment, and our Fifth Army fights valiantly, we still may lose. Therefore contingencies are required. I need you to transfer significant amounts of bullion and cash to accounts in Hong Kong, to begin with. Much less than I have given to the war effort, of course"—he added nuance with a meaningful lift of one eyebrow toward his bald dome—"just what my wives and I would need."

Lin readied his pen, seeing the brilliance of Du's hedge. No one could say he had not done his part to bankroll China's defense, even though what actually happened to that money after he gave it to Chiang Kai-shek was an unanswered question. That was not his problem. He had given, generously.

And he knew his empire, every corner of it. Lin needed his pen and notebook, but the older man could speak from memory not just on his shipping lines but on all the nested tangle of his directorships, corporations, properties, and bank accounts. He knew it all, to the last copper cash, just as he remembered every man he had ever ordered killed, and the terms of every deal he had concluded.

Lin looked at his notes. "So you moved several of Da Da's vessels to Hong Kong?"

"Three to berths in Hong Kong, captains and crews for each steamer. Rent some godown space right away, so we are ready to ship. Even in war, goods must be moved. *Especially* in war." There was some tea left in the pot, and he poured all the rest of it into their cups. *"Hun shui mo yu,"* he instructed his son. Fish in troubled waters, profit by disturbance.

6

SONG YUHUA SAT in front of her mirror Friday evening, August thirteenth, struggling to restore her inner calm as she applied rouge from a small pot. Two days before, Chinese troops had defied the 'thirty-two ban by marching into Shanghai, and were joyfully greeted by cheering crowds, including Song, who waved her handkerchief from the bridge above Suzhou Creek and shouted with the throng— *Ten thousand years to China!* Though she spilled tears of joy at the sight of troops, she also knew somehow that the brown dwarfs would not be stopped, not by these men, or any number of additional Chinese soldiers who might follow them. Demands and reprisals flew back and forth between the two governments as a result of the entering soldiers' having broken the treaty, until the Chinese army promised not to fire first; thus was a fragile calm achieved.

In this pause, this bubble of safety, Du decided to go ahead with a large party he had planned for the evening. Scores of invitations had gone out, opera singers were engaged — Du adored opera, and despite his lack of education had earned the city's respect as a connoisseur — and caterers worked furiously in the kitchens. By seven o'clock, black motorcars clogged the driveway and every room was full, even the foyer, with men and women in evening dress talking in fluid Mandarin and the lighter staccato tap of Shanghainese.

Song was about to rise when her door swung open suddenly, rudely, with no knock. She nearly let out some brusque words, but left them to dissolve in her throat when she saw it was Fiery Old Crow, who was always to be obeyed.

"Number fourteen," he said curtly, and she followed him down the hall, knowing he meant one of the many small wood-paneled, curtained, and bulletproofed studies that lined the second floor. Du scattered his meetings among these rooms, always changing, so that no one outside the building ever knew his location.

Her mask almost cracked when she walked into the room and saw that the man waiting next to Teacher was Dai Li, the infamous head of the Nationalist Secret Police. He was known not only for killing Communists but for stretching their deaths out to be as long and entertaining as possible.

He has come for me. The thought seemed to tear her heart out of her chest. But she steadied herself, watching him, waiting.

Within a minute, she saw there was no danger; he barely perceived her. He did not even glance at her body, tight-sheathed in crimson silk, or her hair, tied back with hothouse gardenias. This fit what was said of Dai — that he did not go with women, and not with men either, preferring to avoid the house thing altogether. He even required all the men under his command to be celibate as well. Whatever the reason, she was apparently invisible to him, and could breathe again.

"Here." Du thrust out a copy of the *North China Daily News*, China's most important English-language paper. "She reads English," he said to Dai Li, as if this rare ability was commonplace among bondmaids.

"Teacher," Song said respectfully, with lowered eyes. Quickly she scanned the article before starting to translate, and her last hopes sank. The foreign powers were calling on Shanghai to simply give up — surrender to Japan!

When she was almost finished putting the article into Chinese, the door clicked open and Lin Ming came in, making a silent reverence to Du and Dai Li. She came to the last paragraph: "However bitterly Japanese aggression may be resented, it can hardly be denied that its extension would be encouraged rather than stayed by physical resistance from the Central Government, and would be accompanied by such complete destruction of China's resources that all hopes of national reconstruction would have to be indefinitely postponed."

The silence of outrage filled the room. Everyone had been hoping the Concession powers would help them — depending on it, in fact.

Du spoke first. "How dare they print such a treasonous demand?"

"They are telling us to what? Form a puppet government?" said Dai Li. "Just like they did in Manchuria, with 'Emperor' Pu Yi!"

"That poor fool," said Du. "Haven't you heard it said? The ghost of one devoured by the tiger helps the tiger to devour others."

Dai Li nodded. "England and France and America do not care if we fall to Japan or anyone else, so long as they can keep making money."

A rustle of movement brought Du's attention to Lin, who still stood beside Song, his face full of pain. "Teacher, forgive my intrusion, but I just heard the news from Uncle Hua that you have been awaiting. Thomas Greene received an invitation today by message boy from Admiral Morioka, to tea."

"Tea?" said Du. "Where? When?"

"Tomorrow, at the hour of the rooster. Café Volga on Avenue Édouard VII."

"It's a trap," guessed Dai Li.

"Trap of what?" countered Du. "Our men aren't going to be out in the open."

"All I know," Lin said, "is he sent his boy with the invitation. And Thomas Greene accepted."

Song wanted to scream and tear at her hair. How could he accept, after he had been warned — by Lin, by her —

Dai Li, with his bulbous forehead and flabby midsection, bounced from one foot to the other in a dark troll parody of childish excitement. "We won't miss. His mother! We'll kill everyone within ten feet of him."

"Not the piano player!" said Lin. "Not the American."

She touched his arm from behind, wanting to get him alone so they could talk.

Du turned toward Lin's voice and saw to his surprise that Song was still there, standing behind Lin, listening. "Go," he ordered, and she obeyed.

It was past eight the next morning when she awoke to the thud of bombs and distant, toylike pops of gunfire. She jumped up. Plumes of smoke were rising above the rooftops far to the north, well beyond Suzhou Creek, in the direction of Japanese Army Headquarters. She prayed their evil command center had been hit by Chinese bombers. Late last night, word had raced through the Party that a full-on Chinese counteroffensive was about to start.

Just as she began to dress, Ah Pan slipped in. "Elder Brother's downstairs."

Thanks to heaven. "Have Lin wait for me in the garden. Bring Dongting oolong and *xi fan.* Tell him by the time the tea is ready to pour I will be there." She paused in front of the mirror to put up her hair. "Go!"

Ah Pan vanished.

On the back lawn she found him waiting, brooding as he stared across the back wall toward the smoke. For the first time ever, he looked old to her, his face sunken, cheekbones bulging. He looked more like Teacher.

"It's going to rain," she said, to lighten things with a joke, for now, even as the Japanese bore down from the north, a typhoon was roaring toward them from the east, its black clouds piling up in the sky.

Lin smiled mirthlessly as servants appeared with *xi fan* and condiments. She ladled the rice gruel into his bowl, and added the spring onion, smoked fish, shreds of river moss, and crisp peanuts she knew he liked. Another explosion boomed from the northeast, where the skies were darkening, though it was morning.

"*Ge,* "she said, Elder Brother. "About Thomas."

"I know!" Lin burst out. "I *warned* him. Nets above and snares below—how could he *do* this?"

"He has to be warned again."

Lin spooned up his *xi fan,* wincing at the far-off grumble of thunder. "They are watching me day and night."

"I'll go," Song said quickly. "No one will suspect me." It was true; though she translated nimbly whenever English was needed, Du saw her mind as capable of containing the two languages, and nothing more. "Why would they connect me to him? He is nothing to me." She watched Lin carefully and saw to her relief that he had no idea she and Thomas had met, not one time, but twice.

Lin said slowly, "Do you think they would let you go out today?" He glanced to the north, where bombs flickered against the storm clouds.

"It's Saturday. Every Saturday I go downtown to buy Taitai's medicine. Taitai needs her medicine." She did not have to remind him that even though the Supreme Wife was incapacitated, in traditional ranking she was still the most important person in the household next to Du himself. "Should I go to his *lilong* house off Rue Lafayette?"

"No. I just telephoned; he is not there. He went to a studio he keeps on Peking Road, just off the Bund, opposite the river. I have told him it's unsafe there."

Her eyes widened; unsafe indeed. That intersection lay directly in front of the *Idzumo,* the Imperial Navy's flagship, a massive war machine and an obvious target. "Don't worry, Brother, I'll go. I'll take care of it."

Normally she left to buy the herbs late in the day, but at one o'clock, seeing the northern suburbs burning, she decided she dared wait no longer. The radio buzzed and chattered: last night Chiang had given the order to begin attacking Japanese positions, and now

Zhabei, Wusong, and Jiangwan were on fire, with the Eighty-eighth Division struggling to hold the Japanese back and sending up plumes over the cityscape. The time was now.

At the front door she was accosted by the guard. "I must get Taitai's herbs."

"Danger. No one goes out."

"Taitai needs medicine. You know I go every Saturday. Her medicine is used up." She raised the prescription. "I must go."

She saw him hesitate. "Give a look." She threw her gaze out toward Rue Wagner. "It is quiet now, safe. In a few hours, who knows?"

"The Supreme Wind is coming." *Tai Feng*.

"I will be back before it is upon us."

She saw his mind working. Taitai's health was no small matter. "If Teacher comes home to find her sick —"

"All right," he said. "But one person, no. Someone must accompany you."

"I'll get my maid," she said, needing to grasp the reins quickly, before he could call one of the guards.

A minute later, she and Ah Pan passed out through the compound gate into Rue Wagner, and instantly were pushed and eddied by a crowd unlike anything either had ever seen. A mass of Chinese made an endless white-shirted column trudging through the sweltering streets, carrying what they could, everyone pushing into the French Concession, another country, neutral, where they hoped to be safe from Japanese bombs or street-by-street attacks. Blocking the tide of refugees were islands of those who had walked as far as they could and then stopped, huddled on the ground to rest or sleep, children and clothing and cook pots shielded from the plodding line by their bodies.

Song and Ah Pan linked hands and pushed through to Édouard VII, where Song's hopes that the trolley might be running soon evaporated, for nothing moved there except the slow streams of people. "We will walk," Song said, wondering how she was going to separate from the maid to see Thomas. They pushed against the human flow, out of the French Concession.

"Come, little one," Song said, when the girl's pace slowed. "Not much further."

But the bondmaid stopped. "I have to go," Ah Pan said.

"Go where?"

"Home."

"Your village? In Hebei? No," said Song. This was impossible, no matter how much Song might have wished for privacy. "Too dangerous! There are no trolleys. What makes you think there are trains? You don't even have money."

"I have money," said Ah Pan, and touched her pocket to make a pathetic jingle of coins.

"Ah Pan, listen to me." Song took both the maid's hands. "You are better off here. In Teacher's house you will be safe, safer than almost anywhere."

"It's my family," said Ah Pan.

Song felt the stab of it. It could hardly be worse for Ah Pan's family; her native place had been overrun. "Listen," said Song. "When this is over, I'll ask leave for you to go see them. I'll take you. We'll go together. Right now —" she gestured toward the explosions, wondering if the maid would even be able to get out of the city alive. Thunder broke and mumbled across the sky; on top of everything else, Shanghai's low-lying streets would soon be knee-deep in water as well. "Come," she said to the girl, "let's walk."

When they reached the herbalist, she turned to Ah Pan. Risky though it was to leave the girl on the sidewalk for a minute, to take her inside was impossible. No one from her life could meet the herbalist. "I need you to wait out here for a moment while I get the herbs. You cannot travel now. I swear to you, as soon as it is safe, we will go." That was all she could say. She believed in freedom, and that meant the girl was not hers to command, in the end.

Ah Pan stood stubborn, and they faced each other like two trees rooted in the earth. Finally the girl said, *"Xia yi beizi,"* next life. *"Ni jin qu ba."* Go inside.

"Please don't go." She didn't want to let Ah Pan leave; it was dangerous. She wished she could command her. Suddenly everything that had drawn her, the rights of the worker, the equity, the higher way of thinking—all of it was *xin luan ru ma,* as tangled as a heap of rope. Her voice was a whisper. "Wait here. Please." And she turned away even as it sliced her to do it, and walked inside.

Uncle Hua stood at the kitchen door with his pant legs rolled up, slapping at mosquitoes on his calf as he peered up at the blackening sky. A siren screamed in the distance, making his heart startle and his flesh jump, turning his thoughts again to Master, who had not slept at home the night before, and still had not returned. Hua had told him over and over that his studio was dangerous, sitting as it did directly across from the *Idzumo,* but Master never wanted to listen. Wooden head, wooden brain. Moreover, it was wrong for him to leave Hua alone with the young brothers now, with the enemy approaching. He was the only servant left. Little Kong, Chen Ma, and Uncle Zhu had all departed the day before, back to their home villages, leaving a lot of trouble for Hua.

Then there was his gambling business, which had abruptly withered. Things had never before gotten so bad that people stopped gambling, and though he was sure they were overreacting, they stopped playing nonetheless, and he could not bring them back. Twice cursed was the fact that just now he was out three thousand, most of which was Master's money. This was a sum he could normally make back in two or three weeks of busy operations, but now he had no operations at all. *Curse the brown dwarf invaders. Curse their mothers. May their guts shrivel and protrude out through their mouths and be gnawed off by rats.*

He heard a noise behind him and saw Ernest in the doorway. "Little Master always look see," he said, pretending annoyance at the teenager, whom he liked.

"Hua Shu," said Ernest, having added "Uncle" to his modest repertoire of Chinese words. "Where's Thomas? He still didn't come back."

"Master stay studio side."

"Not now," said Ernest. "Listen to the bombs."

"Master working."

"Not now. Thomas knows it's just the three of us here. He would have come home if everything was all right."

Hua shrugged.

"I have to go check. Give me the address, catchee chop-chop."

Hua folded his arms. "No can do! Trouble very bad. Many peoples dead."

"That's why I need to go."

"No! Two Little Masters stay here."

"Yes. I am going to look for him."

"No. You stay! I go." Hua rolled down his pants, then huffed and muttered as he poked through the cupboard, finally pulling out an ancient black umbrella which he unfurled with dignity, leaning halfway out the door to open it and stepping out carefully beneath its canopy. Charles had come clattering in behind Ernest, and the two of them watched as Uncle Hua stomped away in the wind, twisting his umbrella this way and that to shield himself. Soon his gown was soaked and clinging to his midsection, and the wind, which the radio said was at seventy-eight kilometers per hour, tore his umbrella right out of his hands. He plodded on in his bubble of dignity, turned the corner, and vanished.

Song made her way north on Jiangsu Road, turned right at the Land Bank, and crossed Yuanmingyuan Road. That was when she saw it, the Bund, the Peking Road Jetty, and the *Idzumo,* the great flag-snapping killer whale, moored right there in the river and surrounded by passenger liners, junks, freighters, and bobbling sampans, all tied down and riding hard at anchor. The first raindrops started to fall on her as she hurried down the block, past the majestic offices of Jardine

Matheson and Canadian Pacific, to the small side door Lin had described to her, opening directly onto the sidewalk twenty or thirty meters in from the Bund. Next to the door was a louvered wood shutter, and behind it the window was open. She could hear the piano.

Inside the room, Thomas had been playing since he awakened, still full of feeling from what he had seen the night before. It had been hot, and the waiters had propped open the lobby doors for air, so that through set after set, Thomas and his fellow Kings had watched the steady stream of people carrying bundles and children and elders on their backs, pouring into Frenchtown, where they thought they would be safe. The band performed to them all night, doors open, and every number they played carried the rootless blues of their homeland.

When he awakened in the studio, he could smell the coming rain, and hear the river churning, boats butting and knocking, warning sounds he knew well from the coves near his grandfather's farm on the Eastern Shore. It was enthralling, a drama, and it drew him naturally to the piano.

He laid his hands on the keys in D-flat major and played the arpeggiated left-hand waterfall of Liszt's concert étude *Un Sospiro*. In his right hand, he added a simple melody, not Liszt's melody, his own, but bent and stretched, with the worried notes added. It grew, drawing energy from the weather. He kept up Liszt's left-hand pattern, and with his right hand, he followed the wind, calling, responding. Then the rain started, first a scattered counter-rhythm of drops, but soon a jackhammering roar. He played to it, swelling the sound, until he heard something.

It was a pounding. Someone knocking at the door.

Who would come here? Quickly he pulled on his trousers, and snapped the suspenders up over his bare shoulders. Where was his shirt? He tilted up the shutters.

Song! He yanked the door open.

She jumped in, out of the rain, her cotton *qipao* plastered to her legs and body.

"How long were you standing there?"

"Since the rain started. I ran here almost all the way, but when I heard you, I was listening."

"Is something wrong?" He took her shoulders, lightly, and feeling how wet they were, reached for a towel and unfolded it over her back. "Why are you alone, with all this?"

"My maid was with me, but she left. She wants to go home. I could not stop her." She drew the rough-nubbed cotton close to her while the rain drummed on the shutters.

"Leaving Shanghai, now? Shouldn't we go look for her?" There was so much *ren qing* in his face, and it slipped its warm and simple arms around her though they stood several feet apart.

She caught her breath. It was that same safe feeling she'd had before, in the teahouse with him. Before her mother died, she had felt this way all the time, protected as if by the laws of nature, but never since, with any other person. "No," she said heavily. "But I thank you. She is gone. To find her is impossible."

"I'll go with you, if you want. We can try."

She shook her head. "It was her choice, Thomas." She softened the words by touching his arm, wanting to let him know how much his kindness meant to her at that moment.

He guided her to the single chair and sat opposite her, on the piano bench, while she took down her hair and then expertly, unconsciously, re-twisted it behind her neck. "I came for Lin," she said, "though no one can ever connect this with him. Swear."

"No one will."

"He says you must not go today. I say the same. No doubt you came to the same conclusion. Perhaps you said yes just to throw him off? But this chance Lin and I can't take. We decided one of us had to come."

"Don't worry. I would not dream of going. And he won't go either. I mean," he added quickly, "not in these conditions." He glanced out at the storm with its bass notes rumbling underneath the random percussion of explosions from the city's north side. "Come." And he stood and held a hand out.

The single room held the bed, a chair, a bureau, the piano, and a screened-off corner for the washbasin, but he led her into the little square of floor between the bed and the shuttered windows.

On top of the bureau the gramophone waited, lid raised. Thomas wound the crank, pushed the lever, and dropped the needle. The song was "Saddest Tale," Duke Ellington's big-band blues; it started with a cry from the clarinet that rose like a breaking wave to start off a slow, heart-thudding rhythm. "Do you want to dance?"

She looked anxious. "I do not dance."

"Neither do I," he said. "I am always at the piano, remember? Try." He opened his arms to her, the gesture marking the slow, stepping rhythm, and guided her into position. "That's it," he said. "Now just follow."

The rhythm was languid, yet the song was anything but simple. Every chorus kicked off a new set of chord changes — one reason he had been listening to it, that and the deep, tinny sadness of the bass-scored trombones. Now he was just glad of the pulled-out beat that let him draw the length of her close to him.

Duke's mournful voice came through, so soft it was almost a bubble from the depths, speaking the song's few lyrics: *Saddest tale told on land or sea is the tale they told when they told the truth on me.* She stumbled and he caught her easily. "Step on my feet. That's right, just like that. You're so light." And he got her moving with him, finally. He could feel her reticence beneath his hands, the little quiver under her skin, so he kept his arms strong but loose around her. He would wait for her.

They stepped apart when the song ended, both a little scared. She busied herself looking through the music on the piano. "What's this?"

"Charts and scores for the band's songs."

"And this?"

"Something I made up."

"What's meaning, made up?"

"Wrote. Invented."

"Play it," she said.

So after resting a split second on the low D-flat, he let go of the rippling, repeating pattern in the left hand he had used before, modeled at first on Liszt, now mutated into something new. His right hand sang with his melody, simple and unexpected in its counterpoint against the complexity of the left.

Then with no warning his right hand started something new, a melody he had not tried before, which came from nowhere and belonged to that moment, making it as much hers as his. As he followed it, the melody became everything he had wanted to show her, his little family of Mother and his grandparents and his father, who had died, and then his mother going too, leaving him. That was pain, and it circled around the melody in every kind of way, crying of loss and sadness. And then, as if following the movements of a sonata, he broke into the passage that answered those cries with resolve and harmony. Here was his odyssey across America, the land for which his father died. He traversed the sweet, tangled woods of Maryland and Ohio, the velvet-block fields of the Midwest, the sheets of sunlight over alpine meadows atop the Rockies, then Seattle, Shanghai. When he came to the last phrase and the final, tonic D-flat chord, home again, it sounded the deep *bump* of their lighter against the wharf, the magic moment they disembarked, he and Lin, the beginning and the end. He let the note hang and then rested his hands in his lap until the drumming of rain once again filled the room, nothing else. He had played as well as ever before.

And improvised. It was a simple feeling, clear as a bar of light on the wood floor, and it had something to do with her being there.

Standing behind him, Song sensed it too; she had never heard him play quite like this. She felt the charge, almost saw it in the air between them.

Everything seemed possible. He was open to her. But she also felt the chill of fear. She was no maiden, yet no man had seen her naked body, and she had little sense of what men and women actually did together. She knew how it ended, of course, because Du had done that, stabbing her distractedly as if relieving an itch. But there was more, surely. Certainly.

Part of her still believed, had never stopped, and from that private place she reached down and slid his suspenders off his bare shoulders. He turned, joy and surprise in his face, searching her eyes, seeking a yes, a sure yes, and then catching her hands in his and drawing her down to his lap.

The wind had dropped back slightly and the rain settled to a steady spit by the time they were quiet atop the sheets, arms and legs tangled in a way that Thomas knew would somehow link them forever, no matter where they went after today.

"Do you know," she said, her hand moving through his hair, "this is the first time I did this of my own desire. If you had rejected me, I don't know what I would have done."

"Never. I dreamed of this." It was true in more ways than he knew how to count. Every girl he had known, even the nice girls back in Baltimore who had been out of reach for him on account of his poverty, had been imperfect. There was always something off, some qualifying streak to mar their appeal. Not her. She was all his hopes, idealized.

So it was a surprise when she continued, her voice tentative. "He did it quickly, and never even looked at me. For all these years I have thought I did the thing wrong. Or that maybe something was not right inside, though I bled the first time —"

"Song." He looked at her exquisite body, yellowed-ivory skin, the strong, frank hips that had urged him higher and higher. "You were wonderful. *It* was wonderful. Couldn't you tell?"

"Yes!" She pressed against him. "But I didn't know. He never even saw me naked." She touched his chest. "You know all my secrets."

"All of them?" He parted her legs. "Did he do this to you?"

Her mouth opened, surprised. "No."

He felt more love, as she arched up to meet him, than he had ever felt before, for anyone. He steadied her hip with his hand, and his voice went down to a whisper. "Let me show you."

Much later he got up and moved to the piano, and once again started to improvise. He played full of happiness, even though bombs kept sending their shuddering blasts up, just a few miles away. *No love without death.* And then just as a sob can escape a man's throat before he is quite aware of it, a melody came up from nowhere through his hands and made a lovely, melancholy little turn.

He left it, played on, and came back to it again. He was riding it more than creating it, and for the first time in his life, he felt the difference. It was a kind of ecstasy, something like being with her. Then he heard something new, a voice—it was her, singing along with him, high and clear and true to pitch. *All that, and this too?*

She sang the line back when he was finished, replicating it perfectly, and asked him what it was.

"Just a melody," he said, unable to stop grinning at her singing. "You pick a name for it."

"My name," she said. "Song."

"No, no, everything is a song. All of America is in a song. Pick another name."

"Tell me the style of the piece."

"The way I was playing it, with that arpeggiated left hand and the melodic, singing right hand—that would be a nocturne. A piece for the night."

"Like *Ye Shanghai*," she said.

"Yes, Night in Shanghai."

"Call it that. It belongs to this city."

"All right." He pulled her naked body to him. "Song, I want to stay here with you forever, but it's bad outside. Don't you hear it? I need to take you back to Rue Wagner."

"I know." She wrapped herself around him. "I was going to say it too."

"Then say we'll see each other again."

"We'll see each other again," she answered, but the sudden dullness in her voice made him bite back what he wanted to say, which was *Tell me when. Tell me how.* Instead, he closed the mahogany lid over the keys and they got dressed.

As Thomas and Song were leaving the Peking Road studio, Zhao Funian, Du's hired assassin, was peering out into the rain from his rented room on the corner of Avenue Édouard VII and Tibet Road. The restaurant where that brown dwarf whore Morioka and the foreign piano player were supposed to meet, right next to the Great World Amusement Center, was ideally located across the street from his window. The only problem was that the Great World had decided to hand out free tea and rice, and thousands of refugees, who had been filling the French Concession for days, were now squeezed into a clotted bottleneck directly in front of his target. He would never get a clear shot without killing a few others, but what did that matter now? One had to be thorough in crushing dry weeds and smashing rotten wood. His rifle was poised, and he scanned through the rain, while Wing Bean, who stood next to him, studied the crowd through binoculars.

"*Ei*, is that leper turd really going to show up here? Today?" The radio was chattering about the fighting in the northern districts, and the bomb concussions could be heard and felt underneath the rain, while the street below roiled with people fleeing for their lives. Morioka seemed unlikely to keep a tea date. It was five minutes to the appointed time.

"The rain is slowing," Wing Bean said, continuing to sweep his binoculars back and forth across the packed sidewalk in front of the restaurant.

Zhao shook his head at the futility of it. "That whore's not coming."

But then Wing Bean staggered, so suddenly Zhao thought he had been hit by some stray bullet, shot, and felt a stab of sadness, such a young man —

But the younger man was only shocked. "Gods bear witness! I see him. It's him. The piano player."

"What!" Zhao snatched the field glasses from him and trained them down on the dense mass of refugees, dialing the focus, frantic. "Are you blind in your dog's eyes?"

"No. I work at the Royal! That's him."

"Where?"

"On the corner. See? He's with a woman."

"A woman —" Now Zhao had him at last in his sights, and his stomach turned over: oh yes. He was with a woman all right.

Song Yuhua.

"Get the camera," he whispered. She was pressed close to the American as they moved together, her dress wet and clinging, her hips sinuous, talking to him, pressed up to him, *touching* him, by all his ancestors. *Touching* him. "Hurry!" he cried to Wing Bean, who saw the same thing and stood with his mouth hanging slack.

"But that whore Morioka could arrive any second. He's the one we —"

"Stupid melon! Get the camera!"

Wing Bean pawed through his canvas bag.

"Give it to me. Is there film in it? Hurry!"

But Wing Bean held it back from him. Something profitable was about to occur, without him. "Why?"

"Never you mind!"

"Why?" Wing Bean repeated, which caused Zhao to swing at him — and miss.

Zhao glanced out across the street. Her clothes were wet and everything of her body was visible. He swallowed back excitement. "The girl?" he said. "Take another look."

Wing Bean's mouth dropped as he recognized her.

Zhao kept his palm open, his eyes hard as steel. "Give."

"Reward. I want half."

"Dog bone! There will be nothing if I don't take a picture!"

"Forty parts of a hundred."

"Twenty-five. And that's generous!"

"Thirty-five."

"Twenty-eight."

"Done," said Wing Bean, pleased, and allowed him to snatch the camera.

"Curse you and that scar of your mother's you slid out from." Zhao yanked off the lens cap, raised it to his eye, and twisted the focus, no, too far. Back again. Now he had lost them in the tide of people. There. Shameless! She was holding his arm. His face would be huge when Big-Eared Du saw these photographs, along with a bonus big enough to take back to Zhejiang and show his brothers how a real man lived. He was the best of the five of them. He had climbed the mountain. There: he snapped. Perfect. Then another. A third. All gods! Now he was pointing down the block, toward the café where he was supposed to meet Morioka, and they were talking—now turning away from the café, hurrying south on Boulevard de Montigny instead. She was whoring with him! He clicked off pictures until they turned again at the first corner, away from the boulevard, and passed out of sight. Zhao's guts went to jelly as he imagined what Du was going to do to her when he saw these photographs. "Any sign of the Admiral?"

Wing Bean did not answer. He wore a strange look.

"Speak! What is it?" said Zhao.

Wing Bean said only, "Look," his voice slow, his finger rising to point. There, against the rumbling bank of storm clouds, a Chinese fighter plane was lit up, one of its engines exploding into flame and hemorrhaging smoke, making it roll and pitch wildly.

Zhao shot a rapid, involuntary glance back to the street. Du's woman and the American were gone. But the pictures were safe in his hands.

Then he heard a word from Wing Bean, soft, barely audible, *"Amithaba."*

Why does he invoke the Buddha? he wondered. Only then, above the avenue, did he see the stepwise line of bombs falling from the plane like pellets, gusting with the rain, drifting sideways, directly toward them. It was the last thing he saw.

Thomas and Song were halfway down the next block when the blast that was to kill a thousand people at the corner of Édouard VII and Tibet Road shattered the air around them, muffling their ears into silence for long pressurized seconds until their drums popped, and a wall of screams rose up from one block over. Plumes of smoke and dust billowed over the rooftops.

"Look," she said. The plane, clearly marked with the Nationalist flag, was wheeling away into the clouds.

"It's Chinese."

"How can that be?" She looked like she might cry.

"A mistake," he said, arms around her. "Listen. You sure you're all right? Yes? Then we have to get you home, now."

"But if the bombs fell right in that crowd—" Cries for help and mercy were carried to them on the wind.

"Song." He took her face in his hands and turned it toward him, because she could not tear her gaze from the corner, where people stumbling away from the blast were already filling the street. "You've got to go inside the compound. Everyone will be focused on this. You can get in."

She slipped her arms around his neck.

"Not here," he cautioned, but before either could move, they heard the click of a shutter. He turned in shock and horror to see Wing Bean, from the Royal.

"Big-Ear Du will very like that one," he said, winding the film on to the next shot.

"Wing Bean," Thomas said, strong. "What are you doing?"

"Taking picture." Wing Bean, still clicking, was clearly hurt, bleeding from a wound to his head, as he stood in the middle of the road, snapping photos.

"Give me that," said Thomas.

"No. So many picture, touch and kiss. How much you give me?"

Thomas saw that the side of Wing Bean's head was caved in, his skull broken. How was he standing up?

"What you give me?" Wing Bean repeated, and started to cough. A second later, bloody foam bubbled from his mouth and into his cupped hand, which distracted him for a second as he stared at it in surprise. One hard lunge, a fast grab, and Thomas had the camera. In an instant he had ripped out the film, unspooling it in the light.

"Doesn't matter!" Wing Bean cried, and tumbled to his knees, gasping, gurgling. Behind him, the crowd stumbling away from the bomb site surged closer. "I saw you! Zhao saw you too, but he is dead—I saw! I am going to tell Du everything."

Thomas took Song's arm and pulled her back a step, out of the way of the human wall barreling up Boulevard de Montigny behind Wing Bean. The waiter did not see them; he was still shrieking at Thomas, his words bubbling in blood.

Neither answered, because at that moment another huge bomb exploded from the northeast, and a smoke-and-debris cloud tufted up from the area around the Bund—where Thomas's studio lay. Wing Bean turned too, and saw the crowd running straight into him, knocking him over. In a short time he was flattened, barely visible but for the rumple of clothes and the blood running out under people's feet. They must have been able to feel the squish and bump beneath their shoes, they must have known, but it was madness, death all around, and no one stopped even to look. Her hand crept into his.

They stood a long minute, and neither needed to speak. "Go home," he said finally, into her ear, and she turned away.

The next day he and Ernest and Charles gathered around the radio to hear the news: three thousand dead from the bombs that fell in the

International Settlement. This was followed by an official announcement made for foreign residents.

"Here we go." Thomas turned it up, and they huddled close.

The consulates of Great Britain and the United States hereby advise all citizens to book immediate passage out. Shanghai is in a state of war and these governments cannot guarantee the safety of their citizens who choose to remain behind.

"Book passage?" Thomas said. "How?" The brothers had only a few hundred saved between them, and all the cash he had was with Uncle Hua, more than two thousand Chinese dollars, another reason they needed to find the old man, because that would be enough to get all three of them out, and Alonzo too, if he was finally ready to go.

But Uncle Hua had not come back. Thomas guessed he had gone home to his family, but he knew it could be worse. Thousands were dead. And what had happened with Wing Bean had shown him that it took only one bolt out of the blue to snatch one's life, or warp one's fortunes. It was like the unexpected ninth in Duke Ellington's "Blue Ramble," the ninth in the bottom of the stacked chord that changed the song, changed everything. The turn. Wing Bean was dead, and they were safe.

That night, at the Royal, he brought up Hua's absence with Lin Ming, who puckered in concern, and said, "Tomorrow morning we go see his family in the Chinese City."

On the way there, Lin scolded him for feigning acceptance of Morioka's invitation in the first place.

"I had no intention of going," Thomas protested. "You warned me. But his boy was standing there. My servants used to handle these things for me, and I did not know what to say." Weak though this was, he was keeping the truth to himself.

"That's stupid," Lin snapped. "Wooden head! I was so worried, I had to send my sister. And then everything happened and she barely made it back!"

"But she's all right?" said Thomas, barely able to breathe now that she had been mentioned.

"Song? Yes. She's fine," Lin said, his brows lifting quizzically at Thomas's interest. Good, he did not know.

They disembarked on Zizhong Road, where Hua's family lived in a third-floor room so crowded Thomas wondered how Uncle Hua could run a gambling operation in it. Lin and Hua's wife talked in light, percussive Shanghainese—*bird talk,* Thomas always thought when he heard it—while the children, two boys and a girl, watched in silence. Thomas relaxed a little, looking around, for Hua's wife sounded normal, which to him meant that she knew her husband's whereabouts.

Ah, there was the gaming table, behind a curtain. The small space also contained beds, a shelf of books, a single charcoal burner for cooking and heating, and a yellow-painted night stool in one corner half-hidden behind another curtain, merely a bucket with a simple lid and a seat on top.

The place was small, but the family benefited in all ways from the city outside. Lin Ming broke off from his chat with Hua's wife for a moment to show Thomas the basket and rope the family lowered to the street to exchange coins with vendors when they heard the cries of their favorite snacks: *Steamed rice cakes made of rugosa rose and white sugar! Shrimp-dumpling and noodle soup!* And—*From the east side of the Huangpu River—beans of five-fold flavor!* The basket went down with a few coins, and came up with food.

And then there was the gambling business, the gaming table. Thomas certainly hoped his savings were safe.

At that moment Hua's wife suddenly released a long, high-pitched wail of grief, shaking her hands in the air as if they burned. It was ice-cold clear that until that moment, she had thought her husband safe at the house off Rue Lafayette.

There were so many dead that most of them had been piled quickly into common graves while the tapering rain washed the gutters clean of blood. Thomas and Lin exchanged a look of pure pain as they realized where Hua must have ended up and, each man holding an arm, they helped Hua's suddenly weak wife to a chair. For a long time that day they sat with her, while she alternated between keening sobs and tearful conversation, none of which Thomas understood as it poured out of her. He felt awful; Hua had gone out looking for him.

"It was his fate," Lin told him, when they finally picked their way back down the stairs to the hot, noisy street.

Before their departure, Thomas had seen him repeat his condolences and then insist she accept all the cash he had on him. Now, it appeared that Hua's unfortunate ending was not his burden anymore. *But it's mine. Just like Wing Bean.*

"I asked about your money," Lin said. "She has no idea where it is, if there is any. Hua was down right before he disappeared, almost three thousand."

"Figures," said Thomas. Was this the first of his many punishments? Because that was his savings, vanished. Everything had happened so quickly—the turn, the discord, the unexpected ninth—and now he was broke, and could not leave. And yet Song had come to him too, which in its own way made it right, all of it.

They went on playing every night, and the crowds kept coming in, even while smoke still drifted from the rubble outside. One of their own was missing, Wing Bean, and Floor Manager Zhou prodded everyone about him. "You see Wing Bean, yes-no?" he asked Thomas, the other musicians, the hat-and-coat-check girls, even the men who worked in the kitchen. It went on for days. Thomas froze every time he had to answer, and barely managed to get out the word *no* before he collected himself and made a promise to keep an eye out for the young man. The way it happened kept coming back to him, like small explosions in his mind. He remembered how, after Song had hurried off down the chaotic street toward Rue Wagner, he threw the film into the carcass of a burning car and watched it shrink and shrivel, ignoring the pleas and screams all around him. Before he turned toward Rue Lafayette, where he knew the brothers would be worried about him, the crowd had thinned for a second, and he had seen for the last time the spreading stain that had been Wing Bean. And now Zhou would not stop asking.

By the next Friday night, the storm water that had flooded the low-lying streets had receded, and huge fires broke out in the Pudong and Wayside districts, big enough to light the sky. On Sunday, heavy shelling could still be heard from Hongkou when the Kings finished their last set at two A.M. A couple of nights after that, huge guns and mortars sounded from Jiangwan. And yet the house kept filling every night, and the six of them performed.

He longed for her, wondered day and night when he would see her again, but when he really felt close to Song was when he was playing. Even simple, affectionate standards like their signature, "Exactly Like You," were now anthems to her. At the piano, he imagined a life with her that could never have been, staying in the studio, remaining in that room forever.

When they grew hungry, he would tip a beggar boy who lived across the Bund in a space underneath the pilings to fetch hot food. "German or Cantonese?" he would ask her.

"Cantonese," she would say with a laugh, and move closer to him.

It was all they would do, love each other. He would play the piano, make tea. Dressed or not dressed, speaking or silent, their together-ness would express itself in thought and laughter, music, the day's routines. "Shall I send the boy for dim sum?" he would say as he held out her cup.

Before, he had mastered his repertoire through practice. Now he closed his eyes, found melodies, and followed them until they grew through their own turns and variations, always as he dreamed of her. He realized this was the same feeling the other fellows had when they soloed, and with only six of them now, everyone except Thomas took long solo flights.

Tonight he might do it, full as he was of love and loss and troubled notes — so that when he signaled a solo for himself, and all the other instruments fell back in surprise, he took straight off into the sky with a rhapsodic ladder of joyfully tinkling dance steps that brought shouts and applause from the ballroom floor, and grins and nods from the bandstand, even Lester and Errol. *Beautiful,* said the voice in his head, and he understood that it was Song's. She was with him.

Applause washed over him in waves. To keep it going, he led a quick chord change into "In a Sentimental Mood" in D minor, and then, in a subtle show of virtuosity, modulated to F major after managing to toy with D-flat major for a moment—but tickling it perfectly, lightly, his beat exactly square. He was true and he was a liar; he had dealt both love and death.

From his end of the stage, Alonzo heard Thomas's playing soaring on its own, and kept his eyes on the piano as his own left hand ranged up and down his fretboard and his right plucked, slapped, and hammered down the percussion and the bass, as one. He wondered about it as his fingers danced the beat up and down, pulling it, popping it, until the truth swam into view: the young man was in love. *That's it, son. Right there.* He caught Thomas's eye and added his own smile to the roar of approval that was washing up from the dance floor. The boy had been to the mountaintop.

On the thirteenth of September, a month after the fighting started, Song met Chen Xing at Café Louis on Bubbling Well Road. Here, the city's most elegant cakes and chocolates were created by chefs plucked from the tide of skilled Jewish refugees pouring into the city. To Song they were an oppressed people, and as *Shanghai ren* she was proud of her city for welcoming them in, while she also enjoyed the fruits of their talents with candid pleasure, such as the signature *ganache* here at Café Louis. Like most places in the French and International Concessions, the restaurant had reopened after the first few days of the battle, even though shelling, bombing, and small-arms fire could be heard almost every day and night, and intermittent food shortages played havoc with the menus.

This time Chen Xing came alone, and they talked in voices pillowed almost to a whisper, since Shanghai was filled with spies. The Communists themselves had moles in the Nationalist government, the French police, the Bank of China, and many other places.

He appeared pessimistic. "We will not hold out for long. The Japanese have been landing reinforcements at Wusong and up and down the Huangpu for days. Thousands of dwarf soldiers have put ashore."

"But the Italians?" she said hopefully. The wireless had been reporting that the Savoy Grenadiers were on their way from Addis Ababa.

"No. Unless one of the big Western powers joins the fight, the city will fall." He looked at her with sympathy. "What will you do?"

"I am a bonded servant," she reminded him.

"If that changes?" He watched her face. "Many people are leaving. You know the government has already abandoned Nanjing and moved to Chongqing," the new wartime capital. "Some people are going to Hong Kong. If they are staying in China, they go either to Chongqing—"

"—if they are with the Nationalists."

"Correct. Or Yan'an."

She nodded. That was the Communists' wartime capital, a dusty, wind-whistling town on the Yan River which was where every true pilgrim of the movement wished to go—including her. Securely behind Red lines, in a part of north China controlled by the CCP, it was that mythic place where she would be able to live openly in her beliefs. Glorious.

She put her gaze back on Chen Xing. "What about you?" she said, for he could either come out now with the Communists, or continue to hide among the Nationalists.

"I'll go to Chongqing," he said.

"So you will stay belowground."

"It suits me."

She nodded. He was the scion of a well-off family; no doubt he wanted to hold on to his wealth and privilege a little longer, too. Living as a double agent would make it possible.

"Your new contact will get in touch with you through a business you already patronize," Chen told her.

Song understood. The Party owned many businesses, everything from furniture stores to tea shops to real estate agencies. Their premises were used for meetings and handoffs, sometimes without managers or employees even knowing. Song loved seeing the pieces fit together behind the surface scrim of reality; she had come to understand that perception itself was power.

So was planning. If Du left, or if he set her free — who knew what this war might bring about? — she would have to be ready to act.

She could go with Thomas to America. The thought brought an onrush of love shot through with the darkness of their last moment together, watching Wing Bean die. He would protect her, she knew that. Even though he had not asked her, and she had not said yes, she knew the door to him lay open.

To go with him, though, meant giving up her cause completely. "I have often thought of going north," she said, this being of course the only version of her future she would present to Chen Xing.

"To Yan'an?" His eyebrows rose. "You're the sort of modern woman I'd expect to run to Hong Kong or America the minute the manacles were off you."

She bristled. "You doubt my commitment?"

"Not at all." His eyes registered her response. "I am impressed by the risks you take. But I warn you, be careful. You will always have the taint of foreignness."

"What about you?" she shot back. "You are 'leaning down' from a well-off family. Your family's wealth is as dangerous as my English. It is a risk for both of us. But if you run from a risk, then how do you call that commitment?"

"*Touché.*" He pronounced the French with a burnish of irony, and she wondered with a jolt if he had been testing her.

But she could pass any test. "If I were free, I might go north. And if I do —"

"You will need introductions. When the time comes, send word here"—and he wrote a few characters on the back of his card for her —"to my brother's house in Chongqing. I will write to them about you."

She took the card, grateful. Everything was a political process. "Thank you."

"Not at all. Are we not the same purpose?" On her way out, she savored this new term he had used, *tongzhi*, same purpose. Comrade. She liked it. She wondered if it would catch on in the movement.

Fighting continued through September, mostly sparing the French Concession and International Settlement, but leaving parts of Hongkou and Zhabei so bombed out that only a few hardy souls were left holed up in the damaged buildings. Thomas crept back and forth to the theater every day, and even the Higgins brothers returned straight home after work. They spent hours on stage trying not to wince at the intermittent bursts of shooting and shelling, and by the time the clock hit two and the lights finally winked up, everyone wanted to shake hands at the door and hurry home. Late at night, when they were all in and safe, and Thomas was alone in his room with his oil lamp, he worried. All of them were saving as much as they could, but inflation was driving things up, and getting enough cash to go home seemed far out of reach.

And there was Song. He ached every day for her, and wondered how he had gotten through all those years before he met her. It did not matter, because they knew each other now, in every possible way, and he had no doubt they would be together every minute if it were not for Du. She would be with him if she could.

By the end of the month, there were signs around the city that a climactic offensive was coming. Fresh soldiers and supplies moved through the streets by the truckload, in vehicles painted with the Rising Sun. The radio reported that separate Japanese divisions were marching simultaneously toward Nanjing. The Americans had doubled the number of Marines in Shanghai to three thousand, hoping to protect American property. Trouble was ahead, and everyone could feel it.

October kicked off the offensive, shooting and explosions from all directions, and the bass thunder of big guns. By late in the month, Thomas had to acknowledge that China was losing. Wave after wave of Chinese recruits had come in, looking pathetically young, fifteen, sixteen—even Charles and Ernest were older. And then Chiang Kai-shek ordered a retreat to defend the rural suburbs, and in a blink, those last soldiers were gone altogether. Japanese flags sprouted at intersections and post offices, and the streets outside the neutral Concessions were littered with eerily abandoned firing nests, sandbags still piled protectively, shell casings on the ground.

A single Chinese battalion stayed behind to cover the retreat. In what was surely a suicide mission, eight hundred men withdrew to the *Sihang,* or Four-Bank Warehouse on Suzhou Creek at the corner of North Tibet Road. Because the warehouse was directly across from the neutral International Settlement, the Japanese were afraid to attack it. By the second day, British soldiers were brazenly crossing the bridge to deliver food, cigarettes, ammunition, and first aid supplies to the warehouse.

When the onslaught against the eight hundred finally began, everyone in Shanghai was glued to the saga of the brave soldiers dubbed the *Gu Jun,* the Lonely Battalion.

On October twenty-ninth the sun came up over the Chinese flag, smuggled in by a twenty-two-year-old girl and miraculously hoisted high above the warehouse roof. Thomas and Charles and Ernest hurried to see it, and found thirty thousand people lining the banks of the creek that bordered the International Settlement, chanting and waving Chinese flags.

They stayed until it was time to go home and dress for work, but then a messenger arrived with a note from Floor Manager Zhou. "The Royal is closed tonight!" Thomas cried, scanning it. "We are to play on the roof of the Gas Works building, right across the creek from the warehouse. They will roll a grand piano out there and put down a dance floor."

They arrived to find the roof transformed into a chilly autumn fairyland of hanging Chinese lanterns and potted chrysanthemums, already filling up with guests in evening wear, both Western and Chinese. Waiters circulated with champagne, and as soon as the Kings swung into "Exactly Like You," couples stepped into each other's arms and onto the dance floor. Pops and spatters of gunfire sounded down below, adding grit and hesitations to their rhythm. Every time there was a large explosion, the air would fill with screams and cries as all the men and women rushed to the roof's edge, to look over and cheer with the crowds below, and on the rooftops all around.

Between sets they took a break, and he saw a familiar elongated shape emerge from the elevator inside the propped-open doors: Du Yuesheng. Thomas barely breathed as he counted out the entourage—until there she was, Song. And then as quickly as they had appeared, they were gone, vanished to a lower floor, it was rumored, to watch the battle from a private room. Thomas steeled himself and focused on playing.

Suddenly, after midnight, the cries of astonishment from the crowd became so urgent that the musicians ran to the parapet to see. Three Japanese soldiers had managed to sneak a ladder over to one side of the building and climb up to a bombed-out opening. Just as they reached it, a man appeared in the opening, the battalion's commander, Xie Jinyuan. Everyone on the roof held their breath as he shot the first Japanese, strangled the second with his hands, and threw the third off the ladder before knocking it away altogether. The rooftop went mad with joy, and for a few precious minutes, chaos reigned. Thomas used this time to move quickly through the crowd, and look for her. But she was absent, along with Du and his bodyguards.

They played out the last set and then kept going, responding to the crowd, pushing further. Everyone sensed this was the end.

It was not until dawn was near that they shut off the lights. Lester and Errol went home, and Alonzo took Charles and Ernest out to help them find a rickshaw, which left almost no one on the rooftop except Thomas and the workmen, cleaning up. So he took some music from his briefcase and played Brahms, because it calmed him.

Then he heard a woman clear her throat, a gentle but specific sound already as close and natural to him as middle C. It was Song, just inside the door, half-hidden in the darkness. "I thought you left," he whispered.

"Careful," she said.

He looked. The only other people on the roof were men folding tables and taking up the dance floor. Not one of them was looking in Thomas's direction.

Six steps, and he was with her, in the shadows. "Where is Du?"

"In a meeting, downstairs. They think I am gone to the restroom."

That meant she had only a minute. "Song—"

"No," she said quietly, putting two cool fingers on his mouth, "Don't." Her other hand sought his, and their fingers linked quickly and naturally. She brought her face so close to his that their cheeks grazed. "I know," she whispered, and they stood for a long moment, until a fresh burst of gunfire startled them, followed by a grenade blast and the rumble of falling masonry.

"All of them will either die or surrender," she said bitterly. "Then it's finished. We will belong to Japan."

"Not Frenchtown. Not the International Settlement."

"Congratulations—a lonely island in an occupied city. And now my time is run out," she said miserably, holding his eyes. "Stay alive for me." And after a brief, desperate squeeze of his hand, she vanished.

Over the next few days, the dominoes fell. The Lonely Battalion was down to 376 men, and Commander Xie Jinyuan had them make a run out of the building and across the bridge into the International Settlement, protected by their gravely wounded compatriots who were dying anyway and had volunteered to cover them from the machine gun nests. British troops cheered them into the Settlement, arrested them, confiscated their weapons to prevent anything falling into the hands of the Japanese, and put them up in a building on Singapore Road they dubbed the Lost Battalion Barracks.

With this last act, Shanghai's War of Resistance shuddered to a close. Through November, Thomas saw brown-uniformed soldiers rolling in by the truckloads, placid, complacent, bouncing along. He saw them down by the river on their time off, walking with a bottle of sake jammed in one pocket and two bottles of Asahi in the other, eating fruits out of hand, taking what they wanted from stores as they passed.

They set up checkpoints at intersections and bridges. At the steel-truss Garden Bridge, which connected the unoccupied Bund to the occupied Hongkou district, everyone had to bow from the waist to Japan, with no exceptions — cars had to stop, the tram down the middle of the bridge halted and disgorged its passengers; everyone had to do it. Thomas adapted with relative ease to this new regime, for all his life, around white people, it had almost always been necessary to defer. And since he was a foreigner, the Japanese went easy on him, letting him pass with the kind of perfunctory bow that would have gotten a Chinese slammed with a rifle butt. Suddenly his race was the right card to hold in the game of fear and death. Sickening. The new slang word for the occupiers, which even Thomas, with his nonexistent Chinese, learned to recognize, was *mo shou*, the evil hand.

One day at the end of November, Lin Ming received a message that he was to be at Rue Wagner, at the hour of the rooster. His first fear was that the conquerors were taking over one of his ballrooms, because the night-world continued to roar, with the drugs, gambling, and liquor flowing so fast that all over town, the abacuses chattered until dawn. Backstage office safes bulged with profits, and he was dreading the day the Japanese decided to take the money for themselves. He had been sensing doom; was tonight the night?

Or maybe there was trouble with the Germans again. The Nazi organization in Shanghai was small but well established, with its own network of spies and agitators, and they were furious about the numbers of Jewish refugees arriving in the city. They also hated the fact that the city's very wealthy Jews, like Sir Victor Sassoon, and Horace Kadoorie, had stepped up to care for penniless arrivals in dormitories and soup kitchens. Small loans were arranged for individuals wishing to open the same businesses they had run in Germany, and soon the Jews had started their own schools and clinics, and even built a synagogue. He and Kung had passed several evenings with Du, urging him to resist the Nazis' demands to restrict the refugees, whose numbers were currently swelling by a thousand a month as they stepped off the Lloyd Triestino ships from Genoa. Fortunately for them, Du was not hard to convince; he had hated the Nazis ever since Hitler told Kung they should surrender to Japan.

Lin Ming arrived at the tightly shuttered second-floor meeting room first, and realized that all these identical red-tufted rooms were another of the old man's superstitions, like the lucky mummified monkey's head that he wore hanging from his back collar inside his gown. Like the ancestral temple he paid to have built in his home village, where the air was clouded by incense and the lights of candles danced along the wall, even though his forebears were nothing but dirt-poor alley dwellers. And like this room, with its dark wood paneling and softly glowing silk lotus-bud lamps, which brought back his brothel boyhood. Of course his father kept his rooms like this. One day Lin probably would too, if he made it through this war.

And he had his own beliefs, his superstitions; one of them was Pearl, and the weeks of battle had shown him that he cared about her, and her safety, too much to leave her in the brothel. He had to save to get her out.

He had been with her the night before, and all her goodness was still there, her sweetness, even though she had passed her twenty-eighth birthday and he had not talked about buying her out. It was over, forgiven, and she loved him just the same, which opened him enough to tell her he had started to save. He did not know how long it would take—there was the war, years maybe—and it embarrassed him to hear himself saying these things, which were still weak and evasive, but she burst into tears beneath him, holding his shoulders, her legs going limp around him in her rush of love and gratitude, forgetting entirely that they had been in the middle of the house thing. He held her, and knew that he was committed; he would raise her buyout, no matter what it took, or how long. The war had made it all clear.

The secret door clicked, and Du entered in a gray silk gown.

"Teacher," Lin said respectfully.

Du responded with a nod of his bald head. "I need you to translate."

"Of course." In some situations, only a male translator would do.

"A Japanese officer has arrived in Shanghai and insists on seeing me now, tonight. Just a few minutes, he says. Doihara is his name."

"General Doihara? Head of the Japanese First Army in north China? The one who calls himself Lawrence of Manchuria?"

"The very one."

"But you need no translation. He speaks Mandarin. And, they say, some Shanghainese."

"I know. I have had him informed that I speak neither language. You and I will speak tonight in Suzhou dialect."

Lin suppressed a smile; *Suzhou hua*, the language of his mother. Du was always a step ahead. "Isn't Doihara the one who set up Pu Yi as puppet emperor in Manchuria?"

"That's right. He has a lot of brass between his legs, coming here. Does he think I am corruptible? Perhaps he does not know that in Shanghai, thieves and police work together. The cat and mouse sleep entwined. We already *are* the government! It is an outrage—as if I would turn against my city."

"When is he coming?"

"He is here now, the dog's fart. I suppose we have kept him waiting long enough." Du opened the room's main door and stepped out into the corridor, at the other end of which was one of the larger studies, with a desk at one end and soft, antimacassared chairs squared around a low table in Chinese style at the other. The room had been deliberately overheated on Du's orders, made stifling, and in the center of it, a compact sweat-beaded Japanese in full dress uniform, heavy with medals, waited uncomfortably on the Tianjin carpet.

As they entered, Lin's father spoke to him in soft *Suzhou hua*. "Look at him. See how he smiles? He's a liar! He pretends to come in civility, but even now they are sharpening their weapons for the fight."

The General had a small, severe mustache and large, sad, droopy-lidded eyes, above which one eyebrow rose perennially higher than the other. He touched his heels with a light tap and bowed.

Lin bobbed his head in return, and said in Mandarin, "Please excuse us that I must translate for you. My master speaks only his native dialect."

"No excuse needed," said Doihara, "and please thank him. I know he is very busy."

"Tell him of course I am," said Du, masking his Suzhou dialect even further with a coarse country accent. "How can I rest for even a moment? Dwarf fiends are running amok."

Lin said, "He says, he has an engagement tonight. But as you said this was a matter of importance—"

"We want to help you keep peace in your city," said the General.

"That's a damn lie. He needs to withdraw from our city."

"We do not require your help," Lin said.

Doihara sighed, as if dealing with a stubborn youngster. "Hostilities may have ceased, but we need a functional government. That is the important thing. Then Shanghai can return to normal. We will run things very well—deferring of course to you, Lord Du." And he lowered his head.

Lin smiled inwardly. He had heard the gaffe, and he knew Du had too. No one addressed Du that way. Papa Du, and Teacher, but never Lord Du. Doihara's Mandarin was excellent but his advance work incomplete.

"Tell him to fuck his ancestors."

"What did he say?" said Doihara, the words in Suzhou dialect being a little too close to those he understood.

"Forgive my hesitation," said Lin. "My master used an old-fashioned honorific, a form used between rulers and diplomats—" Ah, good, at this Doihara's face brightened. "What he said was, *fen ting kang li*." He is so happy to receive you as equals.

Lin was afraid he would not swallow this, but Doihara gleamed. "Tell him thank you. That is why I am here—to find a way to stop all the violence and restore order, which is better for everyone, is it not? But I do not want a Japanese leader for the city. No! For this is China." Doihara stood taller, rising to his prepared remarks. "There must be one supreme leader, all-powerful, answerable only to the emperor. Leadership. Greatness. One man above all."

Lin translated.

Du was furious. "Does he dare to imply that I will be his cursed dog's legs? Am I a traitor, to lick the evil hand? No. He's playing fiddle in his pants. Tell him that. Go on."

"My master regrets his duties leave him little time to concern himself with city politics."

"Not so!" said Doihara, seizing what he thought was an opening. "There is no citizen more august, more widely loved, more *trusted* by Shanghai people than Du Yuesheng."

Lin found this so priceless that he had a hard time keeping the glimmer of a smile off his face while he put the words in *Suzhou hua*.

Du snorted. "He's blowing the ox vagina so hard, isn't he afraid it's going to explode? Translate that."

"My master says, you exaggerate."

"Not at all," said the General. "He is the one to lead. He deserves it. Please ask him to take his time, and think back and forth. Give me his answer forthwith."

"I'll give it to him now, the suppurating pustule! Tell him if he is not off my grounds in ten minutes, I'll have his throat slit. Tell him."

"My master regrets," said Lin. But efforts to sanitize what the boss said had become useless.

Du's face was reddening. He made a curt bow, a deliberate parody of the Japanese gesture.

Lin heard Doihara's gasp. "If I may," he said, and moved to guide their guest to the door, in at least some semblance of dignity.

But Du stopped him. "Flowery Flag will see him out."

Another insult, for Lin was a son and Flowery a thug. Lin watched, his heart hammering, as the bodyguard clomped out the door with the General, every step seeming to seal his father's fate. Of course the older man would never collaborate, having poured half his fortune into the Nationalist war coffers, but this?

The door closed. "I went too far," Du admitted.

Lin bit back astonishment; never had his father acknowledged fault before. He had certainly gone too far, and now there would be retribution. But he had shown courage, too, which Lin admired. "Spilt water cannot be gathered," he said gently. "You handled him just right."

The messenger said Song was to meet Duke Kung in the lobby of the Hong Kong and Shanghai Bank building on the Bund, but he did not say why. She assumed he would be relaying instructions from Du, whom she had not seen since they all fled Rue Wagner in the middle of the night after Du's debacle with Doihara, following which the Japanese military circled the house with loud-droning fighter planes until Du finally abandoned it, bundling them all into cars, and dispersing them to safe houses around the city. He had been the last one out of the mansion, padlocking it before Song saw him climb into another car with Flowery, Fiery, Fourth Wife, and their children.

But that had been three nights ago, and since then Song, like the rest of Du's staff, had heard nothing. At least now the waiting would be over, for Duke Kung would know everything.

Outside the bank, she surprised herself by pausing to give a good-luck rub to the paw of one of the two bronze lions on either side of the door. This was a custom of Shanghai's poor, and the lions' paws were polished to a bright gold by all their hopeful hands. *I'm one of the people*, she thought, but she felt no luck, only trepidation as she strode into the bank.

With its gilded columns and faraway ceilings, the lobby had the magnificence of a cathedral, the sounds of voices and telephones and leather shoes tapping the marble floors hushed by the immensity of space and money. Yet her eye found Kung instantly, his small, portly figure commanding attention. Then she turned and saw Lin Ming walking through the door behind her. *So it was the two of us who were summoned.*

Kung led them to a group of overstuffed chairs, and as soon as they sat down, a young woman appeared with a teapot and three lidded cups on a tray. She poured and retreated to a respectful distance.

"Old Du asked me to call you," Kung said. "He's gone."

A muffle of silence seemed to fall as she and Lin threw shocked looks at each other.

"Gone?" Lin said. "Speak reasonably."

"I am. He left last night on a French steamer."

Song said, "To where?"

"Hong Kong. Eventually, Chongqing. But he has left Shanghai." Kung picked up his tea, looked at it, and set it back on the low table between them, where their cups also lay untouched.

"Forever?" Lin said shakily.

"Forever"—Kung narrowed his expression ever so slightly as he paused, to convey the delicacy of his answer —"well. Naturally he hopes to return. But at the same time, by leaving, he knows he renounces his power over the Green Gang—and over you. That is forever, whether he comes back or not."

"Both of us?" Her voice was sick with hope.

Kung pulled a key from his vest pocket. "Let's go," he said. "I'll show you."

As soon as they rose from their seats, a fawning bank manager materialized to lead them to the safe deposit vault, and in a room with locked metal drawers stacked to the ceiling, they sat at a small wooden table while Kung opened the box. He handed each of them an envelope.

She gave hers to Lin. "I can't. Tell me what it says."

He tore it open. "You're free. He renounces the claim on your family's property." She sagged in shock while he read his own. "Me too, free. He gives us each a thousand in severance pay."

"*Ge,* " she said quickly, Elder Brother. "Take mine. You need it for Pearl."

His face twisted. "I need more than that for Pearl. And how could I take your severance? You have nothing, *Meimei.*"

Her face closed, pulling down the curtain. She could go with Thomas now, or north to join the cause, and in either case a thousand meant nothing next to the diamonds. But what she said was "I don't care about the money. Just being free is enough." And that was true.

"He could have kept you another—"

"Ten years," she said abruptly, because she had always known, every day, every minute, how much longer it was. Now, after they had said dazed good-byes to Kung and stepped back out into the December cold, she tore the flowers from her hair and threw them on the sidewalk; never would she wear them again.

Lin watched the fragile blooms turn quickly to pulp under the careless boots of passersby. "What are you going to do?"

She could be with Thomas, walk into his arms right now, abandon her country and stay with him forever. The thousand was just enough to buy them two tickets, and she could surprise him with the diamonds at sea.

Or she could go north, and reach the culmination of the dream she had been living for all this time.

Not both.

"Well?" he said.

"I don't know yet. But before I go anywhere, may I borrow the key to the padlock at Rue Wagner? I need to go back for something."

"Du cursed the place. He said none were to enter it."

"Du's gone. One hour, and I'll bring the key back to you."

"Gowns, furs, what?" He dug in his pocket. "You always said you hated that stuff."

"I do hate it. It's something else, of no value to anyone but me."
She took the key. "Just a picture on the wall."

That night, when the Kings closed out their last set and came back
for the encore, Thomas was halfway through a highly embellished,
rhythmically arch version of *Rhapsody in Blue* when he looked up and
saw something he had never before seen, Song entering by herself.
Instead of climbing the stairs to the balcony box, she walked straight
into the ballroom, looking different, her delicate frame overwhelmed
by a mannish wool overcoat. She stood watching him as he faltered,
recovered his place in the music, and made it to the end only because
he had played the *Rhapsody* so many times. When it was over, the applause roared up, crested, and dribbled away as the lights winked up
and he flew to her, presto agitato.

"What's happened?" She wore no earrings, no rouge, just her skin,
clean and plain. She had never been more beautiful.

"Du's gone." She took both his hands in hers, something she would
never have dared in public before.

"I ran to the mansion when I heard — it was locked up — I looked
everywhere." He blinked. "What do you mean, gone?"

"He insulted the Japanese General who came to negotiate with
him, and now he cannot come back. I am free."

"And your family's debt?" he said.

"Forgiven."

He took her hand then and led her straight out to the lobby, returning only to get his coat when she insisted. For the first time since
the night they opened, he bypassed the crowds who congregated
around the door, and fled directly into the street. "Du has put me in
a small apartment for a week," she said as she beckoned to a pedi-
cab with an awning-covered seat. They spread their wool coats over
them like blankets and nestled in deep beneath the awning, hidden
from view, for the long ride across Frenchtown and then into the circular labyrinth of the Chinese City. *Finally*, was all he could think.
He knew she had her life, her cause, and he wasn't going anywhere

near all that. But he also wasn't going to let her go again, not if he could help it.

Once inside her room, they did not leave again until noon the next day, when the need for tea and something to eat finally drove them downstairs. Outside, Thomas found the world transformed, animated, vibrant, the lane bright and clattery with vehicles and voices. The winter walls on either side were strung with banners, and the cobblestones coursed with folk in padded coats. On the bottom floor of her building was a rice shop with gunnysacks of grain stacked almost to the ceiling, and it seemed like the center of the world, with customers streaming in and out all day. He was awake to life.

And hungry; he was sure he had never been so ravenous. "Here," she said, stepping into a sesame cake shop, and soon they were sitting on porcelain stools, washing down crullers called *you tiao* with scalding tea.

"I love this," he said.

"Me too," she said, thinking he referred to the breakfast. "It's simple. When I was a child, it made me proud to be rich. Not now. All that time I lived in Du's mansion, I didn't like any corner of it."

"I know," he said. "But I meant you," he said. "Being here. Waking up with you."

Her eyes shone with agreement and her hand sought his. "I have never known anything like this."

"Come home with me. Come meet Charles and Ernest, they'll just be having breakfast." It was disarmingly casual, and to his joy brought a grin of agreement from her. He hadn't expected her to say yes, any more than he had expected himself to ask, but this was Song, and now she was free and everything was different.

He knew somehow during those weeks that no matter how long he lived, he would never feel anything higher or better. First she moved into the studio, after the room Du had rented ran out. Whereas Anya had filled the room to overflowing with her clothes and shoes and hatboxes and assorted treasures, Song brought almost nothing with her, a small square suitcase which held several plain, side-slit *qipao* dresses, and a spare pair of shoes. Aside from her overcoat, she kept everything folded in the suitcase. He said something about the bureau being almost empty, but she used only the suitcase, and he did not suggest it again. It pained him a little to see it there, packed and ready, even when they were naked and she was abandoning herself to him completely. In time this would be something he understood about her, that she needed an out, even from love, even when she told she had been waiting for it all her life, even when they both could feel it growing, in their little room, night after night.

He did not mention the future, and he did not ask her what she did all day, either, for when they arose at midday, she always left, and did not rejoin him until she arrived at the Royal sometime that night. He understood her commitment, so he kept quiet, afraid to ask her to choose.

Outside their door, the city was sliding. The Green Gang was rudderless without Du, causing all the areas of Shanghai life it had once controlled to tip into disorder. The guilds of beggars and undertakers, peddlers, touts, and night soil collectors all ceased to function. Somehow the trains ran, though the station itself was a shell, and every train leaving Shanghai seemed to be full of residents streaming out of the city.

Yet those who remained kept coming to the Royal, frantic, determined, wading through hillocks of rubble in their silks and flashing jewels, crossing into the blessedly unoccupied areas of the French Concession and the International Settlement, now dubbed the *Gudao,* or Lonely Island. The drinks flowed, the restaurants served, *The Good Earth* played at the Grand Theater, and when darkness fell and the Kings stepped out on the stage to a full house, it felt almost like it had felt before.

But soon Japanese men started showing up, peering into things, checking the kitchens, counting the staff. This was the real Shanghai, Thomas understood, not the free-roaming symphony of opportunity and respect he had first glimpsed, but a hard-grinding machine of money and power, the kind you see and the kind you don't, with no music to it at all.

The person he needed to help sort this out was Lin, but he had been in Hong Kong doing a job for H. H. Kung to raise the money to buy out his girlfriend. It was almost New Year's before Thomas finally saw his friend's spindly form in the archway to the lobby. "Call the men over," Lin said. "I have come back to chaos."

"Did you at least make enough to meet your goal?" said Thomas. Lin had revealed how much it would cost him to buy Pearl out, a daunting amount, five thousand.

"Far from it. But I am closer. And you? And Song?"

"We're well." They had gone to Lin, to tell him everything, before he left for Hong Kong.

"Have you been taking care of her?"

"I would take care of her forever, if she would have me."

"She has her own ideas."

"I know," Thomas said, his face pinched by so much yearning that Lin laid a hand on his arm in sympathy.

The men were gathering around. Lin said, "The Tung Vong Company has been dissolved. The Green Gang has fallen apart. Three of you live in housing provided by the Gang." He looked at Thomas, Charles, and Ernest. "That's over. You must be out by the first of next month, by January first, nineteen thirty-eight. I'm sorry."

The murmur went around the group that it was not his fault.

"Charles," he said, "Ernest. You have some place to go?"

"They can stay with me and Keiko," Alonzo volunteered. "We've got the spare room." This brought a murmur of thanks.

"Lester and Errol, you live with your girlfriends—right? Thomas?"

"I'll stay in my studio. But what about the club?" As bandleader, he was responsible for the others and their livelihood. "Japanese have been in here, looking around. And if there's no Tung Vong Company—"

"I know," said Lin. "The ballroom has been running on its own steam, making money. But I have no control over what our new masters do — none."

"Are we safe?" said Charles.

Lin smiled patiently at the same old question. "Yes and no. Anything is possible, and we all know about the massacre in Nanjing that began while I was gone." They all nodded gravely; though none had a personal connection to it, the Rape of Nanjing sounded almost too horrible to believe.

"But here," Lin continued, "the battle is over. Your country is neutral. As long as America is not Japan's enemy, you should be safe here. No promising. But if America enters the war against Japan, that is the difference. You cannot be here. You must be gone before that. Everyone understand?"

Several protested that America would never enter the war, and so there was no chance they could ever be anything but neutral, but they all agreed to the risks anyway.

Thomas had been told this before. Who was it, Avshalomov? Or Anya? He had seen Anya when he was walking up Tianjin Road the week before; she was entering the Grand Shanghai Hotel. He had drawn back, silent, to watch her, thinking it felt as if years had passed since they were together, not months, so different was he now. *No,* he thought as the lobby doors closed behind her, *it is Shanghai itself that has changed.*

In late January, the conquerors got the Royal. Manager Zhou called them together to tell them the theater was being taken over, and he distributed their last pay. Alonzo just stood smiling as if amused by fate. The brothers looked outraged, even though they had already played long past their original contract.

"It is not my say-so," Zhou assured them. "I want to stay. But everything at noontime tomorrow is locked up for good, so take your instruments." And he walked away, muttering to himself, down the hall.

That night, everyone said, the Kansas City Kings put on their greatest show ever. People shrieked and applauded, and one or two men twirled dance partners above their heads. At the close of the last set, Thomas played his usual encore, the *Rhapsody,* and then another encore that put things over the top, the piece he wrote, the piece he had started playing when he was alone with Song on that magical first afternoon, which he had continued to write later, all through the months of battle.

He started it with the undulating, cascading left hand and the cantabile melody in the right, the song of his wanderings. He played his way across the country on freight trains, and he could feel Song listening out in the audience, just as she had listened in the studio on their first day together. He crossed the ocean to the city with its rabid, unruly buildings and its clotted streets, its vigor and its free ricochet of possibilities.

He came to the last part and played it with his eyes closed, barely aware, following the melody and the rhythm out the door and all through Frenchtown, past the waltzing, strutting dancers, the pirouetting waiters, the looping walk of the man who's drunk too much, and the confident toss of the gambler, once, twice, again. The music rose on a crescendo of success and then sank with loss. When he came to the end, he returned as if by jazz magic to the lovely turning phrase on which everything had begun, his home, the place he had loved and left behind. He had improvised, joined their orchestra at last. Too late, maybe, but it was real, and he knew it from the screaming and stamping of the crowd.

Then it was over, and time to pack up. Thomas could make only one final run of his hand over the eighty-eight keys while the others closed their instrument cases. Now the scuffs on the dance floor were obvious, as were the stains and cigarette burns on the velvet curtains. Nothing was sadder than a nightclub when the lights went up, and the magic of darkness was gone — even this one, in which Song now stood quietly, waiting for him.

Lester and Errol had saved their fare; they said good-bye outside the theater. Alonzo took Charles and Ernest home to Keiko's. Above their heads, the lights blinked out for the last time spelling the tall vertical word ROYAL.

That night as they lay in bed, he said, "What shall we do? We can stay here if you like, I can find work. Or we could go to America, if you would do me the honor of marrying me." He said it lightly, so as not to scare her, but still saw the pinch of hesitation in her eyes.

For a moment, she did not speak.

"What?"

"Just — it is too soon. I can't talk about this yet, first I need to go north. It's just for a while," she added, when she saw his face. "My dream for so long, the center of the movement, all the leaders are there, all the thinkers . . ." She pressed closer to him, willing him to understand.

"What do you mean? How long?"

"I don't know, a few months," she said. "After five years in hiding —"

"I understand." She needed the same thing he had needed when he left home and came to Shanghai, but freedom was different for him than for her. Seeing this, he wrapped her in tenderness, and gave his blessing, even though the last thing he wanted was to let her go. "Just promise you'll come back," he said, and she did.

Then she was gone, and he had no work. After giving Keiko enough to cover the first month of the boys' board, he had 430 Shanghai dollars left, not quite enough for a single tourist-class ticket even if he had wanted to go.

The city had gone quiet, no explosions, no war planes, no rattle-pops of gunfire. Even the cold air off the river, the scent of coal smoke, had a new silence to it. There was little boat traffic. Outside, the *Idzumo* still sat there, its flag stiff in the winter wind, and around it were Japanese merchant ships, but for the first time, he saw no Chinese vessels, no lorchas and junks, no sampans. They had fled to other waters.

He himself had only his piano, and fourteen handmade suits. He had chalk stripe, gabardine, seersucker, linen, basket weave, wool tropical, and winter-weight flannel, from three-piece suits to casual single-button sport coats with complementary trousers, suits for every occasion. They hung in a row along one wall, as useless as he was. *You are special,* his mother had told him when he was small. *Opportunities come to those special enough to deserve them.* Not anymore.

Most of the clubs had closed. Only one American orchestra was still playing, and that was Earl Whaley and his Red Hot Syncopators; they had left Saint Anna's and moved to Ladow's Casanova, a cavernous ballroom at 545 Avenue Édouard VII. The place was owned by the Eurasian son of Louis Ladow, an American ex-con and octoroon who, before his death, had run the Carleton Hotel and Astor House ballrooms.

There would be no spot for Thomas, since Whaley had signed on piano F. C. Stoffer, but he thought Alonzo and the two brothers might get positions. Unfortunately Charles, like Earl, played alto, but Charles was good on clarinet, too. Thomas invited the bandleader to lunch.

"The son may be half-Chinese, but he's still an American," Earl Whaley said as they cut into their veal chops at the Park Hotel Grill. "So as long as America stays neutral, the Japs'll let him keep operating. That's the beauty, right there. Because everybody else has been shut down."

Thomas nodded, at the same time mentally quivering as he counted up the bill, five dollars at least, but where else were his band members going to get work? The invaders had taken everything. "I hear Japan is setting up a vice district here in Frenchtown."

Earl lined English peas up along his knife, precise, effortless, a sax man. "I heard about that too. It's going to be rock bottom. Every kind of low-down operation. You stick your arm in a slot with a few dollars in it, they inject you with morphine."

"Music clubs?"

Earl snorted. "If you call 'em that. Nobody's going to play there, 'cept Filipinos." Filipino bands worked the lowest rung of Shanghai's club-world, always with passable renditions of the season's hit songs.

"And everyplace else is closed down?"

"'Cept Ladow's," said Earl comfortably. "We're changing our name, what with the new lineup — Earl Whaley and His Coloured Boys. What do you think?"

"Good," said Thomas, his mind churning. There was no place else. A year ago he would have dismissed Ladow's as a second-tier establishment, since they employed dance hostesses. But that world was gone, Earl's was going to be the only black orchestra still playing, and Ladow's the one jazz place that had not gone Japanese, thanks to its American owner. It was his only shot.

His mouth felt dry as paper. He reached for his tea.

"How about some pie?" said Earl.

"They have lemon meringue," said Thomas, wanting to scream. Two pieces of pie was a dollar. He signaled the waiter anyway, and two wedges were slid in front of them.

Now. They were two dark men in a white-tablecloth restaurant that was deserted save for them, waiters standing idle, in a city of dreams that had crashed into ruins. "Earl," he said. "I need a favor."

Part II

黑暗世界

THE DARK WORLD

· · ·

After the Japanese took over, the Green Gang split apart. Some worked for the resistance, but most crossed the line to serve the enemy. They were dog's legs, the sort of men who had to serve some master, so when the great jazz ballrooms were no more, they turned to enforcing the casinos, dance halls, opium dens, and pleasure houses of the new Japanese vice zone, the Badlands. Our era had been permissive, but the Badlands was vile. Any service could be bought, any form of sex, any wager, any drug, even murder, some said, if the price was paid. It was a cruel parody of what had been.

Yet when it came to what I wanted for my country, which was to stand up to Japan, Shanghai had not let me down. She had fought to the end, laying down a quarter-million lives to the enemy's seventy thousand, putting the lie to their boast that they could conquer Shanghai in three days. Nevertheless, our time was finished, and an exodus of souls had begun, a migration away from what now was a prison everyone called Hei'an Shijie, the Dark World. Some went abroad, to Hong Kong, or to the interior—west into the White areas if they followed Chiang or north into the Red if they followed Mao.

I was reborn first through the movement, and then again, through him. After our time together I knew, no matter where the two of us were, that while he lived, I would never be alone. I knew I would return to him. But just as much, I knew I needed to go north.

. . .

7

I N THE WINTER of 1938, north China was split between areas
controlled by Japan, the Whites, the Reds, and independent war-
lords loyal to one Chinese side or the other. The Communist hub
was Yan'an, a backward settlement in upper Shaanxi Province. It was
carved into dusty loess hills along a sluggish, silt-brown river, but to
Song it was a city of gold.

Even as a Party member, she could not just travel to Yan'an and
present herself. First she had to go to Xi'an, which was in the White
area, Chiang's area, yet functioned as a neutral portal for anyone
who wished to pass into Communist territory as a partisan. Song
was coming on her own, without written introductions; she knew she
would be expected to remain in the hostel of the Eighth Route Army
Liaison Office for a few weeks while they considered her. Operations
were tighter in the north, it being a military center, while the Party
in Shanghai was really a propaganda organization. Maybe she should
have written to Chen Xing for his help after all.

The taxi came within sight of the rambling complex of buildings, and she told the driver not to stop, since ahead she could see
a Buddhist pagoda, rising above the low-slung courtyard buildings.
"There," she said. One hand strayed to the tiny sewn-in pouch she

had carried all the way from Shanghai; it would not do to take twenty-seven diamonds into the Eighth Route Army Office.

She had told no one, and she felt especially bad about keeping the secret from Thomas, but it was only for now. She would pull out the little pouch someday and show him. Right now, though, it had to be put someplace safe.

She walked a while with her travel-bundle, scanning the featureless stone walls. There was no hiding place, not even a small park where she could knock loose enough earth to make a hole under a rock.

She walked back to the pagoda to pray at the temple, and think. After dropping some coins into the earthen pot, which earned an approving gaze from the bald saffron-robed monk at the altar, she lit a clutch of incense sticks and bowed and then sank low, arms outstretched, hoping for an answer. After a minute she stood, and added her incense sticks to the others burning in the dish of sand.

"Sister," said the monk, "you look tired. I must leave for a dot of time, but remain here if you like. See? There is a small meditation chamber. You may rest there." And with the serene purpose of his kind, he left.

The temple was unheated, but it was positioned to give shelter from the winds, so she passed gratefully through the door, and found herself in a smaller room, a sort of side chapel, with a tiny window giving onto a grassy back court. Looking out, she saw the court was crowded with a miniature forest of steles, all erected and inscribed over the centuries in honor of the Buddha; she counted twelve of them along with a gnarled tree, limbs naked now in the February cold. The walls were high, no one could see into the courtyard. Was this the open door, the key, the escape hatch? She did not want to cross the threshold of the Eighth Route Army Office unless she had a way to get back to Thomas. She slipped out and began a search of the walls for a loose tile or stone.

Half an hour later she was back on the street, unencumbered. The package that had seemed to burn a hole in her chemise was gone, she was free, light. She walked into the liaison office like any other believer, shoulders square and purposeful.

When she stepped in, she felt she was slipping back in time. The windows were paned in rice paper instead of glass, filling the room with a milky light, and the only telephone was the old cup-and-cord type. Everyone wore loose trousers and a pajama-style tunic, belted at the waist.

Her plain, long skirt, low boots, and layers of padding against the cold had been carefully chosen to look neutral and proletarian, but suddenly seemed carelessly rich, and attracted stares.

From behind the main desk, a heavyset older woman with a close-cut cap of graying hair gave her a form to fill out. Song reached for the cheap bamboo pen and dipped it in the ink as she scanned the onionskin page. It was easy enough to write her name, and give the details of having been sworn in and commissioned as a member of the Shanghai branch, but there was no space to list anything else. She added a neat, modest note about her language abilities at the bottom and handed it back. The woman stamped it with no expression, and waved her on.

No one asked her about her skills, not even the leader of the temporary work unit she was assigned to the next day. They worked in the laundry, washing the linens and uniforms of the officers. She washed her own tunic and trousers down on the banks of the muddy Yan River with a lump of soap and a rock, but the officers got starch and steam ironing. She didn't mind, and ignored the blisters that formed on her hands and only half healed overnight before opening again the next day.

Nights were the hardest. As soon as she crawled into her cot, beneath the blankets, her dreams were her own again, and she could close her eyes and be with him. Every night they had spent together unfurled in her, and she kept herself awake with it for hours before falling asleep. In the daytime, he receded, a pleasurable secret.

She soon realized that now she was thinking about him the way, in her old life with Du, she had thought about the Party; he had become her private world. As she looked around, she saw young men here, Chinese men, partisans like herself, but she was not drawn to any of them. Her private world was better.

Almost as a challenge to herself, she cut her hair short in the Party style, and let her face become sunburned for the first time ever. Some of the women with good figures could not resist cinching shiny leather belts extra-close around their waists, but Song wore her tunic loose and her hair stubbornly uneven.

In the evenings she attended a newcomers' class at the Party's informal school. There she expected to read Marx for the first time, or discuss Party ideology, but instead found herself pressed by questions about Shanghai. Everyone seemed suspicious of a city whose people all came from someplace else and thus had no real home, and would never commit. This was not exactly true, for almost all Shanghainese, including the wealthy elite, still identified emotionally with their clan seats in the provinces, and even made occasional nostalgic visits to their family tombs and lineage temples. Still, the other young recruits in her class all agreed that the city was a place of spiritual pollution, a *da ran gang,* or giant dye vat so powerful that even jumping into the Huangpu could not clean off the stain—this was the view of Shanghai in traditional China, and here in the class, she was Shanghai's representative. She learned to say little. Such old-fashioned ideas showed Song that in their own way the Reds were just as fundamentalist as Du and Chiang and the Nationalists, only with a different orthodoxy.

At the same time, in other ways, the place was genuinely progressive. She was accepted, made welcome, and given work, even if it was in the laundry. She saw that the other women in her dormitory were grateful to be here too. They were young and, unlike her, mostly not well educated; all were first-timers who'd had no prior contact with the movement. As the days passed and she heard a little about their lives, she realized they were all running from something—one escaped an arranged marriage, another an enslaving mother-in-law, a third the Japanese. They were not so much true believers as girls who had made a dash for their freedom, and all of them, including Song, had found refuge.

One day in early spring she heard shouts and ran out to the side of the building. Singing! And then from around the corner marched a group of students, in step, twenty or thirty boys and girls wearing bright kerchiefs and rucksacks, all singing in three-part harmony.

"They have walked all the way from Chongqing," said the girl standing next to her, drying her hands on a towel.

Song gasped. "That is at least a thousand *li!*"

"Plenty of time to practice," the girl cracked.

As the students marched up the broad street toward the Liaison Office complex, they sounded to Song like a fleet of angels, pure and high. Everything felt squared inside her at that moment, sure and true. Even her feelings for Thomas did not seem to pose a problem.

Walking back into the laundry, still floating on her optimism, she was stopped by the head of her unit, who handed her an envelope. "Your orders," he said.

Finally. Please make it Yan'an, the nerve center, the real headquarters—her fingers shook with anticipation as she tore it open, and then her brain seemed to stall. "Chen Lu Village?"

"Time for you to learn from the peasants," he said.

Thomas had prepaid the rent on his studio until February 1, 1938, and then he lost the room. The piano had to go, since he could not pay to move it, and it felt almost like having an arm or leg taken off to close the lid on those keys for the last time. A piano had been there waiting for him, on the floral rug in the parlor, before he was even born, and now, for the first time, he would have to be without one.

As he would have to be without her. He had known she would go north, had been able to see it in the way her suitcase sat by the bed. But it left a hole in him that never closed.

Luckily, the need to find someplace cheap to live took his mind off her absence. He set himself to scouring the ads in the *Shanghai Times*, and there found a *tingzijian,* a pavilion room, which was really only a closed-off loft above some other room, an eight-by-ten box with a single small window.

He had learned about pavilion rooms a year before, his first winter in Shanghai, when he was walking during Chinese New Year with Lin Ming. They had met an acquaintance of Lin's, and stopped for the two to have an exchange in Chinese before walking on.

"What did he say?" said Thomas.

"He said, 'May you become a second landlord this year.' Everyone says that at New Year's."

"What is a second landlord?"

"A man lucky enough to lease a house and carve it up and rent every room out to other people. Usually the second landlord will live with his wife and children in the kitchen, or the largest bedroom, or the main parlor. And every other corner will be rented, including the little lofts, which are always the cheapest places."

Thomas's new building lay in an alley off a leafy stretch of Route Louis Dufour, and his room hung above the kitchen, in which there lived a family of four, the Huangs, his "second landlords." The loft-cubicle came with one meal a day, and just as he had done when he moved into the studio, he used a considerable part of the money he had remaining to pay his rent out far in advance, so he could guarantee at least his room and the one daily meal, because he wanted to wait here for Song.

Ensconced, he covered the city looking for work, and ate the rest of his meals on the street, parsing out his coins to the vendors who sold hot, sustaining soups of noodles and meat and vegetables, and the large pan-crisped, sesame-bottomed pork buns called *sheng jian bao*. Once a week he put on one of his useless suits and walked to Ladow's Casanova to see Alonzo and Charles and Ernest. That was always a happy hour, talking with them while they set up.

But his cash was disappearing. He spared a few coins every Wednesday morning to get an early copy of the *Shanghai Times* on the day the new employment ads came out, but there were really no clubs left, at least not any that he could play in.

The Badlands, between Yuyuan and Jessfield and Great Western roads, could not even be considered. The Japanese had forced foreigners out of their mansions and then turned them into vice clubs, just as they had done with the Royal. They filled the ground floors with gambling tables and roulette wheels, constantly jammed with customers and patrolled by guards bristling with guns. Everything else was divided into curtained cubicles for smoking opium, or for sex. Thomas noticed the thick haze and the sweet-sick smell when he walked through midlevel places like the Celestial and the Good Friend. The smell hung in the air even at the top club, the Hollywood, a huge low-ceilinged labyrinth of drug dens and gambling halls into which ten thousand Shanghainese streamed every day and night, from motorcars and rickshaws that clogged the streets all around. But there was no serious music.

The rest of the city was unstable, even though the battle was well in the past. The resistance fighters and collaborationists were still attacking each other by bombing the offices of newspapers and magazines, and assassinating anyone who took too strong a position. One day in February, walking down Rue Chevalier, Thomas saw a human head hanging from a lamppost, eyes wide in terror, staring right at the Frenchtown police station. He could not read the note beneath it, but soon learned that it said "Look! Look! The result of anti-Japanese elements," and that the head belonged to Cai Diaotou, who edited a society tabloid. Policemen who investigated the decapitation received human fingers in the mail, and soon other severed heads started appearing around Frenchtown, with warning notes. Still, he had to go out, to look for work, or he would starve.

He tried the pit orchestras at the theaters, film studios, and recording studios, and answered ads for rehearsal and accompanist work. He went to every open call for a piano player, and found them crowded with applicants, classically trained like him, many of them very high level, and all of them Jewish refugees.

He waited for his turn on a long bench next to a man from Vienna named Eugen Silverman. "We came on the Lloyd Triestino Line from Genoa," Silverman said, "and for one whole month we could not leave the ship. Bombay, Singapore, Manila, Hong Kong—all the other passengers could come and go, not the Jews. It's like a punishment from God. No country will take us. Not even for a few hours."

"Except Shanghai," said Thomas.

"Thanks to God. Even though they only let us leave with two hundred Reichsmarks, we are here." Silverman's name was called, and he went into the little room where they had heard the pianists play short excerpts, one by one.

His playing sounded exceptionally good to Thomas, bright and professional, and when he sight-read the selection they gave him— for every man was given two pages of some piece to test his reading—he played with assurance. Yet when he came out, his babyish face, with its soft round features and blond eyebrows, was long and gray.

"Truly?" Thomas said. "You sounded excellent."

"Look what they have to choose from," Silverman said, waving at the long line of pianists. He slumped back down in his seat, and even through his overcoat Thomas could see the hollowness in his upper chest, and the skin loosening beneath his chin, and in one of those intuitive instants he had come to trust, he knew the man had been going hungry.

"Thomas Greene?" said the woman in the doorway.

He gave Eugen a squeeze on the shoulder. "You'll get the next job," he said. "You play beautifully."

Thomas did not do any better. When he was done, they crossed his name off and dismissed him.

To his surprise, Eugen Silverman was still outside, waiting. "No?" he guessed when he saw Thomas's face. "Ach, they are looking for a God, not a man." He stood and brushed at his overcoat, which Thomas saw was worn, and had been mended. *I looked like that when I first came here.* Now his clothes were handmade, of the finest cloth, but it meant nothing.

They left the studio and walked up Zhejiang Road toward the

Grand Shanghai Hotel. "Come with me, Eugen. I know a street cart not far from here with very good noodle soup. I have a few coins. Let me buy you a bowl."

"Are you sure? I wouldn't want to—"

"Come," Thomas said again. He led him north to Taiwan Road, until they came to a small corner between two buildings where great puffs of steam rose into the air and a huddled mob of hungry patrons crowded the small tables, all eating noodles. "Sit," said Thomas, "it's restorative." And he paid the vendor for two bowls.

Song's orders took her to Chen Lu Village, to learn from the peasants. There, the peasants were all ceramics artisans, because Chen Lu was a village that "ate pottery"—in addition to farming the terraces on the repeating hills, everyone worked in clay. Even the houses were made of discarded pots, from whole urns stacked up, to shards and tiles cemented together; some houses were even built in hive shapes, like kilns. People told her she was lucky to be sent there in winter. With all the kilns running, she would at least be warm. She tried to feel swept up in it, but it was not why she had come north. She longed to go to Yan'an.

As she set out in a bouncing, clattering flatbed truck with a group of students from Zhengzhou, she reminded herself that she needed improvement. The students put her to shame with their joy and fervor, and after all, the job they were going to do—dig a new set of terraces on land that had slid in the rains of the previous autumn— was worthwhile.

By the time they came within sight of the town, belching wood-fired kiln smoke into a hazy sky from a string of denuded hilltops, the winter sun was sinking, and the temperature plummeting. As hunger ate at them, they passed houses tantalizingly strung with corncobs, or fronted with tall heaps of drying kernels on the ground, their color leaching away in the fading light. The truck stopped in front of two hives at the top of one of the hills, and was gone almost as soon as they had clambered down, clapping and stamping, into the cold. The hives, one for men and one for women, were as dark and cold as the outdoors, but they soon had the hearths blazing and a minimal meal of mush made from boiling dried corn and millet. The next day, they would approach the locals for vegetables and oil and salt, maybe some pork. The women slept in a huddled row that night, and Song lay on her right side, warm and safe within the accordion-line of bodies. When she woke up the next morning, someone was singing.

It took only a few days to see that there was no man in the group she cared to know any better, and she was embarrassed for having even thought of it. She would return to Thomas when the time was right. Now she had to learn from the peasants.

She loved many things about Chen Lu Village, the way the sun rose red over the hills, as if lifted by the screaming of roosters; the perplexed gratitude of the older potters when the students restored their families' grain fields; the warm feel of the women's hive at night; and the faces of the students by firelight, singing the songs they had learned. It was always in choral style, always about "we" and "us," marching forward. Song recognized it as the same sound made popular by the moving picture soundtracks that had come out of Shanghai's film studios all through the magical time of Night in Shanghai. It was in the left-wing style of composers like Nie Er, who had written the popular "March of the Volunteers." This was the music of the movement, and it was while singing and shoveling dirt all day on the terraces of Chen Lu Village that Song first really heard it and understood it. From the earliest years of her piano lessons with her tutor, to the rapture she had felt hearing Thomas play, she had always loved the music of the West. When she left Shanghai to come north, she had consciously put at least this one foreign-tinged part of her away. But there in Chen Lu Village, digging in the fields and singing beside her fellow believers, she felt music come back to her, in a different way. She added her voice, high and soaring, and they liked it. Thomas would approve. When they came to the end, the others smiled and congratulated her, and she thanked them, but she never forgot that he was the root of her scale. Many nights, she lay thinking of this.

During their last week in the village, one of the men, a dominating personality named Zhu Hongming, moved uncomfortably close to her as they were digging a terrace. He was a leader; she had seen how the other students deferred to him, and how he preened in response. "I have been watching you, Little Sister. You have promise."

Even to Song, who had little experience with men, it was offensive. She emitted a polite monosyllable.

Mistaking her reserve for self-effacement, he pushed ahead. "It's so. Your political statements show intelligence."

She stared. Not a single political statement had escaped her lips. It had taken only a short time in the north for her to see that the safest thing, especially while doing manual labor, was to keep her head down, say nothing, and attract no attention.

"I can help you advance," said Zhu Hongming, his face dotted with blemishes which he had picked at until they bled. "I am well connected." He touched her leg.

She winced and pulled back.

"I know a lot of important people in Yan'an. I am high level. I can help you"—his hand came back to her thigh—"or I can block your way."

She snatched up her shovel and held it poised, point down, above the offending hand, which instantly vanished. How dare he speak to her as an inferior? He was a mere child, no more than twenty-one, while she, an old woman of twenty-four, had already been bought, sold, and reborn. "Don't ever do that again," she spat, and took her shovel with her to another row. Effortlessly, without even having to think about it, she had made a decision: enough of trying to climb on her own. Her first day back in Xi'an, she would write Chen Xing a letter.

By May, Thomas was down to his last few Shanghai dollars. For weeks he had been allowing himself only one small meal a day in addition to his dinner with the Huang family, perhaps a bowl of noodles like the ones he had shared with Eugen Silverman, or a large bun like a *sheng jian bao*. He went on combing the ads, moving quickly from the newspapers and magazines that had been bombed out of existence to new ones, and taking himself to every open call. He failed every time, sometimes even fumbling notes. He never practiced anymore, never played, never touched a piano except to audition while faint with hunger. But there was no help for it, especially after he had spent his last coin. When not at tryouts, he passed most of his time either walking or stretched out in his room, not wanting to impose too often on Alonzo and Keiko.

It was the rituals of the Huang housewife below him that became his clock and kept him tethered to life. First thing in the morning, she did not cook, but went out to the sesame cake store, that fundamental fixture of the Shanghai neighborhood, and brought back fried dough sticks, glutinous rice cakes, soy milk, and sesame cakes, which she had once told him were the "four Buddha's warrior attendants" of a local breakfast. He watched entranced as they consumed these wonders. She bought everything fresh, all day long, buying just enough noodles and wrappers at the rice store, or sending an older child out to buy one or two cents' worth of hot pepper or vinegar at the soy sauce store. She never kept any kind of food. She bought briquettes and coal dust almost every day, and used a paste made from water and coal dust to seal the smoldering fire in after warming the room and making tea with it in the morning, in this way keeping it alight until the evening meal. His loft cubicle was pleasantly warm as a result, though he knew with its one tiny window, it would be unbearable in the heat.

He let his mind go to Song. She was like a locked room inside him, waiting. On days when she held his attention, she was everywhere, leaving a trace of her voice in the laugh of a woman down in the lane, or a note of her fragrance in the air. He let himself drift in and out of the past as if he was slipping in and out of consciousness.

Yet he had also promised her he would stay alive, and when summer bloomed warm and humid, and he found himself weakening, he roused himself to one last audition. It was for a ramshackle club in the

Chinese city that played Yellow Music, the popular local song form that combined singing styles dating back to the last dynasty with jazz and dance songs brought over by the orchestras from America. It was melodically different, with Chinese lyrics; he could never have even auditioned had there not been a written score on hand, which there was — and though it was a strange hybrid, he played it better than anyone else who showed up that day. As Buck Clayton had once remarked to him about Yellow Music, if it can be written, it can be played. He got the job.

The club was called Summer Lotus, and as soon as he got his first week's pay, he went looking for Mr. Hsu to write everything out for him. He found the copyist still living in the same tiny *tingzijian*, with the same piled-high manuscripts, and happy to take the work. Soon, Thomas had all the songs in written form, and was able to keep up.

The club was the kind of place he would never have thought of even entering before. It filled every night with prostitutes and their clients, the latter exclusively Chinese, the prostitutes a regular League of Nations — Russian, French, Ukrainian, and girls from South America and India with long, silky waves of black hair. There was even one who wore the facial veil of an Arab, though he had no idea if it was her native costume or some sort of erotic stunt. So much here was a stunt.

He led the band every night through the summer of 1938, five Chinese musicians including the sinuous singer who carried every song. She did her numbers standing still, her little wrists held out before her in supplication and her small, childlike hips swiveling in plaintive time. The men who came into the club sat at the dimly lit booths all around the wall with their hands up under their dates' skirts, the women blank, bored, unless they were being paid enough to make sounds of pleasure. They were his audience, the ones he played for, because their lives were as hard as any he had seen, despite the fact that they chattered and laughed together like schoolchildren.

One September night at the club, they were in the middle of a song called "Lovely Peach Blossom," a Shanghai standard made famous by Fan Zhang and ably delivered by their seductive singer, even if she was a little thin on the high notes, when the sudden rise of sharp, frightened voices and the crash of a door being kicked in made the music falter.

Thomas signaled the band to keep playing. A few couples still tried to move to the music, but others clutched each other and backed off the floor. Thomas kept the rhythm going, and the singer bravely started the next verse.

But then Chinese toughs tumbled in, pistols waving. Thomas sat dumb on his piano stool, even as the other musicians evaporated like smoke from the stage.

The hostesses were fast disappearing through the exits. One of them, Abeya, a dark-skinned girl from Calcutta who always wore a silk sari and her hair in a glossy braid down her back, saw him frozen there and yanked him off the stage.

"What are they looking for?"

"Resistance music. Hurry!" She dragged him through a short rear hall, and into the fresh cool air of the alley. "They will kill you."

"Resistance? I thought we were playing love songs."

She had already hitched her sari partway up her waistband, freeing her slender brown legs to the knees, and now took off running. He plunged after her, darting through the shadows along the back walls of houses. From behind came shouts and cries from the club, and pops of gunfire.

A block away, they slowed down to a walk, breathing hard.

"You must never go back there," she said.

"They owe me half a week's pay! And what do you mean, resistance?"

"The songs are Chinese to you, you just play them. But some of them are leftist, and they say China must fight. 'March of the Volunteers'? It's from a moving picture, *Sons and Daughters of the Storm*. Nie Er wrote that song—people think of him as a martyr. Yet you play it every night. That's why the raid."

"I never knew what it was about."

"Now you do. Never go back." As she spoke, she twined her hand in his.

His heart rose inside him, right out of the humiliation and loss that had become like a dark cave to him, a place where he was used to living, and hiding from the world. Song was his angel, but she had fled. Abeya was strong and dark and long-limbed; when they ran, it was she who had set the pace. Now she was radiant from exertion, and the warm spicy smell of her enveloped him. Even if she only pitied him, he didn't care. He stepped closer, his heart thumping in her direction. "Do you have a place we can go?" It was blunt, but there was a war raging, and manners seemed to belong to a different time.

She took him to a small room in the Chinese City, up two narrow flights, beneath a dormer. An intricately carved wood-lattice screen covered the single window, but let in the cool night and the predawn sounds from the twisting lane outside. She shivered, and shook a soft, long-used blue blanket out over the bed.

"I want to sleep," she said, and he said he did too, but when he unbuttoned his pants and slid them down and climbed in beside her she turned to him, and opened the strings to her nightdress. He let out a sob of joy, and she laughed as she wrapped her strong legs around him. She was so physically frank, not like Song, whose every touch had carried a world of feeling. But now Abeya was pulling her nightdress over her head, and he was grateful, giving thanks even for the raid that sent him here, though it meant the end of the job at Summer Lotus. When they were done, he turned his head slightly against her neck, and saw that her eyes were open, staring vacantly at the ceiling.

It was early afternoon when he woke up, the light and shadows filigreed on the wall through the wood screen. She was gone; nothing remained of her but a sweet depression where her body had been. He smoothed it with his hand.

He found a note: *I regret there is nothing in the cupboard for you but a few biscuits. Please take what you like. I am never going back to Summer*

Lotus and you should not either. You can come back here, though. Knock and see if I answer. This time was between us. Next time, bring a gift.

He studied her childish looped handwriting, convent handwriting. For the first time he thought about where she had come from, and what she had done to get here. Trying to find her freedom, as he was. *Thank you for saving my life*, he wrote underneath her message, meaning it in every possible way. She was not Song, but she had extended her hand, and every inch of him appreciated it. Because of her he stepped out into the daylight safe, rested, satisfied by a woman, ready for the long walk home.

Lin Ming managed to save 900 dollars more in the first nine months of 1938, bringing his total to 3,200 — still not enough to buy Pearl. Disappointment burned through the scalding cups of tea he downed on the train back to Shanghai, trying to sort out what to tell her. What he really wanted was to take her arm and walk her out of there, watch her give back the furs and silk brocade jackets and dangling earrings of jade and gold filigree; they would leave side by side in their plain cotton clothes. Then he would buy her a set of simple silver wedding bracelets, which he would have incised with their names alongside the dragon and phoenix, entwined in eternal dance.

They could not live in Shanghai; her past would be known to certain people. Instead he would take her to Hong Kong. In doing short jobs for Kung throughout 1938 — the fastest way to get money for Pearl — he had seen the vibrant thrum of life in the streets. He loved looking across the bay from Kowloon at Central's skyline of graduated modern-style buildings in pale stone. He and Pearl could live there, have children, and start a new dynasty, with the name Lin, which had been his mother's name. Take that, Teacher.

But when he was with her, as he was the first night he arrived in Shanghai, he did not tell her all this as she lay in his arms. Surprising her was part of his plan. For now, he just told her to leave everything to him, that he would make it happen. He told her he did not want to die with his eyes open — regretting work undone and promises not kept — and so she could depend upon him. Her eyes shone at these words.

At noon the next day, the time he had paid for came to an end. They embraced long and hard, and he made haste to the address in Frenchtown where he was to meet H. H. Kung.

Since January first Kung had been serving as Premier of the Nationalist government of Chiang Kai-shek, which was now located in Chongqing; as such he had been obliged to slip into Shanghai very discreetly, and seek lodgings in a back lane. Lin arrived to find a *shikumen* house, which literally meant stone-wrapped gate because of the stone lintel that was common in Frenchtown doorways. He would never have suspected this place sheltered anyone special or important. He knocked.

The door was opened by Kung's secretary, a purse-lipped and overly fastidious man who always wore an old-fashioned gown and vest. "Dr. Kung is upstairs," he said, and led the way.

"Duke Kung," Lin said with pleasure, when he saw the older man behind his fog of cigar smoke.

"Young Lin."

"Thank you for seeing me."

"Of course. You said you needed some help?"

"Well" — Lin knew Kung was a busy man — "it's like this. We have known each other a long time, and I am asking if you have any additional work for me. I need money, you see. It's for the girl I want to marry."

"Ah!" Kung's face lit along with the lighter he flicked open to get his cigar going again. "I approve."

"Thank you."

"Let me look around. You were in Hankou, too, recently, doing work for Du, I heard."

"Yes. At the end of April I translated for his interview with two writers from England, W. H. Auden and Christopher Isherwood. He told them he worked full-time for the Red Cross."

"And they believed it?"

"Utterly." They laughed at this, and then sat in companionable silence, built on years of unspoken alliance and a shared understanding of the world. "Any news from Germany?"

"It's bad. Jews had to turn in their passports at the beginning of this year. There are new laws—Jews can no longer be in real estate or banking, they cannot be doctors. Cannot teach or study."

"What about your friends?"

"Dead."

"Dead! How?"

"One was shot, on the street in Geneva, where he had fled. The other was doused with petrol on the street in Hamburg, and set alight."

Lin placed an involuntary hand over his midsection. "How awful."

"Yes."

"It must have shattered you."

"Yes. And they were *powerful*. They ran banks, they were rich, prominent men. If *they* could not escape it, no one can."

"Is no one doing anything?"

"I know of one man," said Kung. "My friend Ho Feng-Shan, in Vienna. He was just promoted to Consul. He has been writing visas to Shanghai as fast as he can dip the pen. They are phony, of course, but they are getting people out of Austria. And if these people don't escape, they'll be killed! You know that, don't you?" He dropped his head, defeated, and ground out his cigar. "Germany won't stop until all the Jews are dead."

The money from the job at Summer Lotus did not last long, but it got Thomas through to the end of 1938, and restored his health. He had not wanted his old bandmates to see him growing thin, but now he resumed visiting them several times a week at Ladow's Casanova.

They noticed nothing. Neither did Lin Ming, who had come through town in October to see his lady friend and attend his discreet business meetings.

But now it was January 1939, and his money was gone again. Thomas conserved his strength, staying home, blessing the warm, prepaid room with its one meal a day. He lived in a world of sounds, and knew every voice in the building. In the first-floor parlor lived a policeman with a wife and two sons, and the dining room housed an older man who was a moneylender for the peddlers in the neighborhood. The kitchen was occupied by himself and the Huang family. In the upstairs parlor was another pavilion room, rented by a struggling actress in Chinese opera, and the main bedroom was let to a sailor and his wife. He was away for long periods at sea, and she was what the other tenants called half-open, meaning she took money from men while he was gone. The other rooms were rented by an opium-smoking woman in her thirties, and a trio of Suzhou girls who worked as taxi dancers. Sometimes he lay in bed and listened for their echoes through the walls, and let their voices conjure Song, feeling the line between dream and reality grow thinner.

The high point of the day was his meal, after which he and the Huang family remained around the table while they played a game of listening to a different radio station every night for one hour; though they lived in a fallen city, most stations seemed miraculously to continue broadcasting. Their original idea had been to get news about the war by starting at the bottom of the dial and ticking the knob up through the bulletins and speeches in many languages. They did that, but they quickly heard an amazing variety of music, too, and agreed to keep listening. They enjoyed Hawaiian steel-string guitars, classical composers, French *chansons*, Cantonese opera, polkas, Russian marches, *kunqu* opera, and everywhere jazzy Chinese pop songs, the Yellow Music he had played at Summer Lotus.

One night in February they happened on an all-Bach chamber performance by German orchestral musicians who had escaped and reassembled here in Shanghai, broadcast live from the Ohel Moshe Synagogue in Hongkou. He knew there were close to twenty thousand Jewish refugees in town now, and so he was able to hear in it a particular kind of blues, a precise and elegant variant on the theme of survival. At the same time he realized they had brought with them a part of home, for Bach was theirs too, no matter how the Germans reviled them. Something lifted in him that night, as he saw he could lay claim to any music he played, no matter where it came from. It was the defiant Bach from the Ohel Moshe Synagogue that made it clear. And in time, as they went up and down the dial, he began to imagine music of his own.

For the first time in his life there were no keys on which to repeat the past, so he let it all go. He had no songs to play, no style to imitate, nothing to do but listen, and he let his mind improvise, his hands moving quickly as if across the keys. He did not play, he only *heard*. He had become a musician of pure thought, straight invention. Music unspooled within him, new melodies, urgent with feeling, shaped and structured. He sat every evening with the Huang family in their kitchen listening to the radio, while his hands played over his thighs and his mind reached out to dream around the world.

Lin was called back to Shanghai in March, for a meeting with Dr. Kung. He went to the address he was given, a different *shikumen* lane house this time, off Mandalay Road, in the consular district. The same secretary answered the door. The rotund Kung emerged right behind him, and instead of inviting Lin Ming in, he quickly donned his own overcoat and stepped outside. "Let us take a walk," he said, something he never suggested.

On the street they spoke of Kung's family and Lin's father as they crossed Bubbling Well Road, and at the right moment, walking in the net of lanes between Carter and Da Dong roads, Kung said, "I have a job for you." He looked around. "But we have to speak privately."

"There," Lin said, pointing to a *laohuzao*, a tiger stove shop, a

neighborhood bathhouse. It was random, local, filled with the constant sound of running water. They passed under the oil-paper lanterns with their brush-written characters saying *qing shui pen tang,*
pure hot water tubs, and paid a few coppers each to enter the men's
side.

Thick with steam and mist, it consisted of one small anteroom
in which clients undressed, followed by another room with a large
wooden tub. High above was a wire cable hung with baskets, watched
over by an attendant; this allowed everyone to see their belongings at
all times. Kung tucked his gold watch and his glasses into his shoes
before they put their clothes in two baskets. As Lin followed the
round naked man into the mist, he was struck by the strangeness of
seeing the richest man in China in a back-alley bathhouse.

They scrubbed at the wooden buckets ranged around the side,
using clean cloths softened by endless laundering, then stepped into
the large wooden tub and inched over to the far side to talk.

It was blessedly hot; Lin sank in to his neck.

Kung said, "I need you to help me with something. It is more
important than anything I have ever done. If I fail, my life will be
worthless."

Lin, who had been floating in the redeeming waters, jerked to attention. "Duke Kung. How can you say that?" Not only rich and powerful, he was also a seventy-fifth-generation descendant of Confucius.

"I told you when my friends died—Shengold and Schwartz—I
realized if wealthy men could not escape, no one could. I call myself
a Christian." Kung stretched his pale, fat form out in the water. "It's
a lie unless I act. I have to do something. Now God has given me a
chance, a way to get Jews out of Germany."

"What?" said Lin. The relationship between Nationalist China
and the Nazis was fragile: Germany was close with Japan, though
not a formal ally. Nevertheless, the Nationalists hoped Germany
might pressure Japan to leave China alone. And Chiang Kai-shek admired Hitler; he had modeled his own secret police after Germany's

SS. "The Germans on the Municipal Council are pressing to get the twenty thousand Jews we have in Shanghai now deported to some-place else."

"I know," said Kung, "but at least they are here already. They are safe. Millions in Germany and Austria still have to get out—that's what I want to discuss. We have a plan—a petition Sun Fo and I are going to present to the legislature in Chongqing on April twenty-second."

Lin Ming sat up with a little splash, because now he was talking about laws. "What? A petition to the Legislative Yuan?"

"That's right." Kung turned in the water. "We'll establish a reset-tlement area, a new homeland for European Jews. They are a boon, not a burden; anyone can see that here in Shanghai. Down in Yunnan, where we have built the Burma Road, we have two whole counties almost empty, ready to be developed, the new road connecting them to the world. And we can bring the refugees by sea to Rangoon, and right through Burma to our border."

"Ah." Lin understood. "Because it's British."

"Nowhere will the Germans be able to get near them. But I need you to set things up as it was done here—barracks, soup kitchens, all the assistance people will need who arrive with nothing. Twenty thousand are self-sufficient in Shanghai; we will multiply that in Yun-nan. The main industry will be farming, at first, but the land is good, the climate ideal, and there is plenty of water. They can build what society they like, within Chinese law."

"Permanent resettlement?" It took its shape in Lin's mind slowly. "Quite a gesture."

"China needs to make a gesture. Naturally we hope to get the sym-pathy of the West against Japan, but that is not the reason. I told you. God wants this done." Kung's face was so radiant through the steam that for a moment, Lin was moved to believe.

But then Kung was himself again, practical. "Meanwhile, we can develop these counties easily, bring in engineers, teachers, horticul-turists, men, women, children. It will lift the whole region up. Look at Shanghai. Now there are cabarets where the satire is every bit as sharp as in Berlin, there are fine Viennese bakeries, and new musicians in the Shanghai Municipal Orchestra."

"How many people are you proposing to bring out of Germany?" said Lin.

Kung paddled his hands in the water and looked at him, the light in his eyes shining. "One hundred thousand."

8

B Y THAT MARCH, Song had been in the Communist headquarters in Yan'an almost a year, thanks to Chen Xing's letter
of recommendation, which got her promptly transferred out
of the Eighth Route Army Hostel.

Her new world had not been quite as she imagined. The town itself, situated on a bend in the Yan River between corrugated hills of
yellow loess, had been bombed to rubble by the Japanese, though its
imposingly high city walls had survived intact. The townspeople and
Communists abandoned what lay within the walls and moved to a
shadow-city of caves hollowed out of the dry canyons, cut long ago
by ancient creeks. The Party University was set up nearby, honey-
combed through the repeating hills, invisible to Japanese planes even
as it housed several thousand students who were learning to organize
and use propaganda. Into this hive of political and military activity
came foreigners, including missionaries, reporters, doctors, and ad-
venturers, almost all of whom needed the help of Song's work unit.
Most foreign visitors did not stay long, but the hospital rarely seemed
to be without an English-speaking doctor from India or Australia or
America, keeping the small team of translators busy.

Song liked using her mind, and translating for doctors and visitors was better than digging terraces in Chen Lu Village, yet she still

felt sidelined from anything important. She was far from the thinkers and leaders in their separate canyons. She once asked one of her fellow translators, a middle-aged woman who had worked for Shell Oil in Shanghai, about climbing the ranks in the Party, and the woman had clucked sadly, as if it would be better for Song to forget such ideas. "You and I are foreign-trained," she said. "That's a bad class background."

So even though Song was in Yan'an, she floated in a sea of separation. No one knew anything about her thoughts, her beliefs, her past. She shared a *kang* in one of the women's caves with two other female recruits, who spoke to each other in Sichuanese and ignored her. She translated for foreigners, who always complimented her on her English before they left, but she had no friends; few Yan'an people even approached her. You could catch sparrows on her doorstep.

She crawled into the *kang* next to the other two girls every night, thinking of Thomas, and plugged through every day. When it seemed nothing would ever change, her superior Wu Guoyong called her in and handed her an envelope.

"Orders," he said. "Special treatment, if you ask me."

She took the envelope, burning, because she knew he meant her English. When he was gone, she slit it open.

She was to escort an American woman writer out of Communist territory and back to the Japanese-held area.

To Shanghai.

She was so excited she ran to the outhouse, closed the stall door, and squatted over the hole without even taking down her pants, just shaking, imagining what she would do when she saw him, what she would say — if he was still there. But he was, she knew it, she felt it. He was there, and she would see him in less than two weeks.

Her feet barely grazed the ground as she hurried that evening to meet the American writer, Joy Homer, in the bombed-out town. Almost no buildings remained standing, and the walled ruins were off-limits during the day, the better to appear abandoned to any Japanese flyovers. At night, though, any roofless space still halfway intact was lit up and turned into a noodle stall, or a shop for the dispensing of necessary goods, or an improvised stage for opera, or a puppet show. People swarmed down from the hills to enjoy themselves.

The meeting place was a snack stall, so when Song saw a plain white woman with a camera over her shoulder walking up the uneven lane of crumbled half walls and foundations, she asked the vendor to go ahead and prepare them a couple of dishes, and walked down to meet her.

"Miss Song!" Miss Homer thrust out her hand.

"Just call me Song," she answered, and they shook. "Come. Let's have dinner." And they pulled two stools up to a box, overturned in the dirt, which served as a table.

"This is some place," Joy said, looking around. "You're all quite young, aren't you? It's a young group."

"That's true, I suppose." Certainly the leaders were older, but Miss Homer would not have seen them. Song herself rarely did.

"The soldiers at the headquarters of Marshall Yan are all older," Miss Homer said. "Did you know we just came from there?" The question was posed with a touch of pride, for the armed camp of this warlord and Nationalist commander was famously difficult to visit. "It's in loess hills, much like your dwellings. Fantastic place! They shaved the canyon sides down into a series of terraces for their caves, all connected by these little zigzag stairways just like a New York fire escape. The cave we slept in was forty feet deep, the *kang* big enough for twenty people. Do you know," she said, leaning forward, "every night soldiers came in and spread out their bedrolls beside us. Why, I thought nothing of sleeping with twelve to fifteen gentlemen a night!" She dissolved in laughter, captivated by her own wit as much as by this strange, exotic world. The vendor set two dishes in front of them, and she reared back slightly. "What's this?"

"Mashed potatoes with wild vegetables, and steamed sweet millet cake." Song plucked out the best morsels and put them on the American's plate. "Tell me what brought you to China."

"Well." Miss Homer picked at the potato. "I was sent by the Interdenominational Church Committee for China Relief, you see, as a press correspondent. I'm to gather accurate news on what's going on, and write a series of articles about it, which will help them raise funds for war relief."

Song nodded, understanding why they wanted this woman leaving with a good impression.

"You know what surprises me most about Yan'an?" Joy said. "No Russians!"

Song looked up, jolted. "Why would there be Russians?" An explosion of laughter rose from the stall next to them. All around, little lights were strung up, and the demolished square had the gaiety of a village market. A man nearby had set up a table from which he sold knitted socks and scarves, another sold flashlights, yet another small cook pots. The rhythmic cries of guess-fingers, the ubiquitous drinking game, sounded nearby. "We broke with the Russians," Song said. "We go our own path." Song knew most Americans were ignorant of this; after all, the official press in China constantly dismissed the Communists as bandits and never reported on their real positions or alliances, much less their real power. The Western public knew nothing.

Yet Joy Homer surprised her. "Unfortunately, Americans are pretty simple. Just you being Communist is enough for them — they all think you are Russian allies, that you have Russian military aid. I can tell them you don't, but it won't make a lick of difference. What's this blob, anyway?" She touched a square cake with her chopsticks.

Song started to like the woman. "Steamed millet cake. Try."

Joy ate some. "Not bad. Well, I for one was certainly in the dark about your movement before coming here. And today I met a whole class full of students from your Party University — so impressive, the girls in their cute Dutch bob haircuts, the boys in their glasses. And they walked here! They walked all the way from Xi'an!"

"Oh yes," said Song. "Students are arriving all the time. You see their idealism." Indeed, the sight of them never failed to stir her.

"To the future," Joy said impulsively, raising her chipped teacup.

Song responded with a smile, but inside she thought, *To Thomas. He will be there. He won't have left. He'll have waited a year. And he won't have another woman.* Everything inside her shimmered at the thought. "To the future," she agreed.

When Thomas first saw her standing outside his house, watching his door, he wondered if he was dreaming. He felt hazy these days, always hungry, one meal a day, dwindling down *a niente,* to nothing. Surely now his mind carried him away.

But when she stepped out and started toward him, and he saw the year they had been apart gather at the corners of her eyes and spill over, he knew. Then she was in his arms again, nothing changed, even her smell the same, although she was the new Song—short hair, a loose jacket, trousers. Beautiful. "Come inside."

"This is the first time they sent me to Shanghai," she said as he opened the front door.

"How did you find me?"

"I went to Ladow's. They knew where you were."

When they climbed the little ladder together, he saw her surprise at his tiny chamber, filled by his bed, his clothes, his sheet music, and one small window that gave out on a sloping rooftop. The ceiling in the little cubicle rose at an angle, just high enough on one side for him to stand.

"Paradise," she said. "I have dreamed of it all my life."

He laughed with her, and pulled her onto the bed, and it was hours later that he asked her how long she had.

"Three days," was her answer, and though he tried to hide his hurt that she would leave again so soon, she felt it, and tightened her embrace. They lay with their arms and legs entwined, the way they both knew it should always be.

"Where do you go for the *yi hao?*" she whispered. "The number one, the bathroom."

"Sorry, I don't have a night stool. I use the outhouse in the lane."

"You just go down, through their room?"

"Actually, no. The roof." He indicated the window. "But you can't do that."

"Of course I can. Let's go." And she was up, pulling on her clothes. "Then we'll come back," she whispered.

He smiled. He didn't want to leave the room either.

But once they were outside in the chilly morning air, she said, "Let's eat before we go back. I remember a place near here for *xiao long bao*."

"I don't have any money," he said quietly.

Song looked at him, top to bottom, thinking that now things made sense. As glorious as the thing had been between them, she had also noticed he was thin, ready to blow over in a puff of wind. "I'll buy you breakfast."

He fell gratefully into step beside her. "How do you have money? Du barely left you anything. Do they pay you, the Party?"

"No. They support me and feed me in exchange for my work. I inherited a little." She appreciated that he fell silent then, and did not ask her any more. It was inheritance, in a way, even though Du Taitai was still alive. She stopped in front of a street vendor, who lifted the lid of a giant flat-bottomed pan to show tight-packed rows of chubby pork dumplings with sesame-crisped bottoms. The vendor turned up a dumpling corner to show them. "You like *sheng jian bao*?" Song said.

"I love them," he answered, and she bought two on the spot, and brushed away his thanks. Money meant nothing to her now.

The diamonds would stay in their stone wall, as long as she remained with the Party. On the day she had left with Joy Homer she had almost done it — taken the diamonds and turned her back on the struggle for good. But she was not yet ready.

So when they awakened together the next morning, and he gathered her to him, she knew, with a bolt of misery, that it was time to be honest about it.

"I know you are committed." He brushed hair tenderly back from her forehead. "I love this about you. So why not marry me and take me with you? I know they don't need piano players up there, but I'm strong. There must be something I can do."

"You're a foreigner," she said.

"I'm hardly from the ruling class. Maybe you noticed."

"Don't," she said. "It's not you, it's everything foreign. Politics, culture, learning."

"Learning?" He raised his brows.

"They welcome doctors and engineers for visits, as long as they side with the cause, but even those visitors don't stay—almost never. And marriages between Party members and foreigners are discouraged." She exaggerated slightly; marriage with a foreigner might be permitted, but the fact was that such a marriage would shut all the important doors to her. It would be much harder to get ahead.

"You're saying I could not live there with you."

"It would not be secure for you."

"For *you*, you mean," he shot back, and she wilted inside. "It would cast doubts on *you*."

"*Shi zhei yang de*," she said in Chinese, unhappily. "True."

"What kind of system is that?" he said disdainfully. "Reject people because they are different? Prejudice."

"Reality," she countered. "It is natural for us to feel this way. Look what Japan has done."

"America didn't do that."

"But America did not help us, and neither did Britain or France. They threw us to Japan like so many scraps of meat."

He switched tactics. "Song. You're foreign-trained yourself. If I cannot be secure up there, how can you be?"

"You have the point," she said, agreeing, but her concession gave him no comfort.

After she left, he spiraled down quickly, getting by on his one meal a day with the Huangs and some money she had left behind for him. In April, when he ran into Eugen Silverman at an audition, he mentioned he was low on money, and Eugen took him to meet a Chinese man named Mr. Pao. This man was looking to hire an American, though the job had nothing to do with music.

"I run a newspaper," Mr. Pao explained over tea in his modest apartment, "the *Shanghai Daily*. You have heard of it?"

"Of course." Thomas and Eugen exchanged looks; it was one of the papers whose ads they followed.

"I need a publisher," said Mr. Pao, and then tittered at Thomas's horrified expression. "No experience necessary. Only the use of your name. With an American publisher, we can continue printing. They will leave us alone. I will pay you the salary. You see?"

Yes, Thomas saw. He also saw that newspaper offices had been bombed, and their employees killed, all over town. Newspapers were magnets. "Sorry, pal. Too dangerous."

"It is a salary," Eugen protested.

"Too high a price." Thomas remembered the words of warning he'd been given in Seattle: *People disagree, they end up dead. Play your music and keep clear of it.* "Can't do it."

So his clothes grew looser on him, and he spent most of his time in his room, waiting for the evening to come, when he got food and an hour of listening to the radio. He lost himself in his dreams of Song, but in his rational moments, he was aware of life slipping away.

Early summer had brought warm days when a man came to the door of the crowded lane house asking for Thomas Greene. He was white, European, underfed, with a shock of brown hair above soft, sensitive eyes. He carried a violin case.

"David Epstein," he said, and they shook.

"Thomas Greene."

"You will forgive my English. Aaron Avshalomov gave me your name—you know him? Arosha?"

"Why yes," Thomas cried, glad to hear of his friend. "How is he?"

"He is well. He said he thought you might be free to play. You see? I have the hope." Epstein smiled apologetically and hoisted his instrument.

Thomas shook his head; he had not played in so long, he was not sure he even still could. "Play what?"

"My desire? My most constant dream since I left Vienna? To play my favorite of Mozart's two sonatas for violin and piano in B-flat."

"Oh." Thomas had never played either, though they were gorgeous. "I've had no piano for a year."

"No? If I find piano, will you play the Mozart with me? I so miss to make music."

Thomas considered.

Epstein looked him up and down, no doubt noticing he was thinner than a man with enough money to eat ought to be. "We could play for tips. Make enough to eat, if we are good."

"I would have to practice."

"We can find something."

He thought again. "Some friends of mine play at Ladow's. Maybe there, in the morning. But I only sight-read, Mr. Epstein. I would need sheet music."

"David. Call me David. I'll come back with music."

A few days later he was back with sheet music, by which time Thomas had been told that Ladow's would allow them to practice in the club early in the day.

The first day they met, on Avenue Édouard VII, under a bright morning sun, David drew out the opening pages of the Largo-Allegro, the first movement of the Mozart, right on the street, before they even went inside. "I would need to read through this once or twice," Thomas said.

"I thought so. You say many months, no playing, is it not? So I bring this, too." The Viennese drew out another sheaf of music, and opened it to the first page.

Thomas saw it was *Liebesleid* by the violin master and composer Fritz Kreisler, a piece written by and for the violinist in which the piano played a lesser role and could be sight-read by any competent accompanist.

"Of course I can play this," he said, covering his embarrassment at having implied he needed something so easy. "Naturally."

"The piano is simple," David admitted, "but that is not why I bring this piece. I need money, Mr. Greene. I have a wife and baby in Hongkou and—"

"You came to Shanghai with a wife and baby?"

"Yes! We are so lucky to get out. We had to leave my wife's parents—I am sure they will die—and her cousin—" He choked for a moment, and recovered himself. "Forgive me. We cannot get the rest of our family out—our friends—we have left so many behind. But now I have my wife and son here, they need to eat, and I need money. And you and I, Mr. Greene, we can make money playing in the hotel lobbies. That's why the Kreisler. His music is very, how do I say, *gemütlich*. German and Austrian people love it, because it sounds to them like comfortable times, happy, before the war. You understand? This Vienna, they want to remember. It will make them tip us well."

They practiced together for several weeks, during which Thomas found himself smiling again, even at little things like the street acrobats and puppet shows now reappearing in the lanes with the warm weather. He was still weak, but music returned, as reliably as any true faith, always demanding, always giving. He still played for Song, too, though she was far away. Those were the moments when he caught a surprised grin from David, and knew he had played well.

By the first week of June, the two of them were ready. They went first to talk to the manager of the Park Hotel, because Thomas had noticed a Steinway there.

The man knew his name. "You were one of the brightest stars of Night in Shanghai," he said, wistfully recalling a time which had ended only two years before but already seemed like it belonged in another century. "Of course you can play in the lobby. I cannot pay you, but you can open the violin case for tips—and, all right, you may each have one meal in the restaurant, free, for every music shift. Agreed?"

They went from one hotel to another, making the same arrange-ment, which had natural appeal for hotel management. Shanghai was full of people living quietly, waiting it out, surviving on little. Hotel lobbies in Frenchtown and the *Gudao* were free, semipublic spaces, and many of the people coming in would order tea and cake.

In this manner Thomas and David started at the Park, kicking off with the Mozart. Later on, they played the Kreisler pieces. David grinned and motioned with his chin — and the whole violin — to people retrieving handkerchiefs to wipe at their eyes. "You see? They hear Kreisler and they get all *verklempt*."

He was right, for the *Liebesleid* and *Liebesfreud* brought double the tips of Mozart and Brahms. When the plaintive strains of Kreisler started, that was when the older men in their moth-eaten suits turned to their wives, took their swollen hands, and steered them out onto the dance floor among the potted palms. *This is what they want from the music, a feeling, a connection to another time.* He glanced at David, who had brought him here. *Thank you.* He poured his gratitude into the passage he was playing, stretching out the feeling with shameless melodrama and rubato, and touched hearts all around the room — if the sudden rainfall of coins in the violin case was any indication. He caught David's eye, and the flash of his grin, its pure happiness, was better even than the sound of the money.

Lin Ming left the town of Tengchong in an open jeep, with a driver of the local Bai minority, on the last stretch of the Burma Road before they hit the border to that adjoining nation. Tengchong was high on a stony plateau, surrounded by volcanoes and smoking, bubbling hot springs that sent columns of steam into the air. Life was simple and pastoral, with hundreds of local families engaged in cutting basalt flagstones for use as pavement in the region's towns. Yet there was energy here, in the hot springs; trained engineers would be able to turn it into electricity.

As they left the cooler plateau and descended toward the warm, low-lying jungles of the border, they stopped in a village called Heshun, with cobbled streets and a river winding around it. Many people from this village had gone overseas and made their fortunes, and then sent money back to build a large library with tall windows and tens of thousands of volumes. Below the village the road descended into a broad, unoccupied valley, fertile and well watered. And as long as anyone could remember, the area had also been home to a lively trade in jadeite and rubies. *The Jews will like it here,* he thought.

They would have to be fed at first, and housed, and that would be his job. Right now, all he could think about was Sun Fo and Kung's petition, which had been passed by the legislature on April twenty-second.

> *Jewish people holding citizenship of foreign countries retain the duties and rights of citizens of those countries, and, if they wish to enter China, they can do so in accordance with the usual practices and regulations ... stateless Jewish people are in a special situation. We ought to do everything possible to assist them in expression of our country's commitment to humanitarianism.*

It was law now: one hundred thousand Jews to be selected and brought here to start over. Looking out over the verdant, empty countryside, he swelled with the rightness of it.

Now Kung was going to pay him all the rest of the money he needed to buy out his *qin'ai de Zhuli.* As they descended through the valley, he thought of his last visit with her, when he held her through the night and told her it would not be long. "My plan is almost ready," he whispered, and she lay against him, content, unquestioning, waiting. She trusted him.

From the very first day he and David played at the Park, Thomas took home enough to start eating more, and he soon rebounded to full energy. The flexing of his musical imagination followed, and he started taking liberties with the scores. He still sight-read on automatic, like riding a bicycle, but now he found himself departing from what was written for more than the occasional ornament. He also pulled the rhythmic accents out of line, the way they had done on stage at the Royal. His little solos never undermined the melodic themes or structures of the piece. He always knew where he was.

At the Park, they ate their meal in the restaurant during a break: steak, whipped potatoes, green beans, and hot, delicate cloverleaf rolls. Thomas relished the Western food even though he knew the Huangs would hold his supper for him until he got back. David, on the other hand, ate quickly, with a barely contained desperation that Thomas knew all too well. *And he's here with a wife and child.*

"What do you gentlemen say to our cuisine here at the Park?" It was the hotel manager, brimming with pride in his high-class service and also happy with the music, having seen a sharp uptick in beverage service.

"It's very fine," said Thomas. "Just one problem. We really should not eat while we play."

David looked stricken.

Thomas pushed on. "It is distracting. So we were wondering, while we perform, can Mr. Epstein's wife and son come to the hotel and have our meals, in our place?" He was bland and perfectly sensible.

"Why not?" the manager said. And across the table Thomas saw David's eyes fill with gratitude. From then on, when they played the Park, Margit and Leo came, rail-thin in their best Vienna clothes, and ate as fine a Western meal as money could buy, while white-jacketed waiters hovered around them. Thomas noticed that Leo was ravenous but Margit ate sparingly, and packed up food to take home for David. All the while, the open violin case accumulated coins and banknotes.

He knew he was himself again when he took Alonzo and Ernest and Charles to lunch at a Russian restaurant, and insisted on picking up the check. He even said he was going to start saving again for their tickets, and get them out.

"Sure you are," Ernest said.

"Forget it, pal," Charles put in.

Alonzo was laughing while they spoke, with his bumping bass rumble that always sounded like it might have come from his instrument, and soon they all joined in, even Thomas, who in the sudden clarity of mirth saw that he had been a fool since the very beginning. Their lives were their own. If they had wanted to save money, they would have. Alonzo sent his money home to his family; Ernest and Charles simply burned through whatever they had. Nothing Thomas had ever suggested to them had made any difference. But they liked their lives, all three of them, and they were choosing to remain, the same way he was. There was a new scent of freedom around them, and him too, when he could finally let them be that way.

In that June of 1939 a woman doctor arrived in Yan'an, a surgeon named Dr. Wei. She was the first woman doctor Song had met, and though she had the broad cheekbones and cheerful smile of a rural girl, she had in fact been trained at Peking Union Medical College in all the latest advances. Long lines of women from throughout the encampment, all eager to consult a female doctor, formed to see her.

Dr. Wei was Chinese and needed no translator, so it was mere luck that Song was assigned to assist her on the day a messenger arrived on horseback from Baoding Village with the news that a nine-year-old girl had fallen from a second-floor window onto her head. Dr. Wei barked out the supplies she needed as she sloughed off her clinic coat and grabbed her medical bag. "You!" she said to Song. "Take this, follow me to the truck. You can help."

"I'm not a nurse," Song said, as the leather cases were piled into her arms.

"Doesn't matter!" Dr. Wei called. A flatbed truck was waiting, and Song climbed up in the big square cab beside her.

It was a hard two hours over a bumpy road to Baoding, where they scrambled out in a grove of cypress trees, and ran into the building where the girl waited. "Here!" the villagers cried. And at the end of the hall they found her, lying on a table, unconscious, with a contusion on the side of her skull just behind the ear.

Dr. Wei bent over the girl, examining her quickly. When she took off the blood pressure cuff, her face was worried. She told the women to boil water, and then turned to Song. "Subdural hematoma. We have to operate right away."

"Here?" said Song, looking around the village meeting room, with its clay walls and rustic wood roof.

"Otherwise she will die. She has only a short time." Wei was terse and crisp now, the scientist, as she set out a tray of instruments for Song to sterilize with long-handled tongs. "Then you will hand them to me with the sterile tongs." Bright lights were brought in and arranged around the farm table, towels and gauze and bandages and suture thread laid out according to rapid-fire instructions. Dr. Wei scrubbed her hands furiously with caustic soap and made Song do the same; they covered their hair and wore masks from her medical bag.

"Get her family out of here," said the doctor, and the village women hustled them out while she shaved the girl's head, swabbed it with iodine, and braced it between rolled towels.

"What if she wakes up?" Song whispered.

"She won't." Wei was sectioning back the skin on the girl's head. "We have to relieve the pressure." The doctor used a hand drill to cut through the child's skull, periodically issuing brief commands to a terrified Song.

The instant she removed a section of the skull, the tissue inside bulged out through the opening. "Dura mater," said Dr. Wei, as if she were a professor, and took a scalpel to cut through it. It was surprisingly tough and leathery-looking. The first slice freed a gush of blood and clots, and she could hear Dr. Wei exhale in relief as the spurting blood released its death grip on the brain. Then the surgeon moved on to the torn bridging veins that had caused the buildup of blood in the first place between the dura and the arachnoid, the layer below—first clamping, then repairing them. Long, tense minutes went by. Several times the family opened the door, and were scolded away.

Finally Dr. Wei said, "That is the end of it. Ready to close up." This part seemed easy for the doctor, and she chatted about the complications of head injuries as she worked, finishing with a clean bandage.

By the time they went to the outer room to talk to the girl's parents, Dr. Wei seemed energized, and ready to explain everything to the parents, whether they understood it or not. "The bridging veins were torn by the head trauma, and they poured blood into the space between the skull and the brain, pressing on it. The pressure was the threat; it would have killed her. Now that it is relieved, and she is stable, she should survive. We have to wait for her to wake up to know more."

"Aren't you going to give them special instructions?" Song said when the parents had left the room.

"Instructions?" Dr. Wei looked at her. "No. We are going to stay here. She must be watched." And though Song offered to stay with the unconscious girl while the surgeon rested, this too Dr. Wei brushed off, and sat by the child herself.

In the end they remained in Baoding Village for five days, until the child was well enough to ride back to Yan'an with them for post-operative care. During those days, Dr. Wei saw all the villagers with health complaints.

In their makeshift clinic, a little gang of four girls, headed by the bossy Plum Blossom, turned up every day to help. When they closed the door in the evening, the girls cleaned everything and asked questions, wanting the use of all Dr. Wei's tools explained to them.

Like most village children, they were illiterate, and the second night Song said, "Would you like to have lessons?" They responded in an eager chorus, and every night, when the clinic closed, they worked on characters. Song wrote them out in stages for each girl so they could practice without forgetting the stroke order. To her surprise they loved it, wanting to stay late and learn more, and every morning they came in with their characters memorized. They were ravenous to read. It was not something that had been planned or scheduled, yet it turned out to be the most useful and joyful thing she had experienced since she came north.

On their last night in Baoding, Song carried a tray of food in to Dr. Wei. "You give so much of yourself," she said admiringly.

Dr. Wei looked up, surprised. "No. It is what your people are doing that will change things. Do you realize — these villagers have never seen a doctor! Just like most peasants in China. No one ever brought medical care to them before — no emperor, no leader — not until you people came. Those girls had never been taught their characters either! That's why I'm here, you know. That's why I believe in what you are doing."

And in the truck the next day, watching the doctor cradle her patient on the ride back to Yan'an, and thinking of Plum Blossom and her friends, Song knew that she believed too. Their movement was the future. Maybe it was meant to be greater than love.

Thomas and David were soon playing six days a week. They developed a following, folks who showed up to listen as they moved from one shabby, war-worn lobby to another, the Metropole, the Astor House, the Palace, and Le Cercle Sportif Français, which was not a hotel but a country club. At each place, they asked for the same deal, a full meal in the restaurant for each of them, and then, when the establishment was happy with the stream of patrons and the busy lobby service, they asked that the meal be transferred to David's wife and son. Thomas saw how David lit up when they came in, his wife in white gloves and her grandmother's necklace, the boy in short pants and socks and a little blazer, clumping in his childish oxfords as if nothing had changed, as if they had not lost their world forever, along with everyone in it.

Yet in playing with David, Thomas saw that the Epstein family and the other refugees in their community had brought some of their world here with them. He felt it every time the aging couples got up from their velvet-trimmed chairs and took a turn around the floor. The two musicians traded a look the first time they saw it, and the next time they met, without words having been necessary, David brought with him Chopin's *Grande Valse Brillante* and one of Strauss's *New Vienna Waltzes*. It worked. More and more men started taking their wives' hands, and once two or three pairs were out there, more tended to follow. The lobby became a dance floor, smiles jumping from one to another, from old to young. As they turned on the floor, he noticed their faded sleeves still bore the outline of the Star of David patches they had worn back home, yet here, dancing, all of them looked happy again.

The crowds grew, and in July, Morioka also began to appear where they were playing — never directly, but by engaging in meetings nearby. It happened too often, and at too many hotels, for it to be an accident. The Admiral did not speak to them, since to do so might put the musicians in danger from the resistance, and Thomas appreciated his restraint. He did not mind that the man came to listen, even though Song would be furious if she knew; to him, music was a separate country, within which war was set aside. And actually, the one time Morioka did speak to them, it was only to ask about David. "Where come from your friend?"

"Admiral Morioka, David Epstein. Mr. Epstein is from Vienna."

"Ah," said Morioka, his eyes widening in understanding. "You are Jew. Many your people live Hongkou."

This hung somewhat frighteningly in the air, until he bowed and walked away. "Ready?" Thomas whispered urgently, with a glance to the music stand. David nodded, raised his violin, and followed him when he counted down.

Lin Ming arrived in Shanghai with five thousand in his money belt, riding high on having reached his threshold at last. But he did not go to the Osmanthus Pavilion right away, where Pearl would be waiting; first he had an important meeting with the Jewish leaders in Hongkou, about the Resettlement Plan.

He hastened out of the train station, still an empty shell. Only the tracks had been repaired, along with the necessary walkways, and trains and passengers came and went as before. Much had been cleaned up and even rebuilt in the two years since the battle, but the city was still missing its spark; it looked to Lin like a prison of sad, huddled brown buildings. Nobody referred to it by *Ye Shanghai* anymore, Night in Shanghai. Now *Hei'an Shijie* was the term people used. The Dark World. Walking to the trolley, he felt the darkness all around.

But even the gloom could not dampen his excitement about the meeting. The Resettlement Plan was no longer a secret, having been passed in open legislative session, and retaliation from the Japanese could come at any time, so he was careful. He changed routes twice, and several times entered shops only to exit through a back door onto some other street. By the time he met David Epstein at the alley door to his building, as planned, he knew no one had seen him.

"Thank you for bringing these men together," he said, when they were inside.

David guided him through long interior corridors past dozens of doors, each marked with a tiny scroll case, each little room housing a family. Most rooms lacked windows, so their doors sat open, and he nodded in polite acknowledgment to the families inside, as they passed. He knew that the Japanese authorities had labeled the Jews "stateless persons" and otherwise left them alone, but this was the first time he had actually seen how they were living. "Thank you for bringing me," he said, but David brushed it off. "You are the friend of Thomas," he said, in a tone which said that settled everything.

Inside, he found three men waiting beside David's wife and son, an older European man with a tonsure-shaped fringe of white hair, a dark-haired European in his prime, and an Asian man, also young and strong-looking.

David introduced Lin Ming, and the older man spoke. "I am Herr Ackerman. This is Amleto Vespa and An Gong Geun. Mr. An is the younger brother of An Jung Geun, the Korean revolutionary martyr. As for Mr. Vespa, he is from Rome, and I from Vienna, and we represent the Sword of David Society. We fought for you here in Hongkou in 'thirty-seven, did you know that? We sabotaged Japanese positions and equipment constantly, and planted bombs in their trucks."

Lin inclined his head. "It is known. No other foreign groups fought with us, and we thank you and respect you for that."

Now that it was recognized, Ackerman waved it away. "We are in your debt for what your government has proposed."

"I am only the messenger," Lin said. "And do not thank me yet, for we need your help. We need money, U.S. dollars and gold bars, at least fifty thousand worth, as fast as possible. Plans are already drawn up for barracks and kitchens and food delivery along the Burma Road."

Lin watched as they looked at one another, nodding, and saw that this huge sum was no problem for them. "There are dangers," he cautioned. "We need this money delivered in Chongqing—and the Japanese will do anything to stop us bringing one hundred thousand Jews to China. They know it will earn us sympathy from the West. They will put a high price on your heads. They are very smart."

An and Vespa exchanged hard, needle-sharp looks. "Not smart like we are," An said, speaking for the first time.

Vespa nodded. He was medium height, dark-haired, wiry, and looked like he had steel cables under his skin when he moved his jaw to speak. "Just tell us where you want that first package delivered."

Before Lin left, Margit took him aside. "Thomas said I could ask you this. Please—I hope it's all right. My cousin Hannah Rosen, in Vienna? She has two children? I am afraid they will die there—the Chinese Consul in Vienna is giving visas, but somehow she could not get one. If you can ask Dr. Kung—if there is anything he can do—"

"I will ask," he promised. Her eyes were brimming, and he took a clean lawn handkerchief from his pocket and gave it to her for a moment.

He left the meeting, still cautious, yet feeling grand too, because they were going to save lives, right under the noses of the Japanese and the Germans. Not a few lives. Many.

And now, Pearl. Life was on his side again.

He boarded a trolley, and found a seat near the rear door, the safest position since one could melt off the car and escape in case of trouble.

But he rode in ease, clacking along the streets, watching people step on and step off, his chest bursting with delight. *I am coming, Pearl. I am almost there.* He dismounted through the back door and walked to Stone Lion Lane.

He arrived to find the Pavilion closed, its gate locked, not entirely surprising at this hour of the morning. He knocked until the old gatekeeper opened a small metal window within the gate.

"Old Feng! Let me in."

"Mister Lin — is it you?"

"Who else? Open up. I want to see Pearl."

"No Pearl here."

"Of course she's here." Lin ignored the frightened pounding in his head. "Top of the stairs, third room on the right."

But Old Feng looked not too clear. Was his mind going dim?

"She wore that red satin jacket in the winter."

Feng's eyes came into focus. "With the fur trim, that one! Oh yes, Zhuli. Sweet girl. But she is gone now. More than two weeks."

The earth seemed to drop out from under Lin's feet, and the old man opened the metal door for him. Lin pushed past the madam, and the girls, who suddenly all looked strange to him, and took the stairs three at a leap to her room.

He opened the door, and everything had changed, the clothes, the smell. A woman lay in the bed beneath a man who turned his head and snarled, *"Ei? Sha jiba!"* Stupid dick!

Lin backed out, running. A minute later he was out the gate with an address in his hand, given him by the madam: the place to which Pearl had been sent. He did not even hear Old Feng's farewell.

The first part of his hope started to shrivel when he realized the address was in Zhabei, a Japanese area. As soon as he crossed Suzhou Creek on the bridge at the end of Carter Road, passing out of the Lonely Island and into enemy territory, he could feel the change. The Japanese were all around, women, children, families, elders, and men in uniform, everywhere. It no longer looked like a Chinese place.

He came almost to the green edge of the Cantonese cemetery before he found the address: a long, low, white featureless building, with a line of Japanese soldiers snaking out the front door and down the road as far as he could see.

It's where they keep women.

A roaring in his ears seemed to drown everything else out, as he pushed his way past the line, up to the desk. "Zhang Zhuli?" he said, over and over, and wrote out the characters, which were the same in Japanese *kanji*.

The man called someone else from the back, who took the name and checked it against a ledger. "Not here," he said, handing the card back.

"Please! She was sent here!"

The first man pulled out another, older book from beneath the desk, and the second man opened it and flipped through it grudgingly.

Just as he was reaching to close it, he saw her. "Here," he said, and turned the ledger to show her name. It had a line through it.

"Where is she now?" Lin croaked.

"Gone away," said the man, and closed the book.

Lin stepped back, reeling. *That means dead.* "Are you sure?" he said, his voice remote, as if it came from somewhere outside himself.

"Sure," the man barked back, glaring. Shanghai was a vassal city, and its whores, living or dead, were not his concern.

A ringing in Lin Ming's ears blocked everything as he pushed out, past the line of men waiting to get in. He walked blindly. But then a shout made him stop short, and he saw he had been about to walk into a cart being hauled by two men. In it were eight or ten girls' bodies stacked like so much cordwood. They had been stripped naked, since their clothes at least still had some value, and their bodies heaped up with a sheet of burlap over them. Their bare white feet stuck out, jouncing with every bump in the road. It was that pitiful sight, the jiggling pile of feet, that cracked his shell and brought out his first long howl of pain.

Thomas had come to know all the voices in his building. He followed the lives of its tenants, their anger and laughter, conversations, the hours at which they came and went. When they had visitors, he knew whether it was someone new or a person who had come to the door before.

So he was surprised one morning to hear a familiar voice outside. It was a man's voice, someone he knew, and he spoke Chinese in clear, bell-like tones that even Thomas, who still understood only a few words of the language, recognized as cultured. He jumped up and threw on his clothes, unable to place the voice. All he knew was that he never expected to hear it in this Frenchtown alley.

Downstairs, he was startled to discover H. H. Kung attracting a fast-growing circle of onlookers to his front door. The Premier was instantly recognizable.

"Dr. Kung," Thomas said. He had met the man several times at the Royal, in what felt like another lifetime. "Please come in."

"Thank you." Kung touched the rim of his bowler in the American style he had acquired in college and never lost. "But if you don't mind—" He sent a glance to the lane-mouth, thirty or forty meters down, where Thomas saw his car and driver waited. He understood.

In the car, Kung explained. "It is Lin Ming. He has been working for the Jewish Resettlement Plan, as you know. He arrived in Shanghai four days ago, conducted a very important secret meeting for the Plan, and then vanished."

"Here? In Shanghai?" the words shook as they came out, for people were getting killed all the time. And it made no sense that Lin would come to the city and not contact him.

Kung raised a hand. "He is alive, but not well. My people found him today. That's why I came to you."

"Where is he?"

"In the *Daitu*."

The Badlands. That was one word Thomas knew. "Was he kidnapped?"

"No." Kung sighed heavily. "Pearl is dead. His intended. It seems he has been out of his senses ever since he learned. I have sent three of my men in to talk to him, but no one can make him leave."

"Drinking?"

"No. Heroin. It's worse than opium." The car pulled up outside the iron gates to the Hollywood, its lights blinking even in the daytime, its grassy front lot already packed with dark, square-topped motorcars.

"He's in there?" Thomas said, dismayed at the sprawl of the complex, where it was rumored customers died every night of some excess or other.

"I cannot go in and reason with him," Kung said, his voice pinched with frustration. "You saw what happened when I stood outside your door for a few minutes. Please. Go and bring him out. He will listen to you."

As soon as he entered the lobby, Thomas felt he was inside some giant machine full of noise and flashing lights. The din of a mediocre orchestra came from behind one set of doors, and the strains of a competing cover band floated from another. Following Kung's instructions, he made his way to a small drug room at the end of the easternmost corridor, where he found Lin Ming on a narrow rattan daybed, one of four occupied by men who were similarly reclining, eyes half-lidded, apparently unaware of each other.

"Lin." He jostled his shoulder. "Time to go."

His friend's head turned so slowly he seemed to trail phosphorescence with his chin. He gazed out through pinpoint pupils, from a far distance. "Little Greene."

"Come on. Car's waiting."

Lin let Thomas lift him by the shoulders until he was sitting up, but when Thomas took hold of both his wrists and tried to pull him to his feet, he crumpled. "Can't go out there."

"Outside?"

"There." Lin's glass eyes went to the door, and Thomas understood. Lin was seeing the place where Pearl had been taken, the place Shanghai whispered about, where Chinese girls were used by a different Japanese soldier every fifteen minutes until they died.

"I know," he said, and gathered his friend into his arms. "But you're not going alone." And he maneuvered him to his feet.

In the car, they quickly realized the best thing to do was to take him to Thomas's room, where Thomas could stay by him as he came out of it. "He's going to be sick," Kung warned. "It lasts three days when they stop."

Once they got him up the ladder and on the bed, Kung tried to give Thomas a small roll of cash, for Lin's expenses, but Thomas refused. "I'm working."

"Please." Kung pushed the cash into his shirt pocket. "He is my friend too. At least you should have cash for his needs." He looked around the small, low-ceilinged room. "And, if I may." He pulled off another bill and stuck it in the same pocket. "Buy a night stool. He is going to need it."

"All right."

"When he comes out of it, tell him I am very, very sorry about Pearl—but also, tell him he did well. The package is on its way to Chongqing. Many people will live because of him—women and children."

"I'll tell him."

"Thank you, Little Greene. May I call you that? That's how he always refers to you."

"Sure. And you're welcome."

Dr. Kung picked up his bowler and turned nimbly, like a large cat, to retreat feet first down the ladder into the Huang family's room as if he did such a thing every day.

Thomas sat through the first night with Lin, and for the next few days traded off with Alonzo, who worked evenings. There was nothing they could do, really, except sponge him down and tell him it would end, calm him when he grew agitated, and cajole him into taking soup, even when it came back up again. By the fourth day he was sweaty and pale, but himself again.

"You've been sleeping on the floor?" Lin's exhausted eyes traveled to the stack of folded quilts and pillows against the wall. "I'm sorry. How many days?"

"Three. Feeling better?"

"No. You should have left me."

"Sure, pal. You think we're letting you go that easy?"

"Who's we?"

"Alonzo. Me. And Keiko, she made soup for you. Charles and Ernest wanted to come, but I didn't want them to see you like you were."

Lin turned his face to the wall. "I wish you had left me."

Thomas argued with him no more that day, but kept him there in his *tingzijian*, and made sure he spent time with Alonzo, too, so that he would never be alone. On many days, Alonzo brought Lin along to hear Thomas's performances with David, and so it was natural that he eventually brought his bass, too, and started sitting in. Alonzo did not read, so he just listened to a few bars and then joined in, creating bottom lines of surprising complexity and even a hint of swing.

When they came to sections that were naturally repetitive, like the call-and-response sequence between the violin and piano in the first movement of one of the Mozart violin sonatas, they would pause on the pattern, and run back and forth over it; once in a while, Thomas and Alonzo flatted the seventh or third, or hesitated extra long to give more syncopation than the composer intended. The audience always cheered at these digressions, but it was the smile from Lin Ming that they were looking for.

One night Thomas was invited to David and Margit's for dinner, and Lin did not want to go. Congested with a summer cold, he said he would stay in, and go to sleep early on the floor, where he insisted on making his bed these days, claiming beds were too soft for him anyway. "Go," he said. "I am all right."

So Thomas took a trolley downtown and walked north along the Bund and across the Garden Bridge—bowing to Japan—to Hongkou, the dense, ramshackle district that was now the refuge of the Jews. David had written out long, baroque instructions with arrows and diagrams, because his apartment did not have an address of its own, tucked as it was into a labyrinth of rooms subdivided from some larger building.

David saw him coming down the long, dim tunnel, and let out a cry of welcome, drawing him into a room with one tiny window, high up in the wall. It had been made cheerful with a checkered cloth on the table, and the good smell of stew rising from the stove.

Thomas hugged Margit and reached down to shake hands with Leo. "Aren't you two brave to bring a youngster so far," he said.

"Brave?" said David. "No, so lucky! You cannot imagine how hard it was to get out, how dangerous. But we are the lucky ones, yes. Mark the words. They mean to kill us, all of us."

"That's awful," said Thomas. "There are millions of you in Europe."

This brought Margit decisively to her feet. "Shall we eat?" she said, and soon was ladling hot stew into bowls, and cutting a freshly baked loaf into thick slices to pair with a crock of butter.

Before they ate, David lowered his eyes and intoned a prayer in Hebrew, of which Thomas understood only one word, *Yisroel*. Then he said, "That was a prayer to give thanks to God, that we are here, alive and free; that so many of us got out of Germany and Austria, and that here we have made new lives—thanks to friends like you."

Margit buttered a piece of bread for Leo. "To see us now, you cannot imagine how impossible it was to get out of Vienna. We were desperate. The Nazis would let us leave only if we had a visa for someplace else."

"And no country would give us one," said David.

"Then how did you get out?"

"God led us out," said David. "God sent us the Chinese Consul General in Vienna, a righteous man named Ho Feng-Shan."

More than a year earlier, on a brisk Saturday morning in March 1938, Ho Feng-Shan had left his home in Vienna on foot after breakfast, thinking he would walk to the consulate and check on the news about Germany. He had watched with concern as calls and demands flew back and forth between Germany and Austria, everything stalled, nothing certain, lines forming at the banks because everyone wanted their money out. Dr. Kung had cabled him the day before, through back channels to be safe, advising him that a Nazi takeover of Austria appeared imminent, but was expected to be peaceful. At the office, he could find out more, and as it was a fine late winter day, he needed no more than his overcoat and fedora for the walk.

As he came close to the wide, tree-lined boulevard, he heard truck engines, a crowd, marching feet. He thought he had misheard until he turned a corner and saw that the boulevard was thick with lines of marching troops. No mistake — the Germans were entering Vienna.

He stopped among the crowds who had gathered eight or ten deep behind the barricades, some of them cheering and extending their arms in the Nazi salute. Fools, he thought. He craned this way and that, and saw only the soldiers, six abreast, hundreds beyond count. His heart sank.

"Consul Ho," said a child's voice, and he turned to look.

"Lord have mercy," he exclaimed, one of the first English expressions he had learned as a child from the Norwegians who had schooled him, and which still erupted from him fairly regularly.

It was Lilith-Sylvia Doron. He knew her family; twice he had visited their home for dinner. "What are you doing out here by yourself, Sylvia?"

"I was with some girls from my class. I got separated." She looked ready to cry, and with good reason, he thought. The Doron family was Jewish, and this parade was a terrifying show of Nazi force.

She was shaking. He slipped his hand through hers. "Come," he said. "I take you home."

He sensibly led her away from the military marchers and the crowds shouting *Sieg Heil,* and down quieter streets also lined with bare-limbed trees, the houses stern and silent with their curtains drawn. Consul Ho could feel the eyes on him as he walked the girl down the street.

When he rang her parents' doorbell and they opened up, they started to cry.

"Now, come," he said reasonably, "she's safe and sound. If you are really frightened, I will stay a little while. I am a diplomat! I am the Consul General. No one will harm you while I am here."

And with that he sat down in the parlor, not far from the welcoming fire, and chatted with Sylvia, and her brother, Karl, and their parents. It was not until evening that Herr and Frau Doron said they felt safe, and that it would be all right if he went home. "Remember," he said before he left. "We are friends. Any problem, come to me."

In the months that followed, actions against Jews became frequent and public. He saw SS men waiting outside synagogues, where they grabbed Jewish men emerging from services, shoved them into trucks, and then forced them to use their prayer shawls to scrub the urinals in the SS barracks. Ho Feng-Shan found it childish and hateful.

In midsummer, people started lining up at the Chinese Consulate. Soon the line stretched all the way down the driveway. People stood there for hours.

Jews.

"Shenmo shi?" he hissed to Guomei, his secretary, when he came in. What is it?

"Visas," she said. "They want visas."

"What do you mean? What sort of visas?"

She shrugged.

He went in his office with its striped wallpaper and reassuringly heavy desk, thinking maybe he could shut out the noise and the line of people. He knew that the Nazis would not let Jews out of the country unless they had a visa to enter someplace else, and since no country would take them, they were trapped.

He saw he had left the door half-open, and when he got up to close it, he heard a familiar voice, asking for him, being told to wait, asking again.

He put his head out. "Sylvia?"

"Consul Ho!" She broke away from Guomei and ran toward him.

"What are you doing here?"

"You have to help! You said to come to you, remember—"

"Sit down, child," he said kindly, and slipped into Chinese to ask the secretary to bring tea. "It's clear you've had a fright. Now." He fixed his eyes on her. He was known for his serene, calming gaze. Maybe it was because he himself was filled with trust, for had not life always been good to him, despite such difficult beginnings? Had not God always treated him kindly? So he was kind in return. "Tell me what's happened."

"They arrested Karl!"

"What! Where is he?"

"They put him on a train to Dachau."

Dachau. Ho Feng-Shan felt the chill in his intestines.

"They won't let him out unless he has a visa to go somewhere else. Can you give him one for Shanghai? Please!"

He felt his brows knit. "The Chinese Consulate does not issue any visas for Shanghai," he said. "You do not need a visa to go there. No one does. There is no such thing as a Shanghai visa."

Tears streamed down her face. He realized she would always be a child to him, even though she stood before him now on the edge of growing up. He would do anything to help her.

His mind ranged over Karl's case. It was true that no one needed a visa or even any form of identification to enter Shanghai. All arrivals were welcome, no matter where they came from or how they got there.

"Give him one anyway," she said through her tears.

"We can certainly try, no? Guomei!" he called imperiously. "Bring me a visa form." And then, to her answering stream of Chinese, he said, "How would I know? Bring whatever you think a visa form should look like."

Twenty minutes later they had a reasonable facsimile of a visa form, and an official-looking series of stamps to make it seem authentic. "You see?" said Ho. "The very first Shanghai visa." He signed with a flourish, and then dictated a stern letter to the Commandant at Dachau advising him to release Karl Doron immediately so that he could leave Austria under this visa, with his entire family included. Etcetera. In the name of the Republic of China. Consul General. And so on.

To his intense embarrassment, Sylvia clung to his arm and sobbed, choked with gratitude, and he dried her tears and scolded her a little, telling her to be strong. "Take care of Karl's envelope. Here is another visa for your family, just in case. Put them inside your jacket. Yes, that's a good girl. Now, Sylvia — don't wait. Pack quickly and get out, just as soon as you get Karl back again. *Hurry*."

"Yes," she said. "Thank you." She moved to the door.

"And Sylvia? God be with you and your family." He meant it. He felt sure the Lutherans would have wanted him to help.

He watched from the tall window, half-hidden behind its heavy velvet curtain, as she ran out the front door and pushed past the line of people winding out toward the gate. He sensed a murmur go through the crowd at her appearance, a frisson of hope.

"Guomei?" he called over his shoulder. "About that visa form." He followed the line with his eyes, estimating the numbers. "I want you to produce as many as you can. Hire an assistant. We're going to need one hundred blank forms, right away. Another hundred by the end of the day Wednesday."

"You could just turn them away," she said.

"No," he said, without explanation. Ho Feng-Shan had been privileged to see God's goodness; he could not expect everybody to understand.

He had been born of peasant stock. Though he was given the optimistic name Feng-Shan, meaning a phoenix that rises from the mountain, in truth he was the poorest of the poor. His father died when he was seven and his mother could no longer care for him. She gave him to the Norwegian Lutheran Mission over his screaming protests, asking of them only that they feed him. They did that and more, educating him in English and in their ways. He believed in God and Christ, after his years with them. They did not have to explain it to him, he saw it; they redeemed him. Raised him and nurtured him and handed him an education, all in the name of doing God's work. Now, as a diplomat, he did the same for others.

And so it was that Ho Feng-Shan said *yes* to the person at the head of the line, the one after that, and the one after that. He sat at his desk all day, signing visas until his hand ached. Each visa was good for a whole family — why not, they were his visas, he was inventing them. One paper per family was more economical, and yet still the line stretched every day, as far as he could see. How many Jews could there be in Vienna? Yes, you're welcome, good luck, *bon voyage,* now please step aside so the next person can come in.

The Ambassador in Berlin heard what he was doing and excoriated Consul Ho for his impudence. He ordered him to stop at once. The Consul put the angry cables in a drawer and ignored them.

Then he arrived in the morning to find Guomei reading even more cables, her sensible skirt clinging to the swell of her hips, her red lips parted in fear. "He says stop or you'll be arrested," she said. For the first time, she looked scared.

"I will not stop," Ho said calmly. "They will have to drag me away." He sat. "You have a fresh stack of forms? Ah, good. Thank you. Now send the first one in."

That summer David watched Margit playing with Leo in their locked room, wondering how long she could keep him inside where it was safe. It was no life for a small boy. He agonized constantly about whether they should leave, and how to get them out, even though he had nowhere for them to go. His parents were dead. Her parents were still here in Vienna, old and infirm. They refused to leave, but urged David to get Margit and Leo out. Her dear cousin Hannah was also desperate to get out with her husband and children.

David and Margit spent hours in bed, planning it out: each would take no more than one small valise, with a third bag devoted to things for Leo. Margit packed the boy's hand-crocheted blankets and miniature satin-trimmed nightshirts, while David lay awake long after she and Leo were asleep and blinked painfully at the ceiling, trying to figure out how it could be done. He had enough money for steerage, now euphemistically called Tourist Class, and a little extra; they would need every last schilling to get started in their new land, wherever that was.

And therein lay the trouble, for no land would take them. He had been to almost every embassy and consulate in Vienna. *Think. Find a way.* He lay for a long time and no answer came to him, except that he must venture out again the next day, to wait in another line.

It was then, standing in line at the Mexican Embassy, that he heard Ho Feng-Shan at the Chinese Consulate was making up phony visas for a free port that required none, and giving them out as fast as he could write them. David left the Mexico line and ran to the Chinese Consulate, arriving there at midday with nothing but his violin case, which he carried everywhere with him. After one look at the line, he considered going home first to get food, but he saw people coming from all directions, hurrying to the queue, joining it, tailing it longer and longer, so he stepped in quickly and took his place, just inside the gate, before the line spilled out of the consulate grounds.

There followed a long day and cold night, one in which he could not dare to sleep, or even sit on the ground for a few minutes, lest he drift off and lose his place, his violin, or both. Instead he stayed upright, stamping, moving, clapping through the hours. He knew Margit would be beside herself with worry, but there was nothing he could do about that; now, with many hundreds in line behind him, he would not leave.

Around eight the next morning, as he stood bleary-eyed, a shiver of excitement swept up the long snake-coil of people stretching down the block: Ho Feng-Shan was coming. And David yawned and popped his ears and then he could hear it too, the approaching automobile.

As it turned in to the long driveway, the square black vehicle with silver running boards was instantly surrounded by people waving, tapping the windows, calling out to the mild-faced Asian man in the back seat. The car ground to a stop, idling, spitting exhaust. The force of the crowd pushed David right up to the car, against the window. He saw that the man in the back kept a serene gaze, despite the chaos outside the car. *Be patient. I will take care of you, all of you.*

Ho Feng-Shan must have sensed him there, because he turned at that moment and met David's eyes. They joined in a bubble of shared silence amid the din of shouts and pleas and cries.

Wordlessly, David raised his violin case to display it through the window. *This is who I am. Help me.*

To his amazement, the Consul on the other side of the glass took a paper from a stack on the seat beside him, signed it, and then cranked the window open a few inches to thrust it out.

David stared, dumbfounded, frozen.

The Consul gave the paper a shake. *Take it.*

So David did, and at that moment the crowd parted in front of the vehicle and the driver inched forward. David looked at the paper. It was a family visa for Shanghai, stamped, signed, the ink still wet, only one line left blank, the one where he would write their names, David and Margit Epstein and Leo. They would sail right away, get on a ship out of Genoa, and trust God to protect them at sea.

Our freedom our freedom our freedom. He tucked the precious paper inside his shirt and pressed his violin case against it all the way home. As soon as he inserted his key in the door, he heard her glad shriek, and his heart twisted again at the thought of all she had suffered through the night, not knowing what had happened, imagining every possible reason why he'd failed to come home — the door creaked open to her face, swollen with tears, happy now, praising God, and then going mute at something too good to be true, a dream fulfilled from nowhere, out of the air.

"Pack, *Liebchen*. We are going to Shanghai." He threw the bolt behind him, pressed the visa into her hands, and fell exhausted, shoes, suspenders and all, across the bed.

She tucked a pillow under his head, covered him with their big woolen wedding blanket, and let him sleep while she dried her tears and prayed her thanks to God.

A humble silence fell over the little group around the table. David's and Margit's eyes were locked in gratitude, while Leo slept in his mother's lap. All of them felt the grace of God, suspended in the room with the last words of the story. "I too am grateful to Consul Ho," Thomas said at last. "That you are here, well and healthy."

At this Margit got up, handed Leo to David, and went out with a short excuse, as if going to use the alley outhouse, except that as she brushed past him to the door, Thomas saw her eyes welling.

"It's her cousin Hannah," David said softly after she was gone. "We write letter after letter, and there is never any reply. No news from anyone in Vienna. The children are just a little older than Leo. We don't know if they are alive or dead." He looked down at his own son, safe in his trembling arms, and held him tighter.

"I'm so sorry," Thomas said. And they sat together in silence until Margit came back, and he thanked them, and embraced them from the deeper well of all they had told him.

In the *tingzijian* he found the light on and Lin awake, leaning against the wall in the corner where he had made his pallet. Before Thomas could even speak, he looked up and said, "I finally reached Duke Kung. He is a busy man."

"Clearly."

"But he left a meeting to talk to me."

"He was worried. He cares about you."

"I don't know why."

"Stop talking like that. Look at all you do. You brought jazz here. You got everyone dancing."

"You did, you and your men, just like Buck Clayton and Teddy Weatherford before you. Not me. But that's finished now. Night in Shanghai is dead."

"We're not, and we are still with you, in case you hadn't noticed. So is Kung. He seems to think of you as a son."

"No surprise, I guess. It's as clear as looking into water that I needed another father." It was the first spark of the old, wry Lin that Thomas had seen since the day they pulled him out of the Hollywood.

Encouraged, he lowered himself to the floor beside his friend, leveling their eyes. "All of us you brought here — we never had this before. I'm not talking about the money. *Respect*. I would say it's something true of every musician you brought here, that he yearned for that all his life. And this is the one place we all found it, because of you. You saved us that way. Even when we go back to America, back to the bottom, we'll know."

Lin nodded.

"And now, you are helping the Jews — including Margit's cousin —"

"Hope can be brutal," Lin cut in. "I advise you, don't hope. Her cousin has not been heard from in too long."

"I know," Thomas said, the sight of Margit's tears still burned into his mind. "But with the Resettlement Plan, you will save so many others. That's why you must regain your strength. A hundred thousand."

"If it works," Lin said dully.

"If it works."

"Then why could I not save one?" Lin whispered, and tears he had held in through all these days rose to his eyes and spilled out. "Why did I not come one month sooner?"

"I know," Thomas said quietly, a hand on his arm. "It's lousy."
And it is the blues, he thought, a realm he finally understood. They sat
together in silence, as only old friends can, until past midnight.

In October of that year, Song was still returning to Baoding Village
every three weeks, bringing new workbooks for the girls and teaching them new characters. Plum Blossom, the group's ringleader,
learned the fastest, and by the time autumn's chill had descended, she
had composed a short letter to Song, proudly sent down the mountain
on a truck hauling casks of vinegar. The phrasing was off and some
of the characters incorrect, but it brought Song perhaps her purest
single moment of happiness since she came north. She expressed
her happiness and pride in large, clear characters and gave the letter
back to the vinegar seller to carry to Baoding, just as a messenger approached her. She was requested at a meeting.

She found herself delivered to a set of steps that zigzagged steeply
up the canyon wall — a canyon she had never been in before, where
higher-level cadres worked. She entered a large cave outfitted as a
meeting room, with a low table surrounded by men in squared-off
chairs, and gas lamps flickering from ledges on the walls. A Tartar
rug covered the floor.

"Interpreter Song," said the oldest man present, "I am Comrade
Feng." He waved her to a seat and continued. "We have news from
our spies in Manchuria."

Her eyes widened. Secrets, like power, had seemed so far from her
in Yan'an.

"The Japanese have learned that the Nationalists have a plan to
resettle Jews in Yunnan, and they have devised their own plan. A
counter-plan they call the Fugu Plan."

"For Jews?" she said, trying to follow.

"Yes. They want the sympathy of the West for themselves, not for
China. So they are proposing to move the more than twenty thousand Jews now in Shanghai up to Manchuria."

"What? Why?" She could not imagine why Shanghai's Jews would want to go to that frozen tundra, when they had already built a successful community in Shanghai.

"They *say* it is to let them farm. A lie. According to our agents, they want them as a human buffer between themselves and hostile Chinese forces. They will exploit them. The problem is that they are going to try to introduce this Fugu Plan as a humanitarian act, so the West will support them in their conquest of China."

"But how are they saving anyone? These people are already safe in Shanghai."

"Exactly. We support the Chinese plan, even though it comes from the Nationalists. Bringing in one hundred thousand more people — to Yunnan."

She nodded agreement. Ordinarily she would not expect the Party to back any Nationalist idea, but this Jewish Resettlement Plan was different.

"Here is where you are needed. We have learned that the Japanese are about to go to all the newspapers and magazines in Shanghai about this Fugu Plan, with a lot of big lies to get the Jewish refugees to accept it and move up there. We understand you knew foreign people in the past in Shanghai — no, no," said Comrade Feng, "do not be frightened, it's all right — and that you may know them still. Yes? Is it so? Then we need you to go there immediately, do whatever must be done to make the right contacts, and make sure Japan's lies are not published. We cannot let the Jews be misled about this Fugu Plan."

She soared inside. Shanghai! And Thomas. "Yes, Comrade. Of course." Her mind raced with possibilities. "You wish to influence the press against the Fugu Plan as well?"

He gave a slight but discernible nod of approval. "If it is possible to plant our view of the matter in the press, even better."

Three days later, having learned Thomas was to play that afternoon at the Central Hotel, she stood waiting in front, on Canton

Road, scanning the crowds in every direction. He was due to appear at two thirty with a violinist, a Jew of all lucky things, whom she had just met inside. Now she waited, anxious, praying she would see joy on his face when he recognized her.

As Song watched, Thomas was approaching the intersection with Lin Ming beside him. He had been listening to Lin tell him about the months he had worked for Duke Kung. "I went looking for my mother, you know." They waited at the intersection for the flood of rickshaws and carts and motorcars to cease so they could cross. "Look," Lin interrupted himself, "old number-three redhead is about to change."

The red-turbaned Sikh on the pedestal stopped the traffic in front of them with wide-swinging hand signals, and they moved out with the flood of pedestrians and vehicles that had clotted up behind them as they waited. "So I went to Jiangsu, looking for her," Lin said, "but she is gone from this world. Old Du lives, but I am finished with him. All I have left is my friends, all of you—and though I do not know exactly where she is, somewhere I also have—"

Lin Ming stood a second in frozen silence before he stepped up on the sidewalk, "—Song Yuhua," he finished.

Because there she was, waiting for them in front of the hotel, her smile so wide it lit the sidewalk. Lin reached her first, stepping quickly into her embrace, and then she turned to Thomas.

As they embraced he said, "How did you learn where I would be?"

She laughed. "*Ye Shanghai* has not been gone for so very long— your name is still known. All I had to do was ask where Thomas Greene was playing, and in two turns of the head I had the answer. As for him"—she smiled at Lin—"I was hoping you might have news of his doings. It was beyond my hope that you would bring him with you."

Thomas felt a stab of sadness, for soon she would hear of Pearl's fate, and Lin's fall. Right now, however, he was late. "The three of us have so much to say, but you must forgive me — my partner and I were supposed to begin playing a few minutes ago. I finish at seven. Could we all meet after that, for dinner?"

"Wonderful," she said, before Lin could speak. "What about De Xing Guan, at the bottom of Dong Men Lu, just off the Bund? It's not far from here."

"All right," said Thomas, and Lin acquiesced too, as pedestrians flowed around them, old ladies in padded jackets, young women with sleek hair, sunburned country people straining under shoulder poles.

"So good to be back," Song said, and sent Thomas a beam of excitement before she took Lin's arm and walked away down the street. Thomas watched from the hotel entrance as Lin stopped her, and spoke, and she cried out and threw her arms around him. So he had told her.

Thomas was so keyed up that day that he forgot where he was several times, and came crashing down in the kind of discord that could not be passed off as creative interpretation. David grinned at him, knowing the reason, as she had come in asking for him.

"I knew it was her," David said. "So beautiful. I see also it is you that she wants to see. She does not expect your Mr. Lin. He is your rival?"

"No, he is her foster brother."

"Ah," said David. "Then you will see her later, and all will be well."

Thomas laughed at this simple forecast, and yet he was able to calm his flutters and play after that, keeping his eyes on the music. But never in all his months with David had he packed up his scores and left as quickly as he did that evening.

Soon he was on Dongmen Road, passing shop after shop where the merchants had folded back their shutters so the whole establishment lay open to the street, lit up now for the evening with tasseled lanterns of wood and painted glass. Shoppers laughed and talked as they browsed each proprietor's goods: pyramids of fruits and bins of autumn vegetables, clothing hanging in rows from rafters, stacked-up enamel bowls and spittoons.

At the bottom of the street, facing the water, he found the restaurant and realized it was the same one in which Lin Ming had given him advice about Anya a lifetime ago; he remembered the rich seafood soup as he climbed the worn-down stone stairs to the second floor. Lin and Song were already there, at a table by the window. Below them, the river cacophony of Asia was subdued, as it had been in the two years since Japan invaded. The merchant vessels, tramp steamers, winged junks, barges, and foreign liners had come back to ply the river, but lights were trimmed and horns silenced. The exuberance was gone.

Yet in front of him now was Song, smiling, more lovely than he had ever seen her. Her eyes shone with humor and self-assurance, and her every move was fluid. Seeing her now, he could barely remember the tight, stiffly brocaded *qipao* dresses Du had made her wear. Her skin had darkened in the sun, and even here in the city, she wore the blue tunic and black trousers of a country woman, yet she was radiant.

Lin was the opposite, gray with sorrow, his constant companion these days. He was bent over the table, studying the *bai jiu* bottle and then measuring out the fiery liquor into three tiny cups. They drank to each other, and then she told them what she had come to do.

"But that is easy," Lin said with a wave of his hand. "I will take you to the Sword of David Society." They were the ones who had dispatched An Gong Geun and Amleto Vespa to Chongqing with the money; they would spread the truth about the Fugu Plan throughout Hongkou.

"And what about Mr. Pao, the editor of the *Shanghai Daily* who I went to see?" Thomas said. "He might like to write an article about the Fugu Plan."

"You are right," Lin agreed. "Don't worry, Sister. Soon everyone in Shanghai will know the facts."

"Thank you." They all drank.

Lin became morose again. "It seems so long ago, *Ye Shanghai*."

"Another world," said Thomas, remembering the three-month battle, stealing glances at Song. Yes.

"The night is gone," Lin complained. "The music. I walked all over last night, even through the *Daitu*, the Badlands — what a joke."

The waiter brought a tureen of the fish soup, which sat between them. Lin shook his head. "We may be here again, the three of us, but this time we make the minor chord." He drained his cup and refilled it. He had forgotten to make a toast.

Song met Thomas's eyes. "Brother," she said, half rising to ladle out the fragrant soup. "Eat something. You've had a terrible loss."

"You need time," Thomas said.

"No one has time now," Lin said, tipping up his cup. "The war has eaten our lives. Though we try to escape it." He poured again.

"Come on," Song said to Lin, again meeting Thomas's eyes. She slid Lin's soup bowl a little closer. "The broth will restore you, the fish, the scallops and sea cucumber, tofu and mustard greens — such a Shanghai taste."

Lin poured more *bai jiu*. "You know what is Shanghai taste to me? The shrimp dumpling and noodle peddler."

"Oh yes," Song agreed.

"He would come through our neighborhood with his own little kitchen on shoulder poles. He had his own song. You always knew when he was coming, for no one else had just that melody. All gone."

"Not gone," she objected. "These things will return in their time. Soon we start a new decade, 1940, and before you know it, the sour plums of late spring will be here, the ones sold on the street with a frosting of sugar." To Thomas she added, "When they appear, it is the start of *huang mei tian*, the yellow plum rainy season."

"Remember the hot roasted ginkgo nuts?" Lin cut in. "The vendor comes through calling — let me think — 'Hand-burning hot ginkgo nuts! Each one is popped, each one is big!'" Putting the chant in English brought at least a small lift to the corner of his mouth.

"Shanghai still lives," Song assured him.

Thomas said, "I agree."

And at last Lin pulled his bowl and spoon closer and began to eat. But after a minute he reached for the wine again and refilled his cup, shaking the last drops out of the small crock. "And the Resettlement Plan," he said morosely. "What if Chiang Kai-shek cuts it off?"

"Why would he?" said Song. "It's as fine an idea as anyone ever had. Even my side thinks so."

"The Germans will hate it. And Chiang wants to please them. Why, he would lick Hitler's running sores if he could get close enough!"

"Niu bi hong hong," Song said, meaning the ox vagina was steaming red, a way of saying he exaggerated.

Lin gave her a laugh as he pushed back and got to his feet, for this was the kind of language she would never have used before. "You've grown up, *Meimei,*" he said, and then he steadied himself against the tabletop and squared them both in the eye. "Don't make my mistake. An inch of gold cannot buy an inch of time. You could die first, both of you." Thomas reached for her hand under the table, humbled by love, while Lin closed his eyes and rocked on his heels, as if trying to remember something else he had wanted to say to them. He gave up, and dropped his voice to a mumble. "I should go."

But then he remembered. "Oh. I know. There's one more thing I miss. The vendor with the new corn, those tender baby kernels — you know — who comes down the lane singing, 'Pearl-grained corn! Pearl-grained corn!'" He shook his head. "Gone."

"It is past the time for corn," Song said.

"I told you, no more time." He turned for the door. A low, sustained boat horn sounded from the river below.

"We'll see you home," Thomas said.

But Lin raised a hand to wave him off. "I'm all right. See you tomorrow. We will go to Hongkou about your business, Song."

"And I'll call on that newspaper editor," said Thomas.

With that, Lin settled his hat on his head with tipsy dignity, stepped out of the dining room, and vanished down the stone staircase.

Her hand trailed up Thomas's leg, which made him tremble. "I know I come and go with no warning," she said. "I never know when they will send me here. It's unfair. I'm sorry. Sometimes I wonder if it is wrong, what I feel with you." Her voice was very soft. "But if you still want, I have a room in a hostel, and—"

"Let's go," he said brusquely.

Much later she lay next to him, watching him sleep. She looked at his hand with love, so skilled, the exquisite fingers now thrown carelessly across her leg, and held her own hand next to it, smaller, paler, crude by comparison. Through his hands he was able to pour all he knew and felt, on the piano, on her body, on the map of her life. She was his, and every time she came back to him, she knew it again.

But. Her head was heavy with uncertainty, and she laid it down next to his on the pillow.

She had once again left the diamonds in Xi'an.

The next day at noon, Thomas came back to the *tingzijian* to change his clothes, and found Lin Ming frantically dressing.

"Where's Song?" Lin said.

"She went down the street to the *laohuzao*." Tiger stove shops, the name used for the local bathhouses, was in his tiny vocabulary, even though he patronized them only when he could afford it, making do in leaner times with a bowl and pitcher. "Half an hour is all she needs. Then she wants us all to have lunch at Sun Ya and—" He stopped short as he saw Lin was stuffing all his belongings into a cloth sack. "What are you doing?"

"Leaving."

"Leaving Shanghai?"

"Leaving China." He pulled the bag's drawstring tight with a sick finality. "The Plan is dead. Hitler threatened Chiang Kai-shek, and Chiang crumpled. A hundred thousand doomed, just like that. They will die."

"And their children."

Lin straightened up, silent.

"But — leave China?"

"I'm next on the list. Kung just cabled me."

"What list?"

"The men I sent out from Shanghai, An and Vespa? With the dollars and the gold bars? Dead, both of them. Intercepted. The Japs want everyone dead who was involved in this."

"What about people here in Shanghai?" Thomas heard his voice rise in fear. "Could An and Vespa have talked?"

"No. They were professionals. Moreover, I heard they were killed by snipers. I know what you are thinking — David and his family. Believe me, if the Japanese knew their names, they would already be dead. It turns out An and Vespa died months ago, almost as soon as they arrived in Chongqing. The Epsteins are safe."

"Then perhaps you —"

"No." Lin's face was stretched tight over his cheekbones with worry, and for a moment he looked like his father. "I worked on the Plan for two months. Everybody in Tengchong County knows who I am."

"I suppose also, with all the press in the last few days . . ."

Their eyes met, and a spark of satisfaction jumped between them. Thomas had called on Mr. Pao, and Lin had approached the Chinese-language newspapers and magazines, which resulted in an avalanche of Fugu Plan exposés. Not a single Jew would now be willing to leave Shanghai for Japanese Manchuria.

Thomas exhaled. "Where will you go?"

"Hong Kong."

"*Today?*" It was usually impossible to buy anything on the day of departure except first-class tickets, and sometimes not even those.

"Kung went through my father. The old man still owns the Da Da shipping line. They serve the Subei ports, not Hong Kong, but I have a transfer from Haimen."

"When do you leave?"

"One hour." Lin stuck out his hand, a last American gesture.

Thomas ignored it and embraced him instead. "I'll walk with you."

"No. You attract attention."

Thomas tried to swallow but his mouth was too dry. He was losing his bedrock. "Are you coming back?"

"Naturally. This is my home! But as long as the brown dwarf bandits are here, I cannot visit except in secret. Remember that."

Thomas drew an X over his heart. "What about your sister?"

"I will stop at the *laohuzao*."

They stood in silence for a moment at the top of the ladder. "Thank you," said Lin.

"Don't even start," said Thomas, which made Lin laugh.

"All right," said Lin, "Then say good-bye in Chinese. *Zai jian*. Means, see you again."

"See you again," Thomas managed, as he watched his friend go down the ladder.

Admiral Morioka was writing a top-secret cable in his office at Naval Headquarters when an aide tapped on the door and announced Major General Shibatei Yoshieki.

Quickly Morioka secreted the cable in a drawer. Yoshieki was chief of espionage at Japanese Army Headquarters, a man who knew China well — he had been born here — but some matters were still between Morioka and Tokyo, and not for his eyes.

No sooner had the aide clicked the door shut behind him than Yoshieki burst out, "It's dead. They killed the Fugu Plan."

"Pressure from the Western powers?" said Morioka. He had been bracing for diplomatic trouble ever since the Shanghai press came out with attacks on the plan.

Yoshieki nodded. "How did the press even get the details of the plan?" he said.

"Do not waste any time on that." Morioka fingered the knob on his desk drawer, knowing that today's secret cables, concerning the terms of the new military alliance with Germany, were infinitely more important than this Fugu Plan — which he had disliked anyway. The Jews in Shanghai were his, and he wanted them left alone. Even if the Nazis were now his allies. "If you will excuse me?"

Yoshieki bowed, clicked his heels, and left.

9

NINETEEN FORTY AND forty-one passed, two years that were hard on Anya Petrova. The Dark World was an occupied city, which no longer attracted international men looking for a sweetheart on whom to spend money the way it once did. The first few years after the Japanese takeover in the fall of '37 had not been so bad, but once all Europe was at war, it seemed the only people in Shanghai with money to spend were Japanese.

In the summer of 1941 she and her friend Li Lan began seeing high-placed Japanese, in secret, since anyone consorting with the conquerors was automatically in danger. They traveled separately to the Japanese sector in Zhabei and met their clients in private spaces, never entering or leaving with them. But the men, military officers, were polite, certainly better than the Nazis, who had been making their presence felt in Shanghai for many months. Next to them, her Japanese escorts seemed desirable.

Anya had her opinions, but her friend Li Lan had a whole different range of motivations—and she had to be twice as careful as Anya, since she slept with Japanese men for another, much riskier reason: she worked for the resistance.

On November 15, 1941, at a Zhabei jazz club, the two of them sat on the floor, on the tatami mats favored by the invaders. Their private room was separated from the club by a sliding rice-paper wall, which kept out prying eyes but not the strains of the jazz quintet from Osaka. Li Lan's date was Major General Shibatei Yoshieki, the Japanese Army's spy chief. He had brought along the top-ranking Japanese in Shanghai, Admiral Tadashi Morioka. Yoshieki knew Morioka loved jazz, so he booked this restaurant and asked Li Lan to bring along the gray-eyed, black-haired Anya as a companion for his friend.

Morioka seemed to have scant interest in her, although he listened intently to the music. He mostly spoke to Yoshieki in Japanese, leaving Anya out.

But not Li Lan. Her Japanese was fluent. Her grandmother was Japanese, and she had grown up in the north, speaking the language at home, a fact she concealed with great care. If Yoshieki and Morioka had any idea she understood them and had come here to mentally record every word they exchanged, they would see her put to death at once. Anya accordingly sparkled with just enough womanly conversation to cover her friend and allow her to follow their discussion, which rose in a heated crescendo before leveling off.

So when Li Lan touched her leg lightly under the table and said, in English, "Please excuse us to restroom," Anya knew she wanted to say something about the intense volley of Japanese they had just heard. Yoshieki and Morioka barely noticed their rise from the table.

The Chinese girl closed the bathroom door and leaned close. "They were talking about someone you were with. Thomas Greene. Remember? It's him, isn't it?"

"What?" Anya knew he was still in Shanghai, playing with a Jewish violinist. "Why would they speak of him?"

Li Lan moved right up to her ear and dropped her voice further. "Something is about to happen. It is something Morioka has known about for a while, and Yoshieki just found out, that is why they were talking. I don't know what it is, but it is big, and very bad for Americans. Yoshieki asked Morioka if he was going to warn Thomas

Greene before it was too late. Morioka became angry at him, and said of course not, the operation is top secret."

Anya's mouth opened in surprise. She kept her voice as soft as Li Lan's. "Could they possibly be planning to attack the International Settlement? But then America would retaliate—"

"I don't know what they are preparing," said Li Lan. "Only that it's about Americans. So if you can find a safe way, and you want him to live, you had better tell him."

Anya squeezed her hand in thanks. They shared a deep breath, re-applied their lipstick, retraced their steps to the sliding screen, and sat again, smiling.

That year, Alonzo and Keiko decided to host an American-style Thanksgiving in their flat, and Thomas went to Hongkou to invite the Epstein family, and explain the holiday.

"You came so far in this war, started life over in a new land," he said. "It's something like it was for those first settlers who arrived in America. To survive was their victory; it was enough. They might have starved, but the Indians helped them. So at the harvest they had food, and everyone sat down together, and gave thanks. And that's why we eat together on this holiday."

"So this is your people coming to America," David said.

"Yes," said Thomas.

"But you were slaves, is it not?"

"Well, it's about the other people, I suppose. But it doesn't matter, does it? Because we are all in Shanghai now, and you three have your freedom." His gaze gathered in David and Margit and Leo, now a solemn boy of five. "So please, come to Thanksgiving."

They did come, and when they first climbed the stairs and walked into Alonzo's apartment, they were made speechless, not by the din-ing table, which was loaded with all Keiko's best dishes and a whole fragrant roast chicken, that being as close as they could come to a turkey, but by the large windows, framed with curtains, showing all the lights in the houses up and down the lane. To the Epsteins, after years in their little room, the simple glass panes were a fairyland of light. They stood there gazing out, laughing and exclaiming in their own language, which pleased Thomas.

He had played with David all through 1940 and 1941, and had long since accepted the Viennese as his brother. He still worried about the family's safety, though so far the only restriction the Japanese had placed on the Jews was to require all the refugees — they now numbered more than 25,000 — to live in Hongkou, where almost all of them were living anyway. The Nazis tried to organize a boycott of businesses employing Jews, but no one paid much attention to it, and if, in the end, a few Aryans ceased to patronize these companies, their absence was hardly felt. Shanghai's Jews were surviving, even thriving. At the same time, their relatives back in Europe were going silent, their letters suddenly ceasing. If the long arm of Berlin managed to reach Shanghai, Thomas knew the same thing would happen here.

But now he had more immediate worries — Anya's warning.

He had not seen her in over two years, when she fell into step beside him the evening before, as he left the Majestic Hotel. "Anya?"

"Let us walk like old friends. Do not make a fuss." And she dropped her voice, and told him what she had learned.

"And you don't know what Japan is going to do?"

"No. Only that the Americans are in danger. They argued about Morioka warning you."

"I can see the buildup, all of us can. But no one knows what it means."

"It means you should leave," she said.

"I wish I could." He took her hand as they walked, a simple gesture from the past, instantly retrieved. "I can't. I don't have the fare. And my friends don't either, and I can't leave them anyway." He stayed for Song too, but he would not mention that now.

"I understand." That was all she said, and when they reached the next intersection, she turned away, as if walking next to him had been a random accident.

He remembered how he had taken a few steps forward through the crowd before he realized Anya had vanished. Now, standing by the window before Thanksgiving dinner, he sent gratitude to her too, since she had taken a risk to warn him. Never mind that he could not act on it.

When the feast was laid out, they pulled their chairs around the table, linked hands for a prayer, and began the happy passing of platters.

In addition to roast chicken, Keiko had made rice and eggplant braised in miso, and hot and sour Korean-style cabbage. When they were finished and David was tamping and puffing on his pipe, Alonzo took out a guitar and started to play a circular twelve-bar blues, a direct, unconscious pattern. Thomas sat back in the chair, listening, giving thanks for the music in addition to everything else. Alonzo caught his eye and sent him the smile of the older friend, knowing, accepting, lighting the long path of the years ahead with his benediction: *It's all right. Somehow it will work, and one day you'll be as old as I.*

After a few minutes Ernest unlatched his case and lifted his tenor from its worn velvet bed, dampened the reed, and mouthed it; then he began to blow atop Alonzo, crying, complaining in short bursts like comments on the guitar lines. Finally Charles took up his alto and joined in, first shadowing his brother in their trademark thirds and later playing off him in their own call-and-response.

Everyone in the room pulsed together, Leo in his mother's lap, Thomas on the chair, Keiko — any sense of separate nationhood had dropped away. This was Shanghai, itself an eclectic improvisation, a loop like this twelve-bar blues, playing again and again, bringing all possibilities to life.

At last David rose and unsnapped his violin case. Thomas felt pride burst out of him, for David had always said he would never improvise, that it terrified him. He looked unsure as he fit his beloved instrument to his chin, and the first few bars he played straight, the way he knew how to do it.

Alonzo shook his head. "Turn the beat around," he said, and used the next measure to emphasize the displacement of accents onto the weak beats.

David understood instantly, and began again, adding the Gypsy plaintiveness for which he was so gifted. After a while he began to grasp their hesitations and use of space, and he left more emptiness as he answered their lines with his.

He said, "So you are flatting the third, the fifth—"

"And the seventh," said Ernest.

"Judiciously," Alonzo added.

And David nodded as his elegant violin shifted the song into something stranger and more mournfully European. Thomas saw Alonzo and Ernest exchange looks, interested. Gunfire sounded outside, and everyone glanced up, then returned to the music, used to the sounds of violence.

The song ended to cheers and laughter, and then Thomas, the only one of the musicians who had not played, spoke up. "My turn. Music is my nation, and you are my people." He raised his glass. "This is our country, right here: America is in a song. We have just proven it. Thank you, pioneers." And they all drained their wine.

The next day, November twenty-eighth, Admiral Morioka left the Japanese Naval Headquarters with a sheaf of freshly decoded documents in a small, stiff leather map case inside his greatcoat. He needed to think, away from the frenzy of cables, the clamoring subordinates. In a few weeks Japan would attack America, and his forces had to be positioned like a clamp around Shanghai, ready to tighten at exactly the same moment. Thousands of his men were garrisoned in the city, and thousands more waited in the rural districts surrounding it. It was essential that he quickly overwhelm the Marines and other foreign troops in the International Settlement, taking the British gunboat *Pe-*

trel and the American gunboat *Wake,* moored in the Huangpu, as his first act. Then he would have his men move through the downtown streets en masse, executing any who offered resistance. *And then it won't be your Lonely Island anymore. It will be ours.*

He would have all the Allied diplomatic personnel in the city detained at the Cathay Mansions in the French Concession, and keep them under house arrest. Their colonization of China was over. He would take the Shanghai Club from the British and turn it into a club for Japanese officers. And those garish bronze lions in front of the Hong Kong and Shanghai Bank, the ones whose feet poor superstitious Chinese rubbed for good luck, he would get rid of those too, just as soon as he had the British flag taken down and the Rising Sun hoisted in its place.

And then there were Shanghai's eight thousand Allied citizens, British, American, and Dutch. As enemy aliens, they would have to wear numbered armbands in public and be barred from all places of entertainment such as restaurants, theaters, and clubs. Their bank accounts would be frozen, their assets seized. They would be restricted and pushed down until they were lower than the Chinese, and then, by January or February, he would have them all moved out of Shanghai and into prison camps. Their villas and apartments would be of use to him and his men.

It still troubled him to think of all this landing on the American musicians he so admired. But he was a man who held loyalty above all things, and breaching the extreme secrecy of this attack was out of the question.

He also believed deeply that Japan's enterprise in taking China was a noble one. It would end British domination of Shanghai after 101 years. China had never been able to liberate herself from Anglo-Saxon tyranny; only Japan could do it. China would be free at last—and cared for, that being Japan's duty as the natural leader of East Asia. The strong should care for the weak. It was correct.

But today's cable from Berlin had sent him to his chauffeured car, to the back seat where he could not be seen, to tell his driver to take him past French Park. What to do? The bare treetops sketched questions against the gray sky, and he studied them as the motorcar rumbled past the park walls.

The Germans were furious that so many Jews were being allowed to live in Shanghai, allowed to work, provide for their families, and form a community. They wanted something done. It was a complaint to which he had always replied simply that Shanghai was under Japan's control, not Germany's. Now things had shifted; the pressure was no longer local. It was coming from Berlin.

He felt the weight of a thousand boulders on him. With their sneak attack about to draw the world into war, it was no time for him to put the alliance with Germany at risk. But Shanghai belonged to Japan, and the tribe of Israelites had flourished here. What was he expected to do, deny them the right to work? And what about the rich Sephardic Jews, like Sassoon and Kadoorie, pillars of the city who had been here since the nineteenth century and lived in vast mansions, off Bubbling Well Road? Surely they were to be excluded from the ugly intimations in today's cable. His hand went to the leather document case inside his coat. The whole thing was impossible.

"Turn right," he said when he saw the Cercle Sportif Français up ahead. Every Friday afternoon, Thomas played in the lobby below the grand curving staircases; to hear music would give him clarity. "Wait for me," he said.

In the lobby, he ignored the barely audible intake of breath, still distracted by the conflict within him. Yet as soon as he heard the music floating across the polished floor, he was righted again. He walked closer, the violin and piano calming him, and took a seat.

The piece contained the world. Morioka found it so moving that he summoned one of the pinch-chested middle-aged men they called boys, who now quavered before him in fear.

"What name this music?" Morioka said, and the boy evaporated to find out. Usually when Thomas and David played, people danced, but today they filled the chairs and settees and all the space in between, listening as silently as he was. He closed his eyes to the music's purity, and everything seemed clear. The maze in front of him was not so difficult; he would find his way through it. He would make the right decision.

When the movement ended, there was a pause, and he opened his eyes to see the Jew, David Epstein, nodding to the boy and writing something on a piece of paper. Then Thomas Greene caught his eye, and sent him a discreet nod, which he returned with a short bow, for they were masters to him, and war or no war, he venerated them.

A second later the boy was at his side, unable to stop the paper from shaking as he proffered it. The Admiral handed him a coin to get rid of him, and unfolded it.

Mozart, Sonata for Piano and Violin in B-flat, No. 454.

A rare smile touched his mouth. Mozart's music was the pinnacle of European culture, and he had just heard a sublime interpretation by this David Epstein, a Jew. Nothing could have made it clearer to Tadashi Morioka that the Nazis were overreaching with their pressures.

He felt even more certain of it as he listened to the third movement, an allegretto full of light-filled, dancing runs, and when it ended, and a storm of applause erupted, he rose and walked out the lobby door. The winter sun was warm, and he felt at peace as he opened his greatcoat and touched the stiff leather document case inside. It was neutral now, the burn of anxiety gone from it.

He would not let the Germans push him, not when it came to his Jews.

Up in Yan'an, reports of the Japanese buildup around Shanghai poured in. The only part of the city not already under Japanese control was the *Gudao,* or International Settlement, for the Chinese had already been beaten, and France was a Nazi vassal state. In Yan'an, everyone thought the signs meant there was about to be an attack on the Settlement. There was no other explanation.

That did not mean there was much sympathy for the unfortunate Westerners who would be caught up in the attack, for they were dismissed as imperialists. The news sparked terror in Song that others did not share.

Alone, she worried about Thomas, for she had not been back to Shanghai since all three of them met there in 'thirty-nine — and that was two years ago. He might be gone, or he might be with someone else and not want to see her. But inside, she felt sure he was still there. And she had to warn him.

So she went before her superior to ask for family leave.

"You have family in Shanghai?" said Wu Guoyong, looking through her file. "I do not see that."

"Friends."

"Foreigners," he said, and she did not deny it.

He turned a few pages. "You have never asked for leave before, and when family is in danger, we grant it. But —"

She just held her eyes on him and let her request stand.

He tapped the file with a sigh. "You know that travel to Shanghai has never been more dangerous than it is right now. Is it worth it?"

"Yes," she said, putting everything she had on the word.

He glanced at a report. "You have done well. I see the children of Baoding Village are very fond of you."

"It is my honor to serve the people," she said automatically, thinking with a pang of Plum Blossom, who was expecting her this weekend, and would wait for her all day.

"All right," he said, and signed the form. "Two weeks."

The next day she was in Xi'an, and this time she went straight to the temple near the Eighth Route Army Liaison Office.

From the outside, it looked the same as when she had first seen it four years before, but anything could have happened. Maybe someone had found the diamonds. If so, it was fate. She entered the main chamber and meditated for a time to calm herself. *If the diamonds are there or if they are not, I accept it. Plum Blossom, I'm sorry to aban-*

don you. The monk came by, nodded to her, neutral, his face empty of recognition. He had forgotten her. She waited until he left, then walked into the empty courtyard and moved close to the wall, heart jumping, until she found the spot and felt the moss intact, grown over the stone she had prised out and replaced so long ago.

Using a small knife, her fingers freezing, she worked the rock loose. There: the pouch, still waiting. The Goddess of Mercy had smiled on her, a fellow woman. She took it and fixed the wall.

Back inside the shadows of the temple, she sat again, heart racing. She was committed now. She had the diamonds and she was going.

She had always had a vision of the moment when she would place the little black pouch in his hands. Maybe she would do it on the ship, or maybe when they docked in the Beautiful Country. She loved the scene no matter where she set it, and she lived it again and again like a moving picture, or a favorite dream. It was her portal, and she followed it now to the Xi'an train station and the steaming, belching Number Twenty-one to Shanghai.

Morioka was irritated by the intrusion of his secretary, who clicked his heels and bowed abjectly. "So sorry, Admiral. We pleaded with him to meet with an assistant, but he insists on seeing you. It is the German, Gestapo Colonel Meisinger. He is here, in the outer office."

"What! Here in Shanghai?" It was Monday morning and he was only halfway through the stack of cables from Tokyo, some of which mentioned this Josef Meisinger wanting to discuss the Jews here in Shanghai. But to arrive here, uninvited . . .

Now he was trapped. "Show him to the downstairs east parlor," he said tightly, "and interrupt us after five minutes."

He pushed back from his desk and saw the calendar — the first of December, 1941. He took a deep breath, steadying himself by imagining the opening bars of the Mozart violin sonata as he had heard it in the lobby of Le Cercle Sportif a few days before. He had to appear normal, smooth, no more agitated than any Admiral in charge of naval operations at the mouth of the Yangtze ought to be. Meisinger must suspect nothing.

Morioka strode into the unfurnished east parlor. If Meisinger found it uncomfortable to stand in the frigid, unheated room, he did not let on. He was blond and solidly built, almost heavy; his features were even and would have been handsome, except for his dissolute mouth.

"Admiral," said the Colonel jovially, as if they were equals.

Morioka hardened. But his voice was neutral as he spoke in simple English instead of calling a German interpreter, which would raise the risk of whatever they said being repeated. "What I can do for you?"

"I have come on a private mission, my government to yours."

"Be brief."

Meisinger blinked, surprised, Morioka's coolness finally penetrating his blond wall of self-assurance. "It concerns our Jews," Meisinger said. "Germany's Jews. The ones in Shanghai."

"Your Jews? *Germany's* Jews?"

"You have twenty-five thousand of them here."

"They are stateless people. You took away their German citizenship, is it not?"

"We did. But they are still our enemies, and we have a new plan for them now. It won't be finalized until our Conference at Wannsee next month, but we are ready to build camps. We'll take care of all the Jews in Europe. We need your help with only one little group—the ones you have here."

Meisinger leaned forward, and his milky European smell wafted over the Admiral. *Batakusai*, Morioka thought with distaste, stinks of butter. "What is it you want?"

"For you to kill them," Meisinger said.

Morioka stared. "All those people?"

The overweight blond man returned his gaze insolently. "Not difficult. They all go to their temples on Rosh Hashanah, and that is when you gather them up. Load them into boats without food and water and send them out to sea, or set up a camp on an island down-river and let them starve."

Morioka stopped trying to conceal his revulsion. "Why?"

"Because they must be eliminated," said Meisinger calmly. "So we cannot leave your twenty-five thousand here." With his words came another gust of sour breath. "You understand."

Morioka's eyes shot to the door. He had seven thousand new troops arriving on warships in the next twenty-four hours alone; teams of assistants awaited him.

Why should he kill them when he had a war to fight?

"So you will give me your decision?" said Meisinger.

"In time," Morioka said, though he had made his decision already, days before, listening to Mozart. *You will not harm my Jews. If you want them, you will have to take Shanghai from me to get them.*

He had less than a week left until the attack.

Song made it to Shanghai on Saturday the sixth. The dark-skinned Ceylonese gem trader she visited in a small side street off the Bund did not even blink at the mismatch between her bedraggled rural clothes and the fantastic value of the single gem she presented, used as he was to the eccentric habits of the rich. A specialist in anonymous cash transactions, he counted out her money with studied disinterest.

She melted back into the crowd. No one looked twice at her in her plain padded jacket, another war-battered refugee fleeing destruction and starvation in the countryside, and this served her well until she tried to ask the doorman at the Palace Hotel where Greene and Epstein were playing, and he barked her right off the steps. The doorman at the Cathay across the street was kind enough to tell her they would be at the Astor House the next day.

There, the British doorman took one look at her on Sunday afternoon and held up his hand, barring her from entry, but he stepped back quickly enough when she slipped a roll of bills into his hand. She could hear them, playing on the other side of the lobby, and just as it had been since the very first time, she felt everything about her lift at his sound, ordered yet unexpected, opening a higher vista of what life could be, if she had the will to see it and hear it.

And then the song stopped, abruptly — they had seen her. They were staring, and so was everyone else in the lobby.

Thomas was across the floor to her in an instant, David behind. "Are you all right?" he said, touching her filthy face, as if two years of separation were gone in an instant.

She covered his hand with hers. "I am well. It is safer to travel like this." She looked around the columned lobby, filled with expensively dressed white people. *All of you have no idea what is about to happen.* "Let's go someplace to talk."

The three of them stepped into a small side room where David and Thomas left their hats and overcoats. "Japan is preparing a major assault on Shanghai."

David and Thomas exchanged glances. "We've seen the soldiers," said Thomas. "And also, I've heard things." He thought of what Anya had told him.

"There are many more soldiers than you can see," she said. "At least five thousand in a ring around the city, waiting to pounce. I came down here because the opinion of our leaders is that they are preparing to attack the International Settlement. The *Gudao*. Any day."

Thomas and David were silent.

"That means British and Americans," she said. "You cannot be taken prisoner by the Japanese. Do you understand? You must leave. Now."

"What about David and his family? All the Jews?"

"This attack is not against them. They are already under the control of Japan, and Japan leaves them alone, as they do the French. The only armed forces here are the British and American soldiers protecting the *Gudao*. If the Imperial Army is sending ten thousand men, it is for them." She paused. "You must *go*."

"I can't," Thomas said. "Don't have the money."

"But I do. A boat sails at nine thirty tonight for San Francisco. I'll get the tickets."

"Stop joking. How could you have enough to buy them?"

"I do," she said stubbornly. "And I will. You too, if you want," she turned to David. "And your family. Though I believe you are safe."

"You are kind, but"—he raised his hands, still holding his violin—"if we sail to the United States, they will send us back to Germany. No, we stay here." He turned to Thomas, his arms open, and they held each other for a long, speechless minute. "Thank you," said Thomas, and David refused to hear it, just as Thomas had refused to hear it from Lin Ming.

He turned to Song. "You're going with me." It was not a question.

She took a deep breath. "Yes." She had the diamonds, they were in her pocket, so why did the words seem to catch in her throat and not want to come out?

He took her in his arms. "But there's a problem," he said, and she pulled back to see him. "I can't leave my men here."

"Get them! What time is it?"

"Around quarter to eight."

"Get them."

"Song! How many tickets can you buy?"

"How many men do you have?"

"Three. And they play with five others. So you see—"

"Bring them all," she said.

"Are you sure you—"

"Hurry! Meet me at the Old Dock off Broadway Road. The anchor goes up at nine thirty—go! Make them believe you." And she gave him a push, away from her.

At the front door of Ladow's, he talked his way quickly past Senhor Tamaral, the Macanese floor manager whose suit hung loose from his whippet frame. The cavernous ballroom was full, and he sidestepped waiters, and silk-clad dance hostesses. Once, this place had seemed grand to him, with its two-story box-beam ceiling, its balcony mezzanines running the length of the room on each side. Now it was all finished.

He waited until the song ended, then whispered to Earl Whaley. "Call a break. Please. Emergency."

Earl's brows drew together. "Who do you think you are? We are thirty minutes from a break."

"Something's happened." He motioned with his eyes toward the door and the outside. "We have to talk." At last Whaley relented, and the men pulled in around F. C. Stoffer's piano, to hear Thomas's explanation.

"Bullshit" was Earl's reaction, when he finished.

"It's true. Tickets for everyone who wants to go. Tonight."

"You know how much money that is?" said Stoffer.

"Who's this friend?" said Alonzo. "Mister Lin?"

"No. Lin's in Hong Kong."

"I know," said Ernest. "His sister. That *fine* woman." His guess was confirmed by Thomas's face.

"Jesus, Mary, and Joseph," said Alonzo. "She coming too?"

But Earl cut back in. "Now listen! This is all nothing, empty as a gin bottle Sunday morning. You don't believe him." His eyes circled his men. "Do you?"

Uncertainty skipped from one to the other. All had seen the buildup of soldiers, and each had found his own explanation to rationalize it, until tonight.

"I been paying you for years," said Earl, "and you're gonna listen to him? Look at all that yellow on him. And he plays their music, too, every day of the week. Classical! With a damn German!"

"A Jew," said Thomas. "From Austria."

This Earl waved away. "Don't believe what he says. He's not one of us."

"He is," said Ernest.

Thomas raised his hands. "It doesn't matter what I play, or who I am. We all came here for the same reason, and I never wanted to leave either. But if they invade the Lonely Island, it's going to vanish beneath the water. You won't be playing anymore. And tonight we can go, all of us, before it happens."

"Bullshit," Earl repeated.

A silence fell as the line deepened in the sand. Finally Alonzo spoke, slowly. "You keep talkin' like that. You go on. You just go right ahead on." He rose, relaxed, flaunting the accumulation of years behind him. "I'm getting my bass."

Thomas almost collapsed in thanks.

"Us too," said Ernest, and he and Charles laid their horns in their cases.

"Listen to me!" Earl thundered. "Any one of you goes down to the dock to try to get on this imaginary boat, don't bother coming back. You won't have a job here tomorrow!"

"Earl," said Thomas. "Come with us."

"You're out of your mind," Whaley retorted. "Well? Earl?" he said to his guitar player, Earl West.

"Not going," said West.

He fixed his eyes on the bassist, Reginald Jones. "You?"

Jones shook his head. "Take more than that to make me leave my Filipina sweetie."

"Stoffer?" Earl said to his pianist. "You going?"

Stoffer said, "No. Staying with you."

Thomas sank inside, his eyes searching the five of them one last time. "You sure?"

No one spoke. The minute hand was advancing. Thomas seemed to hear Lin Ming's voice, as clear as if his friend were not in Hong Kong but still standing next to him. *An inch of gold can't buy an inch of time.* They'd had their inch. Time to go.

He led the way, and the four of them strode past a dance floor full of stilled, silent patrons. As they stepped out into the street, Thomas said only one word to Alonzo, maybe the bluest word he knew at that moment, "Keiko."

"A hell of a thing," said the older man, and turned toward their apartment, which was close.

Thomas waited outside while the three of them ran upstairs, the brothers to grab a few belongings, and Alonzo to say good-bye.

"You don't have your things," said Ernest when they came back down.

"I have my music." Thomas raised his briefcase.

Alonzo came down last, sick with sorrow, and they took off together at a run, back up Rue Vincent Mathieu toward Avenue Édouard VII.

Thomas kept asking people the time on the trolley, until the car clanged to a stop on the Bund and they jumped off, instruments swinging; it was nine fifteen. "It's faster to cross the Garden Bridge on foot. But we can't run," he said. "Walk." And so in an agony of slow, absurd steps they covered the long stretch past Jardine Matheson, Canadian Pacific, and the British Consulate, casual American musicians out with their instruments on Sunday night. Then they came to the bridge.

"*Tomette!*" shouted one of the sentries.

They halted.

"*Ogigi oshite!*" another screamed, and they all understood this too, since no one in Shanghai crossed this bridge without bowing to Japan. Alonzo managed it as best he could with one hand balancing his instrument case.

It was not enough. One of the soldiers raised the butt of his rifle and knocked Alonzo to the ground. He fell awkwardly, and his bass hit with a dissonance of wood and strings.

"*Nanda?*" the soldier demanded, taking a swing at the case to make the sound again.

"No!" Alonzo pleaded. "Please, no, it's an instrument—" And he got to his knees beside the case. "Look. Look. I'll show you. All right?" Slowly, cautiously, because seven bayonet-tipped rifles were now aimed at his head, he eased his long-fingered hands toward the brass latches, unsnapped them, and lifted the lid.

The soldiers leaned forward. Excited spatters of Japanese were exchanged. "Now listen, fellows." Alonzo had somehow regained his paternal calm. "Lemme just show you." And he lifted the instrument, set it on its end pin, and gave it a practiced twirl until it landed light and exact against his hand. The soldiers rumbled, their weapons still poised, and he plucked off a quick, rippling run.

"*Jūbun!*" cried one of the soldiers with a wave of his arm, and Alonzo grabbed the case with one hand and the neck of the bass with the other as the three of them sprinted across, laughing through their fear, flying. They could see the German and Soviet consulates at the other end, and the huddled brown stone walls of Broadway Mansions.

Church bells pealed the time: nine thirty.

Too late too late too late. They ran gasping, heaving, turned right at the Astor House to reach the Old Dock faster. "There it is," Thomas said, and suddenly in front of them was the liner, the sheer black vertical hull of it. Sailors were just working loose the ropes.

Song stood watching them from up above a wooden piling, saw as they came running, and then stopped short at the ship in front of them. The river was deep here, and the liners nestled up to their berths instead of using lighters.

The men looked all around, frantic to find her. She counted four of them, including Thomas. She checked, and counted again. Four.

Life, or love?

She fanned the tickets out in her hands. She always had to choose. Why did fate always force her? When she was young, it was her happiness or her family's survival, not both. Now she could be a patriot, or a woman. But not both.

Four men waited for her below.

Just then she heard a long, low boat horn calling from downriver, and because of where she stood, she could see far. She strained into the night, watching the form of something in the river come closer, something large, until she saw it was a battleship, and behind it steamed another, and another behind that, a whole line of warships coming up the river.

So the attack was starting tonight.

Anger ignited within her, rage she had felt at her father, and at Du, and at those who would keep down girls like Plum Blossom, like herself. Watching the line of ships, she understood that without this feeling, she would wither and die. She would go cold. *And then he will go cold to me too.*

She fanned out four of the tickets, and let the rest drop from her hands to the dark river below, where they vanished. "Thomas!" she called.

He looked up, relief sagging every joint in his body. The brothers had been hopping and Alonzo pacing; sailors were waiting at the top of the passenger ramp.

In a second she was beside him, and in his arms. "Thank you," he breathed.

"I got them." She passed him the envelope, stamped DECEMBER 7, 1941. "But they had only four left."

Her words were transparent to him. "You are going back north."

She nodded. "I can't leave now. Not yet. You knew."

"Just as you knew I would not leave without the others."

"True," she said. "Pure gold proves its worth in a fire. But I have always known that about you." They held each other until a sharp blast from the ship's horn jolted them apart.

"After—" she blurted.

He stopped her. "No more of that. Just stay alive for me."

"I will." He felt her arms go inside his coat, and her hand slip something into his trouser pocket.

"Go. *Ni zou ba.*" Her voice broke.

"Tails!" Charles shouted. Sailors were moving to pull up the ramp. And now he, too, saw something behind them, down the river, a shape—what? He held her face. "See you again," he said, as Lin had said to him, and she nodded in misery and gave him a push, away from her. In a few steps he covered the salt-brined boards to where his men stood with their own America, their instruments and music, ready to go home, and he saw the first warship, its lights blacked out and its engines quiet.

"Hurry," he said, and followed them up the ramp.

· · ·

I watched them steam away that night, passing the first Japanese warship so close they surely could see the rows of soldiers, thousands, rifles at twelve o'clock, bayonets glinting. I shrank into the shadows as they passed, and blessed the ship that bore him away.

I could have left then too, taken a level and more peaceful road to free China, or Hong Kong. But I belonged to the war, I was a creature of its struggle, and so I returned north. I had good years there before the winds changed, and blew fortune away from me. I was a foreign-trained translator, able to read the words of the Westerners and understand their music; maybe it was inevitable that first one comrade, then another, would denounce me as a spy. Now I live alone in a small cell. My punishment is my isolation, hunger rations, and this one, simple masterstroke: I may lie only on my left side. I must always face the door, my hands visible. There is a paradise on my right side, a place of singing angels, and I dream of it every night. Even Thomas waits for me there. But I may not turn.

Despite all this, I am free. I think in English as I like, and roam at will through the halls of memory, still visiting every corner of that glittering world that is gone, never to return, which we called Ye Shanghai.

· · ·

AFTERWORD

Pearl Harbor was attacked just before three A.M. Shanghai time. A Japanese buildup around the city in the weeks prior had been noticed and remarked on, causing some to leave. Earl Whaley remained, and was interned with his bandmates at the Pudong and later the Weixian prison camps. In each place they formed camp bands, scrounging instruments when necessary (one bass player used a cello). Not all the American jazz men survived; Whaley's pianist F. C. Stoffer died in camp. Some say Whaley's hands were broken by his captors, but he is known to have been living in the United States after the war, at least until 1964, working variously at the post office and in real estate. Buck Clayton returned to the States before the war to play with Count Basie; his own account of his years in Shanghai can be read in his memoir. Teddy Weatherford's orchestra continued to tour Asia as the war permitted; he died in Calcutta, of typhoid, in 1946. Aaron Avshalomov lived quietly in Shanghai through the war and later moved to the United States to join his son, the composer and conductor Jacob Avshalomov, who settled in Portland, Oregon.

The Chinese plan for a 100,000-person Jewish Resettlement Area in Yunnan almost came to fruition, thanks to H. H. Kung, Sun Fo, and other Nationalist leaders. The Sword of David secret society did indeed send the Italian Jewish mercenary Amleto Vespa and the exiled Korean revolutionary An Gong Geun with cash and gold bars from Shanghai to Chongqing, where both were killed. Not long after, Chiang Kai-shek gave in to pressure from Berlin and vetoed the Plan. One can only imagine the long-term outcome of 100,000 European Jews surviving and being resettled in 1939 along what is now the China-Myanmar border; instead the Plan became one of history's grace notes, forgotten except in the pages of a story like this.

The 25,000 Jewish refugees in Shanghai did survive. Some of them were saved by Ho Feng-Shan, the Chinese Consul in Vienna, since many of the several thousand specious visas he wrote freed entire families. A vintage directory listing all those in Shanghai's refugee quarter along with their European city of origin confirms the large number of Jews who made it out of Vienna. Ho Feng-Shan died in San Francisco at age ninety-six; in Israel he is honored as one of the Righteous among Nations.

After the Japanese surrender, Du Yuesheng attempted a return to Shanghai, but his health and his power had declined. He did take a fifth wife, though, marrying the opera star Meng Xiaodong in 1948. When he left Shanghai for the last time in May 1949, both she and Fourth Wife were with him.

H. H. Kung retreated to Taiwan with the Nationalists and later settled in the United States, where he died in 1967.

Xie Jinyuan, the commander of the Lost Battalion, was assassinated in April 1941 by the collaborationist city government. One hundred thousand Shanghainese turned out to mourn him.

Other historical characters, drawn as accurately as possible, include Flowery Flag, Fiery Old Crow, Big Lewis Richardson, Julian Henson, the Doron family, Ackerman, Schwartz, Shengold, Sir Frederick Leith-Ross, Dai Li, Joy Homer, Earl West, Reginald Jones, Shibatei Yoshieki, General Doihara, and Miss Zhang, the dance hostess impregnated by Ziliang Soong and murdered for demanding too much money. Admiral Morioka is fictional, but his real-life counterpart in Shanghai also humanely resisted German pressures to kill Shanghai's 25,000 Jewish refugees.

Night in Shanghai is based almost entirely on true events, and many of its characters were living persons, but on two points the novel does veer from the record. First, Josef Meisinger visited Shanghai to demand the murder of the city's Jews in July 1942, not November 1941. Second, the story overstates the role of the Green Gang in the city's jazz clubs. While the Gang wielded enormous power and undeniably controlled drugs, gambling, prostitution, smuggling, protection rackets, and other related industries, it was probably not pulling the musical strings in 1930s Shanghai to the degree depicted here.

The years Song spends in a cell, far in the novel's future, were horrific years for most Chinese, especially for those with foreign training or connections. The hope and optimism of Song's early years in the cause would have been withered by the Anti-Rightist Movements, the Great Leap Forward, the famine, and the Cultural Revolution. Yet in the post-1976 decades that followed these disasters, during which China opened irrevocably to the world, people like Song set about rebuilding their lives. Past traumas were not forgotten — indeed, their associated residues and reactions can often be seen today — but the rest of Song's life would not have been about that persecution. As for the specific punishment she endures at novel's end, it is based on a true story I heard in China decades ago from the American Sidney Rittenberg, who remained in China after 1949, was jailed during the Cultural Revolution, and forbidden for some years to turn over in bed — until the punishment was lifted and he was released.

Of course, Du Yuesheng never had an indentured servant named Song Yuhua, or an illegitimate son named Lin Ming. But he did believe that foreign music such as jazz would weaken China, and so did the Communists, who were later to ban Western music for almost thirty years. The song by Nie Er that prompted the Japanese raid on Summer Lotus, "March of the Volunteers," is now China's national anthem. Shanghai is much changed. Yet the Chinese catchphrase for the city's golden era remains *Ye Shanghai*, Night in Shanghai.

ACKNOWLEDGMENTS

Thanks

... to the historians without whose outstanding scholarship this novel could never have been written: Andrew F. Jones, Paul de Barros, Stella Dong, Andrew David Field, Poshek Fu, Leo Ou-fan Lee, Hanchao Lu, Lynn Pan, Gunther Schuller, and Ross Terrill.

... to those who were there, and whose first-person accounts opened the door to a world that vanished long ago: Buck Clayton, Ernest G. Heppner, Joy Homer, Sidney Rittenberg, Margaret Stanley, Desmond Power, Jacob and Aaron Avshalomov, John P. Powell, W. H. Auden and Christopher Isherwood, and Langston Hughes.

... to the Estate of August Wilson, for generously permitting me to quote a couplet from Wilson's play *Seven Guitars,* part of his ten-play cycle on African American life through the twentieth century; to Farrar, Straus and Giroux, LLC, for permission to quote a passage from Langston Hughes's autobiography *I Wonder as I Wander;* and to Hal Leonard Music for permission to quote lyrics from "Exactly Like You."

... to my researcher Daniel Nieh — whose discovery of an article about the Jewish Resettlement Plan, buried in a Chinese history database, changed the course of the story — for translation of Chinese source material, chasing down endless details, and even coaxing a Japanese steamship line to pull 1937 fare schedules from their archives and e-mail them.

. . . to Kevin Jones, Skip Reeder, Kemin Zhang, and the late Michael Turner for urging me to write this book; to the many readers who wrote from around the world with the same encouragement; and to those friends who kindly read and commented on early drafts: Reyna Grande, Jane Rosenman, and Po-Chih Leong.

. . . to the violist Jody Rubin for answering all my music questions; to Karen Christensen and Steve Orlins for great insight on China questions; to Deanna Hogg for sending me a copy of her uncle's diary, written while he was struggling to stay alive through the Battle of Shanghai; and to Dvir Bar-gal, for his tour of the neighborhood and buildings in which Jewish refugees lived throughout the war years.

. . . to my editor Andrea Schulz for guiding me patiently and brilliantly through the mysteries of creation; and to my agent Bonnie Nadell, possessed of peerless judgment and a great friend besides.

. . . to Paul Mones, always.

And to Ben and Luke, for everything. This one's for you.

For a full bibliography, and extended scenes, visit nicolemones.com.

A NOTE ON
ROMANIZATION

Chinese terms, phrases, and names in this book appear in *pinyin*, except for names of persons and places already well known in the West by alternate spellings, such as Chiang Kai-shek, the Yangtze, and Ho Feng-Shan.